Praise for Matt Johnson

"I thoroughly enjoyed Crow 27. Matt Johnson's detailed research, in-depth knowledge and ability to tell a brilliant story combine to create an important work of fiction. A must read." – **Johnny Mercer**.

"Emergency or armed services, no matter the uniform, if you served or know someone who served, you should read this story." – **Chris Ryan MM**.

"A gripping read I can thoroughly recommend. I read this book with great interest; it has a real aura of reality and illustrates the difficulties faced by an investigating officer in such circumstances." – **Lord Stevens**, former Commissioner, Metropolitan Police.

"Think *Where Eagles Dare* meets *Zero Dark Thirty*. A chillingly-real, rollercoaster read." - **Damien Lewis**.

"Matt Johnson truly nails it in a twisting, turning and authentic story capturing the culture of abuse surrounding female soldiers. I feel honoured at having had the opportunity to read this." – **Jane MacSorley**, Producer, BBC Panorama Documentary *'Bullied to Death'* and 2021 Audible Podcast *'Death at Deepcut'*.

"From a writer at the top of his game. Johnson is a natural." – **Matthew Hall**, Writer of 'Keeping Faith' and 'The Coroner' series.

"Terse, tense and vivid writing. Matt Johnson is a brilliant new name in the world of thrillers." – **Peter James**.

About the author

Matt Johnson served as a soldier and Metropolitan Police officer for twenty-five years. Blown off his feet at the London Baltic Exchange bombing in 1993 and one of the first officers on scene at the Regent's Park bombing in 1992, Matt was also at the Libyan People's Bureau shooting in 1984 where he escorted his mortally wounded friend and colleague, WPC Yvonne Fletcher, to hospital.

Hidden wounds took their toll. In 1999, Matt was discharged from the police suffering with Post Traumatic Stress Disorder. While undergoing treatment, he was encouraged to undertake writing therapy where he described his experience of murders, shootings and terrorism. One evening, he sat at his computer and started to weave these notes into a work of fiction that he described as having a tremendously cathartic effect on his condition. The result was the best-selling thriller Wicked Game, a novel nominated for the CWA John Creasey Dagger and which became the highest rated debut novel on Amazon UK in 2016. In 2018, Matt was voted at No.22 in the WH Smith reader survey to identify the all-time best crime writers, worldwide.

Also by Matt Johnson; -

Wicked Game

Deadly Game

End Game

Follow Matt at www.mattjohnsonauthor.com or on Twitter: @Matt_Johnson_UK

Matt Johnson

Crow 27

'Inside the wire, we make the rules.'

Dedicated to the memory of

Captain Tina Lee Jones, Royal Logistics Corps

(18.01.1977 – 17.01.2019)

And to the inspiring memories of Privates Sean Benton, Cheryl James, James Collinson and Geoff Gray, also of the Royal Logistics Corps, and to their families, friends and supporters who continue to seek the truth about their deaths, to obtain justice, and to experience closure.

And for Anna, who taught me a young soldier's bravery isn't exclusive to the battlefield.

Desolate is the Crow's puckered cry

As an old woman's mouth

When the eyelids have finished

And the hills continue.

A cry

Wordless

As the newborn baby's grieving

On the steely scales.

As the dull gunshot and its after-rale

Among conifers, in rainy twilight.

Or the suddenly dropped, heavily dropped

Star of blood on the fat leaf.

From *Life and Songs of the Crow,* by Ted Hughes.

Chapter 1

'What a way to spend your last day.' Corporal Ellie Rodgers stared dejectedly at her reflection in the window of the NAAFI storeroom. A shiver ran down her spine. The wind had picked up, the rain rattling angrily against the panes as if determined to break through. Behind her, the door from the bar area opened and a tall figure in a grey windcheater appeared. It was Ron Murphy, her Sergeant.

'You ready, Scouse?' he called.

'He'll never come out in this.' Ellie said over her shoulder, half hoping, half praying the job was off.

Ron closed the door behind him. 'It's perfect cover,' he said. 'At least that's what the boss reckons. The last few nights there were too many people around.'

Resigned to her fate, Ellie turned and stretched up to retrieve her coat from the nearby rack. This was her final rodeo, her last operation with SIB – the Special Investigation Branch of the Military Police – and her role was a simple one. She was the decoy, the tethered goat left exposed in the hope she might lure an active sex attacker into the open. She'd been undercover for several weeks, assuming the role of a flirty, civilian assistant working behind the NAAFI counter. To help maintain her cover, the team had also arranged for her to live in temporary accommodation just outside the wire; a walk of about half a mile. Her route home had been planned. She was to use a short cut, one that traversed a woodland area women tended to avoid, particularly when it was dark. Tonight, given the rain, taking such a route might seem an attractive option for someone trying to get home as quickly as possible. It was a ruse they hoped the attacker would fall for. If he did, he'd be in for a shock.

Ron shook his head, and grinned.

'What's so bloody funny?' she asked.

'You trying to reach coat hooks designed for tall folks,' he said. 'They should supply steps for hobbits like you.'

Slipping into her anorak, Ellie swung a playful elbow towards Ron's chin that he easily avoided.

'I'm not letting that connect,' he said, as he smiled again. 'I've seen what it can do.'

Ellie laughed. 'Comms check done?' she asked.

'Roger that. The arrest team can hear everything we're saying.' Ron winked as he carefully pulled her coat straight, made sure her transmitter was concealed and then fastened the zip. The gentle pat on her head at the end of his final check was warm, almost parental. He was concerned, she could see it.

'I'll be fine, Ron,' she said. 'Don't worry.'

'Just being careful, Scouse. You might be a tough little fucker but you'll be on your own. We'll be close by at all times, I promise. If he appears, we'll be on him in seconds.'

Ellie wrapped her hand around the small microphone on the collar of her anorak. 'If he shows, you'll have to pull me off him first,' she said. 'He's getting some summary from me for what he did to those girls.'

Ron grinned and, with a final good-luck nod, headed off into the night, leaving her to lock up. This was the time when their lead investigator had suggested Ellie would be at her most vulnerable. The NAAFI – the Navy, Army and Air Force Institute shop – was the only place on the camp that stayed open so late. With nobody else around, an attacker could force his way in at the last moment, lock the doors and prevent a quick rescue.

As the security door swung to and the padlock clicked into place, Ellie held her breath. Nobody appeared. Heart in mouth, she turned, faced into the rain, and gazed into the darkness. The only light was from the accommodation blocks opposite, the adjacent trees and shrubs throwing a shifting network of shadows, any one of which could conceal a prowler. From an open window came the steady beat of rap music. Inside their rooms, young soldiers would be socialising, watching TV, cleaning kit, doing the things squaddies normally did during their evenings. Warm and safe, some would be sleeping before a guard duty while others prepared for the morning inspection. Someone, perhaps one of those soldiers, might be watching her right now, waiting for the moment he would pounce.

She took a deep breath, turned away from the NAAFI and began the walk to her quarters. She avoided the shadows but then scolded herself for doing so. She wasn't accustomed to being scared. A drunken bully of a father had seen to that. He'd hardened her up, although not in a kind way, and not as a result of any fatherly aspiration to help prepare her to face the world. Danny Rodgers would arrive home on a Saturday night after watching his beloved team, to either take out his anger on his family if they'd lost or, if they won, keep everyone up late, shivering and huddled on the settee, listening to his boasts and tall stories. Her mother, Pat – the human shield who stood between her husband and his petrified children – had eventually found the courage to escape with them to a refuge. In the months that followed, they had endured threats, bricks through windows, assaults on their mother, family court hearings and, finally, a sense of relief when their father was sent to prison.

But that was years ago. Now, she was in a different world. Now, she could fight back and take on men like her father, the kind who saw violence as an acceptable way to treat their wives and children. Now, she was a red-cap; she was Corporal Ellie Rodgers, 110 Provost Company, 1 Regiment, Royal Military Police, and this was her last rodeo because in just three days she was going to be doing something her mother and step-father were proud of and her natural father would never see. She was going to start training at RMAS, the Royal Military Academy, Sandhurst. She was going to be an officer.

'Better luck next time, Rodgers.' Ellie smelt the whisky as she turned from where she'd been standing at the bar of the Sergeants' Mess.

She'd been alone with her thoughts, reflecting on the disappointment of a failed surveillance operation. After half an hour, when Ron Murphy emerged from the darkness with news they were going to call it a day, she'd wanted to carry on. To her frustration, Ron wouldn't be persuaded. They would withdraw and re-convene in the Mess for a de-brief. She'd dumped her surveillance kit in her room, followed on as quickly as she could and, as she'd walked in the door, she'd been met by the whole team, lined up and grinning. The instruction to attend a de-brief had been a ploy, what they'd really had in mind was a bevy, a little party to celebrate a mate's forthcoming promotion.

The camp adjutant, a Major, was standing beside her. 'Hopefully, sir, yes,' she replied, awkwardly. 'It bothers me he's still not there, though.'

Behind the Major, she could see the Sergeants' Mess was now crowded. Her peers were stood in small groups chatting and the drink was flowing freely. 'Can I buy you a drink?' the Major continued. 'I hear you've passed OSB and you're due at Sandhurst on Monday.'

Ellie held up her empty glass and mumbled a thank you. It was her third, and in less than an hour. And, if she knew the lads, there would be many to follow.

***

Someone was shaking her arm.

She was warm, cosy, and in a car. She remembered now. Ron Murphy had offered her a lift. He'd tried to insist she sleep it off at the Mess, but she'd been adamant; she needed her clothes and personal stuff from her room in the civilian quarters. One more night in temporary digs wouldn't matter, in any event.

Senses returning, she thanked Ron for the ride, watched him drive off, and then half-walked, half-staggered through the rain to the door of her room. Rummaging through her coat pockets, she finally located her key and let herself in. She didn't bother with the light, too much effort. Shoes kicked off, anorak on the floor, and then bed – that was all that mattered. Her head was spinning. How many shots had she downed? She wasn't sure. Too many, that was for certain.

Thank God that's over, she said to herself as she slipped into unconsciousness. No more investigating the misdemeanours of her fellow soldiers, no more sucking up to junior officers still wet behind the ears. She'd show them.

When she woke, the room was still in darkness. It felt like she had only been asleep for a few minutes. For a moment, she wondered what might have disturbed her. Then she felt the draft on her face. It was gentle, but it was there. Had she left the window open? No, definitely not. The door clicked shut. You stupid cow, she told herself. You're so pissed-up you left the door to your room open. Some kind soul must have just pulled it shut.

She closed her eyes just as a voice cut though the darkness and she instantly realised this was no kind soul doing her a favour. It was an intruder, and he was close; so close she could smell the dampness of his clothes. 'Thought you'd been clever, did you?' he hissed.

Ellie froze. And for the first time since those awful nights at the hands of her father, she felt afraid.

Chapter 2

Wednesday 21 September 2005, Cardiff Coroner's Court.

'Inspector Finlay.' Floria, my police military liaison, called to me from across the street. 'They're coming out. '

With the inquest concluded, journalists and photographers had gathered in strength behind a line of temporary steel barriers, ready to hurl questions at the first people to emerge through the doors to the Coroner's Court. A loud voice from a security officer announced the emergence of the victim's family. 'Keep clear of the steps, please.'

I kept my distance from the throng, choosing a less crowded area where I'd have a better view. I wanted to observe the family whose daughter had been the subject of the inquest. I was scheduled to interview them the following day because the team I was working on in London had recovered two stolen rifles during a raid on a drug-dealer's home in London, one of which had been in their daughter's care at the time it was taken. I was hoping they would be able to throw some light on how the original theft had happened.

Bill Grahamslaw, the Commander in charge of my team, had sent me to Wales for two days, three at the most, and then he wanted me back. He'd decided to send me for a couple of reasons, an old friendship with Wendy Russell, the local Assistant Chief Constable, and the fact I'd once been a soldier. Bill reckoned that made me a perfect choice to speak to witnesses inside a military barracks. He was also aware that my wife, Jenny, was away from home enjoying a 'girlie break' with our daughters at her sister's place on the Norfolk coast.

'You're the ideal bloke to spot something a civvie wouldn't recognise,' he'd explained. 'And besides, a couple of days in a quiet backwater will give you some time to study for the Chief Inspector board.' I'd laughed out loud when he said that. It was a lumber. He knew it, I knew it. The only thing we agreed on was I should get it sorted quickly.

My escort for the duration of the trip was Sergeant Floria McLaren. Floria was young and looked smart in uniform. As she came and stood alongside me, I noticed she was attracting glances from the attendant journalists.

'It's the Davenports,' she said, as a couple appeared at the top of the court steps.

I recognised the father, Michael, from recent TV interviews and articles in the newspapers. Stood to his left was a woman I took to be his wife. On his other side wearing a dark suit and white cravat, her fair hair tied back in a tight bun, was the family barrister. A set of papers tied with red ribbon was tucked beneath her left arm. Michael held a large, framed photograph of his daughter in Army dress uniform. Although he stood straight with his shoulders pulled back, he looked drawn and I noticed the dark indicators of lost sleep around his eyes.

'I've arranged for us to see them tomorrow, sir,' Floria said.

'Won't their home be surrounded by reporters?' I asked.

'Not unless there's been a leak,' Floria replied. 'The MOD has kept their home address private.'

As I nodded to show I understood, the barrister raised her hand. The effect was immediate. With the exception of the incessant clicks of camera shutters and the distant drone of traffic, the street outside the court fell silent. From behind the barrier, a sound-man pushed a boom-mike forward.

Michael Davenport began to speak and, although he trembled with emotion, his voice remained strong and clear. Suicide, he proclaimed, in a rich West-Wales accent, was a verdict that defied all the evidence the Coroner had seen. It was perverse, he said, and not a conclusion anyone who knew his daughter and appreciated what she was like should have come to. 'People like Angela don't shoot themselves,' he asserted. 'Not when they have so much to live for and are doing so well in their chosen career. A Jury, independent of pressures from politicians and the Ministry of Defence, could not possibly have reached this verdict.' He spoke slowly and deliberately, making sure everyone could hear. 'Prince Albert Barracks must *not* be allowed to go the way of Deepcut. The fight will go on, even if we force a public inquiry.' The reporters lapped it up.

No sooner had Michael Davenport finished speaking than the questions began. Did he have any comment on the similarity to the other deaths? Did he think the Army had failed in its duty of care? Were the family intending to sue the MOD? The barrister fended off all the questions with polite, if somewhat bland, responses.

'That'll put the cat among the pigeons,' Floria said, leaning into me.

'The verdict or the mention of a public enquiry?' I asked.

'The bloody verdict,' she replied. 'How the hell can a Coroner say that poor kid shot herself? Nobody saw it … she didn't leave a note. For Christ sake, who the hell would shoot themselves through the eyebrow?'

'A Coroner can only make a decision based on the available evidence,' I said.

'Is that a dig at the RMP?' she snapped.

'No more than it is at my people, Floria,' I said. My comment had been clumsy. The media reports on Angela Davenport's death had been in the papers at the same time as the results of an official inquiry into the events at a similar barracks in Surrey, where both civilian and military police had been criticised.

'Ok … but spouting that kind of opinion won't win you many friends around these parts, sir,' Floria replied, tersely as she indicated her car. 'Shall we go now?'

Chapter 3

As I opened the passenger door, the Davenport's barrister was still taking questions. I stopped for a moment and leaned on the car roof. 'So, what's your theory about the death?' I said, hoping to remedy my error and build a little rapport.

Floria remained silent until we were inside, the doors were firmly closed and she'd placed her bright red uniform cap on the rear seat. 'Can I speak freely?' she said, straightening her skirt.

'You can say what you like,' I said. 'It'll go no further than me.'

'I hope it won't,' she continued, before taking a deep breath. 'The MOD want all these recruit deaths confined to history because the investigations were a cluster-fuck from beginning to end. No decent forensic was done and witnesses were spoken to by their NCOs before our investigators had a chance to interview them. They put the fear of God in them. Not many would talk.'

'The Coroners would have taken that into account, Floria,' I said.

'The one here certainly didn't side with the family, did he?'

'Coroners aren't on anyone's side and they don't investigate,' I said. 'Their job is simply to decide who died, when, where and how. If there's evidence of foul play, that's for the police to ascertain.'

'So, I was right. You do think it was our fault?'

It was my turn to take a deep breath. I hoped to get my enquiries done and dusted quickly and I'd already managed to get off on the wrong foot with the one person who could help make my visit as expeditious as possible. 'I'm sorry if I gave that impression,' I said. 'That wasn't my intention.'

Floria frowned. 'No disrespect, but you need to understand … although I didn't actually know Davenport … for me and women soldiers like me, she was a sister. She was kin. Think how you'd feel if one of your family wasn't getting the justice they deserved?'

'The Army being your family now?' I said.

She shook her head. 'You're missing the point. It's more about being a woman in a man's world. You can't let them think you're weak, so we become like them and we band together?'

'Like a sisterhood?'

'Exactly ... but it comes at a cost. I've lost all my friends from school, you know? I don't bother going home any more but, when I did, they'd tell me I swear too much or was turning into a bloke. Civvies just don't get it.'

The conversation tailed off as Floria concentrated on her driving and I didn't press the point. I would need to find another way to ensure my escort and I got along.

Our next planned stop was Prince Albert barracks outside a town called Cwmbran, about twenty miles from the Coroner's court. I asked Floria about the place.

'Young soldiers are posted here on Phase Two, the interim period between basic training and deployment to their new Regiments,' she explained. 'Phase Two is when recruits learned their trades. They might be here for just a couple of months if they do well, longer if their progress is slow.'

'Just recruits, then?' I asked.

'Not at all, this is a large camp. On the far side is 25 Signals Regiment and a detachment of Royal Engineers.'

As we approached the front entrance of the barracks, Floria turned off the main road. We entered a narrow lane alongside the camp, next to which stood a high, steel fence topped with razor wire. On the opposite side were fields, rough grass pasture with overgrown hedgerows. 'Short cut,' she announced. 'Our guys use a side entrance as it's easier to get to our HQ building. Do you mind if I ask you a question, sir?'

'Difficult to say if I don't know what it is,' I replied.

She laughed under her breath. 'Yeah, I suppose so. It's just … well, I know you said you're not here to enquire into the suicide … it just seems a bit of a coincidence you turning up now, though.'

'It is coincidence,' I said, firmly. 'I'm just here to follow up on the rifles.'

'Some of the lads I work with think it's a convenient cover story.'

I frowned. 'Think about it logically for a minute,' I said. 'I'm one person on my own. What could I achieve that a whole enquiry team didn't? My job is to find out how two stolen rifles ended up in London, no more. If there's an organised crime group with links to this camp, it's important we close it down, and quickly. Just imagine what could happen if they gained access to the ordnance we're finding in Iraq?'

'Gun running is a specialism of yours then?'

'Far from it,' I said. 'I was sent because the Assistant Chief Constable here is a mate.'

'That'll be ACC Russell, I guess? I heard she was ex-Met.'

'We were at training school together … going back more years than I care to remember.'

Floria slowed the car as we approached a gap in the fence. We turned in, weaved our way through a chicane of red and white fifty-gallon drums and stopped at a lowered barrier. From a small cabin set back from the entrance, a young soldier appeared holding a clip-board. Just behind him came a second, an SA80 rifle held ready in his hands. As the first soldier approached us, I saw his colleague give us the once over and then move to a position where he could cover us without placing his mate in the line of fire. Well trained, I thought. The soldier with the clip board asked for I/D from both of us, checked the photographs and then wrote some details down before raising the barrier.

Ahead of us, through a small copse, I caught my first sight of the barracks. I wondered what kind of reception I'd receive. Formal and not too friendly, I imagined. A case of being tolerated more than welcomed. We made our way slowly along the internal roads and past the freshly mown grass and clean, white-painted buildings. I felt a wave of nostalgia wash over me. Although the camp was quiet with few people moving around, it was all very familiar.

We stopped to park near a small parade square at which point another memorable sight caught my eye. A young soldier in full combat uniform was performing press-ups while a PTI – smartly turned out in boots, combat trousers and red-trimmed white vest – leant over him shouting encouragement in typical military style. On the far side of the square, a number of soldiers stood in lines, all at attention, all with eyes facing front. All would be hoping their turn wasn't next.

Floria saw me staring as we exited the car. 'A lot of people think it's bullying,' she said.

'The discipline, you mean?'

'We call it 'beasting'. What you civvies sometimes don't appreciate is that most of those Crows will be deploying to Iraq and Afghan in a few months, maybe weeks. They're going to find themselves in some scary places where people's normal instinct is to freeze or hide.'

'You mean when the bullets start flying around their ears?' I said.

'Exactly. We expose them to noise, unpleasantness and other trauma. It toughens them up and makes them resilient. Their lives and the lives of their mates may depend on it.'

I smiled to myself. Floria sounded like a Ministry of Defence advertisement. 'I guess so,' I said. 'You called them Crows?'

'It's a nick-name. Combat Recruit of War.'

'So, when does a Crow become a fully-fledged soldier?'

'Officially it's when they get posted to their Regiment but it sometimes sticks a bit longer. Shall we press on?'

I remained where I was, observing the layout of the camp as best I could. 'Does training here take long?' I asked.

My guide huffed slightly, the first sign of any impatience I'd seen since she'd met me at the train station. 'Like I said in the car, it depends,' she replied. 'If they're bright it can be quick but for others, it's slow, like with the Pioneers.'

'The what?'

'The Pioneers. They do the basic jobs like guarding convoys.'

'So, you're saying they're not as bright?' I said.

Floria grinned, mischievously. 'We prefer to describe them as better suited to the physical side of Army functions. Sometimes beef trumps brain, if you know what I mean?'

For a moment, my thinking was distracted as I watched another NCO march past with a second group of soldiers. At first, he appeared to be ignoring us but then his gaze swept in our direction to look me up and down. Grey and penetrating, his eyes studied and assessed. I had no doubt he would be wondering who I was.

I looked at the young soldiers with him. They were a mixed bunch and included several women. Something struck me about them. It was how subdued they were. There were no smiles, none at all. Not one looked to be enjoying what they were doing.

Floria waited until the group were out of earshot. 'Those are Phase Two recruits,' she said. 'It's their first day.'

'Are they all as miserable as that bunch?' I said, as they disappeared into the distance. Floria shrugged but didn't respond.

We turned and began walking towards the Regiment Headquarters building. 'Does the Colonel here have responsibility for both Phase One and Phase Two camps?' I asked.

'He does, yes,' she replied. 'Now, shall we head on in?'

Floria's patience seemed to be reaching its limits. I patted the side pocket of my jacket to confirm I had my notepad and pen close at hand and declared myself ready. Floria donned her cap, pressed it neatly into place and checked her appearance in the reflection from the car window. Seemingly satisfied, she strode ahead of me up the gravel path leading to the steps of what appeared to be the main entrance.

'Looks like something out of an old movie,' I said, as we reached the wedged-open doors. 'An RAF building, maybe?'

'That's exactly what it was,' she replied. 'The cricket pitch behind us was part of the runway. They used to build Spitfires here during the Second World War before flying them to where they were needed.'

Chapter 4

'At last,' the Sergeant said, beneath his breath. 'Fresh meat.'

The young recruits stood to attention, ready for their first inspection. The sergeant licked his lips, his eyes dancing from one face to another as he smiled, indulgently. The growl that followed was guttural, almost primeval in nature, like that of a big cat moving in on its prey.

He knew the type he was looking for, could sense them a mile off. Fresh out of school, early lessons in life not yet sunk in. Naivety was their weakness, his advantage. And by the time they learned, it would be too late. As the intakes came and went, he'd had ample opportunity to practise and refine his methods. He'd reached the point now where he could immediately recognise those who would succeed, those who would struggle, and those who would be vulnerable. Female, young, finding it hard to make the grade and something of a loner were his preferred criteria. And although he liked them pretty, that wasn't essential. The dogs amongst them were often the easiest to control. After a week away on leave – a chance to visit home and show their newly toned bodies to their families – they were now his. From now on, he could either be their best friend or their worst enemy. Soon, they would begin to find out which.

One girl, in particular, caught his eye. Not confident of her position, she was slow to get in line. Eventually, she found a place – second row, third from the end. He watched her face. She had large, dark eyes that, from a distance, appeared the deepest shade of brown. And she looked lonely, like the last puppy from a litter when all the others had departed to new homes. She was perfect.

Before moving in, he glanced back toward the Training Regiment Headquarters building, just to be careful. The man he'd seen with McLaren, the redcap sergeant, looked like a cop. They'd disappeared now, no doubt heading inside to meet the bosses of the headshed. He'd find out why later on.

Starting at the end of the first line, he asked each of the recruits in turn for their name and service number as he drew alongside them and stood in their personal space. One or two stiffened as he breathed down their necks. Others looked nervous, beads of sweat trickling from their hairlines. They didn't move, they knew better than that. He assessed each of them, looked them up and down, all the time searching for a genuine or invented fault he could pull them up on. Inhaling deeply through his nose, he finally stood behind the puppy. Again, a soft growl rolled gently off his palate. 'What's your name, Crow?' he said, leaning in against her ear before flicking an imaginary speck of dust from her collar.

'Richards, staff,' the puppy answered, her voice trembling.

The Sergeant stood in front of her, looked her up and down and scowled. She had a good figure. Small waist. Firm breasts. She was trembling. He breathed deeply, enjoying the smell of her fear. His lips twitched as they curled into a knowing smile.

She was the one.

Chapter 5

Floria held back and, with an open hand, indicated I should enter the HQ building first. I stepped inside. The foyer was cool and, on first inspection, appeared empty.

'Inspector Finlay, I presume?' From behind a glass screen, tucked away in the corner, a rather austere looking woman in a tweed jacket called out from behind a small desk. A sign on the glass told me she was Mrs Brooke, the Colonel's receptionist. She beckoned me over just as Floria appeared in the doorway.

'To see the Colonel, ma'am,' Floria said, formally.

'Can you both sign in, please?' The receptionist indicated an open register resting on our side of the screen. As we signed, she picked up a telephone and, with practiced efficiency, reported our presence. 'Please take a seat,' she continued. 'The Adjutant will be along in a few moments.'

On the opposite side of the entrance foyer, four plain velour chairs had been placed around a small coffee table. I chose the end one, nearest the entrance and facing a corridor into what I assumed were the HQ offices. Floria remained standing. On the table, three pristine Regimental magazines lay, apparently untouched. I hoped this meant visitors weren't normally kept waiting long.

I scanned our surroundings. On one wall, a large wooden board displayed the names of Commanding Officers going back many years. Two smaller boards listed the Second-in-Command and Adjutants. I read through the names, casually wondering if I might recognise any. I didn't.

From a room along the corridor, I could just pick out the sound of male voices, the murmur of a discussion of some kind. A door swung open, and at that moment the conversation ceased. The wooden floor rapped to the sound of metal-tipped heels as someone approached. I counted eight steps before a figure appeared in the doorway. It was a young, male officer. As he leaned into the foyer I saw from the three pips on his shoulder epaulettes that he was a Captain. He looked lean and fit and, although tanned, I saw he had slightly pock-marked skin from what might have been the scars of teenage acne. I stood to greet him.

'If you'd follow me, please,' he instructed, turning away from my outstretched hand. There was no friendliness, no warmth. A request communicated as an order more than an invitation.

Having experienced both sides of the Service divide, the military and the civil, the war-mongers and the peace-keepers, I'd encountered wide-ranging attitudes amongst both towards their opposite number. Some in the police regarded Army officers with an attitude that might best be compared to that a working-class man has towards the gentry; one of guarded respect that sometimes manifests itself as resentment or even jealousy. In turn, Armed Services officers were known, on occasion to be aloof towards the blue uniform, to be rank conscious and elitist. Both groups were often guilty of stereotyping – which is exactly what I found myself doing to the man I assumed was the Training Regiment Adjutant. His voice – public school – and the dismissive manner in which he addressed us meant I immediately disliked him. As I glanced toward Floria, I saw her nod and raise her eyebrows. I smiled, just slightly. It appeared she shared my opinion.

The Captain opened a door and stood to one side to allow us to enter. I made sure to thank him; a tiny gesture I hoped might make a point. As we stepped into a small dining room, the base commander, Lieutenant Colonel Richard Hine, approached with his hand held out in greeting.

Chapter 6

'Do come in, Inspector … you too Sergeant.'

Unlike his Adjutant, Colonel Hine was welcoming. We shook hands and he smiled warmly as he indicated with a wave where Floria and I should sit. The room smelled of beeswax, ancient and aromatic. We were surrounded by Regimental history. Paintings of battle scenes adorned the panelled walls, interspersed with an array of wooden plaques, gifts from visiting senior officers and other dignitaries. One, I saw, was from the local police. Around us, the floor was littered with boxes and a variety of plastic crates, all half-filled with files and documents, as if some kind of audit or search had recently been taking place.

As the Colonel sat down at the head of a polished, mahogany dining table, I noticed how his eyes scanned the boxes and crates. On the table in front of him lay a buff-coloured file bearing the Regimental crest. He flicked at the corner closest to him with his thumb. As I sat down, I wondered if this was what he and his Adjutant had been searching the boxes for. I pulled my notebook from my pocket and placed it on the table in front of me. He didn't say anything, but a fleeting scowl suggested a slight discomfort at its appearance.

'I've asked Captain Pemberton to remain with us, if you don't mind?' Hine said, once Floria and I were seated. 'He'll also be taking notes, of course. One can't be too careful in this kind of situation, I'm sure you understand?'

Before I could reply, the Captain appeared in the doorway clutching a leather briefcase. 'Did you ask Madge to bring the tea, Giles?' the Colonel said to him.

After confirming the request was being dealt with, Pemberton positioned himself on the seat immediately next to his boss. He opened the briefcase. From it, he produced an A4 notebook and a rather fancy looking fountain pen.

As soon as his adjutant was poised and ready, Colonel Hine began. He spoke slowly and appeared to choose his words carefully, as if he were giving an opening address to a more formal meeting. He confirmed he was aware I was looking into a theft of weapons from the base. After that, he went to some length to remind me I was the guest of a military establishment, he commanded it, and that I was to ensure he was kept in the loop at all times. I smiled to myself as I saw Pemberton struggling to keep up.

The introduction was exactly the kind of welcome I'd expected – friendly, but with a reminder who was boss. As the tea arrived, the Colonel moved on, politely asking me a series of questions about my background; how long I'd been a police officer; had I spent my whole career in the Met; did I have family, that kind of thing. It was small-talk before we got onto the reason for my presence. To my surprise, he asked similar questions of Floria. I'd assumed, mistakenly, that he and my escort already knew each other. As Floria politely answered his questions, I learned she was twenty-six, had eight years service – six as a uniformed RMP NCO, two attached to the Special Investigation Branch – and she hoped to be made up to Staff Sergeant the following year.

Formalities over, I explained the nature of my enquiry. 'I'll be honest, Inspector,' Hine said as he tapped his fingers on the file in front of him. 'I'm not really sure how we can be of any assistance. My predecessor and everyone involved made full and frank statements at the time. The base was searched from top to toe by the RMP, and the local police conducted a thorough investigation. I'm not sure there's a lot we can add to this report.'

'You weren't in charge at the time of the thefts?' I asked.

The Colonel coughed as he sat upright in his chair. 'I assumed command here in April. My predecessor took early retirement.'

'Was that anything to do with the rifles going missing?'

'It was after the suicide. Coming just a month after the thefts, well … I'm sure you understand. That kind of thing can be damaging to a chap's career.'

'Do you or the Captain here know enough about the circumstances of the thefts to fully brief me?'

'Captain Pemberton was in post at the time,' he replied, in a tone slightly more curt than he'd been prior to that point. 'But I'm sure I can speak for everyone here when I tell you it was most thoroughly investigated. Suspicions focussed on the families of the recruits who were passing-out that day. Some had some pretty unsavoury family connections, I can tell you.'

'Do you have a list of them I could see?' I asked.

'We do, although I think the RMP may have it?' Hine switched the focus of his question to Floria. She nodded, but didn't speak.

'As I'm sure you've been told, sir,' I continued. 'We found both rifles hidden during the search of a house used by traffickers.'

'Along with other weapons, I heard?' he said, glancing sideways towards where Pemberton was scribbling furiously on his writing pad. No short-hand skills here, I thought.

'Two pistols. Both Russian Makarovs,' I said.

'Not as easy to trace as our rifles then?' Hine raised an eyebrow to emphasise his point.

'No. Illegally imported we believe.'

The Colonel arched his back and then relaxed, easing himself deeper into his chair. When he spoke his voice became steadier. 'What would you like to know, Inspector?' he said.

'If possible, a key-point summary of what happened the day the rifles went?' I said, as I squinted toward the windows. They were closed and, with the room now in full sun, the air was becoming stuffy.

Pemberton pulled a sheet of paper from his briefcase and handed it to the Colonel. Hine only glanced at it briefly before sliding it across the polished table in my direction. It came to rest, very neatly, just in front of me. 'I took the liberty of prepping that for you,' he said, smiling.

'I wonder if I could also trouble you for a list of everyone who was posted here when the rifles went,' I asked. 'And another detailing those still here now. I'd like to check if anyone here has a link to where the rifles were found.'

Hine scowled. 'Do you mind if I ask how long you intend to be around?'

'Two or three days, max.'

'It seems an awful long way to come. Why couldn't the local police have handled it?'

'The rifles were found in London, sir,' I said. 'The prospect of military weapons being used by top-flight criminals worries us. If someone's in the process of establishing an arms-dealing network, we need to identify it.'

The Colonel's eyebrows rose. 'There have been no other losses of the kind to suggest anything organised,' he said. 'But I can see that would be a wise step.' Turning to Pemberton, he ordered the lists be made up for me. 'I can't allow such information about our people off base,' he added.

'Understood, sir,' I replied.

Hine flicked open the folder in front of him, scanned several of the pages and then looked back to me. 'The full report on the investigation is thorough. I'm agreeable to you reading it but it mustn't leave this building.'

Floria shifted in her seat, sufficient to get the Colonel's attention. 'Yes, Sergeant,' he said. 'What is it?'

'We have a copy of that report for DI Finlay to study, sir,' she said.

Hine exhaled heavily. 'Very well. I should tell you this, Inspector. At the end of a passing-out parade, it was customary at the time for recruits to place their rifles on the bed of a lorry before they went to meet their families. That was ordinarily supervised by an NCO. On the day in question, when the lorry arrived at our Armoury, there were two rifles missing. Nobody noticed any of the recruits being absent at the point the rifles were placed on the lorry and everyone present that day made statements saying what happened. Upshot … we were left with no real certainty when the rifles were taken or exactly where from. It may have been a case of theft from the lorry or two of the recruits may have lied in their statements about placing them there.'

'Presumably, the two recruits who signed for the rifles that went on to be stolen?' I said. 'Private Angela Davenport, the girl who shot herself, she was one of them, I'm told.'

I caught an anxious glance between Hine and his scribe, before the Colonel continued. 'A coincidence that hasn't gone unnoticed, I assure you, Inspector,' he said. 'If I can be of any further assistance, you'll know where to find me.' He stood, stretched his back again and then placed his hands on his hips. The meeting was over.

***

Floria was silent as we left the building but I could see something was troubling her. Only once we have reached the privacy of the car interior did she speak. 'Is there something you're not telling me?' she said, as she started the engine.

I was puzzled by the question. 'In what way?' I asked.

'You want to check a list of people on the base at the time the rifles went and compare it to those here now? Do you know something we don't?'

I smiled. 'We have a database of people we suspect are involved in trafficking,' I said. 'I'm just following a hunch someone on that database might be connected to someone working here.'

'Do you have a suspect?'

'We don't. Your people seem to have thoroughly checked family members of the recruits so the next step has to be other people working here at the time. How many were on the base the day the rifles went missing?'

'I don't know,' she said. 'Several hundred, I'd guess.'

'All of whom could be suspects,' I said. 'But I'd be surprised if it was the random act of an impulsive thief. If anyone here has a connection to gangs in London, they'll go straight to the top of my suspect list.'

'I guess,' Floria said, as she shrugged, put the car into gear and we pulled away.

On the short drive to the Military Police offices on the far side of the barracks, we discussed the meeting with Colonel Hine, arrangements for my intended stay – a room in the Officers' Mess – and what might happen if I discovered anything that implicated one of the soldiers. 'It's a sensitive issue,' I acknowledged. 'And I appreciate why Colonel Hine was being a little cagey. The publicity that followed Angela Davenport's death wasn't good.'

'You could say that again,' Floria replied. 'I'm sure he thinks you're here for reasons other than stated.'

I sighed in frustration. If my work was going to be hampered by local suspicions about my agenda, my visit might end up taking longer than I'd planned. 'Even though the Press are suggesting this place could be another Deepcut,' I said, firmly. 'I want it to be clear that's not why I'm here.'

'Roger that, sir,' Floria said. 'Shall we get back to the matter at hand then?'

'That would be great,' I replied.

'Ok. What I can tell you is before Colonel Hine arrived, procedures to account for weapons used to be lax.'

'What improvements has he made?'

'Lots of things, including the way the issuing registers are supervised. Before Hine, there was no secure method of storing them. On the day of the thefts, they were left open in the guard room and that's how it remained until the day Davenport died. That day, we were ordered to seize the registers for both days but they'd gone.'

'You didn't seize the register on the day of the thefts then?'

'It was an oversight. Colonel Hine issued a standing order to make sure that couldn't happen again.'

'So, what record was made of the register for the day of the theft?'

'The RMP Corporal in attendance made a note in his pocketbook that he'd identified which rifles were missing. He recorded the numbers but noted he could only confirm one signature, that of Private Davenport. The second signature was illegible. When we eventually went to seize both registers after her death, the armourer was under the impression we'd taken them. We knew we hadn't. They never turned up, that's all I can say for definite.'

'I'll need to ask Colonel Hine about that,' I said.

This time Floria smiled. 'Hine not only has his own reputation to protect, he's looking after those above and around him,' she replied, ironically. 'Trust me; he'll smile, appear to cooperate, even make sure you seem to get the information you ask for. And he'll offer you every assistance … every assistance short of actual help.'

Chapter 7

'Very nice,' I said, placing my grab-bag at the side of the bed.

Wendy and I had just finished the guided tour of 'Ty Bryn', her home on the outskirts of Usk. We were in what she'd referred to as her 'green room', my bedroom for the next couple of days. The grab-bag was a leather holdall, a keepsake from many years spent doing bodyguard work for the Royal Family. It went everywhere I did and contained all the essentials I needed – washing kit, spare clothes, passport and some cash. Having such a bag would save precious seconds during an unexpected attack or abduction attempt that might make the difference between life and death – discovery or a clean pair of heels.

'Assistant Chief Constables get paid well, it seems?' I added. Wendy laughed.

My first attempt at securing accommodation hadn't gone well. Floria had quietly sniggered at my reaction when the orderly from the Training Regiment Officers' Mess opened the door to the room intended for my use. As we'd checked it over, she'd described it as resembling a 'cell', and she was right. It had been pretty grim; peeling paint from the walls, a carpet that had definitely seen better days and a wrought iron single bed that looked better suited to a prison. A desperate phone-call to Wendy had resulted in the offer of somewhere rather more comfortable.

'Let's just say, the money I made on my house in Ealing went a long way down here,' Wendy replied, with a smile.

I pressed down on the bed. It felt firm and comfortable. 'I appreciate this,' I said. 'The room the Military Police offered was dire.'

'Officers' Mess not as you remember?'

'I have a feeling it was a ploy aimed at persuading me not to hang around too long.'

'Old habits die hard?' she said, pointing to the bag at my feet.

I'd unconsciously placed my grab-bag where I always did, immediately next to the bed. 'You know me too well,' I said, smiling.

It was good to see Wendy again. We'd met on our initial course at the Met Training School and had now been friends for more years than I cared to remember. Her new house looked Victorian and was conveniently situated about fifteen minutes drive from both Prince Albert Barracks and the police headquarters in Cwmbran. The rooms were spacious and to the rear was a mature garden. As Wendy showed me around, I thought it a little too large for just one person. I was right. What I hadn't expected was her new partner to be French and female. Her name was Monique and when she popped her head around the door to introduce herself, the confused expression on my face caused both my hosts to laugh out loud.

Tour complete, Wendy and Monique headed downstairs to allow me time to settle in. I enjoyed a few minutes peace looking through the window at the view across the local meadows. It was a lovely setting. Before dinner, I called Jenny. She sounded up-beat and it was clear she and the girls were enjoying their break. I was slightly disappointed when she revealed our daughters were exhausted and already in bed. True to form, she sensed my reaction and immediately proposed a better plan for the following day. After that, we chatted for several minutes about the comfortable, everyday stuff that formed our glue – the sandcastles Becky had made on the beach, Charlotte's toilet training and how her sister was starting to drive her nuts – before I explained how I'd ended up at Wendy's.

'Typical of the army,' she said. 'No doubt they wouldn't have thought about bedding either. What's the rest of the camp like?'

'Like many others I've seen. There's something about it, though. Something … miserable.'

'Miserable? That's a strange word to depict an army barracks.'

'It's hard to describe. All camps have soldiers getting beasted and screamed at but there's normally some humour. Joshing, joking, that kind of thing. Here, everyone seems so bloody sour.'

'An aftermath of the suicide enquiry, maybe? Are you still going to see the Davenport family?'

'Tomorrow.'

A voice from downstairs announced supper was ready. The smell of frittata had reached me, reminding me how meagre my pre-packed sandwich lunch on the train had been. Jenny and I said our goodbyes and I headed to join my hosts.

Monique had cooked and, as I arrived in their open plan kitchen, I found Wendy laying the table. The food tasted every bit as good as it had smelled. As we ate, our conversation covered a lot of ground from updates on people we had in common through to politics, television and work. Monique was engaging company, intelligent and articulate. Her spoken English was excellent, her French accent adding a pleasant edge to her pronunciation. I discovered how she and Wendy had met. Both had registered with an on-line dating agency, Wendy seeking a male partner, Monique female. It had been Monique who decided to take a chance and send a contact request. The two women had started chatting, arranged to meet and, as Wendy put it, 'I found she rocked my boat.'

After supper, Monique decided to head off to bed and finish a book she was reading. 'You two need to talk shop,' she said, as she kissed Wendy on the forehead before leaving us alone.

Wendy and I moved outside to the garden. Now the sun had set, it was chilly, the sky clear and cloudless, the surrounding fields as dark as ink.

'She's nice,' I commented, as soon as I was sure we wouldn't be overheard.

'I know,' Wendy said. 'It's my first time … you know, with a woman.'

'You seem very comfortable with each other.'

Wendy smiled, warmly. 'I know it's an overused cliché, but it's like we've known each other for years. We're on the same wavelength. I told her about you … about your background. I hope you don't mind. I thought it would persuade her we really are just friends.'

'Did she need persuading?'

'It never hurts to reassure, Finlay.'

'How much did you tell her?' I said.

'I told her the truth, that you're a former army officer who helped me break up a sex-trafficking gang. She liked that. She thinks you're a bit of a hero.'

'I'm a middle-aged cop with a back problem, that's what I am.'

Wendy laughed. 'From what Bill Grahamslaw tells me, you're up for promotion?'

'The selection board is in two weeks.'

'Finding out who's been smuggling weapons out of the base could help you … provided you don't shoot anyone or get into any fights, of course.'

I didn't reply. I didn't need to. I knew Wendy was right. With my fiftieth birthday fast approaching, this would be my final chance to make Chief Inspector. And she was also right about my methods. Whilst skills I'd picked up in the army had served me well in the past, they weren't the kind of thing expected of a modern-day senior policeman. If I was to get a result, it would need to be in a more traditional way.

Wendy stared out into the dark fields for a few seconds, the silence only broken by a distant chorus of crickets. 'Work has been a bit intense lately,' she continued. 'My boss has been having a lot of behind-closed-doors telephone calls with the Ministry of Defence.'

'Secret talks about the inquest, I assume?'

She sighed, ruefully. 'What else? The Training Regiment CO panicked after the body was discovered and while he was flapping about deciding what to do, valuable time was lost. Our investigation was hampered from the start.'

'So, your Chief Constable is making sure the press don't blame the police?' I said.

'We're an easy scapegoat. Keep this to yourself, but we're trying to make up for the initial mistakes by doing a discreet re-investigation.'

'I thought the inquest had seen the end of it?'

'We've kept an open mind. There's something I should tell you about. I need you to promise you'll keep it between us.'

I was just about to ask the all-important question when a snapping noise pierced the darkness in front of us. It sounded like the crack caused by someone stepping on a dry twig and came from a hedge-line about fifty metres across the field butting onto Wendy's garden. I held up my hand to ask my friend to be silent as I listened for any further noise. There was none.

After several seconds, Wendy ran out of patience. 'What was it?' she murmured.

'Someone or something is out there,' I said. 'Do you have a torch?'

'In a drawer in the kitchen.'

'Can you get it? I'll keep watch.'

As Wendy walked quickly into the house, I picked out features in the gloom; trees and hedges, interspersed with the lighter grey of the fields. I knew what I'd heard and knew what it meant. Animals didn't step on and break dry twigs.

Just as Wendy returned with a small torch in her hand, a phone started ringing in the kitchen. 'I'd better get that,' she said. 'Late calls often turn out to be work.'

I took the torch, turned it towards the field and switched it on. A bright, white light illuminated all in front of me for some considerable distance. 'Hell of a beam,' I said.

'It's LED,' she replied. 'Our firearms team uses them.'

'You get the phone,' I said. 'I'll have a quick scout around.'

The edge of Wendy's garden was a low sheep-fence. I climbed over before scanning the fields to and fro, looking for movement. In the light from the torch, I could see that the nearest meadow was small, about fifty metres across, with a hedge on the far side. If whoever had made the noise was still present, now would be their last opportunity to escape into the darkness.

Nothing moved. For several minutes, I searched the area bordering the hedge before moving into the next field. If there had been someone in the hedgerow, it looked like they were long gone.

Wendy was emerging from the house as I climbed back over her fence. 'Nothing?' she asked.

'Not that I could see,' I replied. 'Something made that noise, though. Any idea if someone might be watching you?'

'With what's been going on lately, it could have been a reporter looking for a scoop. Did anyone know you were coming here?'

'Nobody that I know of. Was that work on the phone?'

'It was,' she replied. 'I have to go in for a meeting.'

'Must be something urgent,' I said.

'Just slightly. What I was about to tell you is we've had an undercover officer going through training as a recruit at the camp. That call was to inform me he's gone missing.'

Chapter 8

I woke early to the smell of toast. Wendy hadn't returned until gone three but she was already up and getting ready for work.

As I was getting dressed, I found myself thinking back to our time at the Met Training School, and how we'd first met. Early days as trainee constables consisted of a lot of classroom work, practical assessments and exercises. After that, every evening was spent studying the criminal law, procedures and working practices. As one of the more mature students, I hadn't found the book-work easy. One evening, about three weeks into the course, I took a break from our Instruction Manual to grab a beer in the recruit bar. A young woman with bright red hair had walked up to me and offered to pay for my drink. That redhead was Wendy.

We spent our first evening as friends discussing the course, why we'd joined the police and other, 'get to know you' type things. Despite our differing backgrounds – grammar school and the Army for me, public school and University for Wendy – we soon gelled. Wendy later explained she'd felt sorry for me, standing on my own at the bar, and that was why she'd approached me.

Our friendship was cemented one day during 'restraint' training. One of the PT staff disliked female recruits and also resented what he called the 'Bramshill flyers', the fast-track graduate recruits who would be heading to Bramshill, the police staff college, as their careers progressed. To this particular instructor, women officers were either a 'Plonk' or a 'Doris', and best kept inside the police station to make tea or look after women and kids.

The fact that Wendy was both female and a 'flyer' singled her out for this Neanderthal's attention. On this particular day, he'd chosen her to help demonstrate restraint techniques. As a class, we were being taught how to deal with awkward prisoners using the 'hammerlock and bar' hold. It was a simple technique to learn, but rather ineffective if you were a diminutive female who's overpowering

40

male instructor was set on showing you up. As the rest of the class watched, Wendy was teased, humiliated and repeatedly dumped on the gym floor in a bedraggled mess. She tried hard, very hard, but the instructor was strong, and he was determined to make his point about the value of female officers.

I saw the sheen of a tear forming in Wendy's eye as she lay on the floor following yet another failed attempt to apply the hold to her tormentor. Ignoring her, the instructor ordered us to form pairs and practise amongst ourselves. I went over to Wendy to help her up. 'You ok?' I asked.

She scowled at me as she pushed my hand away. 'One day, I'm going to come back here as his Inspector, then we'll see who's laughing,' she said, angrily.

'Why wait that long?' I said.

'What do you mean?'

'I'll show you.' With Wendy following, I moved to the back of the gym where we would be away from the rest of the class. The instructor, I'd noticed, had nipped out to do something else while we recruits practised. I had also seen how he'd been tipping Wendy on her back as she tried to place him in the hold. He relied on brute strength. He was over-confident, certain of his power advantage and, as a result, was badly balanced on his feet. He didn't consider his adversary to be a threat. That left him vulnerable to surprise.

Over the next few minutes, I allowed Wendy to practise on me. The first time, I dumped her on her back in the very same way as had happened to her in front of the class. She went to storm off, but I held her arm. 'Hold on,' I said. 'Now, try this.'

Using a simple sweeping movement of the leg, I showed Wendy how to knock me off balance and onto my back. By the time the instructor returned, she was becoming quite proficient at it.

'Ok, you lot,' came the call from our leader as the class formed up in front of him. 'Who's going to show me what you've learned?'

For a few seconds, nobody moved. Then Wendy stepped forward. 'Mind if I have another try, Sergeant,' she said, bravely. The instructor and a couple of the younger male recruits laughed, but Wendy continued her approach.

Failing to anticipate his stooge could have improved much in the time he had been absent, our teacher adopted the same casual approach to overpowering her. It was a mistake. Wendy was quick. What she lacked in strength, she more than made up for in speed. In a flash, the instructor was decked.

For good measure, Wendy stood for a moment's celebration, her right foot on her victim's chest, fists in the air. She resembled a victorious gladiator awaiting a command from her audience to spare or dispatch her unfortunate opponent. Two of the women laughed and gave the 'thumbs down' sign. The rest of us cheered and clapped our hands enthusiastically. Wendy looked at me and, as she smiled, I gave her a wink. Justice had been done.

On such memories are friendships made, I thought, as I joined my hosts at the breakfast table. I smiled on seeing the enormous mug of tea put out for me. 'You remembered?' I quipped.

'Of course,' Wendy answered. 'Did you say your driver will be here at eight?'

At that very moment, the doorbell rang. I checked my watch. It was a quarter to eight; my lift was early.

'I've been thinking about last night,' I said. 'Is there any possibility what we heard in the field could be connected to your missing officer?'

Wendy thought for a moment before replying. 'I don't think so but I'll mention it to his handler just in case. We're keeping things low key for now. We don't want to compromise him if it turns out to be a simple comms issue.'

'If I can be of any help, just ask,' I said. I swallowed a large gulp of tea, grabbed my briefcase and, as I walked to the door, Wendy made me promise to get in touch with her later that day. She was arranging a courtesy interview with her Chief Constable, something I was obliged to do as I was working in his area.

Five minutes later, Floria and I were on our way to west Wales and our meeting with the Davenports.

Chapter 9

Private Jodie Baker slumped into the office chair as she read the note. *Usual time. My place.* It was an order, not a request.

Paul's message had been on her desk, tucked beneath the requisitions where he knew only she would see it. Once, she had felt a thrill on finding his notes, knowing he had left them secretly for her to find. Now, she still shivered, but the feeling was no longer one of excitement.

Looking back, it had all started innocently enough. She had noticed Sergeant Paul Slater paying her particular attention on her first Phase Two parade. She'd seen how his gaze lingered on her. Even then, he'd been sending her a message. I've noticed you.

Hers was a large intake of over a hundred recruits. Crows, the training staff called them. They were a mixed bunch, perhaps three-quarters of them male and, with a few exceptions, all little more than children. Slater was the one they all focussed on; he was their instructor, the NCO with the crisp, perfectly prepared uniform. His boots gleamed in the sun and he concealed squinting eyes beneath the neatly slashed peak of his cap. He watched them, studied them. They realised, even then, he was someone to be both wary of and to try and impress. It was he who decided if they would make it as a soldier.

Most of the Crows were fresh from school. During early conversations with her peers on Phase One, she had discovered just how many had been seduced by recruitment teams at school careers evenings. Smart and handsome in their neatly pressed uniforms, the recruiters hypnotised their audiences with tales of adventure, travel and friendship. At Jodie's school, the girls in her year had talked about nothing else for days and, on the Saturday, she had cajoled her best friend into joining her on the bus into Cardiff where they visited the Army Careers Office. Jodie was a year older than her peers, the

44

result of having to take a second go at her GCSE exams. The Recruiting Sergeant pointed out she could sign up there and then, no need to seek the approval and counter-signature of her parents. A ray of hope had brightened Jodie's bleak and hitherto uncertain prospects. She had a chance to make something of herself, to do something all the others in her dreary school would be jealous of. She wouldn't be another single mum pushing a new-born in a buggy around the local estate and living on benefits. She could be a soldier.

Sergeant Slater referred them as cannon fodder and, from day one, he singled out 'Busty Baker', as he referred to her, for attention. She wasn't the fittest or most athletic member of the intake but even so, she'd still puzzled how an NCO could despise her so much. He taunted her and made her perform humiliating drills in front of the others. If they laughed, it only served to encourage him. He denigrated and insulted her physique – she had curves and a cleavage her mother said men should love – and he seemed determined she would fail as a soldier. She wasn't the type, he'd say, more suited to appearing stripped off in some lads' magazine than in the uniform of Her Majesty's Service.

Almost without exception, the recruits hated Slater. Many said as much during the quiet moments when they were certain nobody was listening. One or two even questioned the wisdom of allowing them guns when their animosity toward him was so widely known.

And then, after four long weeks into their Phase Two training, Sergeant Slater had shown Jodie a different side to his nature. It began during an early morning role-call. The Crows were stood to attention on the parade square while the NCOs checked their rooms. Although it was called an 'inspection', the girls knew that was a loosely applied term to justify a search through their underwear and the ransacking of several shared rooms. When the most despised man in the Training Regiment had bellowed her name from the accommodation block entrance door, Jodie almost vomited with fear. As quickly as she could, she'd headed inside. On entering the room she shared with three other girls, she'd been surprised, and not a little confused, to discover it hadn't been turned upside down. Everything was as they had left it.

Her nemesis had been waiting inside the door. He'd loomed over her and ordered her to sit on her bed. She lowered her gaze and, as she fought back tears of dread, her legs shook with fear. When he'd closed the door to ensure they wouldn't be disturbed, she'd feared the worst. Silently, he had then leaned towards her and lifted a foot onto the bed, his highly polished boot resting on the edge beside her. He was so close she'd felt his hot breath on her cheek.

'I despair of you sometimes, Baker,' he'd said softly.

Jodie's stomach had lurched, and she'd tasted acid bile in her mouth. It had been all she could do to simply nod in response.

'Can I share something with you, Baker?' he'd then asked. Once again, he spoke quietly. There seemed no edge to his voice, no threat. Jodie had raised her head, changed her gaze from staring at the floor, and looked up at him. At any other time, such an act would have incurred his wrath but this time … this time she'd sensed things were different.

As he'd grinned, she managed a half-smile in response. 'Yes, Sergeant,' she replied, meekly.

'I'm going to level with you, Baker. But if this goes outside this room then, believe me, I'll make you regret the day you were born, understood?'

Jodie had nodded, all the time wondering if it were a ploy, another of Sergeant Slater's well-known tricks; a way to lower her guard and then launch another bullying attack.

And then, as she listened, the man she'd come to hate more than anyone she'd previously met sat down beside her and sighed. And he spoke to her warmly, told her how he respected her, how he had been impressed with how she'd stood up to the beastings he'd subjected her to, and how she reminded him of a time when he'd been a young soldier himself. At first, Jodie had been dumb-struck,

46

stunned into silence and the sense this was some form of trick, remained. She'd half expected the other NCOs would be listening at the door or hiding under the beds waiting to jump up and ridicule her as part of an elaborate joke.

But they hadn't. And, as their conversation continued, she'd begun to realise her former tormentor was being sincere. He really had grown to like her. He'd been cautious in his praise, though, and warned her that, compared to the others, she still had a lot of catching up to do. And then, he'd offered something she'd never expected. He offered to help.

But, there was one condition – she wasn't to tell anyone. Favouritism, special help to recruits, was frowned upon, he explained. He'd help her with her fitness, her weapon drills and her kit – all the areas where she struggled – but it would have to be done without the others knowing. 'Don't trust them,' he warned. 'They will lie to you and they can't be trusted. If you have a question, wait until you see me and we will get it sorted.'

In the days that followed, Jodie knew she'd made the right decision. Paul gave her permission to use his first name when they were alone and, although he had his own home outside the camp, he also had a key to an unoccupied married quarter, a small house adjacent to the officer's accommodation. While her friends headed to a local pub or the NAAFI during the evening, Jodie would make her excuses and join him. He ironed her dress uniform and even showed her some tricks such as how to quickly bring her boots up to the standard expected for a full parade. He gave her a phone to use, a secret one she was only to use to contact him. In public, he maintained his previous persona and there were times he would deliberately cause upset by rebuking her in front of her fellow Crows for some perceived mistake, or he would make a joke at her expense for the benefit of the other NCOs. But it was all part of their cover, he said, a way to stop people suspecting them.

The beastings stopped too and, in the weeks that followed, she wasn't singled out for attention once. The girls from her intake noticed and one of her friends – a scouse girl called Naomi – laughingly suggested Jodie must have given the Sergeant a blow-job on the day he'd called her back into the accommodation block. A month later following a four-mile run, when he'd screamed 'Good effort, Baker,' to her in the hearing of the other recruits, she knew she'd reached a key waypoint in her training.

When their friendship did, eventually, become intimate, it was a natural development. She'd grown to trust Paul and looked forward to their time together. She began to relax in his company too, as he became the supportive mentor he'd promised to be. He was married, with two young boys, but was separated. He'd confessed it had been a problematic marriage and, if it hadn't been for his commitment to raising his sons, he would have left his wife sooner. One evening, they had been at his family home away from the camp, working on her kit. Not too surprisingly, their conversation had strayed onto other subjects. They'd talked about previous romances and had laughed at their shared experience of having felt awkward around the opposite sex while in school. He opened a bottle of red wine for them to share. Red wine wasn't a drink she'd tried – at school it had always been cheap cider or lager – but she went along with his suggestion and discovered she enjoyed the taste. When he kissed her for the first time, the taste of wine on his lips, she'd thought 'at last'. At last, he had made that final move and done what she had been craving for weeks. It was only when they'd run, laughing together, up the stairs and into his bedroom that she'd realised he'd made some preparations. The bed was made up, the curtains drawn and, just as they reached that awkward moment where they were going to risk a pregnancy or hold back, he reached under the bed to produce a small pack of condoms. He'd thought of everything.

But that had been months ago. Now, he no longer felt the need to treat her with respect. She just did as she was told and made herself available, whenever he wanted. And with almost every member of her original intake posted away to new Regiments, she was one of just three girls from her cohort yet to be deployed. Paul had delayed it, and after what had happened with Davenport, he'd given her what he described as 'a nice little clerical job' in the Armoury where he could keep an eye on her and she could while away her time as the dust settled. She was envious of her peers as they headed off to do courses, qualified on a variety of skills and then boasted of the postings they had received and the interesting places where they were to be deployed. She would talk to Paul but he would remind her how she owed him and that she needed to be patient. In time, he promised, her opportunities would come and they would be better than any of the others.

It wasn't all bad, though. The role brought extra pay and even some kudos in the eyes of other recruits. She was exempted guard duty, no night shifts, no latrine duty and no parades. Some viewed her as lucky. Others, like her friend Naomi, were wise enough to question the price.

The job in the Armoury had been a favour from Sergeant Andy Masters, the camp wheeler-dealer and a friend of Paul's who'd offered to help look after her. Unfortunately, Masters had his own reasons for making the offer. She soon discovered the Armourer was a complete letch. He kept a collection of porn DVDs he hired out to the recruits – mostly the men, but not always – and he regularly made his new charge the subject of his lewd and distorted sense of humour. The atmosphere in the Armoury had become oppressive to the point of being unbearable but when she'd mentioned it to Paul, he'd laughed it off. 'Boys will be boys,' he'd said, 'It's just a bit of fun and you've only got yourself to blame.'

On one particularly awful occasion, Masters had really gone for her. He'd started by pinning her against a desk inside the weapons store-room before trying to coerce her into performing the same kind of favour he reckoned she did for Paul. She'd resisted but his persistence had developed into a wrestling match on the floor with Jodie desperately trying to squirm and wriggle away from him. As Masters' frustration spilled over into anger, he'd lain on top of her, immobilising her shoulders and forcing his hand between her legs. Jodie had used the only weapon she had available to defend herself. She'd told Masters she knew about his money-lending scams, about the stolen phones he dealt in, and that she'd tell the world if he didn't stop what he was doing that very second.

It had worked, and the Sergeant had stopped his attack immediately. Without saying a word, he'd left her on the floor and headed out the door. He'd gone to find Paul, they'd had words and, the result had been that Paul threatened her, warning her what might happen if she ever repeated what she'd said to anyone else.

And she obeyed him, because she knew he was right. Just as he always was.

Chapter 10

25 Signal Regiment, Squadron Offices.

Through her office window overlooking the parade square, 2nd Lieutenant Ellie Rodgers watched as the recruits marched smartly in formation. A drill Sergeant was putting the latest Training Regiment intake through their paces. The young soldiers looked smart and she grunted approvingly as they executed a well-coordinated about-turn. Alongside them, the Sergeant skilfully twirled his brass-tipped pace-stick on the tarmac surface. Resembling a large draft-compass, the hinged stick whirred around in his hand, clicking as the tips hit the ground to mark both the timing and distance – thirty inches – of the 'quick march' tempo he was teaching the recruits.

Whilst her eyes were occupied, Ellie's mind was elsewhere, in a less coherent place she'd rather have forgotten. She'd expected the interview with Private Maria Orr to be routine, an admonishment of a young soldier, a short entry on her personnel record – conduct to the prejudice of good order and military discipline contrary to S.69 of the Army Act – and that would have been the end of the matter. Now, Orr stood silently at attention, in front of her officer's desk, waiting for a response.

Three weeks into her first posting as an officer and this was just what she didn't need. Memories of Germany, vivid and all-consuming, were preventing her thinking straight. 'Don't let it shape you,' her counsellor had warned. 'One day, something like this may happen to someone under your command. You will need to be objective and to put the anger you will inevitably feel to one side.' Incredibly, that day had already come.

What she'd heard was appalling and, if what Orr wasn't exaggerating, a significant number of NCOs on the camp were exploiting female soldiers for sex. Corporal Jackson stood silently near the door. She looked distinctly uncomfortable.

For a moment, Ellie cursed herself for asking the question 'why'. 'What' had been clear. Orr had been caught, for the second time, allowing her room to be used by Private Towler, a female soldier from the Training Regiment. The secretive nature of the use – hiding a note and key inside a boot left in a drying room – had suggested the two young women were in a relationship of some kind.

At first, when responding to Ellie's questions, Orr had been circumspect, even a little evasive. It was only when Ellie had quizzed her about the nature of the relationship that her explanation had been more forthcoming. Amanda Towler was a mate, Orr explained, who worked as a clerk at the Training Regiment. She also explained the reason Towler had been using the room was due to fear. She was afraid to sleep in the accommodation assigned to recruits due to frequent sexual harassment and unwanted night-time visits by several of her NCOs. The quivering in Orr's voice and the way she avoided eye contact told Ellie the purpose of the visits was far more than a simple case of the NCOs harassing Crows. They were visiting the recruits for sex. Orr's friend had become an NCOs' plaything, a young woman bullied and victimised, and then offered a nice, easy job provided she did everything – absolutely everything – her NCOs asked of her.

'Can you get Private Orr a chair, please Corporal?' Ellie said, closing the window firmly. The likelihood of them being overheard by someone nearby was small, but there was no sense in taking chances.

Corporal Jackson disappeared into the corridor for a few seconds before returning with one of the wooden chairs from the HQ Admin office. 'Do you wish me to remain, ma'am?' she said as, with some uncertainty, Private Orr lowered herself onto the seat.

Ellie cleared her throat before replying. 'I think that would be wise, Corporal.'

We're about to open a can of worms, she thought. There's no way I'm doing this on my own.

With Orr seated, Ellie pulled an A4 notebook from her desk drawer. She turned to the next blank page, recorded the date, the time and place, and the presence of Corporal Jackson. A contemporaneous record of whatever discussion followed would be needed.

Orr looked at her, quizzically. 'What are you doing, ma'am?' she asked.

'Making a record, Private Orr. I was a Redcap before being commissioned … a Corporal.' Ellie deliberately mentioned having come up through the ranks in the hope it might produce a little empathy, an understanding they shared a similar background. 'I'm required to make a record of allegations,' she added.

'Allegations?' Orr looked uncomfortable and turned in her seat to glance at Corporal Jackson. Jackson remained deadpan, emotionless. No support there, Ellie thought.

'That's what they are,' Ellie said. 'What you've described will need to be investigated.'

Orr hesitated for several seconds before responding. By the time she spoke, Ellie had already begun writing a summary of what she'd said up to that point. 'Could you stop that, ma'am?' Orr said, firmly.

Ellie looked up from her notebook, saw fear on the young soldier's face and realised immediately the girl had lost her nerve. She wasn't surprised. Young soldiers learned within weeks of commencing training how effective the military grapevine was. If Orr was identified as a snitch, a tell-tale, her life could become impossible and the label would follow her. The fingers on Corporal Jackson's right hand quivered, and then her hand lifted slightly, as if she wanted to speak but felt awkward doing so. 'Yes, Corporal Jackson?' Ellie said.

'With your permission, ma'am,' Jackson replied. 'Private Orr told me before seeing you today that she's happy to explain the reasons behind her misdemeanour but has no wish to take things any further.'

Ellie turned to look Orr in the eye. 'Is this true, Orr. You simply wish to mitigate your offence?'

Orr sat to attention. 'Yes, ma'am.'

'You realise, if we fail to take this any further, these men will continue to do this to your friend as well as to others?'

As the young soldier silently lowered her gaze to look at the floor between her feet, Ellie realised the argument was lost. 'Would you take Private Orr's chair, Corporal?' she said.

Orr stood to attention as Jackson took the chair. Ellie caught another quick look between the two of them. There was more to this, of that she had no doubt. 'Very well, Private Orr,' she announced. 'You'll be fined two days pay.'

As Corporal Jackson marched Orr out into the corridor and then closed the door firmly behind her, Ellie shook with rage. She was angry, really angry; with her reaction to what Orr had said and her inability to progress it. If they had any idea, she said to herself. She stared for a moment at the notes in front of her. They were incomplete and unsigned. Useless, in terms of evidential value, and hardly worth the paper they were written on. Although procedurally correct, starting them had been a mistake that had caused Orr to clam up.

She already knew she couldn't let it lie, though. Not now, not after what she'd been through. Maybe it had been fate, she thought. Maybe it was destined she should be the one to learn what was going on. Maybe, this was her chance to right some wrongs.

Chapter 11

The early part of the drive to the Davenport home near Cardigan gave me a chance to read the investigation report into the theft of the rifles. From what I could see, the RMP had been pretty thorough. Searches had been made of all vehicles and people leaving the barracks and retrospective checks carried out on all movements before the weapons were discovered missing. All potential witnesses had been interviewed. When and how the rifle theft had occurred remained a mystery. Following a parade, all the recruits had been instructed to place their rifles on the back of a flat-bed lorry. The lorry had been sealed – with the tail-gate raised and the rear canvas cover closed up. On arrival at the Training Regiment Armoury, two rifles were found to be missing, one of which had been allocated to Angela Davenport for the parade. Just as Floria had said, whoever signed for the second rifle had never been ascertained as the signature had been illegible and the issuing register for the day had subsequently disappeared.

During the second half of the journey, I decided to try and improve the rather shaky start I'd made with Floria, and also to learn something about her. It was an interesting story. She explained how her Jamaican father, Bruce McLaren – not the famous racing driver – had arrived as an immigrant to the UK in the 1950s, in response to a Government advertisement for workers. Her mother, Virginia, was from South London and that was where the couple had settled. Bruce worked as a bus inspector; Virginia had been a primary school teacher. When I asked about her name, Floria explained, with relaxed amusement, that Bruce was something of an opera fan and had named each of his six children after characters created by his favourite composers. Floria was from Puccini's Tosca. The well-practised delivery of her explanation suggested an oft-repeated story.

To my disappointment, when it came to specific knowledge about the weapon thefts, Floria wasn't able to help much. She had only been on the periphery of the enquiry, she explained, with her normal field of expertise being AWOLs, soldiers 'absent without leave'. When not assigned to help people like me – you're my first, she joked, with a mischievous grin – her normal working day was spent tracking down young men and women who, for one reason or another, had decided to absent themselves from their place of work in the Army. 'Soldiers do a runner and refuse to come back mostly because they're afraid of something,' she said, as we were approaching Cardigan. 'A few are afraid of getting killed but not many. Most of them are more afraid of failure and the treatment some of the NCOs dish out.'

'Did you get bullied yourself?' I asked.

'They like to call it that in the papers, don't they?' she replied. 'When I first joined, the NCOs used to call me 'Nignog'. They used to laugh about it and say it stood for 'New in green, never on guard', but we all knew what they were on about.'

'Did you ever report it?' I asked.

Floria threw back her head in amusement. 'Are you kidding me? My life wouldn't have been worth living. You've got to understand, when you're a young kid starting Army training, these guys are gods. They called me 'black this' or 'black that' to wind me up and try to break me but, to be honest, it did the job it was supposed to. By the time I was deployed, it was like water off a duck's back. In Kosovo, I got called far worse but I was hardened to it, so I guess the NCOs knew what they were doing.'

'Doesn't make it ok, though,' I said. 'Does it still happen now?'

'What do you think?' Floria replied. 'The field Army refer to all Military police as 'monkeys' which makes it a bit hard for people like me to accuse anyone of being racist.' She tapped the three stripes on the sleeve of her shirt. 'What counts once you get to your Regiment is that you do your job and you do it well. We all get banter; it's a way of knowing you're accepted. If you're ginger-haired, a Scot, got a big nose or whatever, people will always take the mickey over something. It's when they blank you that you know your face doesn't fit.'

'What about being female?'

'Not a problem. When I was in training it was like having a huge gang of big brothers. There was the odd one after a bit, but that was no different from civvie street. When someone tried it on, the others would rally round and warn them off. One lad who tried to climb into a girl's sleeping bag while we were on exercise got dragged into the woods by two NCOs and given a right hiding.'

'So, they protected you as well as giving you a hard time?' I said.

Floria grinned broadly to reveal a set of perfect teeth. 'Damn right they did. They were turning us into soldiers.'

We were nearly at our destination before Floria decided to ask about my background. As agreed with Bill Grahamslaw, I was honest but economic in what I said. I told her about my twenty years as a cop, about my time spent on Royalty Protection and how I'd married late. I also explained how I'd left protection work to spend more time with my young family, something she thought a very selfless thing to do. As the satnav announced our proximity to the Davenport home, I mentioned my forthcoming promotion board.

'Do you get promoted based on results?' Floria asked.

I smiled. It was a common misconception. 'We don't,' I said. 'But heading back to London with the names of the people responsible for stealing and receiving weapons from the Army wouldn't harm my chances.'

Floria eased off the accelerator and I saw she was scanning the nameplates of the houses in the street we had just turned into. She pointed towards a large house, partially hidden behind a huge weeping willow tree. Just as she'd promised, there was no melee of reporters, no flashing cameras and no dispirited cops standing guard. We'd arrived.

Chapter 12

As we entered the Davenport home, I thought it prudent to immediately express my condolences over the death of their daughter. I expected the family would still be smarting at the result of the inquest and didn't want any ill-feeling they had towards the police to impact on how helpful they might be. Michael Davenport simply grunted his acceptance before guiding us into the living room.

Michael suggested, before sitting down to discuss the reason for my visit, we look at his daughter's room while his wife, Phyllis, made tea. As we climbed the stairs, I noticed how he moved slowly, his feet dragging heavily on the carpet. I had a sense of a family still in shock, still coming to terms with what had happened. As he gently opened the door to Angela's bedroom, I caught the familiar scent of lavender in the air. The room was large and overlooked the garden at the rear of the house. I looked around and saw the source of the scent. On the windowsill, in a small, glass jar, the flame of a burning candle flickered gently in the draft from the door.

'We've kept it as it was when she last stayed,' Michael said.

I scanned the large number of photographs and posters adorning the walls. Angela appeared to have had two principal interests, pop music and the Army. The single bed was neatly made – a pale blue duvet with matching pillowcase – and there was no sign of dust on any of the shelves or the small bedside cabinet. Narrow lines on the carpet suggested it had been freshly vacuumed.

A single bookshelf displayed two framed photographs and a small selection of novels – all of a military-type – penned by a selection of well-known authors. The photos were both of Angela, one standing proudly to attention in her No.2 dress uniform and a second, larger one, showing her relaxed and grinning with what looked to be her Basic Military Skills platoon from Cwmbran.

'It's a nice room,' Floria commented. I noticed she was edging back towards the door. She looked uncomfortable. A moment later, she turned and stepped out onto the landing.

'Wasn't always this tidy, of course,' Michael said, with a half smile, as he picked up the formal photo of his daughter. 'And your people left it in a bit of a mess when they searched it.'

'Our people?' I said, as I continued to look around the room.

'The Special Investigation Branch came a couple of times after Angela died.'

'Did they find anything?'

'Nothing much. There was some kit under her bed. They bagged it up and took it ... said it was Army property and had to be returned. The second time they didn't say what they were looking for but they left empty-handed.'

'Did the local police come as well?' I asked.

'No. The first time we had any real contact with the civilian police was on the first day of the inquest. Everything else was done over the telephone.'

'Have you done a thorough search yourself?' I said. 'The kind of places we might not think to look?'

'We left it to them,' he said, flatly.

'Did your daughter keep a diary?'

'Not that we ever saw, no.'

'What about a mobile phone?' I said. 'According to what I've read in the investigation report, it seems she didn't have one.'

Michael shrugged and I wondered if he was finding our conversation difficult. 'She did have a phone, a nice one. It was never found,' he said. 'We figured she may have left it at the barracks. Maybe someone stole it?'

As Michael finished speaking, I heard the stairs creak. 'Tea's ready,' Floria called from the landing.

Downstairs, Mrs Davenport had laid out the coffee table with cups, saucers, four small plates and a teapot covered with a brightly coloured cosy. As we sat down, she appeared from the kitchen with a plate of biscuits. She glanced at me, just the once, and didn't speak. It was as if she were simply going through the motions of being hospitable, not really wanting to engage with us. As we sat watching his wife pour the tea, I also noticed how it was Michael who asked our preferences regarding milk and sugar.

'You're from the Met?' Michael said as, in unison, we all reached for our cups. 'I think I should be honest, Inspector. If you'd been from Cwmbran police, we'd not have been minded to speak to you.'

'Yes, I think I can appreciate why,' I replied. And then, to switch the focus of our conversation, I explained about the raid in London, and how one of the weapons recovered was believed to have been a rifle issued to his daughter on the day it was stolen.

'To be honest, I was surprised nobody else came to see us about it,' Michael said. 'Angela always maintained it wasn't her rifle that was taken. She was a scapegoat, she thought.'

'Did she mention that to anyone else,' I asked, as I saw a look of confusion on Floria's face.

'I've no idea,' Michael said, between sips. 'Certainly, no-one ever asked us and when I told the Coroner's people who were dealing with the inquest, they said it wasn't relevant as there were records to show it had been her rifle that went.'

'Did she ever talk to you about what happened at her passing-out parade ... about the rifles going missing, I mean?'

'Talk to us? We were there, for God's sake.' As Michael returned his cup to the table, I saw his hand was now shaking. 'We saw the recruits putting their guns onto the back of the truck. I remember saying to Angela at the time that you'd have thought the Army would be a bit more careful.'

'This was after the passing-out parade?' I said.

'Yes, before we went to have a tour around their accommodation and training areas. She said it was the way things were done and not to worry.'

'And you saw Angela place her rifle with the others?'

'She had to guard the lorry. Until she was relieved, she sat in the passenger seat of the cab while the families had a tour around the camp. I know her rifle was with her at that point because we laughed over the fact it was unloaded. She thought it was ridiculous to expect her to be the guard when she didn't have any bullets.'

'And afterwards?'

'She put her rifle with the others, I believe.'

Phyllis Davenport put her cup on the table alongside her husband's before speaking for the first time. 'She was petrified they were going to kick her out,' she said, after taking a breath. 'The Army police accused her of lying about placing her rifle in the lorry. It was only when an NCO spoke up for her that they left her alone.'

'An NCO?'

'Sergeant Slater. When Angela was accused, he vouched for her.'

'Did Angela or her friends have any theories on what happened?' I said.

'Not that they shared with us,' said Michael. 'They were told they weren't even to discuss it amongst themselves. The same thing happened the day Angela died. They closed ranks, ordered everyone to keep quiet. A wall of silence enforced at the point of a gun.'

'You're saying people were threatened?'

Phyllis Davenport spoke up again. 'They were warned off,' she said. 'The last time Angela was home on leave she told me it had all been cleared up and she was off the hook. But she said it had been made very clear to them they weren't to talk about it to people off the base.'

'Did she ever speak about it to anyone else you know of?' I asked.

'You mean, did she die as a result of what happened that day?' said Michael. 'Well, that's what we're still trying to find out, isn't it? That inquest result was a travesty. How they can say a young woman who loves her job and is looking forward to her future would shoot herself in the head on purpose, is beyond me?'

'So, you don't think it was suicide?'

'We knew our daughter, Inspector,' Michael said firmly, his jaw set hard. 'She was happy-go-lucky and she was doing something she loved. She had no reason to kill herself.'

With our teacups drained, Michael suggested Floria and I join him in the rear garden while his wife cleared up. It was a tactical move. As soon as we were out of earshot from the house, he apologised.

'I'm sorry for spouting off like that,' he said. 'But it's like knocking your head against a brick wall. The MOD seem to think we couldn't possibly understand the pressures our daughter was under. It's clear they want this whole thing to blow over quickly.'

'I wish I could help,' I said. 'But I'm not investigating your daughter's death.'

Michael paused for a moment before taking a deep breath. 'Do you know, for the first time in my life I'm having to take pills. I can't sleep; my blood pressure is off the scale. Phyllis is on anti-depressants. We just need someone to listen to us, someone to take our concerns seriously.' I went to speak but he raised a hand to silence me. 'Just promise me this, Inspector. We've hoped for a long time that Scotland Yard might send someone, at least to take a look at things. If you learn anything, please make sure you do the right thing.'

As I turned to make eye contact with Floria, she remained expressionless. She knew that in a couple of days I would most likely be back in London and the Davenports would never hear from me again. But, as I turned back to Michael Davenport, I said I would, more by way of reassurance than in expectation I could ever deliver.

Floria headed out to the car, leaving me to thank the Davenports for their time. As I handed Michael a card with my contact number on it, I asked if he happened to find something like a diary or a mobile phone, if they would call me. He promised they would.

At the car, Floria was concluding a telephone call as I opened the passenger door. 'That was tough,' she said as she returned her phone to her jacket pocket.

'How are you?' I said. 'I thought you looked upset when you left Angela's bedroom.'

'I'm fine,' she replied. 'It shook me up a bit. It was just like my folks keep my bedroom back home. I had to get out when I began wondering how they would deal with me being killed.'

'An old friend once told me, until you've lost a child, you'll never understand.'

'I would have thought cops get used to seeing death?'

'You get used to seeing dead bodies, Floria. What gets to you are simple things like someone's watch still ticking on the bedside table or a bookmark in a half-read novel. Death can seem surreal when you notice how everything else is carrying on.'

'Well, I don't plan to have my parents find out,' Floria replied. 'But, it was still an interesting visit.'

'In what way?' I asked, as I sensed Floria's eagerness to change the subject.

'To learn more about Angela Davenport. One of the first things we get taught on our investigation course is to find out as much as you can about how a murder victim lived because it may tell you how they died.'

'Except she wasn't murdered.'

Floria shrugged. 'I'll keep an open mind on that.'

'As you wish. I was hoping to learn more about Angela from her mobile phone,' I said. 'The official report made no mention of one.'

'If she had one, we never found it. We did look. The powers that be wanted to see if there was any evidence she'd talked to someone about ending her life. It would have helped prove their conclusion.'

'Is the Sergeant, Mr Davenport mentioned still at the depot?' I asked.

'Sergeant Slater? I'm sure he is, but I'll check. That was my office I was on the phone to, by the way.'

'Anything important?'

'Might be something, might be nothing. I've read both the files, the one about the rifle thefts and the investigation into Private Davenport's death. That call was to confirm a couple of things.'

'Like what?'

'Firstly, there's no record of Davenport ever claiming the stolen rifle wasn't hers. And, secondly, SIB only searched her room here *once* after she died. Whoever came on that follow-up visit, it wasn't us.'

Chapter 13

Ellie Rodgers was about two-thirds of her way through her carefully rehearsed account of the meeting with Private Orr when she noticed Colonel Bullen's eyes glaze over.

'The exploitation of any young person is a tragedy, second Lieutenant,' he said, interrupting her as she paused for breath. As Bullen spoke, his emphasis was on her rank, an apparent reminder of her position as a junior officer, the most junior on the camp. Leaning forward in his chair, he fixed her with a determined stare. 'Such incidents must be seen in the context of the thousands of young soldiers passing through training. You are well aware, especially given your background in the ranks, the Army will not tolerate bullying at any time and, if it is detected, the perpetrators can expect to be dealt with firmly.'

Her Commanding Officer had batted her request away as he might an irritating fly. Ellie glanced sideways at Brian Holt, the Regimental Sergeant-Major. He'd advised her not to ask for this meeting, not to take her concerns 'upstairs', as he put it. The 'I warned you' look on his face said it all.

Removing his spectacles and placing them on the leather-inlaid desk in front of him, Bullen relaxed into his leather chair. 'As I have no doubt Mister Holt will have told you,' he continued. 'We share Prince Albert Barracks with others whose standards are below ours. You'd be best to leave this well alone.'

'May I speak freely, sir?' Ellie asked, as the Colonel paused.

Bullen leaned back and clasped his hands together. 'You may,' he replied, in a fatherly tone. 'I encourage my junior officers to speak up, as you well know. But I'd caution you to engage brain first.'

Determined to ignore the sense of foreboding she now felt, Ellie prepared to deliver her trump card, the one thing she hoped might trigger the response she had been hoping for. Just saying the name

'Deepcut' was certain to provoke some kind of reaction. Whether it would be the one she wanted, she couldn't be certain. But to have your career in any way associated with that place was said to be the kiss of death to a senior officer, and nobody – including Colonel Bullen – wanted their command to suffer a similar experience. It had to be worth a try.

'Sir,' she began. 'If what Private Orr tells me is true, there is a group of NCOs at the Training Regiment who are exploiting female recruits for sexual gratification. We all know what happened at Deepcut. What if the same kind of problem is brewing here? Shouldn't we at least pass this information to their Commanding Officer?'

Bullen's eyebrows rose briefly as she mentioned the name but, to her surprise, he then smiled warmly before folding his arms across his chest. He hadn't reacted as she'd hoped. 'This is not Deepcut, Miss Rodgers,' he replied. 'And you only have the word of one soldier. We all know what goes on in the ranks. Put young, fit people of both sexes together in a close working environment and we should hardly be surprised what happens, should we?'

'But this seems to be a different ball game,' Ellie replied. 'With respect, we're talking abuse and sexual predation here.'

Bullen sighed, just gently, but enough to communicate to Ellie that she was trying his patience. 'Recruit training needs to be hard,' he said. 'We have to know we're producing soldiers who will stand up to the rigours of combat.'

'But, sir. Hard training shouldn't push people to the point where they feel it necessary to hide from their NCOs.' Even as Ellie spoke, she knew she'd over played her hand. She recalled her RSM's words; his advice when she'd sought his guidance on Private Orr. 'Don't rock the boat ma'am,' he'd counselled her. 'Keep it to yourself and think of your career. Think how the CO of the Training Regiment might react if he finds a young officer has reported him for failure to properly supervise those under his command?'

Any officer knew to heed the wisdom of their senior NCOs, and Ellie had thought hard about her RSM's advice. Now, she realised her mistake. Bullen had listened, at first with apparent concern, but subsequently with determination to bring the matter to an immediate close. He'd made it quite clear; he would not be taking Private Orr's complaint any further.

'Ellie,' Bullen said, as he relaxed into his chair. She recognised the switch in tack immediately, resistant senior had become wise parent – I'm your friend, accept my counsel. 'I can understand your concern,' he continued. 'But our role is to maintain discipline within our command. In less than three months we deploy to Iraq, so we need to focus on that, not on the problems of others. We do not, and never will, start poking around in the affairs of others outside our chain of command. To do so would be a serious breach of military etiquette and, to my mind, most prejudicial to discipline. Now, if that's understood?'

'Of course, sir,' Ellie replied.

'Very good. If there's nothing more to discuss, I look forward to seeing you at the Mess dinner. Don't forget it's been rescheduled to Monday to accommodate our guests.'

Beside her, RSM Holt's chair scraped noisily on the floor as he stood ready to leave. The meeting was over.

As she stood, the Colonel had a final word for her. 'I appreciate your concern, Second Lieutenant, but you'd do well to remember that you are no longer in the Military Police.'

***

As Colonel Bullen's door closed behind them, the RSM nodded his head towards the exit. He walked quickly and in silence, encouraging Ellie to keep up using simple movements of his hand. Only once they'd reached the tarmac drive well out of earshot of any nearby buildings did he stop.

'Accept the boss's decision, ma'am,' he said, as he leaned in close to her. 'Between ourselves, I'd say you're not the first to hear stories of what's been going on across the way. Point is, it's not our place to go digging.'

'But nobody seems to be taking it seriously,' Ellie replied. 'You heard what I said to the Colonel. Orr's friend tried to take her concerns through her chain of command and they ignored her. Where are our morals, Mr Holt? Where do we draw a line on what we're prepared to tolerate?'

The RSM eyed her with sympathy. 'If there's a shit-storm brewing like you say, nobody here will want to be caught in it,' he said. 'Don't imagine we don't spot the calibre of NCO posted to run the Phase Two course.'

'Are you saying they're all like it?' Ellie said.

'I've no idea,' Holt replied. 'Some of them must be reasonable, I suppose. But for ages now they've been posting bad eggs to that training depot thinking it will keep them out of harm's way.'

'So, you're saying we should do nothing, so no flack comes our way? I can't do that, I'm afraid. I can't just stand by while that kind of thing is going on.'

'Fact is, ma'am, you're going to have to do as you are ordered. Don't imagine the boss wanted me in there for the benefit of my experience. He wanted me as a witness to the fact he warned you off. He's protecting himself as well as trying to stop you getting in bother.'

'Do you agree with him?' Ellie said.

'I do … and not just for the reasons he said.'

'What else?'

'Try and remember this is the Army, ma'am. Inside the wire, it pays to remember that.'

'I'm not sure I follow?'

The RSM stopped for a moment. He appeared to be looking around for any sign someone may be within earshot. There was nobody. The only people even within sight were a small band of soldiers cleaning the outside windows of a nearby accommodation block. 'Trust me when I tell you there are some very unpleasant individuals in the Training Regiment,' he said, finally, his voice lowered as if he were imparting a secret he felt she should know. 'You really don't want to go pissing them off. And don't imagine those pips on your shoulders will protect you because they won't, and neither can I.'

Ellie sensed there was something more in Holt's voice, something he hadn't yet revealed. 'Are you afraid of them, Mister Holt?' she asked.

'Let's just say I'm wary, ma'am. The best thing for you is to stay clear, that's all I'll say.'

'Is that what happens?' Ellie said. 'We're expected to just give up and leave it be?'

'I'm just suggesting,' the RSM said. 'For your own good, keep your nose from where it doesn't belong.'

Chapter 14

Everywhere Ellie looked in the bar, she saw recruits. A few were dancing but most simply stood around drinking and socialising as they enjoyed a late Summer evening in the Royal Arms. In the corner near the window, a small group were playing pool. They were decent players and had attracted quite an audience.

It had taken her a little over fifteen minutes, mingling with the young soldiers in the pub, before she'd located a small group sat around a table whose accents were similar to her own. There were four of them. She had watched them for a few minutes before deciding they were just what she was looking for – street-wise girls who might know exactly what their NCOs were up to. She'd then followed one of the girls into the toilets where a short ice-breaking conversation in front of the mirrors had resulted in an invitation to join them. Part one of the plan had gone smoothly.

A large number of empty pint glasses now stood on their table. Another four – the most recently acquired thanks to a group of lads at the bar – were full. In addition, Ellie counted ten empty shot glasses. As a cop working plain clothes with the Military Police, she'd been in this exact scenario before. Her eyes darted from face to face, watching and assessing as she scanned everyone in the packed bar for any sign of being compromised. She had to be particularly careful. Despite her heavy make-up and tight, fashionable clothing, if someone she knew came into the bar, they could ruin everything.

As the DJ racked up the volume, she leaned in close to the girl called Naomi to try and make out what she was saying. Naomi appeared to be the oldest of the group. She was tall, had clear ebony skin and wore a tight, figure hugging dress. She also had a broad, beaming smile that turned the men's heads. 'Fancy you being from Woolton an' all,' she shouted to Ellie. 'Where did you go to school?'

Ellie winced. The pitch and volume of Naomi's voice had gone up a notch with each combination of lager and vodka, to the point where her attempts to converse hurt Ellie's eardrums. 'St Julie's', she replied. 'Left at sixteen to sign up.'

It was the truth, and St Julie's was a school Naomi was certain to know. Ellie knew that any Scouse lass worth her salt would soon suss an outsider pretending to be something they weren't.

'There's posh you are,' Naomi said, laughing. 'How come we never seen you in 'ere before then?'

Ellie leaned close once more but kept her eyes on the dance floor. Two lads – both in short-sleeved shirts and sporting cropped haircuts – were sidling up to Naomi's mates. 'I've only just arrived back on camp,' she replied. 'Been deployed overseas.'

'You're not a Crow then?'

'Two-five Signals,' Ellie said. 'Our main detachment is in Germany.'

'So, what brings you back to this shit-hole?'

'A clerical course.'

'Lucky you.' Naomi said, sarcastically, before taking a long drink from one of the full glasses. 'How long you been out of Crow camp?'

'A few years,' Ellie said, as she watched the boys on the floor finally make their move. By the looks of it, the response was as they'd hoped for. The third girl, the one with bleached blond hair, was looking miffed at being overlooked, even though she was possibly the most attractive of the three. She was tiny, hardly big enough to be a soldier, Ellie thought. She was also drunk, something that could easily have put the squaddies off.

'Everyone hates us here,' Naomi said, interrupting Ellie's thoughts.

The rejected girl was walking off, somewhat unsteadily, and was heading towards the ladies toilet. 'Jealous of the Reds, ain't they?' Ellie replied, as she picked up her glass to take a sip.

Naomi laughed at the reference to their city football team and then nodded to where the rejected girl had just fallen through the toilet entrance. 'She's a blue, an Evertonian ... none of 'em can take a drink.'

Ellie switched her gaze back to the dance floor. Their two erstwhile drinking buddies were locked lip-to-lip with their new friends. That didn't take long, she thought. Naomi raised her now empty glass, offering to get the two of them another drink. Ellie smiled and nodded to indicate her acceptance.

As Naomi headed off to the bar, Ellie watched her skilfully weave through the melee of performing figures. She moved like a gymnast, her tight mini-dress accentuating her figure. In contrast, Ellie was of shorter and rather stockier build. She found herself wondering if Naomi could fight as good as she looked. Both their physiques lent themselves well to soldiering but when she'd faced women like Naomi on the Judo mat, her lower centre of gravity proved to be a frequent advantage.

The dance floor was now heaving, the air heavy with sweat and alcohol, the show-offs and posers strutting like peacocks as they attempted to impress the hens gathered around watching. The queue for the bar was slow and the bartenders overworked. Nearly ten minutes past before Naomi reappeared, three small glasses gripped tightly in her hands. She loomed over Ellie, concern in her deep, brown eyes. 'Where's Amy?' she said, her voice only just penetrating the din.

Ellie shook her head. She hadn't seen the girl emerge from the toilet.

Naomi instantly laid the glasses on the table and then forged her way once more through the crowd towards where her friend had last been seen. As she reached the door to the toilets, she slammed into it and barged in. A girl on the dance-floor screamed as the door swung open.

By the time Ellie managed to negotiate her way through the crowd of rubber-neckers, what had happened – or been about to happen – was all over. The music was off and Amy, the drunken girl, was lying on the wet floor of the toilets, half-in half-out of a cubicle, the door jammed open as she threw up into the pan. Her dress was hitched up around her hips, her feet bare. If she'd been wearing underwear, there was now no sign of it.

On the floor near the hand basins, two women – one of whom was Naomi – were laying into a skinny, shaven-headed man with tattoos on his arms. The man was on his back, his trousers half-pulled down around his thighs. He had his arms raised as he fended off the fists Naomi was using and the sharper, more dangerous, stiletto heels employed by the second girl.

As Ellie stepped forward, both women seemed to tire. Their victim saw his chance. He leapt to his feet, hauled his trousers up to his waist and then shoved his way past Ellie and through the crowd. Nobody tried to stop him.

'Bastard was trying to rape her,' Naomi screamed after him.

Amy crawled from the cubicle. Using the back of her hand, she wiped slime-covered hair away from her face so she could speak. 'Leave it … leave it,' she screamed. 'We all know what'll happen if I report it.'

Naomi must have seen the confused look on Ellie's face. 'You don't know that bastard do you?' she said.

'Who was he?' Ellie asked.

'You may well ask,' Naomi replied, as she angrily kicked the cubicle door. 'That paedo skirt-chaser was Doug West … he's one of our fuckin' Corporals.'

Chapter 15

It was gone ten by the time Ellie made it back to the sanctuary of her room in the Officers' Mess. She'd taken her time, making a couple of circuitous detours to be certain she wasn't followed. Following her now established routine, she locked the door, checked the window and then switched off the light. Finally, without undressing, she lay down on the bed. Physically, she was exhausted, but sleep was going to be out of the question. Her mind was filled by a torrent of ideas and uncertainty about what she'd learned from the Crows.

At her suggestion, the group had taken Amy in a cab from the pub to the barracks, before walking the final stretch between the main gate and their accommodation block. Amy and Naomi shared a four-bed room with a third recruit who hadn't been out with them that night. The final steel-sprung bed was unmade and evidently unoccupied. When Ellie had asked about the empty bed, the others had exchanged concerned glances before Naomi elected to respond. The reason for their reticence, she explained, was the bed had belonged to Private Angela Davenport, the recruit who'd shot herself a few months previously. It had remained unused since the day of Davenport's death.

Alongside the beds, standard Army-style cupboards stored all the girls' kit. Ellie didn't need to look inside to know exactly how each would be laid out, where the uniform, shirts, boots and other equipment would be placed, and how it would be presented. Every recruit was drilled in the same method, as they had been for many years. The NCOs did it the way they'd been taught and made sure those that followed them into the service did likewise.

Some things had changed, though. After tying her dark hair into a bun, Naomi had reached beneath the bed belonging to the absent recruit and produced a half-empty litre bottle of vodka together with some plastic beakers. 'She won't need it tonight,' she announced, with a knowing wink.

74

When Ellie had asked how come, the other girls all giggled. 'She's over her fella's place,' Naomi said. 'She'll be kipping there.'

'Not that she seems to get much sleep, wherever she is,' one of the others said.

'Why's that?' Ellie asked.

Naomi shrugged. 'She's got a lot on her mind.'

Amy, the victim of the toilet assault, had continued to drink heavily. Between the tears and expressions of self-pity, she'd eventually managed to explain to her attentive audience what had happened. Doug West, her Corporal, had been pestering her for several weeks. It had started with texts to her phone – he'd obtained her number from her personnel file – and when she'd failed to respond to his overtures, he'd started leaving notes in her locker while carrying out room inspections. On one occasion, she'd returned from an early parade to find a rose resting on her pillow.

Some of the girls felt sorry for West. Although he was much older than them, he was single. His wife had left him for another woman, it was said. One or two envied the attention he gave Amy, suggesting he was her ticket to an easy ride through training. Worn down by the unremitting attention, Amy had started to respond to his texts. She'd figured if she could just be friendly with him, he might leave it at that. She figured wrong. Soon the number of messages built up and, within a week, he was texting her over fifty times a day. If she didn't respond quickly he would ask why, or who she was with. He asked her to send him a picture of something nice – she sent a heart symbol. His response was to ask if she was 'taking the piss'. Then came what Naomi referred to as his 'dick pics'.

'They all send 'em,' she said. 'And they expect something similar from us in return.'

Who *they* were, Naomi didn't explain, but Ellie had an idea.

'He warned me,' Amy said, as they continued to talk.

'How so?' Ellie asked.

'Told me he was going to have me whether I liked it or not. Told me my life could be heaven or hell and what I had to do to make it heavenly.'

'To have sex with him?'

'He was waiting for me in the bogs. I was so tanked up, I gave in. I was beyond caring, to be honest, so I just did what he asked … you know, give him a little blow. I had to stop to throw up and well, that's when he pulled up my dress and got behind me.'

'Did he rape you?' Ellie asked. She was about to try and comfort the young girl when Naomi took her by the arm. 'I think you'd best go,' she said.

Ellie looked at her quizzically. 'It's important,' she said.

'He didn't,' Naomi said. 'We got there before he had the chance. But, even if he'd actually managed to, you know as well as I do it wouldn't go anywhere.'

'She should still report it,' Ellie said.

'Naomi shook her head. 'Waste of time. We'll get her to bed so she can sleep it off. If the officers catch you here, we'll all be for it.'

'We didn't get any of this kind of thing when I was on Phase Two,' Ellie replied.

'Well, you can't have done your training here then,' said one of the other girls. 'All the NCOs and even one or two of the officers seem to think it's their God-given right to shag the Crows.'

'The officers?' Ellie asked.

'Yeah, the officers,' said Naomi, as she stood and pointed at the open the door. 'They're men ain't they?'

Ellie had taken the hint. And she knew if she'd pressed for any more details at that moment, her motives might have become suspect. She was a stranger in their company, after all, and hardly knew them. Only in the case of Naomi had she even learned a surname – Briscoe

– and that had only happened by chance when one of the others used it. Concern for young Amy was natural, the kind of thing many women might express. Being inquisitorial was not.

***

Alone in her room, Ellie now weighed up her options. Tonight's outrageous events had handed her an opportunity as much as it had stoked her resolve. The advice from her RSM was sound, she couldn't argue that. But it was wrong, and on so many levels. It was people like him and the Colonel who turned away from what was staring them in the face that allowed it to continue.

But, as Colonel Bullen had been at pains to remind her, she was no longer an MP. In addition to that, Iraq was looming and preparations for deployment were well underway. Finding time to expose what was actually going on in the Training Regiment would be difficult, to say the least.

She felt angry at what Corporal West had done. She also knew if nobody made a stand, he would get away with it. Seeing Angela Davenport's empty bunk had provided the extra incentive she'd needed. It had caused her to think about why a young girl's promising life had been ended by a bullet through the brain. Ellie wondered if she too had been a victim, just like Amy and her friends, and like she had, on that stormy night in Germany.

Chapter 16

'Time for me to turn in, lads,' the Sergeant said, as he turned away from the bar to address his audience. Every seat was now empty. They'd all left, crept out the main door while he'd been facing the bar. 'Bastards,' he spat.

It looked like he'd be enjoying the whisky chaser he'd ordered from Gerry on his own. Unlike the others, the young barman, had been paying attention to the story he'd been telling about his days as a prison guard, looking after Special Forces prisoners in the first Iraq war.

'I'll have that nightcap now,' he announced, his speech slurred and deliberate. Six or seven pints of the local brew had gone down all too easily. Gerry didn't reply.

'Where's that fucking …' He stopped mid-sentence as he turned back to face the bar and saw, instead of their being a young recruit behind the wooden counter, two new faces stared at him. The first was Andy Masters, the Armoury Sergeant. Beside him stood the familiar face of Sergeant Mick Fitzgerald, just arrived from Germany.

He nodded to the two men in turn. 'Alright, lads,' he said.

Masters stepped out from behind the small bar and walked casually to the main door where he slid the locking bolts home. Next, he closed the only open window. It was a sensible precaution. They wouldn't want anyone walking in on them.

The Sergeant nodded approvingly as he gave Fitzgerald the once over. He remembered the Irishman from Iraq where he'd been a guard at one of the American prison camps. He had a reputation as a hard-man. With dark, deep-set eyes and a face only a mother could love, he was certainly no Adonis. But he looked fit and it was true they could use an extra man.

Masters returned and reached beneath the bar, produced three shot glasses and, pulling a bottle of single malt from the rack behind him, poured a measure into each. 'You ordered a whisky, Paul?' he said, with a grin.

Slater grinned as he reached for the glass and then turned back to face Fitzgerald. 'We like to get to know people here before we decide if we can trust them,' he said. 'When do you start?'

'I see the CO tomorrow,' Fitzgerald replied in a gravelly, Belfast accent. 'The clerk says I'll be working with you, looking after the Crows.'

'That's what we've been told. Andy tells me you requested a posting here and you want to work with us.'

'I do. I've heard you're the lads to talk to if I need help with something.'

'I thought the idea was you'd be helping us. What kind of help are you talking about?'

'The kind that doesn't get talked about ... if you get my drift?'

'You'll need to be a little more specific,' Slater said, with a frown.

'I need to know I can trust you as well.'

Slater downed his whisky and then topped up his glass before turning to Masters. 'Are you going to help solve this little conundrum, Andy?' he asked. 'Why has our friend here asked for this meeting?'

'He wants some help mate, to settle an old score with an officer.'

'An officer from the Training Regiment?'

'From the Signals Depot across the way.'

Slater raised an eyebrow. 'He does, does he?' he replied. 'And who might this officer be?'

'Her name is Rodgers. Lieutenant Ellie Rodgers,' Fitzgerald replied.

Slater looked at Masters who shook his head He returned his gaze to Fitzgerald. 'Never heard of her,' he said. 'But we don't see many of her kind in this part of the camp. What's she done to warrant this?'

'Claimed I attacked her at a camp in Germany. She lied. The Court Martial found me not guilty but she still managed to get my promotion stopped. She shouldn't get away with wrecking a man's career.'

'I see. And you want approval for some form of retribution?'

'I was hoping to have some help as well.'

'What's your plan?'

'I'm not sure. But I want to teach her a lesson. Before that happens, I just want to make sure I'm not treading on any toes.'

Slater thought for a moment. As he looked across at Andy Masters, his gave an approving nod. 'You've come to the right people but now's not a good time,' Masters said. 'There's a copper sniffing around the camp. If you can wait, we've a method that might work.'

'What kind of method?' Fitzgerald said.

Masters laughed before raising his glass in the air and winking at Slater. 'We have a little trick we use to control the women Crows,' he said. 'We've never done an officer before but it's a tried and tested method. You'd need to understand something, though.'

'What's that?'

'If it happens, you pay us and you pay us well. And there'll be no turning back afterwards. You'll be working for us.'

Fitzgerald held out a hand. 'Count me in,' he said. Slater grinned just as there was a gentle tap on the rear door to the Mess.

'I'll get it,' said Masters. A moment later, he reappeared from behind the bar. Two young women wearing smart civilian clothes stood silently behind him.

'Come in girls,' said Slater. 'No need to be shy. We're all friends here. Like I told you earlier, getting to the end of Phase Two can be easy or hard. Tonight, my friends and I will show you the easy way.'

Chapter 17

Jodie had been waiting nearly two hours for Paul to arrive home. It was approaching midnight and she was anxious to return to her room. It was deliberate, she was sure of it. He was probably angry with her for some reason and now she was in the last place she wanted to be; sat in his kitchen, like a lamb, silently awaiting its executioner.

Just once, she had made the mistake of leaving before he turned up. The following morning he'd come looking for her, cornered her on the path to the NAAFI, and then frog-marched her to a deserted area behind one of the male accommodation blocks. There she had seen the old Sergeant Paul Slater, the one who screamed at the Crows, abused and bullied them. Even though it had been daylight and the male block was occupied, Paul hadn't cared. If anything, he'd appeared to enjoy publicly humiliating her. He'd berated her, called her all kinds of names, and then he'd quietly hissed in her ear that if she ever let him down again, she knew what could happen. And he'd been clever. As faces had appeared in the windows to the accommodation block behind them, he'd made sure to raise his voice and refer to her as 'Private Baker'. To anyone listening – and there were many – she was just another recruit at the sharp end of his tongue.

And that night he had been really aggressive as he'd made love to her. Rough sex, he called it. He made her cry. Not due to the violence; that she could handle. It was crude and unpleasant but it didn't last long. What really got to her was what he said as he lay on top of her. For the first time he'd mentioned previous lovers, other women he had bedded, and he'd claimed they were all better than her. She was too needy, he said, she was suffocating him. But, as her tears had flowed, he'd then chosen to comfort and reassure her. He'd even apologised for the way she had made him behave and asked her, nicely, not to provoke him again. She'd readily agreed and promised to be more thoughtful in future.

Alone in the kitchen, she sat at the table thinking how his wife had probably sat in this very spot waiting for him to come home. Stories he had told about her – how she was dirty around the house and never cooked a family meal – were inconsistent with what she had seen after being allowed access to their home. The cupboards had been crammed with the kind of ingredients only someone who prepared food would need. And she had seen things that troubled her. In places throughout the house, fist-sized holes were punched in the plasterboard walls. In the hallway, the ceiling was splattered with what appeared to be food, as if someone holding a loaded plate or a tray had seen it smashed out of their grip. It all served to paint a picture of a home troubled by violence.

Jodie remembered her own home, and how clean and tidy that was by comparison. Her family were less than an hour's drive from the camp but she hadn't seen them in months. Paul had said it was for the best. Away on deployment, cut off from all communication and having your life at risk due to enemy attacks was a lifestyle best not inflicted on people who cared about you, he told her. The kindest thing was not to subject your family to constant reminders of your existence and the dangers you faced. 'Just ease them out,' he'd said. 'The Army is your family now.' It made sense – as did most things he said – even if he was sometimes a little over-zealous in applying his advice. When he'd questioned why she was texting her brother, her first reaction had been one of annoyance that he'd been secretly looking at her phone. He'd explained it though; he was being caring as he wanted the best for her. She needed to learn to trust him.

The clock striking midnight coincided with a need to head upstairs to use the bathroom. She had to be quick, and she was, racing up and down the stairs like a whippet. Paul didn't like her wandering about the house even though his wife had removed the last of her personal possessions from the main bedroom over a month previously. Glancing in through the bedroom door, Jodie was reminded of another of his little oddities. He seemed to get a kick out of knowing he was bedding his girlfriend in the house he'd once shared with his wife.

At ten minutes after midnight, the rear kitchen door burst open. Paul was drunk and not in a good mood.

His interrogation began as soon as he closed the door. It was the same every time. Had she been talking to anyone on the camp? What had they said? Had any of the male recruits been visiting the female accommodation block? As Jodie tried her best to answer the stream of questions in a way that placated him, she found herself shuffling around the kitchen table, keeping her distance, worrying which accusation or response would be the one to eventually spark him off.

After several minutes, he stopped the questions. 'Get me a beer,' he ordered, from his chair next to the table. In silence, Jodie opened the fridge, popped the cap from a small lager bottle and handed it to him. He grinned lustfully and beckoned her closer.

It was a ruse. The moment she was within reach, he shot out his right hand and gripped hold of her coat, pulling her towards him. Her foot caught on a table leg and next thing she was sprawled helplessly across his lap, face down to the floor. He held her tight, pinning her with his right knee hard against her diaphragm. 'You're looking tired,' he said. 'You still not sleeping?'

'It's not easy,' she replied.

'I warned you to trust me. What am I to do with you, Baker?'

'Could you let me go please, Paul?' she begged.

'You've been off-loading to Andy Masters again haven't you?'

'I haven't. I work with him, that's all.'

'I've told you, if you say anything, it will be you in the shit.'

'I haven't, I promise,' she said, more desperately.

Paul's open hand smacked hard and painfully on the back of her head, stunning her. 'Make sure you don't,' he spat.

84

Head spinning, Jodie thought quickly. If she admitted to saying something innocent, he might let her go. She dismissed the idea in an instant. If Paul had been sober and feeling particularly kind towards her, that might have worked. Drunk and in the mood for a fight, definitely not. Her only hope was to distract him. 'Could you let me go, please?' she asked, meekly. 'I could make you something nice to eat, if you like?' Appeal to a basic need, she reasoned. Men are always ravenous after a few beers.

It worked. Swivelling his chair around, the legs screeching on the tiles, Paul tipped her unceremoniously onto the floor. 'Fix me an egg banjo,' he sneered. 'I'll be upstairs.'

As Jodie cooked, she could hear Paul moving around upstairs, doing something in the bathroom. He was crashing about, drunk and clumsy, swearing and cussing about something or other.

She finished the eggs, placed them between slices of thick, buttered bread and added tomato sauce, something she knew would please him. Upstairs was now quiet and as she slowly climbed the stairs, she saw why. In the bedroom, Paul was face-down on the bed, still fully dressed. He was passed-out asleep, his arms thrown out sideways in the shape of a cross.

Placing the plate carefully on the bedside table, she undid the laces of his boots, eased them from his feet and placed them on the bedroom floor. She folded the quilt cover over him and then eased her finger between the slices of bread to burst the yoke. Next, she spread a mixture of egg and tomato sauce across one of his cheeks and onto the pillow where his head rested. It felt good, powerful, and Paul's breathing didn't change, he was so deeply asleep.

Finally, and as quickly as she could, she flushed the remainder of the sandwich down the toilet before returning the plate to the bedside table. The scene was set. When he eventually woke up he would think he must have eaten the sandwich before dropping off.

It was time to leave. She crept down the stairs and was about to close the rear door to the house behind her when an idea popped into her mind. No way would she normally search his home. If he caught her, there would be hell to pay. But, listening to his snores reverberate, and confident he wouldn't walk in unexpectedly, she began to open drawers, just to look, just in case.

After ten minutes fruitless rummaging, she reached his waxed-cotton coat, hanging up in the hall. The noise from upstairs had lessened now and so she waited in the half-light, heart racing, listening in case he stirred. The snoring resumed and she relaxed just a little, her fingers moving nimbly through the pockets. There were car and house keys. In the inside pocket, she felt paper, a letter. She moved towards the light from the kitchen to read it.

It was from his wife, a begging letter. She needed cash for the boys and wanted to know why Paul hadn't sent the money he'd promised. Jodie scowled. The bastard wouldn't even fork out to look after his children. Returning the letter to the jacket pocket she switched off the kitchen light just as the clock on the mantelpiece chimed the half-hour. Silently, she closed the back door and stepped out into the darkness.

It was cold now. Pulling her coat tight, she headed along the alleyway, past Paul's blue Peugeot in the car park, and onto the main road leading to the barracks. Inside of fifteen minutes, she'd be back at the camp and in the comparative safety of the room she shared with Amy and Naomi. They'd chat, like they always did. And they'd drink the vodka she kept hidden under the bead. It would help her sleep, even it couldn't help her forget.

Chapter 18

Motorpool, Prince Albert Barracks.

Slater watched attentively as the last of the boxes was loaded onto the back of the lorry. 'Careful with that,' he called, as he saw a figure in the half-light slip and nearly drop one of the heavy containers. 'They're the latest models.'

'Sorry mate,' Doug West replied, his grinning face appearing over the edge of the flat-bed. 'You look like shit, by the way.'

'Too many shots, mate. I fell asleep.' Slater checked his watch before belching and then shaking his head in frustration. 'It's gone three, already,' he said. 'Check the contents and do it pronto.'

A few moments later, Doug jumped down to the ground. 'They're fine,' he said.

'They'd better be. They're the latest Nokias, so we need to be careful with 'em.' Another face appeared through the window of the driver's cab. It was Sandy Price. 'You remember the RV?' Slater demanded as Sandy opened the door and descended the steps.

'Sure do. Rendezvous zero five-hundred at the phone shop next to the Old Victory. I'll be there in plenty of time.'

Slater held out a brown envelope. 'Your wedge,' he added. 'And a little bonus from Andy, for good measure.'

Shoving the envelope deep into a side pocket of his camouflage jacket, Sandy climbed up the metal steps of the lorry cab, sat inside and started the engine. The heavy beast fired into life; thick, diesel-laden smoke filling the air.

Slater held the driver's door open for a moment. 'Text me when you've made the delivery and again when you get back to camp,' he said.

Sandy gave him a thumbs-up. 'From my phone or from one of the new ones?' he said, jokingly.

Slater threw a playful punch at his friend before stepping back. 'Just don't go tripping any more speed cameras.'

'Roger that. Thanks for sorting it.'

'Andy sorted it. Lucky for you it photographed the tail of the lorry. If it had been the other way round, your ugly mug would have been right in the frame.'

Sandy grinned, slammed the Leyland truck into gear and then gunned the engine. A minute later, Slater and Doug West stood outside the hangar in the darkness, watching its red lights moving down the hill, between the accommodation blocks and towards the side gate. The young recruit on guard duty there had accepted a few quid not to record the vehicle movement in his log. Within twenty minutes, Sandy would be on the M4 heading east to London.

'You think we'll pull out of Iraq then?' Doug asked, once the lorry had disappeared.

'Not in the near future,' Slater replied, as he began placing some unused boxes in a small cupboard. 'The kit I've seen heading off to Basra tells me we're in this for the long haul. By my reckoning, we've got two or three years to make as much as we can.'

'Then Afghan maybe?'

'Place is a fuckin' gold mine, Doug, just like Iraq. They're desperate for phones even before the networks are in place. We can't get hold of them fast enough.' He scanned the hangar as he went through a final check to make sure nothing had been missed. The last thing they needed was some nosy parker asking questions about something they'd overlooked. 'Mick Fitzgerald starts here in the morning,' he added.

'He's here already?' said Doug.

'We had a drink with him in the Mess this evening. He moved some of his kit in today and sees the CO tomorrow.'

'Handy bloke to have onside.'

'I remember him from Iraq. They were prison guards at the Yank rendition camp.'

'And we all know what happened in those places.'

'We saw some things, that's for sure. The CIA don't fuck about when it comes to interrogating people. Fitzgerald has asked a favour of us. He wants us to help square up a woman officer.'

Doug's eyebrows rose. 'How does he expect to do that?'

'He doesn't know. Andy suggested stitching her up like we do the Crows.'

'Fuck me,' Doug replied. 'Doing that to an officer … well, you'd have to be crazy.'

'He is … they both are. Andy reckons we could do it after the cop has gone.'

'Is he a problem?'

Slater laughed. 'We won't have to worry about him. He's from the Met, an old bloke nearing retirement. He's only here for a day or two to ask about the SA80s that disappeared after that parade. Flo McLaren, the half-caste girl from the monkeys is showing him around.'

'Not much gets past you, mate.'

'I hope not. Andy says they found the rifles during a drugs raid. McLaren took him up to see the Davenport girl's family today so, I've no doubt his next call will be the Armoury.'

'Does he have anything?' Doug asked. 'Any evidence I mean?'

'Not so far as I know. I reckon he's here to turn over a few stones and see what pops up. So long as nobody gives him reason to stick around, he'll soon be on his way.'

'What about young Morgan and that piece your shagging? Last thing we want is him talking to either of them.'

Slater winked and half-smiled. 'Morgan's not shown his face since he went AWOL but we're watching his place, just in case.'

'What about Baker? You used to say she went like a belt-fed mortar but you've been quiet about her lately.'

'She'll do whatever I tell her.' Slater turned off the light and, as Doug stepped outside the hangar, he began to pull slowly on the heavy chain that lowered the shutter to the vehicle bay. He placed a heavy padlock through the clasp to the door, pressed it home and then gave it a tug to check it was secure. 'I want you to get the room ready tomorrow,' he said, finally. 'Get a few beers in as well. We might have use of it in a day or so.'

Doug nodded. 'Roger that, mate. Good as done.'

Chapter 19

The next day, I woke early. Dawn had brought a change in the weather. Dark clouds now loomed overhead, the wind had picked up and, from the musky smell in the air, I sensed rain wasn't far away. Autumn was definitely around the corner.

I'd called Jenny the previous evening as promised and, after a quick chat with our girls, she came on the line to ask me how the visit to the Davenports had gone.

'Not too bad,' I said. But, as soon as the words left my mouth, I knew she had seen through them.

'It got to you, didn't it?' she said, knowingly. 'Having a family can do that to you.'

'It was the mother,' I said. 'She hardly said a word. And when she looked at me ... her eyes were dull, it was like there was nothing behind them.'

'Only someone who has lost a child in that way can really understand what it does to you. You did the right thing going, for you and for them. Was it worth the trip?'

'I'm not sure. We didn't learn much other than a question mark over who actually visited them to recover their daughter's kit.'

'A long drive for little reward, then?'

'And something of a cool reception on my return. Wendy's new partner didn't exactly blank me but it was close.'

'Maybe she's uncomfortable with the loss of privacy. If she's insecure about her relationship with Wendy, she may not like having a friend from her past around, especially a man.'

'Any tips?'

'Wine and chocolates might work? It does for me. But for both of them, not just for Wendy.'

I laughed, but it was good advice.

***

Even before my hosts stirred, I was dressed and working at their dining room table. I'd made myself some toast and had my pen in one hand, a brew in the other, as I jotted down some ideas in my notebook. I had two more days to either come up with something tangible about the Welsh end of the stolen rifle operation or cut my losses and head back to London. I was already beginning to formulate one or two theories about the theft. Leaving weapons on a lorry following a ceremonial parade wasn't an uncommon practice so I wasn't surprised the RMP hadn't taken issue with it. I knew what should then happen was a minimum of two soldiers being assigned to guard those weapons. Experience had taught me, however, that just because something was supposed to be done didn't mean it would. It was commonplace for just one sentry to be posted and then, presuming the fenced-off protection of a military camp was security in itself, that soldier might slip away for a quick cigarette or a trip to the toilets. When they returned to the lorry, the rifles would appear just as they had left them. When the shit hit the fan, the accusations and blame-game would start. To avoid being held responsible, the sentry would deny ever having left his post and every other soldier who booked out a rifle that day would testify they placed it on the lorry as ordered. NCOs would swear they had done things by the book, and the Officers above them would confirm their NCOs always followed standing orders. Somewhere within that complexity of denials lay the truth.

But, although I had a workable theory on *how* the theft may have happened, I was still no closer to identifying *who* was responsible. I did have a short-list, and because Angela Davenport had been a guard at the lorry, it included her. The possibility she may have become mixed up in something she later regretted figured highly in my thoughts.

Floria was again due at eight and, all things being well, she was bringing some personnel files with her. I wanted to follow up on some ideas we'd discussed during the return journey from the Davenport home. If I included all the recruits who paraded that day, their families and friends, and the training staff who were around at the time, there would be over a hundred and fifty suspects to interview. With many of those now deployed around the UK and abroad, it was clear I was going to have to prioritise. A read through the files would help me do that.

I also planned a review of the RMP investigation, focussing this time on the statements taken and looking to concentrate on those who'd had the opportunity. I would then email my shortlist of names to London to see if anyone had any relevant criminal history. Floria had suggested, and I agreed, that anyone with the balls to steal two rifles was likely to have been involved in crime before. After all, she pointed out, how many of us would have the contacts to find a purchaser for military rifles? That kind of knowledge only came through having criminal associates.

With that in mind, I'd also asked Floria for details of the Training Regiment staff so I could run their details through the PNC, the police national computer. According to Floria, the names had already been searched on the RMP Central Criminal Record Office without result. I was hoping civilian police data might prove more productive.

Just before Floria was due, my phone rang. It was Bill Grahamslaw, calling from his office at New Scotland Yard. As I answered, I heard the bathroom door upstairs creaked. One of my hosts was moving around.

'Trouble's brewing,' Bill announced, and even before I could say 'Good Morning', he explained how, the previous evening, he'd had a visit from a Colonel Thompson from the Ministry of Defence. He'd turned up unannounced at New Scotland Yard reception and demanded to speak with Bill. Not too surprisingly, I was the reason for the visit. He wanted an explanation why I was visiting Prince Albert Barracks and what I wanted from the Davenport family. He'd also requested reassurance I wasn't re-opening an investigation into the Davenport suicide.

'Could anyone your end have formed that impression?' Bill asked me.

'Quite possibly,' I said, honestly. 'As one of the missing rifles was issued to Private Davenport on the day it was stolen, I'm certain to be talking to some of the people who were interviewed about her death.'

'Have you made it clear you're not re-investigating it?' he said.

'Absolutely,' I replied. 'Although the sergeant who's escorting me said the local RMP are suspicious.'

'That's to be expected,' Bill replied. 'Did you learn anything useful from her parents?'

'Only that she was one of the guards posted to watch the rifles.'

'So, she could be a suspect?'

'Yes. My liaison is due here any minute to help draw up a short-list of other people we can talk to as well.'

'I'll bet the Training Regiment CO made a call to the MOD to report your presence.'

I agreed, and in Colonel Hine's position, it's what I would have done. I asked Bill if there was any news from the lab about the rifles. There was.

'We found sweat traces,' he explained. 'And a tiny blood-speck in the working parts. The lab people are searching the database but they tell us the chance of a match is remote and could take a while. What we really need is a suspect to compare it to.'

'I was intending to ring you this morning,' I said. 'Once I have a list of people to check, I plan to ask Wendy Russell if she could email it to you.'

'Yes, please do that. How is Miss Russell?'

'Pretty good, I'd say. I have a feeling we won't see her back in the Met, though. She seems very settled down here.'

I heard a door swing open behind me. It was Wendy. 'Do I hear the dulcet tones of a certain Bill Grahamslaw?' she asked, a tinge of humour in her voice.

I nodded.

'Tell him I wouldn't transfer back to the Met now for all the tea in China. I'm kept busy, I wake up to beautiful scenery and every day I look forward to going to work. London smog and traffic might appeal to some, not me.'

Bill laughed. 'Tell her we wouldn't have her back,' he said, as Wendy disappeared into the kitchen.

I grinned to myself and, although I assumed my boss was joking, I decided against passing on the message. Wrapping up the call, I headed upstairs to use the bathroom. It was as I was nearing the landing that I saw a movement above me. It was Monique. For a fleeting moment, she looked surprised, as if I'd embarrassed her in some way. Then she was gone, through the door into her and Wendy's room. I stood for a moment, wondering if I was being a little paranoid but, as I looked at the open door into my room I had the distinct feeling it was open a little wider than I'd left it. My curiosity aroused, I pushed the door fully open and stepped through. My suspicions were confirmed when I glanced at where my grab-bag lay on the floor. It had been moved, just slightly, but enough to tell me someone had been there.

Chapter 20

Floria wasn't in the least surprised when I told her about the Ministry of Defence contacting my boss. As the unexpected result of the Davenport inquest was still generating press interest, she thought it virtually guaranteed they would want to know what I was up to.

We were soon making decent progress sifting through the files and names to create a shortlist of people to interview. Another round of cross checking identified just five soldiers remaining at the barracks, all others having been deployed elsewhere. One was Sergeant Paul Slater, the NCO the Davenports had mentioned. Next was the Armourer, Sergeant Andrew Masters. The remaining three were young, female soldiers by the names of Baker, Briscoe and Towler.

To some extent, I was relieved there weren't too many witnesses remaining at the camp. It meant my work could be completed fairly quickly. I asked Floria if she could arrange for us to meet Sergeant Masters and the recruits as soon as practicable. As Slater was the senior NCO, I thought it best to leave him until last. She promised to have appointments arranged by the time I was finished seeing the Chief Constable.

Floria had brought sandwiches from the NAAFI for is so I grabbed some plates from Wendy's kitchen and made us a brew whilst she packaged up the files in a box she'd brought in from her car. As she finished, she opened a briefcase she'd also brought and produced a file bearing the MOD crest. It was an AWOL report, she explained, might I be willing to take a look at it?

'To what end?' I asked, biting into my sandwich.

'I just wondered,' she said, after a slight hesitation. 'This is one of my current cases. I was hoping you could cast an experienced eye over it … see if you can come up with any ideas.'

'Is there something unusual about it?' I said, between mouthfuls, indicating she should also tuck in to her food.

'We find most AWOLs within a few days of them being reported. A lot go home to family because something's happened and they can't get leave. Ever since soldiers started using mobile phones it's been an issue. They get a call in the middle of the night saying their Gran's ill, or something, and then they bugger off without saying anything to anyone. At morning parade, their NCO reports them as absent and we get a call. This is a soldier I haven't been able to find.'

'Family hiding him, you think?'

'I don't know, sir. I check social media accounts of AWOLs and their bank accounts to see if they're using them. This one's off the grid,' she said, pulling a rather tired looking egg-and-cress sandwich from its packet.

I flicked the file open.

'His name's Tom Morgan,' she said. 'He's from a village called Markham, quite near to here. He's been AWOL since mid-March.'

'A long time to be off the grid, like you say. Is he missing from the barracks?'

'No, he trained here but he'd moved across to the Tank Transporter Regiment on the far side of the camp. He actually went missing from Brize Norton. He was last seen in the airport arrivals hall after flying in from Iraq. The lads in our depot put it down to what he experienced overseas but, to my mind, he should have turned up by now.'

I flicked through the pages in the file. Floria had secured my interest and, given the degree of help she was affording me, I figured offering her a little help in return was the least I could do. As I began to read, she finished her uninspiring lunch and reminded me of her offer to have a look around the fields to see if there was any evidence of the prowler I thought I'd heard. I would have preferred to go with her – not that I didn't trust her, more a case of being unsure whether her skill-set included the reading of tracker marks – but I decided it would be quicker to stay where I was and read through the file.

Ten minutes later, she returned with news of a shoe print in a nearby gateway – just the kind of place, she suggested, you might park in if you wanted easy access to the fields and a quick escape if compromised. 'I can't say for definite,' she said. 'But I think someone has been there recently. Might be legit, of course, the farmer or someone rabbit shooting. Or it might be the Press? Perhaps the MOD weren't happy with the explanation your boss gave?'

'It was before their visit to him,' I said.

'I wouldn't rule it out,' Floria replied, pointing at the Morgan file on the table in front of me. 'Any thoughts?' she said, with a smile.

'Not really. I can see why your colleagues drew the conclusion they did, though.'

Floria took the file and opened her briefcase. 'What do you say to a run over to Markham to talk to his family? It won't take long, I promise.'

I checked my watch. 'I'm tight for time, really,' I said, firmly. 'We should prioritise Sergeant Masters.'

I picked up my coat and, as Floria walked towards the front door, I followed her. 'Apart from the fact that he lives locally, was there any particular reason you picked Morgan for me to look at?' I asked.

'I thought you were never going to ask,' she replied, slightly smugly. 'If he'd still been around, Private Morgan would have been one of the key witnesses on our list to interview. On the day of the parade, he took over guarding the lorry from Angela Davenport.'

Chapter 21

As I closed Wendy's front door and walked towards Floria's car, she was sitting in the driver seat talking animatedly on the telephone. I heard her demand to know if the person on the line had double-checked something. Her reaction – an approving grunt – indicated they had.

I dropped my briefcase onto the rear seat and climbed in. Floria started the engine but then paused before pulling out on the road. 'That was my Staff Sergeant on the phone,' she said. 'I thought it best to be sure. He confirmed there's no record of anyone having been instructed to carry out a second search at the Davenport home.'

'Are you saying there was no second search or there's no record of it?' I asked.

'I'm saying all searches should be logged, sir. And we only search twice if evidence suggests we've missed something first time around. We didn't go back.'

'So, we don't know who it was or what they were looking for?'

'It could have been the Security Service, for all I know,' Floria said. 'And, when you add a second unlogged search to the fact a key witness from the day of the thefts is long-term AWOL, I begin to get an uneasy feeling.'

'Ok,' I said. 'I see your point. And one other thing. Would you mind if we cut the 'sir' please? Everyone I know calls me Finlay.'

Floria hesitated and, after a second or two, popped the car into gear. As she released the handbrake she replied. ''Ok … Finlay it is … sir.'

I grinned and then checked my watch. I wondered how we were going to squeeze in the meeting with Sergeant Masters before my meeting with the Chief Constable. 'Relax,' Floria said, as she appeared to sense my concern. 'We'll see Masters afterwards.'

***

With the Chief Constable's previous meeting having overrun, I sat flicking through the reception-room magazines – the latest issues of 'Police Pensioner' – as I waited to be seen. From behind a closed double-door, I could hear a male voice. It was muffled but raised. It seemed the speaker was irritated by something. Eventually, all became quiet and, a few seconds later, the doors swung open from the inside. Wendy appeared. As she looked across at me, I saw she looked flushed. She half-smiled, and then tilted her head to indicate I should follow her.

I was surprised at what I found. The tiny room behind the double-door looked untidy and in need of decorating. The walls were bare, with peeling paint, pale marks and nail holes indicating where pictures had once hung. A single desk, older and smaller than I might have expected, was pushed into the corner of the room to allow a large map to be laid out on the floor. On the map itself, a number of photographs together with several A4-sized sheets of paper bearing hand-written notes were also in evidence. There were no chairs. Two men, both in open-neck white shirts with grey trousers, were hunched over the desk studying a file of some kind. To one side of them, matching suit jackets lay on the floor. Wendy announced my presence, at which both men turned around to face us.

The smaller of the two I recognised from photographs as Martin Richards, the Chief Constable. He introduced himself and then his colleague – Detective Superintendent David Clarke – before extending a hand in greeting. Richards had a hawkish look about him, with a narrow head, thinning hair and piercing blue eyes. As we shook hands, he apologised for keeping me waiting and then grinned as he saw me casting my eyes around the room. 'Not quite what you expected, Inspector?' he said. 'Or may I call you Finlay? Miss Russell tells me that's what most people do.'

Stepping back, I carefully avoided the papers laid out on the floor. 'Finlay is fine, sir,' I said.

'Very well, we'll adjourn to my main office. Dai, could you organise coffees, please?'

As his Superintendent disappeared through the exit to the reception area, I followed Martin Richards through another door on the far side of the room. It revealed an office far more suited to the highest-ranking police officer in Monmouthshire. With a view overlooking adjacent fields – something not often seen in London – a huge leather chair sat behind an equally outsized oak desk. Crammed bookshelves, paintings and a large number of service-related plaques decorated the walls. Beneath my feet, the soft carpet felt expensive. I realised what I had first seen was the Chief's working area, where the nitty-gritty stuff was discussed and debated. Behind the second door, all was orderly and pristine.

Richards sat, and then indicated Wendy and I should use two of the smaller seats opposite him. David Clarke joined us and, as he closed the door, the Chief Constable leaned forward on his elbows, his hands clasped hard together. 'Miss Russell has told me a lot about you, Inspector,' he said, warmly. 'It would appear Commander Grahamslaw made a good choice in sending a former soldier to make enquiries at an Army depot.'

'My boss thought it might help,' I said, cautiously.

'I'm also told you're ex-SAS Regiment, a veteran of the Iranian Embassy siege, no less.'

As I shot a fleeting look toward Wendy, I saw she appeared embarrassed. She knew more about me than almost anyone and, although I hadn't specifically requested she keep my past secret, I'd assumed she would be discreet. 'It was a long time ago, sir, another life.' I replied.

Richards noticed my glance. 'I understand your reticence, Mr Finlay,' he said. 'Personally, I find the fact you have such a pedigree to be reassuring and it would have concerned me had that information been withheld by one of my officers. It may interest you to know the

Ministry of Defence telephoned this morning. They asked me to keep a close eye on you and to report back on any progress you make.'

'They've been in touch with my boss as well.'

'Understandable in the circumstances. Please be assured, what we've learned will go no further than this room. I'd also appreciate your discretion concerning what we're about to share with you.'

I now understood the raised voices I'd heard earlier. Richards must have been pushing Wendy for an explanation as to why her friend – a supposedly run-of-the-mill Detective Inspector – was attracting such high-level interest. As I confirmed my willingness to keep what I was about to learn to myself, there was a tap on the door. Richards called out and we were joined by his secretary carrying a tray of coffee mugs.

Wendy stood up. 'I'll be mum,' she said, as she took the tray and placed it on the desk in front of us. The offer was unusual for Wendy. Although she had never lost her femininity to the tough world of policing, she had always struck me as being mindful of equality and not likely to play the role of 'mum', as she had put it. The explanation was soon forthcoming though. As she leaned in front of me, she gave me a furtive wink accompanied by a nervous half-smile. It was an apology, I thought, and one I appreciated. I flashed a quick smile back, hoping she realised I wasn't annoyed with her.

Richards turned again to his Superintendent. 'Over to you, Dai,' he said.

As I listened, David Clarke explained he was leading a small team quietly investigating alleged abuses of recruits at Prince Albert Barracks. He went into some detail, giving me a full run-down on the resources they'd committed, their safeguards and what they hoped to achieve. The maps and papers I'd seen in the adjacent room were part of the enquiry.

'You're aware I've been told to keep away from anything unrelated to the rifle thefts?' I said, as he finished.

As Clarke opened his mouth to respond, Richards interrupted. 'We're aware of that, yes,' he said. 'And this morning's call from the MOD rather reinforced the point. But I understand you're also aware our investigation has run into difficulties.'

'You have an undercover officer missing?'

'Correct. I've no doubt you're aware police came in for some criticism following the deaths at Deepcut?' the Chief Constable continued. 'Sadly, with this Davenport case, we didn't do much better.' He turned to look at Wendy but she remained silent. He placed his hand on a document file sat on the desk and then pushed it towards me. 'ACC Russell had persuaded me your presence inside Prince Albert Barracks may be timely. Please open the file,' he said.

I turned over the front cover. There wasn't much to see, just a photo of a young, male soldier attached to a short report.

'What you're looking at is a brief report on the absence of Private James Summers from 16 Regiment of the Royal Service Corps based about forty miles away from here, at Sennybridge. Summers is our missing officer.'

Richards allowed me a few moments to read through the file before he continued. 'His real name is Simon Liverick' he said. 'He's a Detective Constable, eight years service, one of our specialist undercover officers. He'd finished his course at Prince Albert Barracks and was posted to Sennybridge the week before last. If everything had gone to plan, he should have resigned from the Army this week and would have been debriefed before returning to his normal duties.'

'Did he find any evidence of the kind you were looking for?' I said.

'Nothing we're aware of. He reported a number of relationships between recruits and NCOs but nothing abusive, so far as we could ascertain. And, although there's no immediate evidence to suggest he was at risk, he's now failed to meet two scheduled check-ins with his handler.'

103

'Enough to cause concern,' I replied. 'Does the MOD know you've had someone on the inside?'

As the two senior police officers glanced nervously toward each other, I knew the answer to my question even before the Chief Constable replied. 'They don't,' he said.

David Clarke turned on his chair to face me. 'Despite what the press have said, we've been doing our best.'

'We don't want another Deepcut here, Inspector,' said Richards.

'And the RMP at Sennybridge have no idea where he's gone?'

'They're based in nearby Brecon and have him labelled as an ordinary AWOL. We've managed to confirm that personal effects like his wallet and driving licence were missing along with some kit he might have needed if he were planning to live rough.'

'But you don't buy it?' I said. 'Because Sennybridge is only an hour's drive from here and one of ours would surely find a way to let his handler know if he was going off-grid for any reason?'

'He's normally very reliable,' Clarke said, as he exchanged another concerned glance with Richards.

'Does he have a family? Could he have had enough and decided to head home?' I asked, wondering if the simplest answer may be the right one.

'He's married with a young child and we've made discreet enquiries … his wife hasn't heard from him. As you seem to appreciate, we have standard procedures an undercover officer should follow if something unexpected comes up … such as the loss of his mobile telephone. He didn't follow them.' Richards leaned across his desk, his gaze focussed on me. 'Having you inside the base has created an opportunity.'

'You want me to ask around?'

'That could raise suspicions. While we focus on finding our officer, we simply want you to keep your eyes and ears open and report anything useful to us. I'm sure you appreciate the conundrum we face.'

'Having the civilian police trying hard to locate a particular AWOL would draw attention to the fact he's no ordinary recruit?'

'Exactly.'

'I'm only here for another couple of days,' I said. I have to get back to London for a selection board at the end of next week.'

Richards smiled. 'I've arranged with Mr Grahamslaw that you can take as long as you … as long as *we* need. I'm certain you won't miss the board.' He looked me hard in the eye as he finished his sentence; the emphasis on the 'we' clearly designed to let me know who was in charge here. My heart sank. My cooperation, although requested, wasn't optional. Any ideas I'd had about having some quiet time to study before seeing my family for the weekend had just flown out the window.

As I left the meeting to walk back to meet Floria in the car park, Richards' final words lingered with me. 'At the moment, we're keeping an open mind,' he said. 'But the longer this goes on, the more I fear for DC Liverick's safety.'

No pressure, I thought.

Chapter 22

Floria and I arrived at the Armoury at 4pm – the pre-arranged appointment time with Sergeant Masters – only to be told by the Guardroom staff that the Adjutant had changed his duties. Masters had returned to his home to get some sleep before supervising guard duty that night. Although the Armoury was locked, Floria offered to show me around using the spare set of keys kept in the guardroom. I declined. It was Masters I wanted to see, not the place he worked.

By now we were hungry so we headed into town, to an American-style diner Floria knew. Hoping for an improvement on our rather dismal lunch, I ordered a chicken dish with fries and, as we waited for our food to arrive, I took the opportunity to slip outside and ring Jenny. I'd timed it just right this time. After a busy day, she had both our daughters bathed and awaiting my call before bed. I managed a quick kiss-blowing exchange with Charlie, our two-year-old, before her older sister, Becky, decided enough was enough and it was time to tell me about her day exploring rock-pools at the beach. I was enthralled, overflowing with fatherly enthusiasm as my daughter described the limpets, barnacles and other sea-life she had found. Eventually, as she began to wind down, her aunt took both girls off for bedtime stories, leaving Jenny and me to enjoy a few precious minutes catching up on our news of the day. I returned to my table enthused by the call.

Our food had arrived. 'They do great scoff in here,' Floria said, as I sat down. 'Do you call home every single day?'

'Every day I can, yes.' I glanced around the table looking for the salt and pepper.

'I thought you might,' she added, passing me a paper salt sachet. 'The look on your face, it's like you just did a line of coke.' I didn't think it prudent to ask Floria how she was able to make that comparison but I knew what she meant. Touching base with my family always gave me a lift.

By the time we'd finished eating and were on the road towards Private Morgan's family home, it was already getting dark. Floria explained the house was a terraced property in a former mining village at the edge of a steep, fern-covered hillside. The mountain roads were dark and unlit and I only became aware we were close to our destination as we past the 'Markham' sign. As we reached the centre of the village. I saw a single, brightly-lit convenience-store at the end of an unkempt row of shops. Next to the store was a fish-n-chip shop come Chinese take-away, a working man's social club and, at the end of the terrace, a bookies. The communal areas adjacent to the shops looked deprived and uncared for. Abandoned furniture and other debris littered a grassed area, and a solitary bus-stop shelter – a rusting hulk devoid of glass – was covered with spray-painted graffiti.

I knew a little about the area from Welsh lads I'd worked with in the Regiment and what I saw, depressed me. A century before, men had journeyed for hundreds of miles seeking work in nearby coal mines. Wealthy owners had sent men, women and even children deep into pitch-black, dust-filled underground tunnels and, to make sure they stayed, built homes for them. Those mines – the pits, as they referred to them locally – were now closed and the jobs they'd provided were no more. But the people who had worked underground, those that survived the work, the accidents and the diseases that befell them, they and their descendants were still here. The Morgans were just such a family, I imagined. They were amongst the leftover and forgotten remnants of an industry that had promised much, fuelled the industrial revolution, but which had ultimately failed to build beyond its short-lived existence.

As we parked outside a terraced house sitting beneath the steep, grey slope of the adjacent mountain, I could see light from a huge television screen flickering colour and shadows around the living room. 'They're definitely expecting us?' I said to Floria, as she locked the car. I glanced up and down the empty street. The smell of coal-smoke filled the air.

'They used to get a visit most weeks after Morgan first went,' she said, opening a rusted garden gate leading to the front door. 'We don't get over here much these days.'

Five minutes later, we were sat side-by-side on a small settee in the Morgan front room. The television seemed even larger now we were close to it. Mrs Morgan had offered us tea before heading out back to the tiny galley kitchen. Twin boys, younger siblings to their absent brother, sat on the floor with their backs to us, eyes glued to the screen. From the moment their mother had politely asked us to take a seat, neither child had so much as acknowledged our presence. A film was showing. It was some form of zombie apocalypse movie, a hero with a powerful and destructive gun battling against a horde of slow-moving people who he disposed of through increasingly violent and bloody means. Just at the point where I was beginning to wonder how on earth we were going to have any form of meaningful conversation, Mrs Morgan re-appeared in the doorway carrying a large brass-handled tray laid with what I guessed might be her best tea set. She also held a remote control in her hand. The TV screen flicked off.

'Go watch in your room, boys,' she said, as the two youngsters finally tore their eyes from the television. I guessed this might be a familiar occurrence – visitors to the house, up to your bedroom to watch another TV – as both boys stood without speaking and headed towards the stairs. I smiled to myself as, in the doorway, I saw their mother move her hand from the tray to drop a handful of sweets into expectant hands.

Floria introduced me and made out our visit was routine. From Mrs Morgan's reaction as she sat down opposite us, she appeared no more than mildly curious about my presence. 'Makes a change to have civilian police involved,' she said to me, as she sipped from her china cup. 'So, what makes you think you can find our Tom when this lot haven't?'

'I was wondering if you can help us with a couple of things,' I said, without responding to the question. 'Was Tom enjoying the Army before he went missing?'

A slight scowl crossed Mrs Morgan's face. 'It was all he ever wanted to do,' she replied, resting her cup and saucer on her lap. 'He used to spend hours up the mountain, camping out. Joined the cadets at school and signed up before he'd even done his GCSEs. But if you're here to ask again where he is, then all I can say is I've no idea.'

'I'm not here for just that,' I explained. 'I'm looking into the theft of some weapons that went missing on the day of Tom's passing-out parade.'

Mrs Morgan nodded, approvingly. 'Well, I did wonder when that might come up. To be honest, I'm surprised nobody ever mentioned it earlier, being as Tom was there, like.'

'Did he ever talk about that day to you? Express any opinion as to how the rifles went missing?' I asked.

'All he said was they'd worked out who'd had them.'

'The Army had worked it out?'

'No, not the Army. Him and the other recruits, they had it worked out. They were sworn to say nothing, though.'

'Did Tom tell you that as well?'

'Yes … and, to be honest, Tom said it had to have been one of the visitors. He said someone could easily have snuck in the back of the lorry while he was sitting in the cab.'

'Was there some reason he was posted as sentry?' Floria asked.

Mrs Morgan scowled. 'He was in some kind of bother over something. That was why he was told to keep watch over the guns in the lorry whilst all the others got to spend more time with their guests. One of the officers – Tom said he was sometimes ok but mostly a bastard – he fixed it so Tom was the guard.'

'Did your son ever mention that NCO's name?' I asked.

'He was warned never to speak about it. When those guns went missing, Tom was told to say nothing to anyone. Either that or he'd be in big bother. Warned him he'd go to prison, they did.'

'So, the statement he made to our Special Investigation Branch wasn't quite true?' Floria said. She'd put her cup down, I'd noticed, and was pulling a small notebook from her pocket.

Mrs Morgan didn't reply but, as I watched I saw her glance at Floria's red cap where it sat on the arm of the settee. I had a sense she was already thinking she'd said too much.

'Did he tell *you* the name?' I said, gently.

'I'm not being funny, Inspector, because I'd help you if I could. But, like I said, he was told not to.'

There was a lack of conviction to Mrs Morgan's response that suggested she knew more than she was prepared to say. For some reason, probably a wish to not get her son in yet more trouble, she was holding back. I decided to change tack. 'Did he mention Private Davenport to you at all?' I said. 'I don't know if you were aware, she was guarding the rifles before Tom. One of the rifles taken was issued to her.'

'Not really,' Mrs Morgan said. 'Tom knew her, of course, they all knew her. She was well-liked, if you know what I mean. Pretty girl she was. Very sad. A tragic waste of a life … there's a lot don't think she killed herself, you know?'

Floria jotted a note down before asking a question. 'Tom didn't express any suspicion she might be involved in the rifles going missing?' she asked.

'Involved? Her?' Mrs Morgan replied, with a slight laugh. 'God, no. Nice family she was from. Not the kind to go stealing guns from the Army. It'd be different if she'd been from around here.'

'What makes you say that?' Floria asked.

'People around here are flat broke. It wasn't so long ago there were a thousand men down our pit. Now, look at us. The local school keeps a supply of shoes for the children who turn up without any. Our community is dying … if Tom has chosen not to come back here, who could blame him?'

'Were the recruits told not to speak about Private Davenport's death as well?'

'You know very well they were,' Mrs Morgan said, scowling. 'The Army closes ranks on things like that. We look after each other, was what our Tom said.'

'Did he say who gave them that order?' I asked, as I tried to stop Floria taking over. It was clear she hadn't given up on her Davenport theories.

'It was the NCOs, but don't go asking me any names. If he told me, I don't remember. All I will say is Tom was really scared of them … like many of them were. If they told him to keep quiet, then he'd do just that.'

I felt Floria's hand touch me gently on the forearm. She had another question. 'Your son still hasn't been in touch?' she asked.

Mrs Morgan shook her head, again. 'Not so much as a word. Not a phone call, a letter or anything. Same with his mates in the village. Good boys they are … in the main. They'd tell me if they heard from him.'

'Would you mind if we looked over his room?' I asked.

My question was met with a resigned shrug of the shoulders as our host stood and then led us up the stairs. Tom Morgan's room was the small bedroom at the front of the house. It was surprisingly tidy and, as Floria began looking around I thought how unused it appeared. It was almost too tidy. There was one small bed, neatly made up and covered by a red, Liverpool FC duvet. As I looked over the poster-covered walls and at the selection of football trophies on the shelf – best player 1999, league winners 2001, and others – I saw Floria surreptitiously slide her hand beneath the bed covers. She was checking for warmth, an indication the bed had been used and to see if the sheets were fresh. She shook her head before lifting the matching pillow. Moving it revealed a small torch.

'We left it ready for when he comes home,' Mrs Morgan said, as I flicked open the top magazine of a pile lying just inside the door. Floria turned over a pair of well-used Army-issue boots sat at the end of the bed. As she looked at the soles, I noticed a slight scowl flicker across her face. I wondered. From behind the closed door to another of the bedrooms, I could hear a second television blaring. I was tempted to open it; just to take a look, but another idea was forming that I hoped might prove more productive.

With our cursory look around the bedroom complete, we headed downstairs, thanked Mrs Morgan for the tea and her time, and then made our way back to the car.

It didn't take long for Floria's reaction to examining Tom Morgan's boots to be explained. With his mother safely out of hearing, she told me. 'The soles had damp mud in the treads,' she said, as she opened our car doors with the remote key. 'Someone has been wearing them, and quite recently, I'd say. And for a mother whose son has supposedly been missing for several months, she seemed remarkably cool about it.'

I closed the car door, attached the seat belt and waited while Floria started the engine. 'I thought that too,' I said. 'Those football magazines in the bedroom? The top one had been read and was from this month.'

'You think he's around then?'

'Definitely, and I've a feeling I know where we'll find him.'

Chapter 23

On the return journey to Wendy's, I asked Floria if she could arrange some kit for me – I would need some boots, trousers and a decent outdoor jacket. I also suggested we could use some help from a couple of uniformed military police officers.

'Are we going up the mountain behind the house?' Floria asked. She'd guessed my intentions.

'We'll need to be back before first light,' I said. 'Morgan used to spend all his time camped up on the hillside. I think he heads out the back door as we arrive at the front. I want to ask him why he's so desperate not to be caught.'

It was getting late by the time we arrived in Usk. The dining room light was on and, through the front window, I could see my friend was still working, a mass of papers spread out on the table in front of her. I knocked the front door gently in case Monique had gone to bed and, after opening up, Wendy asked if I had time for a chat. I agreed, and she disappeared to the kitchen, returning a moment later with two large glasses of red wine.

As soon as we'd sat down, Wendy revealed she had an apology. I'd been right about how her Chief Constable had learned of my background.

'It's really not a problem,' I said. 'Things worked out OK in the end.'

'I've been worrying about it all day,' she replied. 'I felt I betrayed a confidence but I had to do something to persuade him to keep you inside the camp.'

'It was your idea?'

'Well, you said you'd do anything you could to help. As an ordinary DI, he wasn't persuaded to let you help us. As an ex SAS officer, he became very keen.'

I smiled. I could see how Wendy's trump card had helped her win the argument. 'Presumably, there's no further news on your missing DC?' I said.

'None.'

'There wasn't much in the report from what I could see.'

'It's an impossible situation. The military police deal with AWOLs so we can't ask them a thing without raising suspicion.'

'The press would have a field day if they found out.'

Wendy paused for a moment. 'There's something else I need to explain,' she said, hesitantly. 'It was my idea to put an undercover officer into the barracks. I recruited him ... I set up his fake identity. His absence is my responsibility.'

I immediately understood the looks that Wendy's Chief had exchanged with his senior detective and the pressure Wendy must now be feeling. 'He'll turn up, I'm sure,' I said, as I tried to reassure her.

'Let's hope so.' Wendy opened her briefcase and began collecting the files together.

'Busy day?' I asked.

'Nothing out of the ordinary. You'd be amazed how much work an ACC has to do. How are you getting along with the RMP Sergeant? She seems nice.'

'Not too bad. We got off to a sticky start due to a difference of opinion over the Davenport inquest, but we seem fine now.'

'A difference of opinion?'

'She's convinced the girl was killed by someone.'

'She's not the only one,' Wendy said, as she finished packing her files away. 'Bullied to death is what people are saying.'

'So I hear,' I said. 'How old is DC Liverick? It can't have been easy to find someone who didn't stick out among the recruits.'

'Late twenties but he looks younger. If something's happened to him …'

'It won't have,' I said, interrupting. 'There are all kinds of reasons why undercover officers drop off the radar temporarily. I took a large sip from my wine glass and smiled. 'In the meantime, do you want to hear my theory about the Davenport suicide?'

'Fire away.'

'The descriptions of what happened during the incidents at Deepcut and here reminded me of something that used to occur quite frequently at a barracks I worked at in Germany. We had this particular NCO who liked to try and catch the soldiers out when they were on guard duty. He'd creep up on them in the night to test them, as he put it. What he was actually doing was having fun scaring them.'

'Bit risky if they were armed,' Wendy said.

'In those days, the guards patrolled with an unloaded rifle. Sometimes they would carry a separate magazine containing a few rounds but often they didn't even have that. He wasn't in any danger of getting shot.'

'The weapons carried by guards here are loaded,' Wendy replied. 'Wouldn't doing that now be a bit of a recipe for disaster?'

'You don't know soldiers,' I said. 'A lot of them get turned on by danger. The same qualities that produce acts of incredible bravery can see them doing stupid things they think are great fun, particularly if they've had a few beers beforehand.'

'So, what you're saying is Davenport's suicide may have been horseplay? Some idiot trying to scare youngsters for fun?'

'That's my theory,' I said. 'Something went wrong, the kid got shot somehow and now the NCOs are keeping quiet about it.'

'Have you shared that theory with your RMP friend?'

'I haven't and I don't intend to. I want to finish this job as quickly as possible and then get home. So, how's Monique? Has she gone to bed?'

'She's fine … why do you ask?'

I shrugged, not wanting to make a mistake or to highlight an issue where there wasn't one. 'I just wanted to make sure she was OK with having me around,' I said. 'I sensed a bit of an atmosphere last night.'

Wendy smiled as she closed her briefcase. 'You're more astute than most men, Finlay. I'll give you that.'

'She's not keen then?'

'It's nothing she can't handle. Having someone from my past, especially a male friend … shall we say it gave her a bit of a wobble?'

'Is she the kind of person to want to check me out for herself?'

Wendy scowled. 'I'm not sure I understand what you're saying. Has something happened?'

'I met her on the landing this morning. It looked like she'd been in my room and when I checked, I saw my grab-bag had been moved.'

Wendy shook her head. 'I'm sorry. And you're right. She is unsettled by you being here. It wasn't helped by the hang-ups she had this evening.'

'On the telephone?'

'Twice, both times she heard someone breathing but nobody spoke.'

'Did she one, four, seven, one it?'

'Number withheld. She thinks it may have been Jenny.'

'It wasn't,' I said. 'She's not like that.'

116

'It'll have to remain a mystery then,' Wendy replied. 'And don't worry about her going in your room again. I'll have a word.'

'If you're certain?' I said.

'I am,' she replied, firmly, but with a warm smile that seemed to come from deep behind her eyes.

As I sipped at the wine, an idea came to me. 'About your missing lad, I could ask Sergeant McLaren, possibly?'

'Without raising suspicions?'

'She told me on the way to the Davenport's that she's an AWOL specialist. We've just been following up on a missing soldier who was present when the rifles were stolen. I think he's living at his mother's home and hides on the mountain nearby when the MPs come looking. It's about half an hour from here so we're going to have an early start in the morning to try and catch up with him.'

'How will that help us?' she asked.

'It won't directly. But I could ask her to let me have a look at the files of all other AWOLs who've have gone after recently leaving Cwmbran. Your man would be on that list.'

My friend beamed at me as she drained her glass. 'That's fantastic, Finlay, really brilliant. Thank you. And, if you can, the sooner the better.'

Chapter 24

From her seat in the corner of the NAAFI bar, Ellie Rodgers had a decent, if slightly restricted view of everything happening around her. She'd been watching a group of lads playing pool. They were tipsy, not drunk, and the banter between them and a mixed group watching the game had been friendly. One of them had looked her up and down and, if she'd read his signals right, he'd been looking to see if she was interested. She hadn't reacted. No smile, no nod, not even a look of recognition. The last thing she needed was a young squaddie on the pull.

She'd picked a good spot to watch the comings and goings in the bar, but not good enough for her to see what had caused a glass to smash near the pool table and the atmosphere in the bar to suddenly become very tense. And with everyone now still, it was impossible to move position without drawing attention to herself. One of the players looked towards the entrance door where an area of the floor had begun to clear as young recruits shuffled back towards the walls. Just inside the main door, she saw an older man had appeared. He stood glaring at those around him. Ellie didn't need to recognise him to know what he was. Early thirties, cropped haircut, fit-looking with faded tattoos on both arms. He was an NCO and he looked angry.

The crowd parted as the newcomer walked slowly forward, placing himself in the centre of the cleared floor area. He stopped, fists clenched by his sides, staring aggressively in the direction of the players. All four nervously placed their cues on the table before stepping away, the crunching sound beneath one of them revealing the location of the smashed glass. They looked uncomfortable, as if they'd been caught doing something reprehensible rather than enjoying a simple game of pool.

Apparently satisfied he had everyone's attention, the NCO pointed at one of the players, a skinny, shaven-headed youth who could have been no more than seventeen or eighteen. With a jerk of his thumb, he pointed to the door. Gaze firmly fixed on the floor in front of him, the chosen recruit quietly shuffled towards the exit. The NCO hissed something in his ear as he passed.

Even though Ellie wondered what the recruit had done to secure the wrath of an NCO, she knew but the situation wasn't without precedent. She'd seen lads who were barred from the NAAFI or late for guard duty suffer a similar fate. What had surprised her, though, was the fear this particular NCO's appearance had generated amongst everyone present. There'd been no banter, not even a wink or a smile. They were all petrified.

She was curious, enough to want to have a look outside, but aware if she moved first it would be noticed. For twenty or thirty seconds, nobody moved or spoke and then a voice from the far side of the bar broke the deadlock. 'Tucker's in the shit again.' One of the pool players reached for his abandoned cue and then laughed, nervously. Then, almost as if a game of musical chairs had re-commenced, conversations started up and everything returned to the way it had been before the NCO had appeared.

'He'll go the way of Davenport if he's not careful,' a female voice said, although Ellie couldn't see where it came from. She seized her chance. As quickly as she could, she headed to the door. She was just about to open it when a grey-shirted arm barred her way. 'Best not love. I'd give it a few minutes.'

The accent was Geordie, the voice hoarse. She looked up at the young man who now stood between her and the exit. He was long and lean, with a wide jaw and large nose. Ellie thought to push past him – he didn't look to be too much of an obstacle – but she decided a trick might be more expedient.

'I'm gonna throw up,' she said. 'Want it over you?'

The arm pulled back quickly out of her way. Shoving the door hard, Ellie stepped out into the cool evening air. There was nothing to see.

A combination of experience and instinct told her where to look. She turned to follow the narrow gravel path leading around the back of

119

the building towards the staff entrance. As she turned a corner, from the darkness, the sound of a muffled, yet angry voice caught her ear.

'Once more Tucker, once more,' the voice screamed. 'She's ours and you do not fuckin' touch, is that clear?' A groan followed, suggesting the man making the threat was relying on more than just words to make his point.

The next moment, three figures appeared from the shadows, running directly towards her. Ellie stalled. There was nowhere to hide. She was stood in the light coming from the NAAFI windows and would have to front it out.

As the figures approached, she saw they were all in dark overalls. They moved like men but the indistinct nature of their facial features confused her. As they drew closer she saw why. They were wearing respirators, gas masks designed for protection but equally effective at concealing identity. As the first two ran past, she turned to watch where they headed. Then, as she turned back, the third man stopped. In one swift movement, a strong hand wrapped around her throat and she was pinned against the wall of the building. A deep, metallic voice roared at her through the air filter. 'Who are you fuckin' clocking?' the man screamed, as he forced the mask against her face.

Ellie didn't reply and, although all her instincts and training demanded a reaction – to put this bastard down and find out who he was – she resisted. In the light from the window, she strained to peer through the eye glasses of the mask, to pick out some features she might recognise or recall. Was it the same man she'd seen in the bar? It was useless; the glass was misted up from the physical efforts of the wearer. There was one thing though, one clue. It was a smell. Not sweat, much sweeter. He smelled of aftershave, a familiar one, a scent she recognised but couldn't name.

Fingernails bit into her skin as the hand around her neck tightened so much breathing became impossible. She felt light-headed, giddy, as her vision blurred.

'Say nothing or you know what'll happen,' the man screamed at her.

With her legs weakening, Ellie felt the grip around her throat lessen and then stop completely. She sunk to her knees, coughing, and furious with herself for not having fought back. Then something that felt like a hand touched the top of her head.

This time she reacted instinctively, grabbing the hand then twisting it forward and down. Quickly, she swung her foot around his weight-bearing leg. He toppled and lost balance. Clenching the fist of her free hand, she pulled her arm back. She had him.

'Whoa ... steady on, love,' he called out. 'Only trying to help.'

The Geordie from the door, Ellie realised. Skinny arms, grey shirt. No respirator. She fell back, let go of her grip and screamed in frustration. And then to her horror, and before she could hold back, she began to sob.

Chapter 25

A wave of intense burning clawed angrily at the lining of Ellie's throat as her stomach convulsed once more. The spasms intensified and she braced her shoulders ready for the next opaque mixture of bile and half-digested lager to be ejected into the pan.

A moment later, it was over. Sinking back onto her knees, she collapsed against the wall of the cubicle. Be calm and breathe, she told herself.

Using a loose bundle of toilet paper, she began to wipe the bile clear from her mouth. It was a mistake. The action triggered another spasm. Quickly, she lunged forward but this time she was fortunate, the heaving subsided almost as quickly as it had arrived. Her prayers were being answered. Opening her eyes, she tried to stand. Overhead, the single naked bulb in the NAAFI toilet shone bright, the glare blinding her, preventing her from seeing the mess she knew she must have made. As her feet lost grip on the slippery floor, she leaned against the walls to prevent herself from falling. The effort caused her legs to tremble.

Loud music from the bar reminded her where she was and the predicament she now faced. First things first though, she needed a drink, something to wash away the awful taste. Only then would she be able to think how she was going to get past the recruits without being noticed. Easing back the door to the cubicle, she lurched towards the sinks. Thankfully, nobody had followed her into the ladies toilet. Small mercies, she thought, as she winced at the sight staring back at her from the mirror. With her face as white as a sheet, a mixture of sweat, bile and tears had conspired to spread the remnants of her makeup across her cheeks and forehead. Red, puffy eyes peered back at her. Again, she felt the muscles in her upper body spasm, this time in an unproductive aftershock. She spat into the sink before swearing at herself. 'Get a fucking grip, Rodgers.'

With the tap full on, Ellie pulled her hair back before thrusting the whole of her face beneath the flow of cool water. She drank deeply. Her eyes and nose cleared, the taste of the vomit fading with each gulp. Finally, with water dripping from her face, she stood and looked once more into the mirror. Her ribs were sore and her stomach ached, but it was over. Strength was returning to her limbs and the shakes had eased. Time to check the damage. She straightened up, took a deep breath, and lifted her chin.

The half-moon nail marks were clear, and on one side of her neck, three long, parallel scratches. They looked raw and angry. Anyone who knew anything would see them for what they were, the evidence of some bastard's hand having been around her throat. She touched the skin gently and winced. It was tender and already showing signs of bruising. She cursed again, angry with herself, angry with what she'd let happen. And, of all nights for this to happen, this was a bad one. The following Monday was the Regimental Mess dinner requiring her to wear a formal evening dress with an exposed neck. Hiding the injuries and avoiding the inevitable questions would be almost impossible.

But that wasn't her most pressing problem. Returning to use the NAAFI toilets had been a mistake born of urgency. She now had to get out the door and back to her room before somebody saw her. 'Before somebody sees me?' she repeated to herself, angrily. Of course, someone would see her; how could they not? There would be a gauntlet of concerned and gossiping Crows still drinking in the bar. Some of them would have seen her rushing in from outside and heading straight to the toilets. One or two might even have thought about following her. Fear of those responsible would have stopped them.

But, even if they had come to help, they would probably have concluded it was just the lager. She wouldn't explain and would see no point in explaining to them why she had reacted so badly to what had happened and why she felt so angry at herself for not fighting back. The memories the hand gripped around her neck had triggered were hers alone, personal and not to be shared. She took a deep breath and reached for the handle to the door leading to the bar. 'Now or never,' she told her reflection.

The door burst open. Ellie jumped back, the sudden movement making her giddy. A shape appeared, abstract at first but soon morphing into a figure, female and tall, and reassuringly familiar.

'What the hell happened to you?' Naomi said.

***

Half an hour later, Ellie embraced Naomi outside the NAAFI before heading back to her quarters. 'Are you sure you don't know who he was?' she asked.

Naomi huffed. 'Nobody's prepared to say. They're all shit scared, believe me. Are you sure I can't come with you?'

Ellie smiled and shook her head. Although the idea of some company was appealing, it couldn't happen. If Naomi saw her accommodation, it would immediately bring an end to a very promising relationship.

The bastard in the respirator had unwittingly done her a favour. Where Naomi had been unwilling to talk to a stranger, as a fellow victim enjoying several sympathetic vodkas, she had learned more in half an hour than during the whole of the previous evening. A door had been opened, just a chink, but she was in. Outsider had become friend, a fellow sufferer, someone to comfort and share the load with – someone to tell.

She now knew what the NCOs were up to, about the favours they expected to be done for them and about their enforcement team; euphemistically known to the recruits as the 'respirator gang'. It was them she had inadvertently run into. It was made up of NCOs and, according to Naomi, a small number of Crows the training staff used to spy on the others. The spies helped make up the numbers when the respirator gang needed them for a particular job, like putting the frighteners on a troublesome recruit. That was what had been happening outside the NAAFI. Private Lee Tucker had been singled

124

out for attention after becoming friendly with a female recruit one of the NCOs wanted for himself.

'It was platonic,' Naomi had insisted. 'Even Tucker isn't stupid enough to touch one of their girls.'

Before leaving, Ellie seized the opportunity to ask a final question. What had the girl in the bar meant when she'd said what happened to Davenport could happen to Tucker.

'Best we don't go there,' Naomi said. 'When the NCOs tell us we're not to talk about it, they mean not to anyone … even other soldiers.'

'But why is Davenport's bunk still empty?' Ellie pressed.

Naomi hesitated, as if unsure what she should say. 'We don't really know,' she said, finally. 'But I'll tell you what we think.'

'What's that?'

'It's a reminder. A reminder from the NCOs that, if it could happen to her, it could happen to us.'

Chapter 26

Saturday was the day it hit me how much I was missing home. I should have been waking up in my own bed, Jenny beside me, as we listened to our daughters chattering in their shared bedroom. Before my plans for the week had been changed, I'd had a little morning brunch in mind for them as a welcome home treat. It was my signature dish, and something I enjoyed doing. I even had a floppy chef's hat and an apron to make them laugh. Eggs, bacon and all the trimmings was something I'd enjoyed, ever since my Army days. Even our youngest, Charlie, had grown to love it – provided she could add plenty of red sauce, of course.

At 5am, as my alarm woke me, I'd not slept well, either. I rarely do when I know I have an early start ahead of me. The habit was formed in the Army where I grew used to bedding down exhausted, late at night, only to be on stag – sentry duty – a couple of hours later. Officers in training, such as I had been, soon learned the best way to ensure you weren't late was to oversleep once, just once. The experience of being dragged forcibly from your sleeping bag by an angry NCO tended to leave you with a lasting reminder not to let it happen again.

The house was in darkness as I crept along the landing and into the bathroom. If everything had gone to plan, Floria would soon arrive with two uniformed MPs to provide help. I had a quick wash, pulled on a t-shirt and trousers, and then opened the front door. In the street, I could just make out the sidelights of Floria's car with a second parked close behind. I gave them a wave and a few moments later I was changing into the camouflage jacket and trousers Floria had brought with her. She watched attentively as I fed laces through the eyelets of a rather worn pair of military issue boots before trying them on. 'Just the job,' I said.

'Don't ask where I got them,' she joked, her lips breaking into a broad grin.

I didn't. 'Did you get my text last night?' I asked.

'Why do you want AWOL reports from Sennybridge?'

'It's a hunch I'm following up on.'

'Want to share it with me?'

I grinned, stood up and stamped the boots on the floor to test them. They were comfortable. 'If they reveal anything useful you'll be the first to know,' I said, as we headed to her car.

***

The roads were quiet and the closer we got to our destination, the mistier it became. When she noticed me peering through the mist, Floria explained the roads and altitude were deceptive; it didn't appear we were climbing but the mining villages in the area were several hundred feet higher than the Usk valley where we'd begun our journey.

The MPs in the second car had brought radios, two for them, one for Floria. On the journey I used the time to share my plan with them. The idea was simple; they would knock on the front door of the Morgan household once Floria and I were in position on the mountainside behind the house. I should like to have laid in wait a little closer to the house but the layout of the terrace – tight against a steep, fern-covered, slope – made that impractical. I also had a feeling we would find a track somewhere behind the house that Tom Morgan used to escape onto the mountain whenever someone came looking. If all went well, we'd be there waiting for him. The two MPs seemed au-fait with my approach and, as Floria explained, the method wasn't a new one.

A quarter of a mile short of our destination, I was pleased to see step one in action as our companions pulled over and their lights turned off. Floria and I continued, branching off onto a steep road leading up the mountain behind the houses. With the mist drawing in around us, we soon found ourselves struggling to locate anywhere suitable to leave our car and make our approach. Eventually, we compromised on a pull-in Floria probably would have missed had it not been for an abandoned fridge picked out by our headlights. As she killed the engine, I opened the passenger door. Immediately, the dank, morning air enveloped us. I shivered and pulled the collar of the camouflage jacket tight around my neck.

'Bit colder than you're used to, sir?' said Floria as we scrambled up a rock-strewn slope away from the road.

'Are we to have this debate again, Floria?' I said.

She grinned and held up a hand to acknowledge my reminder. 'Sorry … not used to calling officers by their name.'

We headed east – at least what I thought was east. The mist on the higher levels was even denser than in the village and I relied, to a large extent, on my sense of direction and the diffused light from the moon. Floria didn't quibble, so I figured she either trusted my judgment or agreed we were heading the right way. Underfoot, the grass was short and slippery with tussocks and stray rocks conspiring to create ankle-breaking terrain for the impatient. Picked out by the dew, delicate silver cobwebs laced the bracken and every visible surface was wet. Every so often, a ghostly apparition would loom out of the mist. The first such encounter startled us momentarily until we realised it was a sheep, one of few animals capable of eking out an existence on the mountain.

After a few minutes, I was relieved to find my rusty navigation skills were still functioning when a silhouette of the houses at the edge of the village appeared through the mist. Perhaps sensing our presence, a small dog further along the row began barking excitedly. It was quickly silenced by a curse from its angry owner. Someone else was up early.

I'd counted the houses the previous evening and was looking for the twelfth one from the end. To my frustration, even though dawn wasn't far off, I now struggled to distinguish them through the mist. I was glad we weren't intending to do a forced entry from our side. With no house numbers or effective landmarks to use we could have ended up breaking down the wrong door. As I knelt while thinking how best to overcome the problem, Floria joined me. 'Having a problem picking out the Morgan place?' she whispered.

I nodded.

'It's difficult in this,' she added. 'All the houses look the same. Why don't we split up? I can cover a few, you watch the others. If he tries to escape out this way, we'll likely hear him coming anyway.'

It seemed a decent compromise. Although, if Tom Morgan did try and sprint for freedom, I had serious doubts whether I'd have much joy catching a fit young soldier who knew this area a lot better than I did. In an ideal world, I'd have preferred to be waiting on the other side of the correct gate as he walked through the tiny back yard of his mother's house and into our arms. As Floria and I separated, I heard her talking quietly into her radio telling the MPs to move in. The mist was closing in once more, the silhouette of the buildings disappearing into the chilled, damp cloud. Every colour, the rock of the mountain, the grass, even the skyline, all was now leeched to a grey monochrome that disguised detail and masked movement. To my left, I heard the sound of a back door opening. I tensed, and then heard the sound of a woman swearing at a cat who appeared reluctant to leave the warmth of his home. It was a false alarm.

A moment later, the rapping sound of a door knocker caused me to turn to my right. It was nearby, maybe just one or two houses away from my perch. Keeping low, I monkey-ran nearer to the sound, moving carefully down the slope towards the back gates. As the dark shape of the buildings appeared once more from the mist, I became aware of a slow-moving figure close by. It was Floria. She'd heard it too.

Again, there was the sound of knocking. Three raps this time and more urgent. Muffled voices followed the sound. One was male, the other older and female. One of the RMP cops talking to Tom Morgan's mother, I guessed. Then ... silence.

The seconds passed and became minutes. I rubbed my hands to keep the circulation going. Beside me, Floria tensed, and a fraction of a second later I heard the reason. There was movement at the rear of the house. A door was opening. We readied ourselves.

Floria's radio burst into life. *'House is clear.'*

That was quick, I thought. Floria responded, asking for a *sitrep*, a situation report. The MP reported Tom Morgan wasn't home and the bed in his room was cold. It was them we'd heard at the rear door as they'd been checking the back yard. We'd drawn a blank.

'Ask them to check if the boots we saw are in his room,' I said to Floria. 'And tell them to look under the pillow. See if the torch is still there.'

We waited and thirty seconds later had our answer. Tom Morgan's boots and torch were missing.

I turned to Floria. 'He's up there,' I said, looking back up the mountain. 'He was one step ahead of us.'

'Or someone told him we were coming,' she replied.

Chapter 27

Had I known the scale of the task ahead of us, or had I heeded the raised eyebrows that met my proposal, I may not have insisted we immediately head up the slope to search for Tom Morgan's hideout. Markham Common, and the mountain area it joined, was a great deal larger than I realised.

The MPs returned to their car after making sure Mrs Morgan thought the attempt to locate her son had met with another failure. We didn't want her phoning a warning to her son. A few minutes later, we met them at the lay-by. Following a quick discussion on how best to cover the mist-shrouded hillside, we agreed to split up. I smiled to myself as the soldiers took over the planning. 'No disrespect, sir,' one of the MPs commented. 'But this kind of terrain is where we do our training and we know the kind of places Private Morgan will find shelter.'

I followed Floria along one of several well-trodden sheep trails. Although dawn was breaking, visibility was still very limited. 'Just keep close,' she said. 'I don't want to have to explain to my boss how you fell off a crag and broke your neck.'

'The morning sun might lift this mist,' I replied, as once more I rubbed warmth into my hands. 'What are you looking for?'

'Nothing specific,' Floria said. She stopped for a moment at a fork in the track, pulled a small, yellow crayon from her pocket and marked a small letter 'f' on a rock face next to the path. 'Easy to get lost in this,' she added. 'Just look for anything out of place. Maybe a discarded ciggie or a sweet wrapper. Anything that suggests a human has been here rather than an animal.'

I smiled to myself as I watched Floria scanning the ground. What we were doing took me back to a time, many years previous, to a survival course in Kenya when I'd first been taught to track by people who could spot an unnatural bend in a blade of grass. My knowledge was now rusty, to say the least, but I was still hopeful I'd see things my escort might miss. Millions of years previously, in the place we now walked, south-moving glaciers of the ice age had scraped deep gouges through the rock. Those channels – the Valleys – became the route for further water erosion and, as industrial-age man discovered, the means to access deeply-buried deposits of coal. Where money was to be made, commerce and people moved in, and pockets of habitation soon established. But here, on the mountains, the windswept, upland plateaus remained as they had been for aeons, inhospitable and barren. With only four of us searching, we were going to need a healthy dose of luck if we were to be successful. As we reached a conifer tree-line high above the village, I called a halt to our climb. Floria contacted the others on the radio and requested they rendezvous with us.

'If it was me, this is where I'd hide,' Floria puffed.

I was also breathing quite heavily by this point and it took a few moments before I could answer her. In the meantime, I saw the two MPs approaching. They walked slowly, rummaging in the carpet of pine needles beneath the trees as they searched. I looked ahead. The heavy tree canopy blocked the ambient light making the spot ideal to hide from an aircraft but, devoid of undergrowth, it offered no opportunities for concealment at ground level and no warmth or protection from a prevailing wind. 'If he were here, he'd be easy to spot from our level,' I said. 'And there's no shelter.'

Floria frowned, her gaze resting on me for several seconds before she spoke. 'Fair point … but he has to be somewhere he can reach quickly. Maybe best we keep fairly close to the village.'

The suggestion we restrict our search parameters met with an eager response from the two MPs. I wondered if they truly agreed with Floria, or if it were the prospect of a brief amble around the hills followed by breakfast back at camp that persuaded them. Either way, with daylight now making our presence much easier to detect, we needed to be careful if we were going to find Tom Morgan before he spotted us.

After a cursory search of the trees, we climbed into an area of heavy bracken I thought looked more promising. Find a nice little hollow beneath the heavy leaves and I could see you'd soon be able to create a hide that gave you concealment, warmth and shelter. Floria seemed to agree as she decided this was the point to spread out again. One of the MPs moved away to our left, the second went forward. Floria and I broke off to the right.

We all moved more slowly now, scanning the ground and then stopping every so often to listen and to observe. Tiny stonechats darted nimbly amongst the fern leaves, each uttering a quick warning call to let others know of our presence. If Morgan was any good I thought, he'd know what those little birds were telling him. Ahead and further up the slope, I also caught a glimpse of the occasional rabbit amongst the purple flowers of moorland heather. It was a lovely area, one that I could have enjoyed exploring had the circumstances been different.

'Flo from Jim.' One of the MPs was on the radio, talking in a low voice. Jim, I recalled, was the smaller of the two men.

Floria answered him.

'I've found a hexi wrapper', he continued. *'On a sheep track about two hundred metres north of our last RV.'*

'We're close,' Floria said to me, quietly. She clicked the transmit button on her radio twice. It was the agreed acknowledgement signal and, in response to a find, it would let Jim know we would head towards his position.

Five minutes or so later, in a narrow clearing between two rocky outcrops, I saw the grey outline of a figure crouched down and waiting. It was the second MP. He stood as we drew close. 'Jim's gone ahead,' he murmured. 'We found a track further along this gulley. I said to wait for you but he wants the arrest.'

I heard Floria swear under her breath as the MP handed her an empty Hexamine fuel-block wrapper. It looked to be the exact kind soldiers used with a compact solid-fuel cooker. I'd burned many of them in the field – they could produce enough heat for a decent brew in a couple of minutes – and once I'd even seen a block sliced up, placed into a Kendal Mint-Cake wrapper and then given to another soldier as a present. The look on the recipient's face as he bit into his 'cake' had been memorable.

Although it was now light, the mist had yet to fully lift and our visibility was still limited to thirty or forty metres at the most. Floria tucked the cardboard wrapper into her jacket pocket and we pressed on. With the second MP between us, I brought up the rear. After about a hundred metres we came to another split in the path. Floria stopped, and seemed to be scanning the ground around her. After a few moments, she stood upright, hands on hips, and inhaled deeply. She beckoned us over.

'Wanker hasn't marked his route,' she said, bluntly, keeping her voice soft and quiet. 'Lloyd, you take the left, we'll take the right.'

Lloyd nodded and, without replying, headed in the direction he'd been given. We waited until he was out of sight before moving off. Then, just as we turned onto the right-hand path, a fast-moving figure loomed out of the mist to our left. I expected it to be Lloyd but, as the figure drew closer, I saw it was Jim, the MP who'd made the original radio transmission.

'I've found him,' he said between heavy breaths, making no attempt to lower his voice. 'He's under a basher about a hundred metres along the track.'

'Is Lloyd guarding him?' Floria demanded.

'He's with him, yes,' Jim said. 'But he won't be trying to escape. He's dead.'

Chapter 28

Tucked up in his army-issue sleeping bag, it would have been easy to assume Tom Morgan was asleep. He'd made himself a basher – a small shelter – using a tarpaulin he'd tied to the branches of a small tree. There was no obvious sign of injury on his face or upper body, no blood stains and no indication of any struggle. Floria grinned at me as I did a quick check for signs of life and then began explaining to her and the two MPs about scene preservation, cross-contamination and the need to treat what appeared to be a 'natural causes' death as something more sinister until we knew otherwise. As I paused for a breath, she reminded me, politely, that the Met aren't the only police service to attend forensic courses. I felt suitably chastened.

Fortunately, from our position high up on the mountain, I had a good enough phone signal to call in help. The '999' telephone operator answered immediately and, after being transferred to a police call-handler, I explained who I was, what we'd found and that we'd need the local CID, a SOCO – Scenes-of-Crime Officer – and some uniform assistance to help manage a crime scene. With Floria standing guard over Tom Morgan's body, I then sent the two MPs to stand at waypoints we'd marked during our search so the first police officers to arrive at the scene could use the same approach route.

The local response wasn't the quickest. About forty minutes after I'd made the call, one of the MPs radioed to say a single uniformed PC had appeared. He'd been sent from the nearest police station at Tredegar and, to be fair to him, the only information he'd been given by his control room was to look for a man who claims he's a detective from the Met and says he's found a body on the moor. Even then, it was only after he'd walked along the track to check the scene for himself that he agreed to call in further help. He warned us it may take a while, it was a Saturday, most of the CID were off and a lot of his uniform colleagues were in Cardiff, policing a 'bluebirds' home game. Then, to my surprise, and without so much as a word, he walked back along the track, climbed back in his car and left us to it.

'So much for inter-service co-operation,' Floria said, with some irony, when I returned to wait with her.

An hour and a half after I'd made my initial call, an unmarked car containing two detectives arrived on the nearest of several mountain roads, about four hundred metres from us. From that point on, things moved more quickly. The only notable exception being when I found myself explaining to one of the DCs, and then on the telephone to his DI, and then again to a DCI from the Force Headquarters, exactly why an officer from the Met was working on their patch without their knowledge.

Jim, the MP who had found the body, was brought in from his place on the mountain to sit in the back of the CID car with one of the detectives and make a statement. With that formality over, the MPs returned to their barracks and the Scene of Crimes specialists took over the crime-scene. I was hungry by this time, so Floria and I decided to drive to the nearest local police station at Tredegar to get some breakfast.

It was as we reached the point on the track where Jim had first told us of his discovery that I saw an unexpected movement near some gorse bushes about two hundred metres from where we were walking. 'Is there anyone else up here that you know of?' I said to Floria, as she stopped to see what I was looking at.

'It's probably just another sheep,' she replied.

I stood watching for a few moments and then, just as I was about to give up and accept Floria was right, I saw what looked like a crouched figure moving between two outcrops of rock.

'Did you see that?' Floria said.

'Someone's out there,' I replied. 'Let's split up. I'll make my way straight toward them. You take the track back to the road and see if you can cut him off.'

'What do you want me to do if I catch him?'

'Play it by ear. If it's a nosy hill walker just dust him down and send him on his way. There's only one road off the mountain from here so, if they get to it before you and they've got a car, try and get the index.'

For a second, I was tempted to summon help from the cops dealing with Tom Morgan's body, but there wasn't time. We had to move quickly. Floria ran towards the road and was soon out of my sight. I half-walked, half-jogged across the boggy grassland towards where we'd seen the figure. Although it only took me a couple of minutes to reach the point I was aiming for, not too surprisingly, I found it deserted.

I was scanning the ground, looking for a sign of someone having been there when I heard a scream from the direction of the road. It was Floria.

Chapter 29

'I'm telling you ... all I saw was a blue car,' Floria said angrily as she brushed dirt from the sleeves of her jacket.

I was still catching my breath, having run, slipped and jumped a couple of hundred metres of wet moorland in my efforts to try and reach the lane quickly.

'What was the scream?' I said, between gasps.

'That was me diving out the way. Bastard nearly ran me over.'

'Are you ok ... did you get part of the number maybe?'

Floria stared at me as if I'd personally insulted her. 'I was concentrating on not getting killed. I didn't even see whether the driver was male or female.'

'You sure they tried to hit you?' I asked.

'Course I'm bloody sure,' she said. 'When I got to the road I saw nothing until the car came hurtling around the corner. I was about to try and get the number when it swerved towards me.'

'I'm going to call it in,' I said.

The police telephone operator put me through to the local police station at Tredegar. After recording as much of a description of the car as we were able to provide, a CID officer I spoke to requested Floria should come in to make a quick statement. I offered to take over the driving but she declined. She was bruised, she said, not broken.

By the time we arrived at Tredegar, we'd agreed Floria would report what had happened as factually as she could without putting forward any theories as to who may have been in the car or what their intentions had been. The driver could have been connected to Tom Morgan, they might have been keeping an eye on what we were up to, or they could easily have been someone local having a nose at what was happening on their mountain who'd panicked when we'd given chase. While she headed to the CID office, I went straight to the canteen to order food. By the time she joined me, I'd been doing some thinking and had decided we should have a straight talk.

'If you're right, and Morgan was murdered, I don't think that was his killer we saw,' Floria said, as she tucked into her meal. 'I reckon he'd have been long gone. I think someone's watching you.'

'My host's partner had a couple of hang-up calls yesterday,' I replied.

'Maybe you'd best tell Miss Russell what we found, then?'

'I will.' I was about to continue our conversation when the telephone in my pocket began to ring. The caller identity was withheld which meant it was almost certainly from London. After a quick slurp of tea, I pressed the answer button. It was Bill Grahamslaw again, and he wasn't happy.

'I thought I told you not to get involved in anything outside of your brief,' he said. Again, there was no opening 'hello' or 'how are you'. Bill had a point to make and he got straight to it.

'What the hell caused it to be you to find another dead soldier?' he continued. I held the phone away from my ear. Across the table, I saw Floria grimace. If she hadn't picked out the detail of my Commander's words, she'd certainly heard the tone. I judged it best to find a space to hear the rest of Bill's call in private and smiled my excuses at Floria as I left the table.

'The dead soldier was assigned to guard the rifles before they were stolen,' I said, as I reached the nearest corridor and the first opportunity to get a word in presented itself. 'He was a potential witness I was hoping to interview. '

I heard a deep breath at the other end of the phone line. 'Are you absolutely sure about that, Finlay? Because, if it's not correct, I'll have you back in my office today to explain yourself. I've already had the Permanent bloody Secretary from the MOD on the phone and to say they are not best pleased is an understatement. They want you recalled, and pronto.'

'Perhaps you could ask if they are having me followed?' I said.

'I'll do no such bloody thing,' he replied. 'Are you being followed?'

'Since I arrived.'

'Are you certain?'

'Someone was outside Wendy's house on the night I arrived and just now on the moor where we found the body, Sergeant McLaren and I spotted someone watching us. It probably explains how the MOD found out so quickly.'

'Is it another suicide?' Bill asked.

'We don't know,' I said. 'He was AWOL and hiding on a mountain near his mum's home. We found him dead in his sleeping bag. But, what I can tell you is he was the best line of enquiry I had regarding the stolen rifles. '

'Anything to suggest foul play?'

'Too early to say, really. I'm hoping to speak to the SOCO when she gets back from the scene.'

'Ok,' he said. 'But be careful what you do and who you speak to down there. I'm happy for you to help them but I don't want you being used as some kind of scapegoat for a failed operation.'

'So, you're happy I help the local Chief find his missing DC?'

'Just as a short-term favour, Finlay, not indefinitely. We're not there to do his bloody job for him and if I'm ordered to pull you out, you're out.'

'I'll get things wrapped up here as quickly as I can.'

'Where are you at the moment?'

'The local nick in a town called Tredegar.'

'Ah,' Bill replied. 'The home of Aneurin Bevan.'

'The politician?'

'Founder of our National Health Service, Finlay.'

'I'll make sure to thank him.'

Bill laughed. 'You do that. The reason I asked where you are is because I've had your mate Harry Davies from MI5 on the phone.'

Learning Harry had been trying to call me was a pleasant although unexpected surprise. He was an old friend who, for a number of reasons connected to his previous life in Special-Forces, had been given a new identity and a role within MI5. In the early eighties, he'd been my troop Sergeant and, as the years had rolled by, he'd also been the only mate from that time I'd kept in contact with. He now ran an office in MI5 resettling special-forces soldiers and knew everything about me it was useful to know. 'What did he want?' I asked.

'He wants you to call him,' Bill said.

'He could have used my mobile.'

'Apparently he tried but couldn't reach you. Give him a call.'

As we ended our conversation, Bill seemed in a much better mood. I sympathised with him. There was only so long he could stall people as influential as a Permanent Secretary before a call would be made to those higher up the police command chain. Then it wouldn't be a question of asking, we'd be told.

I returned to the canteen, finished my cooling breakfast, and then apologised to Floria again as I disappeared into the corridor once more. As soon as I was on my own and out of earshot, I called Harry's work number. He picked up straight away. 'About time you got yourself a mobile that actually works,' he said, with a laugh.

'You're always uppermost in my thoughts too, mate,' I replied.

He chuckled again. 'Sure. Now listen, I've got something for you. Someone's been running checks on your name. Two searches have been made on the Army personnel database within the last twenty-four hours. One was made at Army HQ, Whitehall, and the other from within the Prince Albert training establishment in South Wales.'

'I'm in South Wales doing some enquiries at that barracks,' I said. 'And I seem to have picked up a shadow. I spotted someone the evening I arrived and again this morning.'

'What are you doing there?' he asked.

'Trying to find out who's been smuggling military weapons to London gangsters.'

'Well, if you managed to clock your shadow that easily, he must be a right plonker,' Harry said. 'Given what happened there recently, it'll probably be someone sent by the MOD to keep an eye on you. That would also explain the Whitehall check.'

'I have an RMP escort working with me. About an hour ago, whoever is following us nearly ran her over.'

'Fuckin' amateurs,' he said. 'Did she clock a face?'

'No. And she was too busy diving for cover to get the registration. My Army record is definitely deleted, isn't it?' I said.

'Correct. Whoever did the search, they won't have found anything. But someone wanted to see if you've served. What are you doing down there anyway? I hope you're not shagging that Wendy Russell. I told you before, she's more my kind of woman.'

It was my turn to laugh. 'You're not her type, mate,' I said.

'Never mind, I live in hope. So, what's the weapon connection to London?'

'A search we did south of the river turned up two SA80s stolen from the barracks a few months ago.'

'Really? Well, excuse me if I'm not surprised. Ever since Joe Public found out you could put civvie 223 rounds into the Mark-One version, there's been a black-market trade in them. The MOD keeps pretty quiet about how many have gone missing but I reckon there's a few.'

'I think it's possible a local was involved.'

Harry sighed. 'The Army's full of bloody crooks, Finlay, as we well know. Be careful, that's all I'll say. There's something not right about that barracks. You might want to check if there's any connection with that suicide from a few months ago … the Davenport girl.'

'One of the rifles was booked out to her on the day it was stolen.'

'What did I tell you?' he exclaimed. 'Well, it's no wonder the MOD don't want you nosing about. If you prove there's a connection, the shit will really hit the fan. Have you examined the registers or are they the ones the Inquest was told are missing?'

'The weapon logs from the day of her death and the day of the theft are both absent,' I said.

There was a pause as Harry seemed to be thinking. 'Both days, eh? Someone's trying to hide who booked them out, maybe?' he said. 'Have a look at the registers that are still there. You never know what that might turn up. Soldiers tend to have their favourite weapons; makes it easier for zeroing in, that kind of thing. And they know if they cleaned it themselves, they're not gonna get blamed for a weapon someone else left in shit order.'

I agreed. Harry knew Army procedures inside-out so it was a good tip, one I hadn't thought of but would do the moment Floria managed to pin Sergeant Masters down for a talk.

'One other thing,' Harry said. 'The MOD can't afford another Deepcut, especially with Iraq and Afghan keeping us so busy. The slightest whiff of another suicide scandal and Army recruitment will drop through the floor.'

'They're really that concerned?' I said.

'Enough to want it hushed up? Who knows? But I'd bet my life they'll put a stop to your investigation in an instant if they need to. Some big names lost their jobs after Deepcut. There'll be people at the MOD not wanting the same to happen to them.'

We ended the call with a promise to meet for a beer on my return to the city. I was curious about the news from Harry but not too alarmed. The searches of the Army personnel records might be routine; people doing some background checks to find out who they were dealing with. Or they might mean something more. In any event, I was relieved my service record was now deleted. Previously, with MI5 policy being to just remove reference to Special Forces postings, the simple fact there were gaps in a service record was enough to generate suspicion in the minds of those who knew how such things worked. Now, whether it was a senior officer in Whitehall or a military police officer at the barracks – possibly even Floria – it mattered not. They had nothing to go on.

Chapter 30

Without doubt, Sergeant Masters was avoiding us.

After a third telephoned request left with his clerk at the Armoury and with none so much as acknowledged, Floria and I decided on a more direct approach.

'It's often like this when they know the Redcaps want to talk to them,' she said, as we pulled up outside the Armoury building. 'They think we'll get bored, give up and go away. They duck and dive and generally keep a low profile knowing full well we have other priorities.'

'So, you try and catch them unawares?' I said.

'It hacks them off, but it's either that or we give them a night in a guardroom cell to help them decide.'

'Do they ever choose the cell?' I asked, as I closed the passenger door of the car. I glanced towards the single-storey building in front of us. At one of the barred windows, a movement caught my eye. Someone had been watching our arrival.

'To be honest, yes,' Floria said, laughing. 'Some would rather do that than be seen talking to one of us. Do you want to watch the side door while I go in the front?'

'You think he might sneak off?'

'I'd put money on it.' Floria reached in her pocket and pulled out a set of keys. 'Remember I said the spare set were in the guard room?' she grinned.

'You took them?'

'One of the benefits of being a cop. This way, even if Sergeant Masters has locked himself in the back, we can reach him.'

'Clever girl,' I said.

'And if he hears me unlock and tries to disappear, that's where you come in. It's a little trick I learned in Markham.'

I laughed at Floria's reference to our attempt at catching Tom Morgan leaving his home. As she walked through the Armoury entrance, I held back and watched the side of the building. A minute or so later, her arm appeared through the front entrance to wave me in.

'He's in one of the weapon stores,' she murmured, as I joined her. 'No external door.'

We walked swiftly through the empty reception area and past a door to an office overlooking the front. A lone, female soldier was sitting at a desk. I guessed she was the clerk we'd asked to get Masters to contact us. She had her head down over some paperwork, pen in hand, and appeared to be ignoring us. I could see just enough of her face to realise how young she looked. Floria stopped in front of the outward-opening steel door to the weapon store. It was ajar.

'Any problems?' I said, indicating the clerk.

'She's a Crow ... name of Baker. Same intake as Davenport, out of interest. She's been given a job here while she waits for a place on a course.'

'Did she pass on our messages?'

'Yes ... at least she says she did. I got the feeling she and Sergeant Masters aren't exactly mates. She saw us coming and did nothing to warn him.'

The steel door swung open to reveal a typically laid-out Military Armoury. To my right, a heavy desk sat adjacent to a lockable hatch through which weapons would be handed out and returned. A grey, steel cabinet on the far wall contained what I surmised would be ammunition and pistols, the Browning 9mm hi-power, most likely and possibly the Glock. On the left wall, a long, double-height rack of black, SA80 rifles stood in individual stands, barrels pointed toward the ceiling. Further along, I could make out a small number of

'Gimpies', the general-purpose machine guns that, although old in design, were so robust and reliable they had yet to be surpassed. As Floria closed the steel door behind us, from another, half-open door at the furthest end of the store, I heard a familiar metallic slide and click, the sound of a weapon being re-assembled. We approached the door and, as we entered the large room behind it, I smelt freshly applied gun oil. A lean figure in faded green overalls was standing at a wooden bench with his back to the door cleaning the working parts of a Browning pistol. It looked like we had found the elusive Sergeant Masters.

'How many times do I have to tell you to knock first, Baker,' the man called out, angrily, as he turned towards us. His facial expression was immediately deadpan as he registered the fact his visitors were not the clerk he'd been expecting to see in the doorway.

'Sergeant Masters?' Floria asked, although the question was almost pointless. With soldier's names clearly displayed on their clothing, I could see we had found who we were looking for. Masters turned back to face the scarred, wooden bench behind him. With practised skill, he quickly reassembled the pistol he'd been working on. The process only took a few seconds but, in that time, I had the feeling he was measuring us up, deciding how he was going to react to our intrusion.

Floria did the introductions and, with formalities complete, she then closed the door to allow us to continue without interruption. She began politely, explaining the reason for our visit and asking why Masters hadn't responded to the messages she'd left. The Sergeant was hesitant and claimed not to have received any such message. As he spoke, he continued what he'd been doing, placing the Browning alongside several others in a steel cabinet which he then locked.

There was only one available chair, an old wooden one at the end of the table. It looked distinctly unsafe so I tested it carefully for any sign it may collapse. Satisfied it would support my weight, I made myself comfortable and started my pre-planned questions. To begin,

I wanted to know about the procedure for issuing weapons. 'Do you have a log to book rifles in and out?' I asked.

Masters pulled open a drawer below the pistol cabinet he'd just used. He seemed more confident now he'd recovered from the surprise of our appearance. 'A register, yes,' he said. 'Everyone issued a weapon has to sign for it. Them's the rules … there you go.' He pulled out a large A3-sized binder and dropped it with a heavy thud on the desk before me. On the front cover, I saw it bore the MOD logo.

'You're aware I'm looking into the two SA80s that went missing some months ago,' I said, as I slid the binder towards Floria.

'Word has got around, yes.' Masters nodded his head towards where Floria had begun flicking through the pages. 'These guys were all over it at the time,' he said.

Mindful that Master was either a suspect or a key witness, I determined to keep our conversation friendly. Having read his statement, given to the SIB investigators at the time, I was well aware of what he'd said previously. I therefore wanted him to run through it again to see if anything changed, to see if his recollection bore the hallmarks of genuine memory. Put in simple terms, it's harder to recall a lie created than an event lived through.

'Would you mind going over that day again for me?' I said. 'I haven't had the benefit of seeing your statement and, as both weapons turned up in London, I'm trying to trace the route they may have taken to get there.'

Masters huffed a bit, as if impatient at the inconvenience. But, as he ran through his recollection, he reproduced his statement almost exactly. After summarising his duties and movements on the day, he explained how he'd booked rifles out to all recruits against personal signatures. After the parade, it had become accepted practise for the rifles to be brought back to the Armoury in the back of a covered lorry while the recruits joined their friends and families for a get-together. On arrival at the Armoury, he'd unsealed the rear of the lorry and, as he'd counted the rifles in, he'd noticed two were missing. He'd immediately contacted the Adjutant who had then taken over the unsuccessful search to locate them.

'Who drove the lorry back to the armoury?' I asked.

'Sergeant Slater.'

'And the rear was definitely sealed with the rifles inside when he reached here?'

'Tight as a duck's arse.'

'And then, when the MP checked the register later – before it went missing – he saw one of the rifles was signed out to Private Davenport?'

'Correct, sir,' he replied. 'It was the following day before I noticed the relevant page from the register had gone from the binder. I assumed the Military Police had taken it … that was until they reappeared later to seize it.'

'Reappeared?' I said.

'The first MP to look didn't take the register with him. It was only because he remembered reading Davenport's name that we knew she'd signed for one of them that was stolen.'

'What about the second signature? Did you ever take a look at it to see if you could identify the soldier?'

'I did and, if we'd had time, I reckon we could have worked it out by a process of elimination. The system is better now they have to write their name as well as sign.'

'And, after Private Davenport died, someone stole the entries for both days? Was it ever established who?'

'Not to my knowledge.'

'Did anyone else apart from you check the returning weapons to identify which were missing?'

'No sir, just me.'

'Do recruits still do the same thing after a passing-out parade?' I asked.

A knowing smile quirked the corners of Masters narrow lips as he shook his head. 'Not a chance. It's now their personal responsibility. On return, weapons must now be signed in by the soldier and the entry countersigned by the Armourer on duty.'

'So, what's the local theory on what happened? Things like this tend to generate ideas so, have you or your mates come up with anything the MPs haven't explored, perhaps?'

Masters glanced across at Floria before turning back to me and answering the question. 'Look no further than the families of the Crows,' he said. 'Loads of 'em have form of one kind or another.'

'I understand that Private Tom Morgan took over from Davenport guarding the lorry,' I said.

'So I was told. I wasn't there to confirm it, though.'

'I've also been told someone might have covered for him so he could have some time with his family.'

'News to me, sir,' Masters said, as he raised an eyebrow. 'If Morgan sloped off when he should have been watching the rifles he might claim that to avoid being on a charge. It might explain how the rifles were taken ...'

'Although, not who took them?' Floria interrupted.

'Did you know Private Morgan?' I said. 'Enough to know whether he was trustworthy, I mean?'

Masters shrugged. 'Tom Morgan is a decent lad. If he hadn't decided to go AWOL, I'd have backed him to earn a lance-corporal stripe before long.'

'Not someone you'd expect to be involved in stealing Army rifles, then?'

'Not a chance.'

I turned to Floria. 'I thought your guys checked criminal records of the families at the time?'

'We did,' she answered. 'One or two had some minor stuff, but nobody obvious came up.'

Masters wasn't finished. 'If it was me, I'd definitely be looking at the Crows who have connections in South London. Records could get you the names better than me. As soon as we get a new intake I forget them.'

'Who do *you* think took the page from the register?' Floria demanded.

The Sergeant shrugged nonchalantly. 'No idea,' he said, pointing to the bunch of keys in Floria's hand. 'Maybe someone used those?'

Again, I flicked open the front cover of the record. The date of the first entry was just a few weeks before. 'Do you have the older registers,' I asked, recalling Harry's advice.

'Sure,' he replied, before turning on his heel and marching towards the main store.

Floria looked at me quizzically. I held up an open hand to ask her to bear with me. Once in the store, Masters pulled several similar binders from a large filing cabinet. The records were a little grubby but looked to be complete, with all entries showing weapon type, serial numbers, times of issue and return, the soldier's signature and a corresponding scribble from the member of the Armoury who booked the weapon out or accepted its return. Most of the returned weapon counter-signatures seemed to belong to Masters. I pulled my notebook from my pocket, flicked through the pages and found where I'd noted down the serial numbers of the two rifles found during our raid.

With Floria and Masters watching, I then started to work my way back through the registers, starting on the day of the theft. The numbers of weapon movements and the poor standard of the writing made my progress slow. After a few minutes, Masters seemed to get bored and asked if we had any objection to him using the toilet. I didn't. As soon as he was out of earshot, Floria asked me what I was doing.

'I'm looking to see who booked the two SA80s out in the weeks prior to the theft,' I said. 'I want to see if any particular names pop up.'

'That'll take ages. Have you seen how many entries there are?'

'Got any better ideas?' I asked.

'I'll take the registers back to our offices. We can have a look when we have more time.'

I nodded in agreement as I continued to scan the pages. With Masters gone for a few minutes, I had a chance to see if anything obvious could be seen. There was nothing. 'Ok,' I said, finally. 'Do you have any paperwork showing Davenport's signature?'

'What are you thinking?'

'Maybe something, maybe nothing. I'd just like to see if those two weapons were anyone's personal favourite.'

The sound of returning footsteps brought an end to our conversation.

***

After informing Masters we were taking the registers, we gathered them up and headed back to the car. The Sergeant declined to help us, excusing himself with a mumbled explanation, the only words of which I caught were something about 'security'.

No sooner had the double door to the Armoury closed behind us than Floria leaned in close to me. 'He's brickin' it,' she said. 'Did you see his face when he saw it was us?'

'I'm not sure,' I answered. 'He became more confident the longer we were with him.'

'Maybe he thought we were there about something else?' she said. 'The current register looked fine, by the way. No more missing pages as I could see.'

'Let's go and see if Colonel Hine has those personnel lists ready,' I said. I held back from answering Floria's suggestion until we were in the car and the doors closed. She beat me to it, and had a light-bulb moment before I was able to speak.

'Everyone thinks the register going missing afterwards had to be linked to the thefts,' she said, excitedly.

'You don't agree?'

'I'm not so sure now. The MP who saw the register before it went missing remembered Davenport's name but that's all. We've always assumed whoever stole the rifles must have destroyed the record to hide their identity. I'm wondering if the page was taken to hide something else, something that's unrelated to the theft but might have been apparent if we'd taken a closer look.'

I glanced back towards the Armoury. Again, there was a face at the window, just as I'd seen when we arrived. I was certain it was Baker, the female soldier we'd seen alone at a desk. She seemed to be watching us. I wondered if she'd been told by Masters to let him know when we had left. I turned back to Floria. 'Not wishing to state the obvious,' I said. 'But people mostly tend to hide things if they have a reason. Any suggestion what that might be?'

Floria shook her head as she turned the ignition key. As the engine burst into life, the phone in my pocket began to vibrate. Someone was trying to call me. 'It's a decent idea,' I said, ignoring the interruption. 'And it's another reason to check the old registers. I also think it might be a good idea to arrange to speak to that clerk in there.'

'How's that going to help us?' she said.

As we pulled away I turned and saw the face in the Armoury window was now gone. I had also noticed how Floria had used the word 'us'. If I'd been in any doubt before, it was clear she was now as interested as I was to find out who was behind the thefts. 'I'm hoping she might help answer a question,' I said. 'You asked me about Masters' rabbit-in-the-headlights reaction when he saw us?

Nobody here, apart from you and me, should have been aware those rifles turned up in *South* London. So how did Andrew Masters know?'

Chapter 31

Jodie Baker stood silently at the window, deep in thought as she watched the cops drive away. Their visit to see Sergeant Masters had to be something to do with Paul's warning. 'No way is it coincidence,' she said, under her breath. 'No fuckin' way.'

'What's no way, Baker?' A gruff voice came from the doorway behind her.

'No way that older man is a soldier, Sergeant,' she said, quickly.

'He isn't,' Masters said. He's a detective from the Met, an Inspector. He's been sent here to ask about the two SA80s that went missing a few months ago. They turned up in London.'

Jodie hesitated. 'The rifles taken from our passing-out parade?' she replied. 'So, he's not here about Davenport?'

'Don't listen to rumours, Baker. And if he tries to speak to you then you say nothing and refer him to me, understood? I've sent him and his redcap friend away with some paperwork to make them feel like they're getting somewhere.'

'Will he want to speak to me, do you think?'

Masters had turned away from her to head out of the building when he stopped in his tracks. 'Just remember what I said, Baker. You don't speak to anyone. Now, get back to those chits and when they're done the officers' weapons could do with a clean.'

'Yes, Sergeant,' Jodie replied, as Masters retrieved his beret from his desk and walked out towards the exit. 'Three bags full, Sergeant,' she added, quietly, as the door slammed shut behind him.

Alone at her desk, Jodie began to think. Paul had been right about how tired she was. She wasn't sleeping well and every time she looked in the mirror and saw the dark shadows beneath her eyes, it reminded her why. For Paul, it was easy, he had no conscience. Not so for her. Having those cops around was the last thing she needed, even if she'd been wrong about the reason for their appearance. She had to come up with an escape plan before it all became too much to bear. Paul had accused her of being careless when talking to Masters. She hadn't, but she wondered now if the Armoury Sergeant's close connection to Paul was the key she needed.

There was plenty of time; Masters was often gone for ages, talking to people, doing little deals like he did. His tentacles of influence stretched throughout the camp and it was said there wasn't anything a soldier might need he couldn't get hold of – at a price. Kit, food, booze, even a little spliff, Sergeant Masters could source it. There was one thing though, one thing he wanted that he didn't have. It was the one thing that might persuade him to help.

***

As Jodie heard the sound of Masters' bicycle against the outside wall to the office, she flicked on the kettle. The water was already hot and, as he walked through the door she placed a mug of tea on his desk – strong, two sugars, just as he liked it – before giving him her best puppy-dog smile. A pit instantly formed in her stomach. Don't bottle it, she told herself.

Masters saw the tea. 'What are you after, Baker?' he said. A mocking grin crossed his face as he tossed his beret on the desk and slumped heavily into his chair.

'I need a favour,' Jodie said. She gripped her fists tight to hide her trembling fingers. The hollow feeling was worse now.

'What kind of favour?' he replied.

'I want to go to Leconfield … to do my driving courses.' She tasted bile. An unexpected wave of revulsion had rushed from the very depths of her torso up her throat and into her nostrils. Beads of sweat trickled slowly down her back. I'm going to do this, she told herself. It's now or never. 'Some of the boys on the new intake have dates for theirs,' she continued. 'I should have done mine ages ago.'

'Sergeant Slater decides who goes on courses,' Masters replied with a smirk. 'And we both know why he hasn't put you down for one, don't we?'

Jodie saw the knowing expression that accompanied the question. Ignoring Masters' rebuff, she moved closer to where he sat, aware his gaze was already switching between her chest and her face. 'I was kind of hoping you might have a word for me, Sergeant?' she said, demurely.

'What kind of a word, Baker?' He swung around in his chair to face her, his legs splayed open, his eyes now firmly on hers.

'I was hoping you might know a way to persuade him to let me go. I want my HGV ticket and a posting to a Regiment.'

Masters paused for a moment, looking her up and down as if weighing up what doing such a favour might be worth. 'You've got some front, Jo,' he said, quietly. 'I'll give you that. What's in it for me?'

Jodie smiled broadly and raised an eyebrow. Masters hadn't used her first name since the day she'd rebuffed his advance. She knew exactly what he was hoping for.

'I'd owe you a big favour, Sergeant,' she said. She met his look, widened her eyes slightly and then, just for a second, allowed her gaze to move across the front of his trousers. She saw him swallow. She breathed deep and opened her fists. Her fingers no longer trembled and the hollow feeling in her gut was easing. She felt empowered. It was working. Men were so fucking predictable.

Chapter 32

Before heading back to Wendy's, I asked Floria to drive me into town so I could buy some wine and a box of chocolates for my hosts. I produced my purchases as we sat down for supper. Jenny was proved right. The gesture broke the ice and, as we ate, conversation with Monique became friendly and relaxed. The hang-up calls hadn't been repeated, which she was pleased about, and I was able to reassure her that Jenny definitely hadn't been making them.

It was after supper when I remembered the phone call I'd ignored while Floria and I had been talking outside the Armoury. My phone showed it was from a land-line, a number I didn't know but which seemed familiar. Flicking back through my notebook I'd only scanned through two pages when I saw why. It was the Davenport home.

I nipped upstairs, closed the door to my room and called the number. After a few rings, an answer-phone cut in. Just as I began leaving a message, Michael Davenport picked up. 'Thanks for getting back to us, Inspector,' he said. 'We've found a phone.'

When I asked where, Michael described how he and his wife had heeded my words and, feeling they needed to be doing something, they'd decided to check through some of their daughter's personal effects. They'd discovered the phone inside a small teddy-bear.

'How come the search teams didn't find it?' I asked.

'The first lot told us they were coming and why. Angela's mother insisted we remove the kind of things a young woman keeps that a mother wouldn't want men rummaging through. We still had them in our room when the second team turned up unexpectedly.'

'So, the bear wasn't checked?'

'When Angela was a little girl, it was a hiding place she used for her treasures.'

'Is the phone working?'

'The battery was flat but we found a charger,' Michael said, flatly. 'In many ways, I wish we hadn't looked.'

'Do you want me to arrange for someone to collect it?'

'We'd prefer you came yourself … this evening if possible? We want it out of our house.'

'I'm stuck without transport,' I explained. 'Can it wait until tomorrow?'

'It can't,' he replied, this time more forcefully. 'There's a recording on it you have to see.'

'A recording?'

'A video. It's imperative you come straight away. And please … just you. You'll understand, I promise. Please don't bring the young RMP sergeant with you. We'd rather they weren't involved.'

I didn't argue the point. If Michael Davenport preferred to limit his contact with the Military Police, it wasn't for me to try and change his mind. I pressed him for more information on why he needed to speak so urgently but he wouldn't be drawn.

'Angela had to have been forced into it,' he kept repeating. His voice sounded defeated but I had a sense of underlying anger behind the words. His closing comment, after I'd promised to find a way to get to him, was the most disturbing part of our short conversation. 'I don't know if you're a father, Mr Finlay,' he said. 'But if you are, you'll understand why I simply cannot bring myself to describe what we've found.'

I returned my phone to my jacket pocket as there was a knock on my bedroom door. It was Wendy bringing me a glass of wine from the bottle I'd bought. 'Great timing,' I said, as she handed me the glass. 'I wonder if you could do me a huge favour.'

Ten minutes later, after persuading Wendy I could be trusted with her car, I was on my way back to west Wales. I texted an apology to

Jenny, asked her to give the girls a kiss for me and promised I would call her later. Driving as fast as the winding roads would allow, I made good progress and by nine o'clock I was pulling up outside the Davenport home.

***

Michael Davenport opened the front door as I walked up the drive. 'You came alone?' he said, as he scanned the darkness behind me.

I noticed how crushed he looked, as if he had aged several years in the short time since I'd last seen him. 'As requested,' I said.

In the living room, I sat in the same spot on his settee I'd previously used. As Michael joined me, I saw he was carrying a new-looking mobile phone with a large screen. Of his wife, Phyllis, there was no sign.

'This is it,' he said as he turned the phone on. 'There's a video recording on it. I didn't even know you could use these things to send them.'

'I'm a bit of a dinosaur when it comes to technology,' I replied, as I watched Michael's wavering fingers navigate the phone menu. Finally, it appeared he had found what he was looking for.

'You can find what I'm about to show you in the messages folder,' he said. 'It looks like Angela received it a few minutes before a series of texts sent on the same day.'

'Is this video the reason you couldn't explain things over the phone?' I asked.

'You'll understand in a moment,' Michael replied, somewhat grimly. 'I chose to call you because you sounded sincere when you promised to do what you could. Do you have children, Mr Finlay?'

I recalled Michael's words as we'd ended our earlier call. If I was a father, I'd understand. 'Two girls, seven and three,' I said. 'I started late.'

'Well, I hope you never have to see either of your daughters in this kind of situation.' Michael pressed a button on the phone and handed it to me.

Having spent two years working on a police team specialising in sex-trafficking, I thought nothing I'd see on video of a sexual nature would ever shock me again. I was wrong. Something I'd never imagined experiencing was being in the presence of a father as we sat watching two men abusing his daughter. Several times, I lifted my gaze from the tiny screen to look at Michael. He looked ashen. He kept his face turned away from the phone screen but I could see the tears in his eyes. He couldn't see what I was watching, but the sound alone was enough to turn anyone's stomach.

Two men – one naked and heavily tattooed and the second wearing just an Army PT vest – featured in a clip that lasted perhaps four or five minutes. Whoever had made the recording appeared to have been very careful to ensure only one face was visible, that of the solitary female, Angela Davenport. One of the men even referred to her by surname several times, in a way that suggested he was an NCO. He gave her orders; do this, do that, lie here … open your eyes. Angela was compliant, but it was clear to me she was either drunk or drugged. As the clip ended I offered to return the phone to Michael.

'Look at the texts,' he said, rather than accepting it. 'The ones from the same day.'

The phone was new and not a model I was familiar with. It took me a moment or two to work out how to operate it but I soon found what Michael was referring to. There were three texts, all sent in the minutes that followed the message containing the video attachment. I read them.

My my didn't we have fun Angie?

Then, just a minute later. *Bet the camp would love to get a look at you performing? Sweet little Angie is actually a ho.*

My chest had tightened. The messages, especially when read against the background of the video, were sickening and disturbing. Worse

161

was to come though, as it was only when I read the third, and final, text that the reason for sending the video became apparent.

Tell anyone and this goes public.

Angela Davenport was being blackmailed.

Chapter 33

'I think they used her by name so it would be clear who it was,' Michael said, as turned off the phone. His face was expressionless, his eyes staring into space. I couldn't begin to imagine how he felt.

'Any idea who the sender was?' I asked.

'None at all,' he replied. 'Someone wanted our daughter to keep a secret and this was how they enforced their wish. Phyllis went to her sister's before you got here. She couldn't bear to hear it again. Before she left, we agreed I would ask something of you, Inspector.'

'Of course, anything,' I said.

Michael's focus seemed to turn inward as he continued. 'We were very proud watching Angela at her passing-out parade,' he said, solemnly. 'She'd talked of becoming a soldier for years. It may not surprise you to learn ... I think the greatest joy afforded any parent is to see their child realise its dreams. To have that snatched away from us, and in such a despicable manner ... it was a nightmare no parent should ever have to deal with.'

'I hope I can help,' I said.

Michael nodded. 'So do we, Mr Finlay. We need you to find the scum who did this to our daughter. Find out why they were threatening her and make sure they are punished. But ... and this is something we must insist on ... do *not* let that video go public. We don't want our daughter's memory further tarnished by anyone else seeing that disgusting betrayal of her ... not even a jury. If you can't agree, then we will destroy that phone, together with its contents, and you'll not hear from us again.'

I held the Nokia tight. What Michael was asking of me was going to be far more difficult than he realised. Even if I could identify the men behind the blackmail, gathering enough evidence to prosecute them without using the video would be tough. But I as I thought about it, I knew I had to try. 'I promise,' I said. 'I'll find them.'

***

My mind was in a hundred places on the return journey as I thought about the Davenports, what they had been through and how I could now solve the conundrum they'd presented me with. Two parents, still grieving for their daughter, had witnessed a Coroner's verdict they couldn't believe and now they'd discovered the most harrowing video imaginable hidden in their child's most secret place, her teddy bear.

The Nokia now sat in an envelope on the passenger seat of Wendy's car. I'd already worked out that whoever had sent the recording had to have planned it and somehow lured the poor girl into their trap. Whether they'd drugged her, or she was simply drunk, I couldn't tell. But one thing was certain, she was too far gone to consent. She'd been raped.

Every so often, I took my eyes of the road to glance down at the envelope, hardly daring to think of the horror Angela must have experienced on opening the video, let alone when she read the texts that followed. Even putting the motive for sending it to one side, she'd faced an awful dilemma. She could report it – by handing the phone to the military or civil police – and then she would have had to deal with the subsequent investigation, the rumours and publicity, a trial, and the kind of allegations that would inevitably be levelled at her. Or she could ignore it, give in to the threat, and live in fear it might one day resurface. It was a nightmarish scenario, and one that could easily have resulted in a young woman deciding to end her life.

Floria had told me there were no other enquiries or even rumours relating to Angela Davenport. She was a decent recruit, doing well, and looked to have a good career ahead of her. That put her link to the rifle theft uppermost in my thoughts when it came to a blackmail motive. She had to have known something.

I was about half way back to Usk when it dawned on me time was pushing on and I hadn't yet called Jenny. I pulled in and stopped in a lay-by on the Heads of the Valleys road, a link joining Swansea in the

164

west to Monmouth in the east. Even though it was late, Jenny was awake and waiting on my call. I was pleased she had. Truth was, I needed to talk. After confirming Becky, Charlotte and Jenny's sister were all asleep, I told her what had happened.

'Pound to a penny, whoever sent it was behind the theft,' she said, after listening to me describe the video and texts.

'That's what I thought,' I said. 'Finding them won't be easy though, especially given the time constraints.'

'Then hand it over to Wendy,' she replied, firmly. 'She'll understand the need to be discreet.'

'I gave my word to the Davenports that I'd not let it be used as evidence.'

There was a pause as Jenny seemed to digest what I'd said. 'You also swore an oath to uphold the law without fear or favour,' she replied. 'Nobody ever said that would be easy. You have a duty to make sure those monsters can't do that kind of thing to another young girl.'

'It knocks my theory about horseplay into a cocked hat,' I said.

'If that's what had actually been going on at these army bases, somebody would have said something by now. You need to consider the possibility that video may have driven her to suicide.'

'That had crossed my mind. And I think it's what Michael believes,' I said. 'The texts establish an explanation lacking at the inquest.'

'You might find yourself having to apologise to Sergeant McLaren.'

'It certainly looks that way.'

'How about you, Robert?' Jenny asked, softly, as she changed the tack of our conversation. 'It can't have been easy talking to another father after he'd found such a horrible thing?'

'I'm hanging in there,' I said. 'Michael told me how special it had been to see his daughter realise her dream of becoming a soldier. A short time later she was dead.'

'Now is your chance, Robert. You have an opportunity here to achieve something for the family. Ask yourself, if you were Michael, wouldn't you prefer to see the truth come out, to see justice done and those responsible prosecuted?'

'He made me guarantee it wouldn't go public,' I said. 'Why say that if he didn't mean it?'

'Did you explain that using the video might be essential to convict his daughter's attackers?'

I paused for a moment to switch on the ignition and clear the windscreen. It was misting up slightly as a light drizzle dotted the glass and blurred the outside world. 'I didn't,' I replied. And I was beginning to see the wisdom of Jenny's argument. 'So, you really think I should hand it over to Wendy to deal with?'

'At least talk to her. She has a right to know it exists.'

'She won't be happy with just knowing about it.'

'That's hardly surprising. You can't expect to achieve much on your own and she has the resources to make sure it's properly investigated. Nobody ever said being a cop is easy, Robert.'

I took a long, deep breath as I came to a decision. 'You're right,' I said. 'I'll do it soon. I need to speak to her anyway ... to find if there's been any news on her missing officer.'

'There's been no developments, then?'

'Not so far as I know. If it turns out to be connected to this ...'

'You could be opening a real can of worms,' Jenny interrupted. 'If he's come to harm as well you could be dealing with something far more ugly than blackmailing a recruit to keep quiet about the theft of some guns.'

'I spoke to Harry earlier on,' I said. 'He said something similar.'

'How is he?'

'Doing well. Seems life in MI5 suits him nicely. He called this morning to tell me someone at the MOD has been checking my name on the Army database. When Floria and I found Private Morgan's body on the moor, there was someone up their watching us. My guess at the time was the MOD. After seeing what's on this phone, I'm less certain.'

'If people at that camp have some kind of a racket going on, they'd want to know what you know. You should make a back-up of that video.'

'How would I do that?' I asked.

'Play it and then record it using your phone. Take pictures of the texts as well.'

It was a good suggestion, so good that as we ended our call, I did it straight away. Although I'd never previously used my mobile to make a video recording, I was surprised by how simple it was. I was glad I'd called Jenny and was grateful for her advice. Although she knew little about criminal investigation, she had a naturally inquisitive brain and a structured approach to problems that helped me focus.

On the remainder of the journey, I thought more about what she'd said. She was right. I had to look at this from Michael Davenport's perspective and ask myself what he would really want me to achieve. By the time I reached Wendy's, it was almost midnight and I'd also made a second decision. I was going to help Floria discover the truth.

I parked on Wendy's drive and it was at that point I noticed Monique's Audi was missing. Thinking nothing of it, I locked Wendy's car and walked towards the front door. It was open, wide open.

Chapter 34

The house was in darkness. Cautiously, I leaned in through the doorway and flicked the hallway light switch. Nothing happened. I tried it again. The result was the same, a hollow click but no light. The air temperature had dropped, but that had little to do with the shiver of uncertainty that ran down my spine as I stood in the doorway, listening for any sign of movement. As my eyes adjusted to the darkness, I peered into the gloom and saw the door through to the kitchen was also ajar. Groping my way along the walls, I located the light switch just inside the kitchen. It too failed to work.

Wondering if Wendy and Monique had retired early to bed due to a power cut, I called out. 'Anyone home?'

There was no response. I tried once more, louder, and enough to disturb anyone asleep upstairs. Again, nobody replied. A thought occurred to me the power cut may be connected to the absence of Monique's car. Perhaps my hosts had nipped out? Remembering the torch Wendy had lent me to look around the fields a couple of nights previously, I felt my way along the kitchen counter, opened the drawer where it lay and retrieved it. As the narrow but powerful beam lit up the room, I immediately felt more confident. Playing the light around the floor and walls, I noticed a mobile phone left on charge on the counter. It was then I felt a cool draft coming from the far end of the room. I shone the torch towards the garden door. It too was open. Nobody goes out and leaves both doors like that, I thought. Quietly, I retraced my steps through the hall and out onto the front drive. It was time to call in some help.

***

Cops often have to put themselves in harm's way. Whether it be searching a building for a night-time burglar, wading into a pub fight or chasing an armed robber, it's part and parcel of the job. We know that, and it's something we do willingly. Rarely, if ever, though, do we want to take that kind of risk on our own. It's for that very reason, if a colleague radios for 'urgent assistance', every nearby officer will drop whatever they are doing to go and help. It's also the reason cops can sometimes be reluctant to make such a call, as they know their colleagues will risk everything to get to them.

And so, as I spoke to the emergency telephone operator, I chose my words carefully, making sure I used terms I knew response officers would understand. 'Off-duty officer requires urgent assistance' would have implied I was at imminent or actual risk of injury. I wasn't, and although I wanted help on the hurry-up, I didn't need anyone breaking their necks to try and get to me.

'Premises insecure, possible suspects on', I said. I heard the telephone operator type my words on her keyboard. It was sufficient to bring about a prompt reaction from the local team, especially when I added that the house belonged to their Assistant Chief Constable. I ended the call, stood back from the house and decided it was there I would wait. I could see enough to at least watch the front and side of the house, and if anyone moved nearby, I figured I would hear them. There was no pressing need to go back in, and I'd heard many stories of lone officers coming unstuck while searching buildings on their own.

I'd been waiting for less than a minute when my phone began to ring. It was Wendy. 'I've just been told about a call to the house,' she said, as I answered. 'What's happening?'

'I think you may have an intruder,' I said. 'I arrived home to find both front and back doors open.'

'Where's Monique?' Wendy demanded.

'I assumed she was with you. Her car isn't here.'

'I borrowed it to come into work. Have you tried calling out to her?'

I hesitated. If Wendy was at work and Monique was alone inside, perhaps lying injured, I wouldn't be able to wait for back-up. I'd have to go in and check. 'The house is in darkness,' I said. 'It looks like the power has been turned off. I called out but nobody replied.'

169

'She could be hurt,' Wendy said, the anxiety clear in her voice. 'The main fuse box is in the kitchen. The walk-in cupboard in the corner near the door. Use my torch, you know where it is.'

'I already have it,' I replied, as I flicked the beam on. 'Stay on the line while I go take a look.'

Holding the phone to my ear, I walked back into the house. Once more, I tried the light switch. 'Power's still off,' I said.

'Maybe she's hiding upstairs,' Wendy replied. 'I'm worried, Finlay. I can't think why she hasn't called me.'

'I think her phone's on charge in the kitchen. Maybe she couldn't get to it.'

'All the land-line phones are cordless. They need mains power to work.'

I crept further into the house and, as I located the cupboard Wendy had directed me to and began to open it, I sensed, rather than actually saw movement behind me. Instinct is a hard thing to describe and whether I reacted to the body heat of another person, a subtle variation in air movement or a sound that registered before my conscious brain could alert me, I don't know. All I can say is something I'd describe as instinct caused me to turn quickly around. The first thing I saw was the blade of a kitchen knife, as it glinted in the torchlight.

When you're attacked with a knife, it doesn't pay to stand on ceremony. 'Put the knife down, sonny' is the stuff of Hollywood, as is fast-moving unarmed combat skill to disarm your opponent. In the real world, you have to strike first and hit hard, the probability being your life is going to depend on it.

And with that thought in mind, I kicked as savagely as I could into the centre of the shadow framed in the doorway. The heel of my shoe connected with soft tissue. It sank in. There was an explosion of breath, a thud as what sounded like a head striking the side of the door. A woman's scream filled the air.

It was Monique.

***

Half an hour later, after copious apologies from me and many tears from Monique, she had stopped shaking and we were sat drinking tea in the dining room alongside Wendy and a local detective. Two response cops and a dog handler from the local station were outside checking the gardens and surrounding area. By then, we'd pieced together what had happened. After Wendy had borrowed her car to head into work, Monique had gone to bed. She had been cat-napping, listening out for Wendy coming home, when she'd heard what she'd assumed was me creeping back to my room. When the noise hadn't settled down, she'd got up, intending to remonstrate with me, only to find the landing light wasn't working and it wasn't me making the noise. She'd opened my door, seen the torch-light and silhouette of someone going through my drawers, and had then had the presence of mind to stealthily return to her room, close the door and dial 999. Just as Wendy had surmised, without mains power, the cordless phone in the bedroom couldn't function. Fearful and unable to call for help, she'd decided to hide and, only after a period of quiet had she decided to risk venturing downstairs to retrieve her mobile phone. When she'd heard me looking around and seen the torchlight, she'd been convinced I was the burglar returning and had armed herself with a knife from one of the kitchen drawers.

'Nowhere else in the house has been touched,' Wendy said, as she sipped at the tea I'd made. 'Just your room.'

'There's no doubt,' Monique replied. 'He was looking through your stuff for something.'

'There was nothing for him to find,' I replied. 'Everything apart from some spare clothing was with me.' I saw Monique look at Wendy, a combination of mistrust and concern in her eyes, and I guessed what she may be thinking. 'I think I should move into the room I was offered on the camp,' I said.

171

Wendy drew breath to respond but was interrupted by a knock at the front door. 'We'll sleep on it, if that's ok?' she said, as she stood and walked toward the hallway. 'Meanwhile, I think it best you stay.'

It was one of the response cops. He confirmed their search was over. The police dog had followed a trail up the lane to a lay-by where it appeared a vehicle used by the intruder may have been parked. With that car now gone, there was nothing further they could do.

Eventually, we all headed to bed. Wendy gave me strict instructions not to touch the chest-of-drawers and said she would be arranging for a SOCO to give it the once-over the next day. It was only as I removed my jacket that I was reminded Angela Davenport's mobile phone was still in the side pocket. I needed to find a better time to show it to Wendy, though. She had Monique to reassure and a decision to make about me – whether I continued to stay in her home or not.

Chapter 35

Ellie opened an eye. It was dark. Someone was tapping the door of her room. Two knocks … repeated but gentle, and not too loud. The deferential approach of a subordinate, she decided. What on earth did they want at this ungodly hour? Although this was a Sunday, it was undeniably a wake-up call. Had she booked it? She struggled to recall. God forbid, she may have forgotten an early duty of some kind. That would be guaranteed to put her in the CO's bad books.

A dreadful thought rushed into her mind, her heart beginning to pound as it gained traction. Someone had spotted her with the Crows and reported it. The CO now wanted to see her and had sent a lackey to wake her up, to catch her off-guard when she was half awake and vulnerable. What would he say? Could he sack her? Did he have that power? She wasn't sure.

Three more knocks on the door, louder this time, more insistent. No chance of ignoring it. She pushed back her quilt, allowing cooler air to waft over her chest. Better to face it than hide, she mused.

'Wait one,' she called, her voice coarse and dry. She needed something to quench her thirst, the legacy of a good Saturday night in the bar with the junior officers. 'When will I learn,' she muttered, her head pounding as she sat up.

Kicking the remainder of her bedding away, Ellie swung her legs off the bed and then fumbled around the floor to locate her dressing gown and slippers. She found them and, with the gown in place, shuffled unsteadily across the thinly carpeted floor, located the light switch and flicked it down. It was a mistake. She winced, first in pain and then in horror as she caught her reflection in the mirror. It wasn't a good look.

With the light extinguished again, she smoothed her hair back and felt her way towards the door handle. The key turned easily and, as the lock released, she twisted the brass knob to ease the door open, just slightly. There would be no need to show herself to hear whatever message the caller had been sent to deliver. Through the gap, the glare from the corridor revealed the sleeve of a green tunic, one stripe on the arm. She saw what looked like a female hand and, finally, a polished black shoe. The caller was a junior NCO.

'Beg pardon, ma'am,' a voice said. 'Colonel Bullen has requested all officers in his office by oh, five hundred.'

Ellie focussed on the wording; wanting to be sure she hadn't misheard. 'All officers' were the words used. Not a personal summons, then; not her day to be carpeted. She said a silent thank-you for having been spared that particular humiliation. 'What time is it?' she asked.

'Zero-four-fifty, ma'am,' came the crisp reply.

Ten minutes notice. Sometimes, Bullen could be a real bastard, she thought. Ten minutes to get cleaned up, dressed and to appear in the CO's office looking bright-eyed and bushy-tailed. Ten minutes to make it appear as if you weren't hung-over and hadn't just been dragged out of your pit. Thank God she wasn't a bloke, she thought as she mumbled a 'thanks' to the NCO, at least she wouldn't have to shave as well. As the door clicked closed, she heard another door along the corridor being knocked, another sleeping officer being dragged from their slumber. And they'd have only nine minutes, she thought. Half-closing her eyes, she flicked the overhead light back on and turned on the cold tap at the sink, lowering her face into the water. As the cold flow woke her, she drank thirstily.

Six minutes later, she closed her room door behind her, ready to face whatever the CO had in store.

***

Maybe Colonel Bullen wasn't such a bad bloke after all, Ellie mused. The coffee from his office percolator had warmed her to the core and looked to have gone down well with the others. Unusually, their CO was late. Normally, he was a stickler. When he ordered your presence, it was woe betide the unfortunate junior officer who failed to make the appointed time.

174

She was checking her watch for the third time in as many minutes when the door to the adjacent conference room burst open and Colonel Bullen strode in. He looked tired and, as he saw what Ellie was doing, he glared at her. The ante-room fell silent, as if a switch had been thrown to end all conversation. 'Follow me,' he ordered the assembled group.

Ellie tucked in behind Wayne Corbishley, a Captain from Headquarters Squadron. Wayne was a huge man, easily six-four with his boots on; and perfect for a diminutive subaltern to stand behind in the hope she wouldn't be singled out for attention. Some of the older and more experienced officers had quietly resumed their conversations as they filed into the Colonel's office. She did a quick headcount as the door was closed behind them. There were fourteen present, in total. Apart from the Colonel, both Majors were here, three out of four Captains and most of the junior officers. These were the Lieutenants and included – at the lowest end of the command chain – her peers, the subalterns or 'subbies' as they were affectionately known. They were the lads she'd been drinking with the previous evening.

'Listen up, everyone.' The room fell silent as Bullen stood up from behind his desk and began to address them. 'I make no apology for dragging you from your pits on a Sunday morning. And I'll come straight to the point of my doing so. A few hours ago, I received news that Private Thomas Morgan, an AWOL from 18 Tank Transporter Squadron was found dead yesterday morning. Morgan did his Phase Two here with the Training Regiment which means, in the aftermath of the Davenport inquest, we are in for another shit-storm from the Press. I want you to be aware of the facts as they are currently known. Yesterday morning, members of the Military Police, acting on intelligence, carried out a search of a mountain area adjacent to Morgan's home village. He was found in a basher having apparently died in his sleep.'

As Bullen addressed his audience, Ellie began to appreciate why they'd all been summoned. This was no ordinary 'morning prayers' meeting of the kind the Colonel had with his Senior Command

Team. 18 Tank Squadron was also based at the barracks. The media interest could be huge. Silently and to herself, she breathed a sigh of relief. The tension she'd been feeling was now easing. Even up to the point where Colonel Bullen had started his briefing, she'd continued to fear the worst, that she was the reason for his summons.

'Was it natural causes?' The question came from Harriet Hall, one of the acting squadron-commanders and the only female Captain.

'Too early to say,' Bullen replied. 'Local plod are treating the death as suspicious until proved otherwise.' He paused, casting an eye around the room to ensure he had everyone's attention. 'It goes without saying that to have this happen just a couple of days after the Davenport inquest concluded is an absolute PR disaster, particularly for the Training Regiment. Despite the fact Morgan wasn't one of ours, our ops room is already fending off telephone calls from the local press and I'm damn sure the nationals and the bloody TV people will soon be on to it.'

Another of the senior Captains, Michael Young, raised a hand. 'In a moment, Mike,' Bullen said, in response. 'Suffice to say, everyone, we need to present a united front to the outside world. Soldiers and junior NCOs will be confined to barracks for forty-eight hours and you will tell those under your command not to discuss the matter with anyone outside this camp without my express authority ... on pain of death should they do so. I will not have the kind of shit that could be heading the way of the Training Regiment landing in our laps as well. All press enquiries of any kind will be handled by the Adjutant in the first instance and then by me, if required.'

Ellie listened attentively as the Colonel deftly handled the plethora of questions that followed. What were the instructions with regards to soldiers on leave or a course? What was to be the method of cascading the order down the ranks? Mike Young was Welfare Officer and had raised his hand to offer to act as liaison with his counterpart at Morgan's regiment. Bullen approved the idea but stressed tight lines of communication were to be maintained with Major Leith, the Adjutant. By the time the meeting closed and all present headed off to start the process of containment, everyone was clear what needed to be done. Filing out with the others, it was only as her hand touched the polished oak door to the corridor that Ellie discovered Colonel Bullen hadn't finished with her.

'A moment, if you please, Miss Rodgers,' the Adjutant called out. Ellie turned, just in time to see Wayne Corbishley wink at her. He knew she'd been hiding behind him and now he seemed highly amused she'd been singled out for attention. She waited as the others shuffled past and, within a few seconds, was alone with the Regiment's two most senior officers.

'Come and sit down, Ellie,' Bullen said, indicating the empty chair opposite him. His tone was informal, even friendly, she thought, as she closed the door. The sense of foreboding returned, though, as she glanced across to Tom Leith. He was sat on the only other chair for guests. In his hand, she could see he was holding a white envelope.

'The letter is for Private Orr, Ellie,' the Colonel said, as she sat down. 'I've read the disciplinary report you prepared and support your recommendation. A fine of two days pay is confirmed and to that, I've added seven nights additional guard duty. For your first such case, I think you handled it well.'

Leith passed the letter to her. It felt crisp, new. The envelope was sealed, Ellie noticed, and had Orr's name hand-written on the front. 'Thank you, sir,' she said.

'I've also written to Colonel Holt at the Training Regiment regarding Private Towler,' Bullen continued. 'Possibly against my better judgement, I decided it's appropriate he should be kept in the loop so I've apprised him of Private Orr's claims. It may also assist with Towler's mitigation.'

'Very good, sir,' Ellie replied, although her feelings were mixed. A part of her would have preferred to have kept Colonel Holt in the dark, at least for the time being, until she'd been able to secure irrefutable evidence of what the Training Regiment NCOs were up to.

177

Bullen's facial expression changed from one of benevolence to one of concern. Here we go, Ellie thought. 'I need you to be frank with me, Rodgers,' Bullen said.

'Sir?' Ellie shifted uncomfortably on her seat, aware Major Leith had also begun watching her carefully.

'You'll no doubt be aware that, despite its size, this camp can be a very small place? People talk, rumours get around … stories spread.'

Ellie felt the muscles in her neck tighten. 'Of course, sir,' she said, politely.

'I'm aware of certain rumours concerning NCOs within the Training Regiment. Would you happen to have heard anything similar, perhaps have an idea of the source?'

'Nothing, sir,' she said, keeping her voice as steady and convincing as she could. 'The detail of Private Orr's information was all I've been privy to.'

Ellie was confident she'd be believed. Even as a child she'd made an art of lying to her teachers and she knew how to look believable. In more recent times with the RMP, she'd interviewed soldiers accused of all manner of misdemeanours and she'd learned how they too could convincingly play the innocent, even when the truth was so obviously at variance with their claims. As Bullen leaned back heavily in his chair it creaked loudly and, for a moment Ellie thought it may give way. An ancient, yet sturdy, piece of mahogany furniture, it was said to have followed the Colonel for many years, on deployments around the world. Hands clasped together as if in prayer, he breathed in deeply through his nose and then exhaled with equal vigour. 'Very well,' he said. 'The last thing we need at the moment is a loose cannon spreading stories among the Crows. Should you hear something along those lines, I hope I can trust you to be discreet and to bring it to my immediate attention?'

So, you can make sure it's swept under the carpet, Ellie thought, although she made sure to answer the question with a more reassuring response. It was as she spoke that she saw the Colonel's gaze focus on her neck.

'What happened to your throat?' he asked.

'Free practice on the judo mat, sir,' she replied, with a relaxed smile. 'My opponent got a little carried away with a choke hold.'

Bullen nodded, seemingly reassured by the explanation. 'Of course. You were champion judoka at Sandhurst, I recall reading? Unbeaten in your weight category for an entire year, is that right?'

'I don't like to lose, sir.'

'Very good.' The CO paused for a moment, as if he were about to say something before changing his mind. 'Well, do make sure you wear something to cover those marks up when you parade your soldiers this morning,' he said, ultimately. 'You know how they can gossip.'

Meeting over, as Ellie went to stand up, a gentle cough from the Adjutant was enough to remind her to salute. She stood straight and threw up her arm. Bullen simply grunted.

***

Back in her room, Ellie lay on her bed. She'd been lucky, she thought, very lucky. That meeting could have been so much worse. There was still the problem of her neck to deal with, though. Hiding the marks in preparation for muster parade was going to be a challenge. An idea came to her, and a rummage through her wardrobe produced a solution. It was a norgi, a form of Norwegian roll-neck shirt, left over from her time in Germany. It was a little warm for the time of year but, with its zip done up tight, she realised it would be perfect. The fact she was wearing a slightly different uniform from the troops could be explained by pretending she was off on a reconnaissance trip to plan a day on the ranges after the lock-down was lifted.

The norgi did its job. Muster parade passed without comment and the indifferent reaction from both soldiers and NCOs when she followed it up with the news about Private Morgan's demise and Colonel Bullen's resultant orders, told her they already knew. Stories like that spread quickly. News of the lock-down decision nevertheless produced some sullen and disappointed looks, particularly amongst the youngest of the soldiers who'd been planning to head home to their families or spend some time in one of the local nightclubs.

A few minutes after the parade, Ellie was back in her office when Private Orr appeared at the door. 'I was told you wanted to see me, ma'am?' Orr said, politely. The young soldier glanced around the room and then over her shoulder. She appeared nervous, possibly as a result of having to enter the Headquarters building twice in a week. Routine or otherwise, the soldiers would talk if Orr's visits became unusually frequent.

Ellie instructed Orr to shut the office door behind her and sit down before she produced Colonel Bullen's letter. Too late, she realised Orr was staring at her neck. Away from the parade square, she'd automatically unzipped the overly warm norgi to cool down.

'Judo,' she explained, as she ran her fingers over the scratches. 'I lost.'

Orr didn't comment, but it was clear she had seen. 'I wasn't expecting anything like this,' she said as she peeled open the envelope.

As Private Orr read through the letter, Ellie found herself struggling not to touch her neck again. The skin felt tender and bruised, every turn of her head triggering a reminder of the bastard in the respirator. One day, she promised herself, she would find out who he was and she would have him. He'd pay for that. Nobody humiliated her, not any more.

The sound of paper being crushed brought her back to the present. Private Orr was squeezing the Colonel's letter in her fist.

'Not what you were hoping for?' Ellie said.

'May I speak frankly, ma'am?'

Ellie nodded. 'The door is closed so anything you say is between us.'

Orr held up the scrunched letter. 'This is bollocks,' she said. 'To be honest, I can't even understand most of it. Why do they have to use such posh language?' She unfolded the paper slightly and pointed at some wording. Ellie leaned forward to read it.

I must reiterate most strongly that bullying or sexual harassment is not tolerated in any form in this Regiment and is always investigated fully.

'Who is he trying to kid?' Orr said, as Ellie finished reading. Orr's voice croaked with emotion and, for a moment, it appeared she might burst into tears. 'They never take us seriously. To them, we're just … just nothing.'

'Does it explain what action he plans to take?' Ellie asked.

'How should I know? I only passed my GCSE English because my mam helped me with the coursework.'

Ellie held out her hand. 'Would you like me to take a look,' she said, softly.

With a flurry, Orr slid the letter across the desk. 'I'm not the first girl to complain about the NCOs from the Training Regiment. Nothing ever gets done … they just shove it under the carpet,' she said as Ellie began to read.

The letter was two pages and on the Commanding Officer's official headed paper. At first, Ellie was impressed to think Colonel Bullen may have carried out a thorough investigation of Orr's concerns but the more she read, the more she realised the content was so bland, so impersonal, it might easily have been a standard template with the names and dates changed to fit the individual concerned.

As she looked across to where Private Orr sat staring out the window, she wanted to apologise and to reassure her something would be done, that her concerns wouldn't be ignored. But she didn't, because now it was personal and she didn't want Orr saying anything to anyone. Now, she wouldn't be stopping until she'd identified the men in the respirators and they'd been made to pay.

181

Chapter 36

Sundays were a day I normally treasured. Jenny and I would sit up in bed and put the world to rights over a mug of tea while listening to our girls playing in their room. We'd get up late and then take them for a walk in the woods to work up an appetite ready for lunch. Charlie had some new Postman Pat wellies. They were bright red and she loved to stamp them in muddy puddles. Becky was curator to a collection of forest-floor treasures and was becoming quite adept at following my tips on identifying edible mushrooms. It had become a familiar, enjoyable routine. I missed it and was hungry to be home.

I'd had another disturbed night as I walked up and down the corridors of my mind, a mêlée of thoughts spinning on discordant cerebral hamster-wheels as they conspired to keep my brain alert but unproductive. I'd thought a lot about Floria's comment on the anonymous calls Monique had received, and how they could have been an attempt to discover if the house was unoccupied. I was now convinced she was right. Someone was trying very hard to learn what progress I was making. As I pulled back the curtains to let the daylight in, I saw the scribbled notes I'd made during my half-awake state.

Soldier girl / Wendy - Phone. Written in the dark, the letters were uneven and barely legible, but they did their job.

Soldier girl. A reminder to speak to the young soldier Floria and I had seen at the Armoury.

Wendy. I mustn't forget to tell her about the blue car that had made off from the moor and to ask Floria if she'd managed to obtain the additional AWOL files I hoped might include the missing detective.

Phone. I needed to find the right moment to show my friend the video.

Satisfied I hadn't forgotten any of my late-night thoughts, I lay back on the bed and pulled the duvet over me. Through the window, I could see wispy white clouds moving steadily across the pale blue sky. For several minutes, I watched them drift across the window. I was about to throw back the covers ready to surface when there was a gentle tap on my door.

'You decent?' said Wendy, from the corridor.

I heaved myself from the bed opened the door. A steaming mug of tea was thrust through the opening towards me. Wendy was already dressed in a smart suit and looked like she was ready to head off to work. 'You work Sundays too?' I said.

'No rest for the wicked, Finlay,' she replied. 'We decided to let you sleep. Sergeant McLaren is downstairs having some toast.'

'She's early,' I said. 'What time is it?'

'A little after eight.'

'Did you tell her what happened?'

'Just the basics. I thought I'd leave the detail to you.'

'Is Monique ok? I really think I should move out.'

'Look ... whoever it was, it's pretty certain they won't come back. Monique and I had a long talk and we've agreed she'll adapt her working hours to match mine for a while so she won't be here alone.'

'Is she sure?' I said. 'I don't want to be the cause of any issues between you.'

'You're not, Finlay, trust me. What's done is done and we can't change it. Right now though, we need to have a chat.'

'What about?' I asked.

Wendy stepped quietly into my room and closed the door gently behind her. 'It's about Private Morgan,' she said. 'I've just had a telephone conversation with the SIO from the enquiry team. The initial Post-Mortem result was inconclusive but there were no injuries on the body to suggest homicide. We found an empty pill container in his sleeping bag, though, so we might be dealing with an

183

overdose. It'll only be after we get the toxicology report on the blood and tissue samples that we'll know what we're dealing with.'

'So, we're talking suicide?' I said.

'We're keeping an open mind. There was no drink container anywhere near the body. So, if he took pills, he swallowed them dry. One other thing ... a police dog picked up a scent trail that headed away from the scene in a different direction from the approach you used. They followed the trail to a lane where they think a car may have been parked.'

'That'll be the car Floria and I saw as we were leaving. They nearly ran Floria over.'

'What kind of car? Why the hell didn't you tell me?'

'I thought you knew. We reported it at the local nick and asked them to forward it to the enquiry team. I was planning to ask if you'd made any progress.'

'Nothing reached me. Did you get the registration?'

'All Floria could say was it was blue. We think it was the same people who've been shadowing me ever since I arrived here.'

'You mean the noises in the field and what happened last night is part of a pattern?'

'Someone seems to consider it very important to know what I'm doing.'

Wendy sat down on the edge of the bed as she mulled over what I'd said. 'I'll let the SIO and my Chief know,' she said, finally. 'I also have some news I imagine Jenny won't be too happy to hear. The Chief has been in touch with Bill Grahamslaw again. Until we're certain the Morgan case isn't homicide, Bill's authorised you to remain here.'

I sighed and shook my head. 'I guess I'm destined to miss that promotion board.'

'You'll be fine, I'm sure,' Wendy replied. 'But you'd best let Jenny know as soon as possible.'

'She won't be up yet,' I said. 'I'll let her know when I call her.' I glanced at my jacket where it hung on the back of a chair. I wondered if this might be the right time to show Wendy what was in the pocket. Before I could overcome my hesitation, she checked her watch, announced she was running late, and then strode off down the stairs. The opportunity was lost.

As I took a quick shower, I thought through the implications of what Wendy had said. Lack of injury to Morgan's body didn't necessarily mean he hadn't been murdered. He might have been coerced into swallowing pills or even tricked. I hoped the post-mortem would tell us more. I also wondered about the second scent trail she'd mentioned. Locating Morgan on the mountain would have presented the occupants of the blue car with the same kind of problems we'd faced. I wondered if they'd followed him or been watching his home. To make that possible, they'd have needed an OP, an observation point.

More questions rattled around my brain as I dressed. What had caused them to take the risk of entering Wendy's home? Was I close to discovering something? Had they been watching as we'd arrived to speak to Mrs Morgan? Had they anticipated us coming back again? I knew one piece of the jigsaw might be found if I went back to the mountain to look for an OP. I also knew from experience, the sooner Floria and I looked for it, the easier it would be to find.

***

'We're going hill walking again?' Floria said between finishing her toast and reaching for the last remnants of tea in her cup. She'd looked up from reading Wendy's newspaper and had noticed my camouflage trousers. The boots she'd provided me were in my right hand.

'Before we do anything else,' I said, placing my empty mug on the table. 'I want to take another look behind the Morgan house to see if anyone had been up there watching him.'

'You think his death is suspicious? Miss Russell said she thought it might be accidental.'

'We assume it's connected to the rifle thefts until we know better. I'm wondering if whoever was in that blue car was watching his house.'

'Ok, sounds like a plan,' Floria said, with a smile. 'I hear you nearly got yourself skewered last night.'

'Luckily for me, I saw Monique coming.'

'Can't have been easy disarming someone in the dark?'

'I got lucky.'

Floria scowled before moving the conversation on. 'Do the police have anything on the intruder?' she asked.

'The forensic people are coming today. I think you were right about the phone calls, though. And, at a guess, I'd say it might be the same person we saw on the moor and I heard in the fields on my first night.'

'They seem pretty determined.'

'Given their desire to have me brought home, the MOD are high on my list of suspects.'

Wendy appeared in the doorway through to the kitchen, a document folder in her hand. 'I've got to run' she said. 'Scenes of Crime will be here soon to have a look around outside and at your chest of drawers. What time shall I tell DCI Mostyn you'll be there?'

'Who's DCI Mostyn?' said Floria.

'He's the SIO, the Senior Investigating Officer for the Morgan case,' Wendy replied.

'Where does he want to see us?' I asked.

'At Ebbw Vale nick. We've set up an incident room there.'

I turned to Floria as I suggested sometime between 11am and noon would allow us enough time to do a reasonable search. She nodded in agreement.

With Wendy gone, I sat down opposite Floria. 'Any joy with the lists from Colonel Hine?' I asked, as I pulled on the boots. She didn't reply. I looked up and saw she was watching me lace them up. I used a method taught to me during the jungle-phase of SAS selection that was supposed to help reduce pressure on your ankles and keep out leeches.

'You ever serve?' she asked, as I pulled the second set of laces tight, double-knotted them and tucked the ends neatly away.

'Not personally,' I lied. 'If it's the boot technique that made you curious then you can thank my father. He taught me the way his father taught him.'

Floria's face screwed upwards slightly, as if her curiosity was only partially satisfied. 'Colonel Hine has left the lists with his Adjutant,' she said. 'We can collect them later.'

'What about those AWOL files from Sennybridge?'

'There's just the two of them. How did you know one would be a male soldier who trained here?'

I grinned and winked at her. 'I didn't. Like I said, it was a hunch and sometimes you get lucky. What's his name?'

'I forget. They're faxing copies to our main office later today.'

Good news, I thought. Hopefully, I'd be able to pass whatever was in the reports on to Wendy without incurring undue attention. 'Presumably, everyone at the barracks now knows about Private Morgan?' I said, changing the subject.

'Yup, the soldiers and junior NCOs are confined to base. And no talking to anyone; not the press, not even to relatives.'

187

'Is that a normal reaction?' I asked.

'Not really. To my mind, it makes it look like the Army has something to hide. But, after what happened at Deepcut, the MOD are mega-sensitive about any potential scandal. That's probably why they're watching you.'

Chapter 37

Half an hour later, Floria and I were again entering Markham village. I wanted to have a quick look at the mountain from outside the Morgan home, to see if I could spot somewhere promising to begin our search. What I hadn't anticipated was to find the Press camped outside.

'Shit,' Floria exclaimed, as she too saw the melee of reporters. She braked heavily and, as our car skidded to a halt, faces turned in our direction. The subsequent reaction was instant as, without exception, the whole group began sprinting towards us. Fortunately, we were the best part of two hundred metres away and none of them looked fit enough to cover the ground very quickly. As Floria checked the road was clear behind us, I could see several had already slowed down to a walking pace. 'Best we go up the mountain road,' I said, as we began to reverse.

Floria executed a neat three-point turn and, with the rear tyres throwing up grit from the road surface, we soon left the approaching journalists behind us. 'They didn't hang about,' she said, checking the rear mirror.

I nodded, and said a silent thank-you. Having my face on the evening news wouldn't have been what Bill Grahamslaw had in mind when he'd warned me not to wind up the Ministry of Defence.

With the car safely parked in the same lay by we'd used the previous day, Floria and I tracked slowly back through the crags and grassed areas above the village. Keeping low, avoiding being seen from the streets, whilst looking for evidence of an observation point would have been a challenge at the best of times but it soon became clear my companion had little relevant experience. As I scanned the ground, looking for an indication of recent activity other than our own, I noticed how she watched me attentively.

'You think whoever was driving the car I dodged was watching from here?' Floria said.

'I hope so,' I replied. 'If someone was here it reduces the likelihood of a leak from your office.'

Floria stopped walking and stared hard at me. 'I'm not sure I like what you're saying.'

'Face it, Floria. Either someone told our watcher where to find us or he'd been here all the time.'

'My team are straight, I'd bet my life on it.'

'Let's hope we find an OP, then.'

Floria shrugged. 'So, what exactly are we looking for?' she said.

'Look for somewhere hidden that gives you a decent view,' I said. 'And then check for signs of recent occupation.'

It didn't work. After a few minutes searching, Floria gave up in frustration and suggested I searched while she kept an eye on the village to make sure we weren't spotted.

Left to my own devices, I found the OP in less than fifteen minutes. It was a perfect spot, wedged between rocky outcrops and about a hundred metres higher up the slope than where Floria and I had lain in wait the previous morning. Crushed grass told me someone had been in situ for some time, and they'd used a groundsheet as protection from the cold.

I waved at Floria to join me. 'It's here,' I said, as she came within earshot.

'How can you tell?' she asked, scanning the ground in front of where I stood.

'I'm no expert,' I replied. 'But I reckon this grass is crushed.'

Now on her knees, Floria ran her fingers over the rough ground. 'No leak then?' she said, raising her eyebrows.

'I guess not. Look there.' I pointed to a line on the grass created by the groundsheet where the crush effect was at its most apparent. 'See that hard edge?'

Floria scowled, stood up and ambled towards the slope leading down to the village. 'You'd need night-vision kit if you were to do the job properly,' she said, casually.

'Someone who knew what they were doing, you think?'

'Maybe, yeah' she answered. 'Someone who hadn't catered for an expert like you being on their tail.'

I had a feeling Floria had chosen her words deliberately and there seemed to be an edge to her tone. 'An expert like me?' I said.

'Ok,' she said, looking askance at me. 'Confession time. I ran your name through the Army HR database. It came up with no known records.' She paused for a moment, seemingly waiting for me to react before continuing. When I didn't, she carried on. 'Normally, I'd have accepted that but I happen to know, in certain circumstances, Army records can be deleted. Soldiers who've joined MI5, for example. I once had to check on a retired senior NCO … even had his paperwork on my desk, but there was nothing on the computer.'

'What does that have to do with me?'

'This morning you laced up your boots in a way that I happen to know some soldiers do and … I know, you say your father taught it you, but … well, let's just say there's no way an ordinary plod from the city could have found this OP so fast.'

'Do you have a theory to go with your suspicions?'

She shook her head. 'I thought Secret Service, maybe? You're too old to be a soldier.'

'You think I'm MI5?' I said, my eyebrows raised.

'Or maybe it's you who works for the Ministry of Defence, who knows? Monique told me how you disarmed her, so it's apparent you can look after yourself, and you seem to know military stuff like second nature. You never missed a beat when Colonel Hine used acronyms only a soldier ought to know. I gave you that one, I thought maybe you're well prepared or you might be ex-services even. But when you said you're not … well, that just doesn't stack up, does it?'

'Sometimes, when the pieces fall into place, the picture might be different than you expect,' I said, as I stalled for thinking time.

'Meaning what, exactly?' Floria asked, harshly. Before I could explain, she continued. 'Look, I don't know who you are Mr Finlay, if that is your name? What I do know is there's more to you than meets the eye … and I think you should level with me.'

'Have you shared this with anyone?' I said, before looking up.

'Is that it? Is that all you're worried about,' she said, her eyes now blazing. 'Who else might know you're not what you seen? Try trusting me, sir. We're supposed to be on the same fuckin' side.'

I stood up and was about to begin my explanation when Floria turned on her heel and marched off towards the car. I had a last check of the grass, satisfied myself the users of the OP hadn't left anything behind, and then jogged after her. The moment I caught up, she turned to face me, her top lip raised in a snarl. I stepped back, fearing she was about to throw a punch.

Then, in an instant, her body language changed. She exhaled loudly and the anger disappeared. She was back in control.

'When did you check the HR database?' I asked.

'Yesterday,' she said, frostily.

It was my turn to take a deep breath. 'Ok, I'll explain. And this isn't an admission. You're half-way right in what you think. I was Army a long time ago. I really am a DI from the Met and I'm definitely not working for the MOD. I've been keeping quiet about my background in the hope the soldiers we meet might talk in a way they thought I wouldn't understand.'

'So, someone deleted your Army record in case anyone here checked?'

'Temporarily, yes.'

'Hiding your identity seems a bit extreme for a couple of missing rifles, or is there something else going on I don't know about? Maybe the reason someone broke into Miss Russell's house last night?'

'It wasn't my idea to hide my identity,' I said. 'I just do as I'm told. And as to who's been following us, I'm as much in the dark as you are.'

'What mob were you in?' she asked. It was a standard question every soldier seemed to ask someone who'd also served.

'Royal Artillery. But, like I said, it was a long, long time ago … a previous life. Before you were even born, I'd bet.'

'What rank were you?'

'Captain.'

Floria snorted in satisfaction before ramming her hands hard onto her hips. 'An officer?' she exclaimed. 'Bloody hell, I knew it. You know the biggest giveaways?'

'Try me.'

'It was when we sat down with the Colonel. Me, I'm so in awe of being in front of a Colonel, I'm even trying to sit to attention. You, well you relax in your chair like you'd been there a hundred times. And you watched everything like a hawk. I could see you, taking it all in, sussing them out. And then, when we were in the Armoury. Civvies are fascinated by guns. You weren't, didn't even want to hold one like every civvie I've ever known. Reason … you'd seen it all before.' Floria paused for a moment, then looked back towards the hide we'd found. 'You knew exactly what you were looking for over there, didn't you?'

'I've set up similar OPs in the past.'

'I thought so. That's what got me so mad. I'm trying to help you do this enquiry properly and you won't level with me. You need to start trusting me.'

193

'Perhaps, I do,' I said, with a grin. 'And now you've shown you have detective ability, are you going to help me find out who has been watching me? I'm starting to think these stolen rifles are just the tip of a very ugly iceberg.'

Chapter 38

Floria decided we would take a short-cut to Ebbw Vale Police Station using one of the winding, narrow roads that took a direct route over the mountain. The gradients were severe, the slopes steep and with road edges that were frequently unprotected, it wasn't for the faint-hearted. As we gained altitude, the occasional house appeared through the mist. These were grey, desolate places occupied I imagined by hardy folks well used to life at this altitude. With the air between us cleared to some extent, Floria and I enjoyed some light-hearted banter as I attempted to pronounce some of the local place names and work out their meaning. Cwmbran, I learned, meant 'Valley of Crows', which seemed highly appropriate and led to a friendly debate as to which had come first, the name of the town or the barracks.

The car rattled as we crossed several steel cattle grids designed to keep sheep on the upper ground and away from the populated valley areas. They weren't completely effective, as I soon learned. As we left the mountain and approached a conurbation fittingly called 'Hilltop', I saw a small flock of sheep, most of which were grazing on the sparse meadows above the cattle grid. A few were enjoying richer pickings from grass verges on the lower, more urban side. Disturbed by our car, the larger section of the group suddenly charged at the steel framework of one grid and leapt fully ten feet across it and into the land of plenty. One or two trailed a single leg into the gap but the vast majority cleared it easily. Sheep, it was clear, knew their physical capabilities far better than the designers of such barriers.

Steep grassy slopes soon gave way to neat rows of red-brick homes laid out in parallel and virtually identical terraces that followed the contours of the valley sides. Lazy smoke trails drifted skyward from many of the chimneys and, with rain-bearing clouds blocking out the sun to create a grey, diffused light, the town of Ebbw Vale had what I would describe as a 'monochrome' look. Nothing vibrant stood out.

'The area is still in shock from the steelworks closure,' Floria said, as we approached our destination. 'It was on the cards for years, they say, but nobody thought it would actually happen.'

Ahead, I noticed a small, blue 'Police' sign on a high wall. It looked like we'd arrived. Next to the wall, a young woman in a green parka – hood up to protect from the chill wind – was using one hand to rock a small child in a buggy. Her free hand gripped a smouldering cigarette she repeatedly held to her lips, wispy puffs of smoke lingering in the damp air. 'You know this town well?' I said to Floria, as she slowed before turning into what looked to be the police station yard.

'I spent a lot of time up here in uniform,' she replied. 'The lads from the camp used to come for the nightclubs and cheap beer. There were always fights with the local studs when our lads chatted up their girls. All those clubs are closed now.'

As Floria parked the car, a young PC who'd been loading some traffic cones into the rear of a police car gave my warrant card a quick once-over before pointing us in the direction of a rusted, iron fire escape that led up the outside of the building. As unlikely as it looked, the PC assured me this was where we would find the CID team we were looking for.

The area below the staircase was littered with cigarette stubs. Floria turned her nose up as she also saw the debris. 'You don't, presumably?' I asked.

'Never have. Parents smoke, a lot of soldiers as well. Not for me though. First one I tried made me feel sick.'

'Likewise,' I replied. 'The first was one too many.'

At the top of the metal stairs, we found an unpainted wooden door with a single, opaque wired-glass window. I was pleased to find it open. Inside, we found a large room with eighteen desks, only four of which were occupied.

Behind me, the door swung closed with a loud clunk. I rubbed my hands to ease the cold in my fingers as four sets of eyes turned towards us. Immediately, as if a switch had been thrown, the room fell silent.

Four grey-suited detectives looked us up and down. They were weighing us up – threat or friendly, nuisance or welcome, ignore or react. It was a typically cynical police response. Three of them returned to what they were doing with just one continuing to study us. I figured he was more curious than his peers as to why his office was being invaded by two strangers in rather tatty looking military clothing. At the far side of the large room, adjacent to a closed office, a fifth man waved at us. He appeared older than the others, and was dressed in a rather worn looking suit with his tie loose around his unbuttoned collar. I guessed him to be a supervisor, perhaps the man we had come to see. 'Can I help you, butt?' he called.

'DI Finlay,' I called back. 'Here to see DCI Mostyn.' Floria tucked in behind me as I squeezed through the narrow gaps between the desks. The detective who greeted us had pushed open the door to a smaller office with his foot. I heard him say something under his breath to someone inside before turning back to face us. 'Step this way,' he said.

***

Unfortunately, I made the error of assuming the older detective was the man in charge. To be fair to me – as I pointed out to an amused Wendy Russell later that day – the door had displayed a small brass plate bearing the acronym 'DCI' and I presumed he was the Detective Chief Inspector. A young fresh-faced man in a blue pin-stripe suit who was perched on the corner of a desk inside the office, I took to be his subordinate. I couldn't have been more wrong and to say DCI Luke Mostyn wasn't happy about my mistake would be to rather understate his reaction.

What Mostyn lacked in years, he more than made up for in his command of anti-Met vocabulary. Once he and his colleague had finished attempting to humiliate me over my blunder, he really tore into me. My failure to properly report the figure we'd seen on the moor and the fleeing car came first, then my apparent lack of crime-scene awareness followed by my elitism – quite where he got that one from, I don't know – all came in for criticism. Floria looked bemused as she stood watching in the doorway. My jaw tightened as I fought hard not to bite back but, given my promises to both Wendy and Bill Grahamslaw, I decided it was wiser to keep quiet and allow what I guessed was inter-regional rivalry to wash over me.

Thankfully, things relaxed a little when I mentioned the OP we'd discovered. Mostyn had me mark the site on a large Ordnance Survey map pinned on the wall and then asked me to indicate the route we had used when looking for Tom Morgan. It was only as I saw the scale of the mountain that I appreciated how lucky we'd been to find the young soldier so close to his mother's home. If he'd headed further onto the moor, it would have been like looking for a black cat in a coal cellar.

By the time we finished, it was after lunchtime. Floria led the way as we headed in silence down the stairs, past the discarded cigarettes and back to the police yard.

'Sorry about that,' I said, as I climbed into our car and closed the door behind me.

'Don't be,' she said. 'It gave me an insight into how seriously they're taking things ... not.'

'How do you mean?' I said.

'A total of just six detectives?' she replied, dryly. 'Every other squad I've seen investigating a death had a shed load of people on it.'

'It's early days. If the death is confirmed as suspicious they'll bring in more.'

Reaching into her jacket pocket for the keys to the car, Floria rummaged around for a few seconds and, having found them, pushed the ignition key home. 'So, they're not even sure it's a suspicious death at the moment?' she continued. 'What happened at the PM?'

'They'll know more when the lab tests come back.'

Floria frowned as she started the engine. 'Next stop Colonel Hine then?'

I laughed. 'Not quite. Next stop is to get out of this dirty kit.'

The girl with the buggy was still outside in the street, and still smoking. I wondered if she may be waiting for someone to be released from custody. As we headed towards Usk and a change of clothes, I also found myself thinking about Floria's comment on the small number of detectives assigned to the case. Although I'd done my best to reassure her, my own experience of murder investigations was also of large numbers of detectives being involved right from the beginning. It was the reason most murders are solved within forty-eight hours of occurrence. Here, it seemed, things were done differently.

Chapter 39

Ellie walked as if she were on a mission as she approached the town shopping precinct. She was determined to identify the aftershave worn by the man in the respirator. Unfortunately, although the name was somewhere in her memory, it hadn't come to her. It was expensive, she was certain of that, and probably not the kind soldiers might buy for themselves. There had to be a possibility it had been purchased in town, perhaps as a present from a wife or girlfriend and, with Cwmbran being a place where an expensive aftershave wasn't likely to sell in great quantity, she hoped a tour of the chemists and department stores might produce a result.

Although it was now something of an anachronism, Cwmbran had once been a 'new town', one of several Government-sponsored projects to replace poor quality and bombed-out housing in the aftermath of the Second World War. Conversion of the redundant RAF base to accommodate a barracks had begun not long afterwards. Soldiers soon became part of the fabric of the community. They shopped, socialised and sent their kids to local schools and, in the aftermath of the Iraq and Afghan conflicts, they had witnessed an unmistakable and growing wave of popularity. All around the country, wearers of the Queen's uniform were no longer regarded as a nuisance, as rival suitors for local girls or somebody to pick a fight with on a Saturday night. Now, they were heroes, people to be envied and emulated, and with every story of bravery and every heart-rending body-bag that arrived at Brize Norton airfield, the esteem in which they were held grew exponentially. The cat-calls had long since ceased to be replaced by expressions of appreciation and the occasional request for a hand-shake or photograph. Women soldiers, in particular, were received very warmly and, as a result, Ellie encountered willing help in every shop she called at, as the staff willingly indulged the 'young lady soldier' attempting to identify her boyfriend's favourite scent. To her frustration though, every sniff test proved fruitless. She remembered the aroma as spiced, almost woody. A few ideas were close but not quite there. They were either too mellow or too sweet. After nearly an hour of trying, a large family-owned department store was her final port of call.

The girl behind the perfume counter was enthused and helpful – if a little amused – and soon bought in to Ellie's story. She also proved to be very knowledgeable on the subject and, following a series of questions aimed at narrowing the possibilities, she came up with a name. It was a top-of-the-range scent created by an Italian fashion house. 'We haven't seen many soldiers in town today,' she commented, as she used the tester bottle to spray onto a strip of paper.

'There's an inspection,' Ellie said, cautiously. 'Only officers are allowed off camp.'

'But, you're not … oh, sorry.'

Ellie smiled as she saw the assistant's eyes glance at the rank insignia on her chest. She leaned forward, sniffed the litmus paper and, as she did so, she felt her stomach lurch. There was no doubt. It was the same. 'I think this may be it,' she said, her heart pounding. The shop assistant was about to return the bottle to the display cabinet. 'Is there any possibility you can check your sales to see if he's bought it here before?'

The assistant hesitated, as if unsure. 'I'm not sure if I should,' she replied. 'You know … company rules and all that. We're not allowed, to be honest.'

'You'd be doing me a real favour,' Ellie said, sensing she was nearly home. The answer wasn't a *no*, more a case of *I shouldn't*. 'His birthday is tomorrow and I'm running out of time.'

The girl glanced nervously towards the till check-out area. Without speaking, she bent down and pulled a small book from beneath the counter. Flicking through the pages of hand-written entries until she found what she was looking for, she then placed it open in front of Ellie before walking casually away towards what looked like a curtained-off staff area.

Ellie looked down. The open page showed a date in January. It bore the heading of the designer and revealed just one entry. As she'd hoped, not many people were prepared to stump up the cost of such expensive cologne. The name was female – Jodie Baker. And there was a telephone number, a mobile by the look of it. She was just about to try and memorise it when a hand appeared and flicked the book closed.

'I'm sorry, that's confidential.'

Ellie looked up to see the face of an older woman, a supervisor by the look of her. She returned the book to its place below the counter, enquiring, with a frosty smile, whether Ellie wanted the aftershave gift-wrapped.

'I just need to go to the bank,' Ellie lied. 'My credit card's been playing up.' She half-smiled at the woman before turning tail and heading back to the stairs. As she left the exit, the smile had become a fully-fledged grin. She was getting close. She had a name. The next step would be to find the girl and ask who the aftershave had been for.

Chapter 40

We'd been waiting for nearly ten minutes before Pemberton finally acknowledged our presence.

'Gotta scoot, chap. Plod are at the door.'

The HQ receptionist cringed in response to the Captain's loudly-spoken words. Floria rolled her eyes. We'd been listening to him droning on to someone about the arrangements for an upcoming Mess dinner. It was a deliberate move, I was sure of it. He was sending a message he considered us a nuisance. 'Come,' he called in a shrill voice. It was a simple enough communication, although normally aimed at subordinate soldiers to say their senior officer was ready to receive them.

As Floria and I approached his door, it was slightly ajar. The temptation was too much. Knowing it would antagonise him, I walked straight in rather than knocking as he would have expected. The irritation on his face as he looked up to find the two of us standing in front of his desk gave me a sense of profound satisfaction.

The game continued as Pemberton dismissively waved a hand in the direction of a large brown envelope sitting on his desk. I picked it up, muttered a 'thank you', and peeled it open. It contained both lists we'd been promised – Training Regiment staff and recruits posted to Prince Albert Barracks on the day the rifles went missing, and a shorter record showing those still at the base.

As I quickly scanned through the names, the door swung open behind us. It was Colonel Hine. The sleeves of his shirt rolled up, he looked to have been hard at work. 'Thought I heard familiar voices,' he announced. 'Timely visit, Mr Finlay. Giles, do you have that notice from the Safety Camera people?'

Where he had previously slumped indifferently in his seat, Pemberton now sat upright, alert and oozing efficiency. He reached into the top drawer of his desk and pulled out a letter. I noticed the heading – Police Camera Partnership. I smiled; one of them had received a speeding ticket.

'Any tips on how best to handle this?' said Hine. 'With all the crap flying around since you discovered Private Morgan's body; this really is the last thing I wanted to be dealing with.'

Taking the letter from Pemberton's outstretched hand, I had a quick read. As I suspected, it was a Notice of Intended Prosecution. It was already two weeks old, and I saw from an attached note that it had only been forwarded by the Ministry of Defence to Hine's Regimental HQ a couple of days previously. A Bedford Lorry had been clocked at forty-two in a thirty limit. 'Is it one of yours?' I asked.

'One of our eight-tonner medium mobility units. Did you note the time it tripped the camera?'

I hadn't. Re-reading the details I saw it had happened at a little after 3am. 'Early hours of the morning,' I said. 'Unusual time for a lone military vehicle to be out, I'd have thought?'

'It's from our squadron lines,' Hine continued. 'Used for training and troop movements generally. According to the log it was still parked here at that time.'

'Have you checked the ten, thirty-three, sir,' Floria piped up. It was a decent suggestion. The G.1033 form had to be completed by the driver when they signed out the equipment pack that accompanied every vehicle.

Ignoring Floria, the Colonel addressed his answer to me. 'Captain Pemberton has spoken to Corporal West from Transport Squadron. He assures us no vehicle left the camp that night.'

I raised an eyebrow and scowled. 'False plates or someone moonlighting?'

Hine took the letter from me. 'I have no idea, but I'm sure we'll get to the bottom of it, in time. My immediate problem is I have to identify the driver within twenty-one days of that notice. I now have just two remaining days to fill it in and return it, or risk prosecution.'

'If it were me, I'd write and explain.'

The Colonel smiled, broadly. 'I've never actually known a camera unit bother to send such a thing to us.'

'Possibly because the lorry was on its own and not part of a convoy.'

Hine shrugged. 'I was rather hoping you would know somebody who could kill it off?' he said.

I thought for a moment. Having the local Commanding Officer indebted to me could work in my favour. That said, Safety Camera Units were very much a law unto themselves and I'd even heard tales of drivers of emergency vehicles on 'a blue-lights shout' having to produce proof it was a genuine call before a ticket was cancelled. Killing off a speeding summons – even in the case of a military vehicle – might take more than a single phone call. 'If it helps, I'll certainly give it a go,' I said.

'Excellent,' Hine said, in response to my offer. 'I'll get Rosie to run you off a copy.' He took a step closer to me and lowered his voice. 'I'd be most grateful if you'd keep this between us,' he said. 'I have to dash now. I'm due to interview a Sergeant just transferred in and I think I've probably kept him waiting long enough.'

I smiled to reassure Colonel Hine I understood and then passed the brown envelope to Floria. As we followed him out the door, I made sure to give Giles Pemberton a wink and a big smile. It wasn't returned and, as I headed back along the corridor, I could have sworn I felt the heat of his glare on the back of my head.

Sat on one of the chairs in the reception area, where Floria and I had been waiting a few minutes earlier, I spotted the Sergeant, Colonel Hine had mentioned. He looked very smart in his No.2 dress – tunic, pressed trousers and polished shoes – his cap resting on his lap. Floria ignored him and headed outside. As I diverted towards the reception office to collect a copy of the Speeding Notice, he looked up, made eye contact and nodded politely. He seemed a little old for the rank, maybe late thirties, but looked every inch a career soldier.

Behind me, Giles Pemberton appeared in the doorway to the HQ offices. The Sergeant stood crisply and to attention, his cap neatly tucked beneath his arm. 'Sir,' he barked, before turning smartly to march behind the Adjutant.

***

After collecting the photocopied form from Colonel Hine's secretary, I found Floria outside waiting for me. Something was wrong. She looked to be in a state of shock as she stared back in the direction from where I had just appeared. 'Are you ok?' I asked, curious to discover what had brought on her change of demeanour.

She hesitated for several seconds before speaking. 'Did you see that Sergeant waiting in reception?' she said, her voice little more than a whisper.

I nodded. 'The one Colonel Hine mentioned he was about to interview?'

Floria shuffled around me, pushed the door into the HQ building firmly closed and then looked all around us. 'Yes, *that* one,' she snapped, so unexpectedly I stepped backwards away from her in surprise. 'His name is Mick Fitzgerald. He's not supposed to be posted to this camp.'

'How do you mean, not supposed to be posted here?' I asked.

Floria tilted her head towards our car. 'Not here,' she said, as she pushed past me.

Only once the doors to the car were shut did she continue. 'He's banned from here after he was arrested a year or so ago for attacking an SIB Corporal in her quarters.'

'In *her* quarters?' I said. 'Are you saying it was sexual?'

'It happened in Germany a little over a year ago. A girl called Ellie Rodgers.'

'So, if this happened in Germany. Why is he banned from here?'

'I'll come to that, if you'll give me a minute. It was Ellie's last day before going to Sandhurst to train as an officer. Her team were running a surveillance op and she was the tethered goat, the bait to try and lure a sex attacker out into the open. To cut a long story short, the suspect didn't appear so everyone adjourned to the Sergeants' Mess for a piss-up to celebrate her promotion. She went home drunk and Mick Fitzgerald was waiting for her.'

'How bad?'

'Real bad. She woke up to find him standing over her wearing a ski mask. I'm sure you can guess what happened next. He was caught within a couple of days but there was nothing to tie him to the other attacks and at the trial he claimed what happened with Ellie was consensual; they were both drunk and knew what they were doing. Net result, he got off and Ellie went a bit off the rails.'

'How far off the rails?' I asked.

'She can be a bit of a hot-head. She was nearly kicked out of Sandhurst when she decked another officer-cadet who made a comment about her having a cute arse. They convicted Fitzgerald for being in her quarters without authority. He lost seniority and a note was supposed to have been made on his file so he wasn't posted anywhere she was.'

'He lost seniority?' I said. 'So, his chances of making it to Senior NCO are virtually nil?'

'No less than he deserved. Lying shit should be serving time.'

'And I assume Ellie Rodgers is posted here? That's why you're surprised to see him?'

Floria punched the driver's wheel. 'Yes, she is, and surprised doesn't half describe what I'm feeling at the moment. Sometimes, I think the army couldn't organise a piss-up in a brewery. It won't be a coincidence him turning up. He'll have wanted it.'

It was clear from what Floria was saying she felt she was going to have to do something. 'Is Ellie on the Training Regiment as well?' I asked.

'No, thank God. She's at 25 Signals on the far side of the camp.'

'Perhaps your unit commander can get something sorted before it's too late and they bump into each other?' I suggested. 'Did he recognise you?'

'No, I don't think so. But he clocked the RMP badges straight away. I reckon he'll think we were with the Colonel to talk about him.'

'That explains the look he gave me as I walked past him,' I said.

'If I drop you off at the police headquarters, could you get a lift home with ACC Russell?' Floria said.

'To give you time to go and see your boss?'

'Yes. If I'm quick and he's agreeable, they might be able to sort something. I won't be the only person to know Fitzgerald shouldn't be here. God forbid Ellie should bump into him. She'll do her nut.'

Chapter 41

I called Wendy who readily agreed to give me a lift and suggested I wait in the police HQ canteen until she finished work. I'd only been there about ten minutes when my phone beeped. It was a text from Bill Grahamslaw. *MOD here again. With AC this time. If anything odd happens let me know.* The Ministry of Defence had decided to up the ante and go to the Assistant Commissioner. As I needed to secure Bill's help to deal with Colonel Hine's NIP and tell him what had happened the previous evening at Wendy's home, I called him immediately.

'It'll be someone working for the fuckin' MOD,' Bill said, as I finished explaining about the intruder. 'From now on, make sure you don't do anything more to hack them off. And don't worry about things this end; the AC is old-school. He won't be brow-beaten by them any more than I was.'

I asked about the speeding ticket. 'Consider it done,' he said, after I'd read him the reference number. 'It'll help to have the locals on side. Meanwhile, tie everything up as quickly as you can and get the next stage out of town.'

We ended the call just as Wendy appeared behind me, coat on and briefcase in hand. 'Something important?' she asked.

'Updating Bill on progress. I told him about last night.'

'Does he have any theories?'

'The MOD are at the Yard as we speak, trying to get me pulled. He thinks they might have decided to check on what I'm up to.'

'Have they been putting more pressure on him?'

'Just a bit.' I held the phone up so Wendy could read Bill's text it.

'I'm not surprised,' she said, as she finished. 'They've been on to us as well.'

'The uncertainty will worry them,' I said. 'How's Monique?'

'She'll be fine. She went to work as soon as the SOCO had done his stuff.'

'Did they find anything?'

'Nothing of use. They think it was one person and, from the marks they found, they're certain he wore latex gloves. He got in through the unlocked back door and escaped through the front when Monique disturbed him. It's a good job I'd kept the Security Conference paperwork with me.'

'It was me they were interested in, not your conference.'

'We assume,' Wendy replied. 'Just in case the break-in was a ruse to plant a listening device, I had our techie boys do a sweep after the SOCO finished. All clear, they said.'

'You wouldn't think the MOD would take that kind of risk.'

'We have no idea what goes on in the corridors of Whitehall, Finlay. Huge reverberations hit the MOD after Deepcut. The last thing they need right now is another series of unexplained deaths.'

I walked over to the canteen till, paid for my tea and then joined Wendy at the exit. 'What about your missing officer?' I asked, as we walked to her car. 'Is there any news on him?'

Wendy's expression relaxed a little. 'There is actually,' she said. 'He rang his handler's number and left a message asking to take some outstanding annual leave.'

'So, he's ok then?'

'We're still not certain. It's most unlike him. We've had someone make discreet enquiries with his wife and she's not heard from him.'

'You think he might have been coerced into making that call?' I asked.

'Until we speak to him, we just don't know.'

'But your Chief will only keep the MOD at bay while he thinks I'm inside the camp helping you?'

'Correct,' Wendy replied. 'Your enquiry into the rifles is just a convenient excuse. If Liverick turns up you'll be on your own, I'm afraid. Do you know how to use MMS, by the way?'

'Send pictures by phone, you mean? I've never done it. Why do you ask?'

'When you get to see the AWOL file, I want you to take photos of it rather than making notes. It's far more accurate.' As we left the building, Wendy took my phone, confirmed it was a model that could send photographs and then gave me a quick run-through on how. After a couple of abortive attempts, I soon had the hang of it.

'Not as tricky as I thought,' I said as we reached her car. It occurred to me as I spoke, just how easy it would have been for someone to do the same to Angela Davenport. 'I need a favour,' I said, reaching into my briefcase for Angela's phone. 'But before I ask, I need to show you something.'

Wendy frowned. 'Like what?'

'Better inside the car.'

She looked confused. 'Is this anything to do with you borrowing my car yesterday?'

'Do I have your word?' I asked.

She paused for a moment before replying. 'Ok,' she said, finally. 'We can talk inside if you prefer. But nothing illegal, mind. Friendship only carries so much weight, Finlay.'

The car hazard lights flashed as Wendy unlocked the doors. Once inside, I held the phone in my open hand so she could see it. 'Nice,' she said. 'The latest Nokia N90. I take it this is what you wanted to show me?'

'I had a chat to Jenny before I got back to your place last night,' I replied. 'Showing it to you was her idea.'

'Is this what last night's intruder was looking for?'

'I don't think they were looking for this,' I said. 'It was given to me last night by Michael Davenport. It was his daughter's.'

'His daughter's?' Wendy said, scowling. 'It belonged to Angela? The RMP told the inquest she didn't own one.'

I began flicking through the phone menu. 'She did, and this is it. I need to show you something on it … and I need you to keep what I'm about to show you between us, at least for the time being.'

'You're being very secret squirrel, Finlay. What is it?'

I took a deep breath. 'It's a video … a recording of Angela Davenport having sex with two men.'

'You want me to watch a sex video?' Wendy frowned and shook her head. 'Are we talking non-consensual or something?'

'Maybe decide after you've watched it? It's nasty, so maybe brace yourself. I can't begin to imagine what it must have been like for her father to see it.'

'Don't patronise me, Finlay. I spent two years as a DCI running a cyber crime unit. Trust me, there's not much of a sexual nature I haven't seen before.'

'Sorry,' I said. 'I didn't mean to infer … it's just I promised Michael Davenport I wouldn't show it to anybody.'

'But you're going to let me see it?'

'I need your opinion and also your help,' I said.

'Ok,' she replied. 'You have my word … for now. But I repeat, I'm not doing anything illegal for you or anybody, end of.'

I found the video file, held the screen up and pressed 'play'.

***

As Wendy watched, I saw her mouth set in a hard line. She was quiet, unusually so and, on a couple of occasions I noticed her hands form into fists. 'Jesus, fucking Christ,' she said, as the play-back finished. 'And her father saw that?'

'I think it was made for a specific reason,' I replied. 'Hold your thoughts until you read the messages that came after it.'

I flicked through the phone menu again, found the texts and held the device up once more so Wendy could read them. We sat silently for a few moments after she'd finished, the car engine running, both of us staring through the windscreen. 'Are you ok?' I asked, a little surprised at my friend's stunned reaction.

When she finally spoke, Wendy was measured and calm. 'I'd say Davenport is drugged,' she said. 'I've seen enough recordings of girls on rohypnol to recognise the signs. What you've got there is a video of a recruit being raped. And I'd be willing to bet from the texts those two are either fellow recruits or NCOs. They sent her a copy of the video to blackmail her into keeping quiet about what they'd done.'

'Definitely rape?'

'Well, I can't say absolutely,' Wendy snapped. 'But not many young girls take a date-rape drug of their own volition, do they? Are you aware what happens procedurally when a servicewoman is raped by a fellow soldier?'

'I assume they refer it to us, the civilian police?'

'That's what most people think. The reality is, if both victim and perpetrator are serving soldiers, the allegation is investigated by her Commanding Officer. And all they are interested in is the damage such an allegation might do to army reputation and to their careers. Unsurprisingly, not many cases get to a military court. Result … women feel they're not taken seriously, they're not believed and even reporting they've been attacked is a complete waste of their time.'

'So they keep quiet about it?'

'That's what we believe … and listen to this, because it gets worse. The army has what it calls a Service Test. Basically, that means a woman runs the risk that if she's not believed she can find herself interviewed as part of a disciplinary investigation aimed at prosecuting her for making a false allegation.'

'So, they prosecute the complainant? That's crazy.'

Wendy sighed. 'The whole system is loaded against the victim. Believe me, if I had the power to do something about it, I would. Sending an undercover officer inside the camp was a way to do my bit for those women.'

'So, what happened when you investigated Davenport's death?'

'We met a wall of silence from everyone, and not just the NCOs. The MOD weren't exactly helpful and the senior officers at the camp just wanted it over with. Nobody in the military seemed the slightest bit interested in the notion that young soldiers could be bullied into killing themselves. What you've got there is dynamite, Finlay. Combine the video with those texts and it would have changed the whole course of the inquest.'

'I agree someone was blackmailing her,' I said. 'But not to keep quiet about the video itself. I think it's related to the rifle theft.'

'You could well be right, there may be a connection. Presumably the favour you want is authority for a subscriber check to find out who sent it?'

'Exactly.'

Wendy huffed and shook her head. 'No can do. Not unless you hand over that phone. We both need to discover who they are, Finlay, not just you. In case you'd forgotten, we still have an ongoing enquiry into her death and an undercover officer whose fate remains uncertain.'

'If anything comes of this, you'll be the first to know,' I said.

'Are you saying you won't hand the phone over? I could give you a direct order?'

'I will, I just need a little time. For now, I need the name of the man who owns the phone used to threaten her.'

'Even though you can't see their faces, the snake should help identify one of them,' she replied, referencing a distinctive tattoo one of the men had on his back. 'Do army personnel records list tattoos?'

'They're only recorded at enlistment. Besides, if we go around at the camp asking who has a snake tattoo on their lower back, he'll soon be warned we're looking for him.'

'So, you want a way to identify them on the q.t?'

'I had to promise to her father the video wouldn't be disclosed. It was the only way he'd let me have the phone.'

As Wendy shook her head again, I could see I was losing the argument. 'You shouldn't have done that,' she said. 'If you want a subscriber check to go through me it would have to be as part of the official investigation. And what are you going to do with the name once you have it?'

'Speak to them, of course. Maybe put them under a little pressure.'

'You'd better not be planning any Met-type stunts, Finlay. Your methods may work in London, they won't get any support here.'

'I know that. I promise to be good.'

Wendy through her head back and laughed, ironically.

'It's a no to the check, then?' I said.

'The rules are very tight nowadays, you should know that,' she answered. 'Your sense of loyalty to a wronged father may be commendable but it's also misguided and I can't now undo what I've seen. I want that phone, Finlay, and I want it now.'

'Could you at least buy me some time?' I said, although I knew I was struggling.

Wendy breathed a couple of times as she thought hard before replying. 'Ok,' she said, finally. 'You can have a day … but no longer, and that's only because you're a mate to whom I owe a great deal. After that, you hand over the phone, despite what you promised the girl's father. In the meantime, can I suggest you use your old friends to run a check?'

'My old friends? How do you mean?'

'Do I have to spell it out, Finlay? I mean ask the people you know can trace a phone. Call MI5 ... ask your old mate Harry Davies.'

Chapter 42

After arriving back at Wendy's, I decided to head upstairs to my room for a quick catch-up with my family before calling Harry. I updated Jenny on the break-in and, with the notable absence of swearing, our conversation somewhat mirrored my earlier discussion with Bill Grahamslaw. There was one noteworthy exception though. Jenny showed far more concern for the effect it might have on Wendy and Monique than Bill had. It was only after I promised to check the house and gardens before we retired for the night that I was able to let her know I'd shown the video to Wendy.

'She's dealing with it now, then?' Jenny said.

'She's given me a day to see if I can turn something up. If not, she's going to take over.'

'Well, you be careful. If someone's covering up a murder, they might get desperate.'

It was an astute warning.

Next, I rang Harry and, to my pleasant surprise, he picked up straight away. 'Twice in as many days, Finlay?' he said. 'At this late hour, something tells me you either need a favour or you have a problem.'

'The former,' I said, as for the third time that day, I found myself describing the break-in.

'I agree with Bill,' Harry said, as I finished. 'The MOD have to be favourite, even though their operator sounds a bit gung-ho. And Wendy was right to do a sweep, even if they didn't find anything. If that had been me, putting a bug in place is what I'd have done.'

'Are you busy?' I said.

He laughed. 'I have a post-op report to get to the Assistant Director by midday tomorrow; I'll give you one guess.'

I didn't need it. Put a Browning 9mm pistol in Harry's hand and he was outstanding. Writing, even the simple act of using a keyboard, had never been a skill he'd truly mastered. To save on time, I got straight to the point; told him what I needed and why.

'There are some nasty bastards in this world,' he replied, as I concluded my description of the video on Angela Davenport's phone before reading out the accompanying texts.

'You're telling me,' I said. 'Until recently I didn't know it was possible to make videos with a phone let alone transmit them. These people are way ahead of us.'

'You're a dinosaur, boss, with respect. We've been using that kind of technology in the Service for some while now. Bit expensive for the average Crow I would have thought, mind?'

'Wendy said that as well. And she suggested asking you to trace the sender. She couldn't help without making it part of the police enquiry.'

'Does she want the phone?'

'She's given me a day,' I said. 'Then I have to hand it over.'

'And best you do that. I'm amazed the Davenports let you have it.'

'If it had been a daughter of mine, I would have thrown it on the fire.'

'The Robert Finlay I served with would have found the bastards and ripped their fuckin' balls off,' he replied.

'That was twenty years ago, Harry. I've changed.'

'People like us don't change, boss, we just get older. Make sure you give them something to remember on behalf of the girl's father. My guess is you won't have to look far. It has all the hallmarks of something another recruit or an idiot among the directing staff would do.'

'So, can you trace the sender's phone for me? On the hurry up, I mean.'

'No dramas mate. Tomorrow lunchtime, do you? I'll do a subscriber check and see what it reveals. I might even be able to tell you what area the messages were sent from.'

'How's that?'

'We can trace the transmission route, where the nearest mast was at the time it was sent. It's not precise but it'll give you a starter for ten.'

A creak on the stairs alerted me to the fact that Wendy was close. I ended the call, stepped out onto the landing and found her waiting for me. I was about to suggest a quick check of the garden when I saw she was wearing a latex glove. In between her thumb and forefinger, she was holding a small piece of paper.

'That was Harry,' I said. 'He'll have something for me by tomorrow.'

Wendy faked a smile, but I could see she was upset. She held up the note for me to read. 'This was on the windscreen of my car,' she said. 'They came back.'

***

Thirty minutes later, Wendy and I were sat with Superintendent Dai Clarke in the warmth of the police laboratory at Cwmbran. What Wendy had forgotten to mention when she told me her home had been swept for listening devices was that the techie had also installed two battery-operated CCTV cameras as a temporary security measure while a full risk assessment was being carried out. One had been placed to monitor the rear of the house; the other covered the front garden and driveway.

With the CCTV footage downloading from an SD card onto the techie's laptop, we were sat in another laboratory watching a Scenes of Crime Officer examine the note. It was hand-written, on a sheet of lined A4 paper that had been folded into four. The wording was clear and unequivocal.

To Detective inspector Robert Finlay

if you know whats good for you family

BACK OFF

'If my spelling was that bad, I wouldn't have signed it either,' Clarke laughed, as the SOCO ran a UV light over the note. Wendy glared at him. She was not amused. Eventually, the SOCO shrugged and then placed the note carefully into a paper evidence bag. 'Nothing,' she said. 'Probably wore the same kind of gloves as the intruder.'

'Pity,' Clarke said. 'I'd hoped we might strike lucky. '

As Superintendent Clarke and the SOCO went in search of the camera technician, Wendy turned to me. 'These people seem very amateurish considering you think they're from the Ministry of Defence,' she said, softly, so we wouldn't be overheard. 'Do they think something like this could be enough to make you quit.'

'The MOD shouldn't know I have family,' I said. 'They don't have access to Met personnel files.'

'I'm wondering if that was an after-thought' she replied. 'Whoever it was added the word *family* to a note that read *what's good for you*?' I'd bet ninety-five percent of coppers your age have family. The note doesn't say names so it could easily have been a guess hoping you'd bottle it.'

'So, all we can assume is it was designed to send me back to London with my tail between my legs?'

'Exactly, and I'd be willing to bet they left it on my car because they saw you arrive in it last night.'

'They don't know me then, do they?' I said, aware I was sounding angry.

'Not yet they don't, but if it is the MOD they soon will, it's only a question of time. The effort they're putting in convinces me there's something to be found.' Wendy raised her eyebrows as she stared hard at me without commenting further. I knew what she was getting at. She wanted the phone handed over. 'Don't imagine they won't be doing deeper checks on you,' she added, when I didn't respond.

What Wendy said made good sense and I was sufficiently unsettled to be reassured by the fact that Jenny and the girls were still away from home at her sister's.

The door behind us opened. 'Ok, we're ready,' a voice announced. It was the CCTV techie. In his hands, he held a laptop computer. Superintendent Clarke followed him through the door.

What we now needed was a break. We needed the camera footage to show us a face. Wendy, Dai Clarke and I formed a semi-circle behind the techie's chair. On the screen in front of him, a small video began playing in the bottom corner. It enlarged as he pressed a button on his keyboard. The play-back was a grey-green colour, suggesting some form of night-vision or infra-red device. Although grainy, the definition and the picture displayed was decent quality. It showed Wendy's front garden looking towards the lane, with her driveway and parked car on the right-hand side of the screen.

'I've started it at the important part,' the techie said. 'Watch the dark area on the far side of the car.'

I noted the time on the recording. 10.14 pm. I'd been on the phone to Harry.

As we watched, a dark silhouetted figure appeared from behind Wendy's car, heading toward her front door, face-on to the camera. The moment of truth.

I leant forward, hoping I would recognise him.

Chapter 43

As the first rays of Monday-morning sun brought dawn to my room, I was already awake. The examination of the CCTV footage had ended in disappointment. Although the figure had been close enough to the camera to be recognised, his face was covered by a dark balaclava. Dai Clarke had cracked another misjudged, but well-intentioned joke suggesting it could even have been Wendy's undercover officer dropping off a sick note to explain his absence. The gag died beneath her withering glare.

Before heading to the shower, I had another read through my note book. I was missing something, and I was sure of it. Top of my priorities for now was the video and the inevitable conclusion it was connected to Angela Davenport's death. Extortion gave us a motive, but what was it? Was she murdered or had someone pushed her to the point of suicide? As I drew two lines beneath Angela's name on the final page of my notes, I knew she was where I had to focus my efforts. She was the key. Unlock the truth behind her death and a house of cards would soon be tumbling down.

As I put my pen down, my phone burst into life. I fumbled around as I tried to recall where I'd left it. Finally, after just a little swearing, my groping fingers located it on the floor at the side of the bed. I pressed the answer button and grunted a hello. It was Floria. Was I awake? 'Yes,' I said. 'I tend not to answer the phone in my sleep.'

Floria didn't laugh. She had her serious head on and got straight to the point. Could I meet her at the base RMP offices as soon as possible? I asked why and she promised to explain as soon as I arrived. I hung up the phone, checked the time – 6 am – and after gathering my senses for a moment, staggered to the bathroom.

***

The Military Police offices were housed in a series of portakabins on the northern edge of Prince Albert Barracks. At the main gate, several reporters were standing around chatting so Wendy dropped me off at the side entrance Floria had shown me. I thanked her profusely for yet another favour and then made my way on foot through the gate. The sentry checked my warrant card, compared my name to a list he had on a clipboard and allowed me through. By the time I'd reached the path to the security door of the RMP building, the chill morning air had woken me up and I was feeling more alert. I knocked on the door and was 'buzzed in' immediately.

My first sight inside the RMP Headquarters revealed a small office crammed with desks and lockers. With ancient, stained and rather threadbare carpets, the walls were decorated with posters and a range of photographs and prints. Everywhere you looked there was kit piled up; on desks, against the walls, on the seats and on the floor. At the far side, a fully loaded bergen and a set of body armour lay blocking a corridor. Floria was alone, sitting at one of the desks nearest the door. 'What took you?' she said, as she saw me approaching.

'The main gate is heaving with reporters.'

'They'll be here for days,' she said. 'We can walk from here.' She levered herself up from her chair and reached for her camouflage jacket.

'Walk where?' I asked, quizzically. 'And what's the rush?'

'To see Lieutenant Rodgers,' she replied. 'She's expecting us. I spoke to my CO last night … he's going to try and get Fitzgerald moved. In the meantime, I've volunteered to tell her what's happened and warn her to keep away from the Training Regiment areas for a while. The boss thought the presence of a civvie copper might help demonstrate we're taking this seriously.'

'You got me out of bed at six in the morning to help deliver news to your friend?' I said, rather too sharply. My lack of sleep showed.

Floria grinned in response. 'I knew you wouldn't mind,' she replied, a mischievous edge to her voice. 'Shall we press on? She'll just be getting into work now. I'll make us a brew when we're done.'

Before I had a chance to mention the note left on Wendy's car or to even think about objecting, Floria was on the march. Within a few minutes, we were walking into a part of the camp I hadn't seen before. A long path cut through a small copse of trees revealing an imposing two-storey building that looked a cut above the other accommodation I'd seen on the camp. A large sign on a neatly mown grass lawn out front told me it was the HQ of 25 Regiment Royal Signals, Officer Commanding – Lieutenant Colonel R Bullen, OBE.

We walked on and, as we arrived outside the Officers' Mess, I gently took hold of Floria's arm. I wanted to get something straight before we went any further. 'Let me check before we go in,' I said. 'You want me to pretend I'm a local cop to make it appear the RMP are taking the Sergeant Fitzgerald issue seriously?'

'We *are* taking it seriously, Floria replied, impatiently. 'And you being Met is even better. Your lot never come this far west unless it's something big. You can reassure Ellie, we can listen to her concerns and then I'll report back to my boss.'

'So, this is simply an exercise to give your friend some reassurance?'

'In a nutshell, yes. You've got to understand, she's had a tough time of it. If she even suspected we weren't going to sort things out, she'd take things into her own hands.'

I shook my head, frustrated at the use of my limited time. But, I was still very much in need of Floria's co-operation and I had to accept that, up to this point, her help had been invaluable. 'Ok,' I said, as she turned and walked on. 'I'll play along for now but don't forget … you owe me.'

***

Floria had mentioned the barracks being built on a redundant RAF base. The home of 25 Regiment looked like it. Old hangers nearby that I imagined once held Spitfire and Hurricane fighter planes now provided shelter to many types of ground-based vehicles including Land Rovers and a number of much larger types of transport. Many of the newer buildings, she'd described as being cheap and impersonal; a mixture of standard and not very imaginative military architectural styles. That wasn't the case here. Although showing signs of wear, the neat, former RAF accommodation, was much smarter than the remainder of the base.

The Officers' Mess itself could have been lifted from the set of a WWII movie about the RAF. As we entered the foyer, an open door revealed a tiny bar, heavily panelled in oak, with ancient leather seats and walls decorated with plaques from other Regiments. It would have been very easy to close your eyes and imagine pilots sat around waiting to be scrambled into action or winding down post-flight over a beer. As an NCO, Floria wasn't allowed further than the threshold without permission. An orderly reacted quite quickly to our knock and, after listening to a brief explanation, instructed us to wait.

A minute or so later, a young female officer appeared through a doorway ahead of us. I presumed this was Ellie Rodgers. She was dressed in desert camouflage and had fair hair pulled back from her face in a tight bun. She was also very short, just as Floria had mentioned to me, although she looked solid. Where her sleeves were rolled up I saw well-muscled forearms. Floria stepped forward, threw out her hands and the two women greeted each other with a warm hug. She and Ellie were clearly better friends than I'd realised.

Floria said something I couldn't make out and then, as the two women pulled apart, Ellie playfully smacked the top of her head. 'No way,' she said, grinning broadly. 'You take that back this instant. Stevie Gerrard will be a red 'til the day he dies.'

I guessed what had brought the reaction. It had been on the radio the previous day that Liverpool footballer Steven Gerrard was once again rumoured to be making a move to Chelsea.

Floria then seemed to remember I was with her. She introduced me as Detective Inspector Robert Finlay from 'The Met'. Ellie leaned forward and shook my hand. 'What brings you here, sir,' she asked, rather more formally than she'd spoken to her friend.

'Some news,' I replied. An immediate look of concern appeared on her face. Coppers don't come bearing good news, I thought. I asked if we could go somewhere quieter than the Mess bar.

'Follow me.' Ellie pushed open a door behind her beckoning us to follow. We entered a short corridor with a polished parquet floor and oak panelled walls adorned by two huge oil paintings depicting Napoleonic battle scenes. Silently, we then made our way through a double door into an ante-room to the main dining area. Here, our host paused and pulled the doors closed. As she turned and walked back to join us in the centre of the room, I found myself staring at her neck, at bruising that resembled finger marks. She saw me and, in response, casually stated her Judo opponent had suffered even worse. 'We don't do things by half here, Inspector,' she said. 'So, what's this news?'

Floria frowned, and I saw a bead of sweat had formed on her brow. 'Perhaps we should sit down,' she said, with some uncertainty, pointing to a circle of armchairs near the window.

I left the talking to Floria. She handled it well and, given the circumstances, Ellie's reaction was remarkably composed. She'd feared this would happen one day, she said. She also seemed happy about the steps being taken to remedy the situation. We were about to wrap up when one of the mess staff knocked on the double doors. He came with a message. Ellie had to see her Commanding Officer. Our visit was at an end. Job done and not too much time lost.

On the walk back to the RMP offices, Floria was very subdued. She didn't speak, not even to say thanks as I held doors open for her. I opted to hold back for a while before mentioning the note left on Wendy's car and the CCTV recording. On our arrival, she located an unoccupied office for me to use, offered to make the tea she'd promised earlier and then left me with Colonel Hine's lists.

After several minutes alone, I'd failed to spot any soldier with an address or next-of-kin in South London. When Floria returned, she seemed to have regained her normal composure and, as she placed our teas on the desk, she gave me a look that told me she'd registered my disappointment. 'Nothing useful?' she said.

'Nothing,' I replied.

Floria pointed at the files lying on the desk. 'Shall we make it a little easier by looking for people who are still here on camp?'

'That would help, you think?'

She moved the list to her side of the desk and sat down opposite me. 'Definitely,' she said. 'I mean, you're not exactly going to fly out to Iraq to interview people, are you?' She pulled a highlighting pen from the desk drawer and began marking the sheet. It didn't take long. Inside of a couple of minutes, just four names were marked.

'All female,' I said, as I spotted a common denominator.

'Yes,' she replied. 'All women … and all still here many months after they should have been posted to their Regiments.'

'Back-squadded because they're below par, possibly?'

'I doubt it,' she said, sceptically. 'I'd put money on this little group being the NCOs favourites. And I'll tell you something else interesting.'

'What's that?'

'These girls were all on the same intake as Angela Davenport.'

Chapter 44

As Colonel Bullen repeated the exact news Floria had relayed, Ellie realised just how grateful she was to her friend. The intervening period, although only ten minutes, had been sufficient for her to compose herself. Bursting into tears in front of the CO was an experience to be avoided and, although the revelation of Mick Fitzgerald's appearance had generated deep-seated emotions now simmering beneath the surface, those few, vital minutes walking to the Colonel's office had been enough.

'I've been tasked with reminding you about your agreement with the MOD, Miss Rodgers,' Bullen added, his grey-blue eyes staring at her over the top of his spectacles.

Ellie looked past him, focussing on a group photograph on the wall. He had to know about the NDA, she thought, the Non-Disclosure Agreement she'd signed as part of her settlement. So much for it being a secret. As painful memories flooded her thoughts, the muscles in her neck grew tight. It was only interrupted when the Colonel coughed.

'Of course,' she answered, as she returned to the here and now. She could feel her body temperature rising. Not now, she said to herself. Not here. 'The NDA, I assume you mean, sir?' she replied.

The Colonel frowned at her. 'If you ever reach this level, Miss Rodgers, you will realise how little goes on within a Regiment without the Commanding Officer knowing of it, provided he … or she, is doing their job, of course.'

Ellie managed a thin smile. 'And what about Fitzgerald?' she asked. 'I was assured our paths would never cross again.'

'I suspect whoever it was made that promise to you had little understanding of the improbability of it being achieved.'

'It was a Brigadier from Whitehall,' Ellie replied, bluntly.

Bullen raised an eyebrow but didn't respond. Ellie understood why. She'd been misled, that was clear. The reality was, so long as both she and her assailant remained in the Army, there was a possibility their paths would one-day cross. 'Will he be re-posted, sir?' she asked, rather more politely.

'That will be for the CO of the Training Regiment to decide.'

Ellie tugged at the collar of her shirt. A trickle of sweat ran slowly down her spine. It was those early signs her counsellor had warned her about. Slow your breathing, she recalled the woman telling her, and try to relax. Quell the panic attack or outburst of temper, control the symptoms before it happens.

Bullen appeared to sense the anxiety their conversation had created. 'I'm confident matters can be brought to a satisfactory conclusion,' he said, hurriedly. 'I've tasked Mister Holt, our Regimental Sergeant-Major, to act as liaison on this. He has arranged an appointment with the Training Regiment Adjutant to allow you to state your case regarding Fitzgerald.'

'With respect, sir,' Ellie said. 'I shouldn't need to *state* my case.'

The Colonel breathed deeply, leaned back in his chair and removed his reading glasses. 'I do understand, Rodgers, I really do,' he said. 'But there are protocols that must be adhered to. Go and see their Adjutant. I can't order one of their men be re-deployed. They can.'

'Does Mister Holt know everything?' Ellie asked.

'Not in detail, no. But he's been fully apprised on what happened and about the existence of the NDA. When I spoke to him a few minutes ago, it was clear he'd heard about the incident but wasn't aware you were the victim. I can't think of a better man to be at your side, frankly.'

The incident, Ellie thought. Is that what people like Bullen thought of the attack on her? A man rapes a fellow soldier, he lies at his court martial, the all-male jury swallow his shit story and he walks away a free man; and that is described as a bloody 'incident'.

As she re-focussed, she realised the Colonel was staring at her. He seemed transfixed, but not on her face or neck this time; he was looking at her stomach area. She glanced down and saw what had distracted him. Resting in her lap, her fists were clenched, the knuckles of both hands white and bloodless. She hadn't noticed and now found herself embarrassed, aware her struggle for self-control was showing.

The meeting ended uncomfortably and rather abruptly as Bullen stood, muttered something about needing to press on with another matter and then strode purposefully towards the door. Politely, he held the door for her but, as he went to place a reassuring hand on her shoulder she saw him hold back. As they made eye contact momentarily, he looked away as if uncertain of himself. It was all Ellie could do to mutter a thank-you.

***

Ellie headed straight to the HQ ladies toilet. She needed some privacy, a few minutes to cool down, to recover, and to think. Only once the door to the tiny room was safely secured and she had sat down on the toilet lid did she allow herself to react. She kicked the door in frustration. How dare they ask her to state her case, she fumed? The NDA was supposed to have been her protection, a fail-safe mechanism to prevent further harm, not something she had to bring up whenever the Army failed to deliver on its promise.

Everything had seemed so straightforward at the time. In the immediate aftermath of the trial, with Fitzgerald's family and mates all whooping it up in celebration, a Major who'd led the SIB investigation thrust a business card into her hand. It was the contact details for a firm of solicitors in the City. 'Call them,' he'd said, before walking off and allowing her to handle the shock of the result on her own. Ellie had followed the advice, and her phone call had been expected. At first, she'd been hesitant – the prospect of facing her assailant in a second, civil trial didn't exactly enthuse her – but time, and a growing sense of injustice, had played its part.

At Sandhurst – the Military Academy that trained all officers – the course staff had either bent over backwards to provide support or had treated her as some kind of pariah. The Army was a small world and word travelled fast. Everyone knew the story of the scouse RMP Corporal who'd cried 'rape' and was now suing the MOD. Two versions did the rounds; one where she had been ambushed in her quarters by a predatory NCO, the other where she'd supposedly allowed an innocent fellow soldier into her room and then claimed assault when it looked likely to affect her Commission. It had been that latter version – the one Fitzgerald's defence team had pursued – the Court Martial board had believed.

Not long into the course, after a small altercation with a fellow officer-cadet, Ellie had been approached by another Major, this time a woman, who was Head of the Academy Education Department. She'd told Ellie about the Sisterhood, a group of servicewomen who were also victims. Ellie had realised then, for the first time since the day of the attack, she wasn't alone. There were many others in the same situation as her. As she got to know them, she discovered their unswerving and unified advice. 'Take them to court and, no matter how hard they fight, don't back down.'

Exchanges of documents, letters and reports had begun in earnest as soon as the 'notification of intended legal action', was filed by her lawyer. Solicitors for the Ministry of Defence, well-versed in defending such claims, placed every conceivable obstruction in her way. Veiled threats of a ruined career, unpleasant postings and other reasons to drop the case were brought to her attention through both official and unofficial channels. Friendly chats with the Academy Adjutant where her 'best interests were paramount' were supplemented by frequent appointments with both the Padre and Welfare Officer. No stone was left unturned in the campaign to persuade her to give up. Her lawyer was supportive though, assuring her that with the burden of proof lower in a civil trial, the case against her attacker would be more straightforward. Where individual accounts conflicted, juries found it easier to order an employer to pay compensation than to convict a man and send him to prison.

And then, quite out of the blue, the MOD stance changed completely. They wrote to Ellie's lawyer with a conditional offer of settlement. Ellie nearly fainted when she read the eye-watering amount. It was more than enough to change a normal person's life. No mortgage, no debt worries. Just sign an NDA where she agreed to never disclose anything about the case to anyone or to allow the detail of the agreement to be made public. There was a sting in the tail, though. She had to agree if she ever breached the terms it would mean paying back the entire settlement, plus additional costs.

By the time of the Sovereign's Parade – the day she was commissioned as an officer – she still hadn't fully made up her mind whether to accept the NDA. But, as the Chief of the General Staff addressed over two hundred of her fellow cadets, he'd talked of pride and family loyalty. She'd allowed her thoughts to wander back to Liverpool, to her childhood and to the street of terraced council houses she still thought of as home. The settlement would mean she could buy her mother and step-father's home for them, clear her debts and theirs, and still have more than enough for a place of her own. In that moment, as she listened to the General's words, she'd looked across to her beaming family standing proudly in the audience, and made her decision. She would sign.

And, until this moment, she'd never regretted it. The Sisterhood had continued to provide support and, through them, she'd met others who had accepted similar settlements. They make it a large amount, her fellow recipients explained, to seriously focus your thoughts should you ever be tempted to speak out in the future. To the best of her knowledge, no-one had ever succumbed.

When Ellie finally emerged from the HQ building, she found Mr Holt waiting for her outside. The Regimental Sergeant-Major had his back to the door, his feet at a classic ten-to-two stance. A closed pace-stick nestled in his hand, the polished brass points resting on the path next to his right boot. She could see the outline of his muscular frame where the thin material of his shirt clung tight to his torso. As she closed the door behind her, he turned around.

'When you're ready, ma'am,' he said, warmly. 'If you'd follow me?'

Chapter 45

Twenty minutes later, Ellie was sat with her RSM in the reception area to the Training Regiment HQ, waiting to be seen by yet another senior officer. The day wasn't panning out quite the way she'd hoped, her intention having been to visit the Training Depot that day but only to find out as much she could about the after-shave buyer, Private Jodie Baker. Convincing their Adjutant to re-deploy one of his NCOs hadn't figured in her plans.

An oak door to the offices swung open. As quickly as she could, Ellie stood to attention, eyes forward, hands clasped to her sides. Sergeant-Major Holt smoothly matched her timing. Inwardly, she smiled to herself. At least I look the part, she mused, even if I don't feel it.

'Enter.' The instruction came from a Staff Sergeant who stood to one side as she and Mr Holt marched smartly into a small office. She stood to attention in front of the Adjutant's desk and, having waited for her RSM to draw up alongside, threw up her best salute. 'Second Lieutenant Rodgers, sir,' she announced.

The door closed behind them as Captain Pemberton leaned back in his chair. 'At ease, Rodgers,' he said, warmly. 'As you probably know, I'm Giles Pemberton. Now … please sit down and relax, both of you. We're all friends inside these four walls and I'm aware why you're here. I hope we'll be able to speak frankly.'

Sergeant-Major Holt lifted a small, wooden chair from the side of the room and handed it to her. He nodded, and she thought she caught a tiny wink from his right eye. Relax, he seemed to be saying. We're here to help you.

Just as Colonel Bullen had been, Pemberton appeared sympathetic yet uncomfortable. He made no mention of knowing about the NDA but quickly deduced the request to move Fitzgerald had a sexual angle. Several times though, he hummed and hawed as he probed for a fuller explanation. Ellie began to wonder if he was also wary of her. Eventually, and unexpectedly, he revealed he had also spoken to Mick Fitzgerald.

For a moment, Ellie closed her eyes in despair. 'He knows about this meeting?' she said, despondently.

'Fairness is only achieved by knowing both sides of the story, Miss Rodgers,' Pemberton said with a thin smile. 'He already knew you were based here.'

'Are you saying he engineered this move?'

'I have no idea. But, he tells me the allegations were dealt with and he was simply disciplined for being in female quarters. He thinks it's time to move on.'

Ellie felt a surge of anger. She bit her cheek, breathing in deep gulps as she fought to control it. To her right, she sensed rather than saw the RSM moving in his chair. She turned her head slightly to him and their eyes met. Say something Mr Holt, she urged, silently.

Holt had been quiet up to that point. The reason for his presence – to provide support, to act as her chaperone and to report back on the outcome to their CO – was obvious. What he hadn't chosen to do until now was to contribute to a conversation between two officers. 'Permission to speak, sir,' he said, politely.

Ellie breathed a sigh of relief as, out of the corner of her eye, she saw the Adjutant nod. She turned back to face him and, as she did so, caught his gaze move rapidly upwards towards her face. For an uncomfortable moment, she had the impression he'd been staring at her chest.

'We're talking serious allegations that went to trial, sir,' Holt continued.

'And which resulted in an acquittal, I believe?' Pemberton replied.

Ellie went to interrupt but her Sergeant-Major hadn't finished. 'The MOD subsequently saw fit to promise that neither party would ever be deployed to the same base,' he said, politely, but firmly.

Pemberton hesitated for a moment, as if processing the RSM's words. His gaze flicked between the two of them. Ellie wondered if the penny had dropped. 'A promise you say?' he replied, his words slow and deliberate.

The penny *had* dropped, Ellie thought. At last, we're getting somewhere.

Holt nodded. 'From the Chief of the General Staff, sir.'

'And you want me to enforce this promise, I presume?'

'With respect, sir, someone messed up. Someone within your staff failed to run a full check on Sergeant Fitzgerald before processing his move. For all our sakes, it would be easier if he could be spirited away.'

'He'll know why, of course?'

'Do we really care what he thinks, sir?'

'No, I suppose not.' Pemberton breathed deeply and turned to face Ellie. 'Could you leave us for a few moments, Mister Holt?' he said, in a resigned tone.

'My orders are to accompany Miss Rodgers, sir,' the RSM replied.

Ellie saw another opportunity to speak but, even as she opened her mouth, the Adjutant cut across her. 'My order, Regimental Sergeant-Major, is that you will remain outside for a few moments while Second-Lieutenant Rodgers and I discuss an unrelated and confidential matter.'

Holt was too experienced a soldier to believe there was any further point in continuing. He stood, saluted and marched quickly out through the door, closing it gently behind him. Ellie watched him go. An unrelated and confidential matter, Pemberton had said. That could only mean one thing. She'd been recognised.

Chapter 46

As Ellie turned back to Pemberton once more, his gaze again moved upwards away from her chest.

There was no mistaking the familiar move. Experience had taught her what to look for. A lot of the men did it. The understated glance or the longer stare when it appeared the object of their attention was distracted. Most were subtle, others less so. A few, she'd caught staring at her quite overtly and on one occasion just recently, as she'd been checking beneath a bed for cleanliness, the occupant had stepped quietly forward and pretended to spank her. Although she saw what had happened in a mirror, she'd ignored him. Afterwards, having failed the soldier on his room inspection, she'd had her revenge by ordering his Corporal to beast the cheeky bastard around the parade square for the next two hours. She'd stayed on the square for the whole time to make it clear to all and sundry what the punishment was really for.

'Ellie,' Pemberton said, quite slowly. 'You'd very much like to see the back of Sergeant Fitzgerald, I assume?'

He'd used her first name. Why had he switched? For the second time that morning, Ellie felt her neck and back muscles tightening. 'I would, yes,' she replied, tight-lipped, as she glared back at him across the desk.

'I have the power to make that happen, as I'm sure you know,' he continued.

'And I'd be most grateful, sir, if you'd do that.'

Pemberton pushed his feet towards her beneath the desk before leaning back in his chair and staring hard into her eyes. 'I'd need something from you,' he said, his lips curling into the faintest of smiles.

'I'm not sure I understand what you're saying, sir,' Ellie replied. The feeling of discomfort wasn't easing and, for a fleeting moment, she

237

felt quite angry with herself. Had he been staring at her or not? What was he playing at?

Pemberton held her gaze as his smile broadened, but it wasn't a look of warmth or friendliness. His face had taken on a lustful, predatory appearance. He seemed to be playing with her, like a cat tormenting its prey. 'Do I have to spell it out?' he said, one eyebrow raised, as if the answer to his question should have been obvious.

Ellie felt her jawline harden and, without thinking, she snapped a response. 'Perhaps you should, so we're quite clear where we stand?'

The Adjutant inhaled deeply. 'I'm a man, Ellie,' he said. 'You're an attractive woman. I have a marriage that doesn't meet my needs. I think an arrangement between the two of us could be mutually beneficial in many ways …'

'You want to fuck me?' Ellie replied, angrily.

Pemberton stalled for a moment, seemingly taken aback by her forthright response. 'If you want to put it in such coarse terms …'

'You cheeky fuckin' nob,' she said, before he could finish. 'You're saying you'll move Fitzgerald, but only if you get to sleep with me?'

'A quid-pro-quo arrangement, Ellie,' he replied, with surprising composure. 'You get what you want, I get what I need. And afterwards, I would naturally remain in your debt.'

Her fists clenched tighter than the lid on an ancient pickle jar and with every bone in her body crying out to grab the bastard sat smugly in front of her by the throat, Ellie held back. There was no hiding her anger, though. Unless Pemberton authorised an immediate re-deployment, Mick Fitzgerald would remain at the camp. The bastard was banking on her fear of the Sergeant being enough to persuade her.

But he didn't know her. Ellie stood up, stepped forward until she was hard against the Adjutant's desk and then leaned across into his face. 'You … can fuck off … *sir*,' she said, her emphasis on the small three-letter word at the end of her answer giving her a sense of intense empowerment. So close were their faces, tiny flecks of her spit landing on Pemberton's face.

He shrank away. 'You're dismissed, Rodgers,' he said, angrily. 'And take that fucking pace-stick with you.'

Ellie turned to see where Sergeant-Major Holt had left his stick resting against the chair he'd been sitting on. She picked it up, controlled an immediate urge to smack Pemberton around the head with it, and then stormed out of the room without uttering another word.

Chapter 47

Ellie slammed the exit door to find Mister Holt waiting outside, a concerned look on his face. As she handed him the pace stick, he asked what had happened. She didn't reply. There seemed little point. There was nothing he would be able to do to help. She strode on in silence as she dreamed up all manner of unpleasant fates for Giles Pemberton. Holt marched beside her, fiddling with the pace stick as they walked. He seemed to be having trouble with the mechanism. As they reached a quiet spot adjacent to a small copse and about two hundred metres away from the nearest buildings, he held out an arm to stop her. 'Want to tell me what actually went on?' he asked, his tone now almost fatherly.

'Not really,' she replied.

'Is he going to re-deploy Fitzgerald?'

'Not exactly. Well … I don't know … I'm not sure.'

The RSM smiled, knowingly. 'He made a pass at you, didn't he?'

She stood back, confused. 'How did you know?' she asked.

'Colonel Bullen sent me with you because he feared something like that might happen. Did he give you his little speech about not much happening in the Regiment without him knowing?'

'He did, yes.'

'It's one of his standards. Thing is, it's true, and not just within his own Regiment. Bullen keeps his eyes and ears open with very good reason. He knew about Pemberton's reputation. The Army doesn't just send problem NCOs to the Training Regiment; they post their challenging officers here as well. They have this back-to-front reasoning that soldiers unfit to serve in front-line Regiments can be gainfully employed teaching new recruits.'

'He told me his wife didn't understand him.'

Holt laughed. 'That's an old one. The boss wanted me with you to make sure nothing like that happened.'

'He was clever enough to send you out, so the Colonel's little plan didn't work, did it? You know I nearly hit him ... I came that close.'

The RSM looked at her reassuringly. 'The Colonel gave me this ... just in case,' he said. Lifting the pace stick to head height, he pushed on what appeared to be a thin, brass name-plate at the top near the hinge. It moved, and from within he pulled a metallic object. It was about two inches long, with a small screen.

Ellie looked at the device he now held out for her to see. It was a digital recorder. Her jaw dropped. 'You bugged our conversation?' she said.

'Does that bother you?'

'I think I'd have preferred to know.'

Holt paused for a moment as he checked their immediate vicinity. Apparently satisfied they wouldn't be overheard, he pressed a small button on the front of the recorder. As Ellie leaned in closer to listen, the first thing she heard was her own voice, the conversation where she'd marched in and introduced herself. Then Pemberton could be heard quite clearly. She and the Sergeant-Major listened for a few minutes until, at the point where Holt left the Adjutant's office, she held up her hand. 'Could you stop it, please?' she asked. 'It's already starting to make me feel a little sick.'

Holt paused the play-back. 'Colonel Bullen is a good commanding officer, ma'am. He has his faults but he places the welfare of soldiers very high on his priorities. He'll deal with this, trust me.'

'Will he actually use that recording?'

'You're family, ma'am, one of his,' said the RSM. 'To keep you out of it we'll explain to Colonel Hine at the Training Regiment it was made by me without your knowledge. Hine won't like it but there'll be bugger all he can do about it. To avoid any unpleasantness, he'll no doubt order Fitzgerald be re-deployed. He'll probably do the same with Pemberton.'

'That'll take ages.'

'With the right incentive, they could both be on a plane in a day or so. I suggest you keep a low profile until we're certain Fitzgerald has gone.'

'That makes sense,' Ellie said. 'But what about you? Won't you be in hot water for making that recording?'

'I don't think Colonel Bullen will make a fuss, given the circumstances. I heard what happened to you in Germany and if you were to label all of us blokes as over-sexed, predatory rapists-in-waiting, I'd understand. Please try to appreciate, the Army has bad apples but most of us are ok. People like Fitzgerald and Pemberton are a rarity.'

'And we don't want this camp turning into another Deepcut do we?' Ellie said, quoting Colonel Bullen's words from their earlier meeting.

'We don't … and it won't,' said Holt. 'And the sooner the Press stop thinking we're heading that way, the sooner we'll be able to get on with our lives.' The RSM slipped the recorder into his jacket pocket and then smiled warmly at her. 'Shall we go and see Colonel Bullen, ma'am?'

Ellie returned the smile and, as she did so, she realised that in the few minutes they'd been talking her body temperature had normalised, her heart rate had slowed and she no longer felt a burning desire to thump someone. 'Yes, Mister Holt,' she replied. 'Let's do that.'

Chapter 48

When Floria suggested we break off to eat in town again, I expressed reservations. I wanted to press on and had a call booked with Bill in London to discuss how best to react to the note left on Wendy's car. With time limited, we compromised on a take-away lunch, courtesy of the NAAFI canteen.

The files on the four recruits remaining at the base were thin, consistent with soldiers at the beginning of their career. Each contained a small head-and-shoulders photograph together with a selection of paperwork including medical records, some written and physical test results, and their progress reports from Basic Course and Training Regiment. I was reading one of the files at the same time as tucking enthusiastically into my all-day breakfast sandwich when Floria appeared from the main office, two additional files in her hand. 'The AWOL paperwork you requested from Brecon,' she said, dropping them on the desk next to my tea.

'Thanks,' I said. I left the new files where they were in the hope I'd soon get a few minutes alone to photograph the contents in the way Wendy had requested. Floria pulled a handful of crisps from her packet, crushed them between her finger and thumb and then sprinkled them into her sandwich. There was a satisfying crunch as she bit into it.

I flicked open the nearest file. 'Can I ask you about this?' I said. I'd noticed all bore a five-digit number on the front cover. The first was for a soldier named Briscoe, Naomi P. It was numbered 194/11. I asked Floria what the numbering referred to.

'It's the intake number followed by their Crow number,' she replied before taking a gulp from her drink and, with the back of her hand, wiping away the damp crumbs that remained on her lips. 'Briscoe is intake 194, recruit number eleven.'

I thumbed through the pages. 'Says here she's been knocked back from driving courses twice for minor disciplinary infringements,' I said.

'Funny how it's mostly the good-looking girls that seems to happen to,' Floria said, cynically.

'You think the NCOs hold them back deliberately?'

'I know they do. I'm not saying it doesn't happen to the boys but, if it does, it's handled different.'

'In what way?'

'If one of the staff decides a male recruit isn't good enough, they simply keep delaying his courses until he gives up and quits. I know Briscoe, by the way.'

'You've had dealings with her?'

'I make a point of speaking to the black recruits so they know they got someone to talk to if an NCO starts giving them any racist shit.'

'Have they?' I asked.

Floria shook her head. 'They seem to like her.'

I flicked through the second file, numbered 194/44. The picture was of another pretty girl, blonde this time. I'd recognised her during my earlier look through. 'The girl from the Armoury,' I said.

'Jodie Baker. I thought that would interest you. All four are from the same intake and should have transferred to their new Regiments months ago.'

'The same intake as Angela Davenport. Do you have *her* file available?'

'It's next door in the CO's filing cabinet, under lock and key,' said Floria, with a nod toward the door.

'Do you think we'd be permitted to see it?' My thigh muscle twitched, almost as if it was reacting to the presence of Angela Davenport's phone sitting deep in my jacket pocket.

Floria pulled the files on the desk towards her, stacked them neatly and rested her hands on top. 'If you had a good reason … but I thought you weren't interested in the Davenport case?'

I winked at her and scowled. 'We'll see. And that reminds me, how far did you get with the issuing registers from the Armoury?'

'Not very far. Why do you ask?'

'I was wondering if the register might have shown her returning her rifle?' I asked, recalling what Michael Davenport claimed his daughter had said.

Floria paused for several moments, as if running the implications through her mind. 'Are you suggesting it might not have been her rifle stolen from the lorry?'

'Think about it … what if the rifles weren't actually stolen from the lorry? Maybe someone told her to say that's what happened. Perhaps she was being threatened? What if the rifles went from the Armoury itself … after they'd been booked in?'

'I don't understand. The rifles were driven back to the Armoury by one of the Sergeants. He handed them to Masters who noticed two were missing and reported it immediately.'

'I'm trying to work out why someone stole the register. Do you remember the name of the Sergeant who drove the lorry?' I asked.

'Yes, it was Paul Slater. If you recall, I told you he also corroborated Davenport's claim she put her rifle on the lorry.'

'He was the NCO her father mentioned as well. Do you know anything about him?'

'He's a bit of a chameleon. Some of the recruits hate him, others think he's wonderful … anyway, thinking it through, why would

Davenport admit in her statement it was her rifle that was stolen if it wasn't?'

Floria had stopped what she'd been doing, looking to me for an answer. As I ran my hand over my pocket and felt the outline of Angela Davenport's phone, I could almost hear the cogs whirring in her brain. I knew I'd reached a point where I was going to have to decide whether I trusted her or not. Once again, I thought back to the undertaking I'd given Michael Davenport and the fact I'd already stretched that promise by talking to Jenny and Wendy about the recording. 'Because someone had something on her and made her do it,' I said.

'Like what?' she asked.

Now or never, I thought, although I hesitated.

'Like what?' Floria said again.

I pulled the phone from my pocket. 'Let's step outside,' I said, as I pressed the power button. 'I think I need to show you something.'

Chapter 49

Floria swayed awkwardly on her feet and, for a moment, I thought she was about to be sick. 'Where the fuck did you get that from?' she said, her voice shaking.

I explained. She swallowed before puffing out her cheeks. 'Why didn't you call me to go with you?' she asked.

'He asked me to come alone,' I said. 'He wanted to talk as one father to another.'

'I can see why,' she replied. 'Do you think that phone is what they were after during the second search?'

'I'd put money on it,' I said. 'You saw the texts. The sender was threatening her. They were trying to make sure this didn't fall into someone else's hands.'

'So, you think whoever sent that wanted to make sure she stuck to a story about the rifle thefts?'

'It's a theory that seems to fit.'

'I've heard the rumours, you know, we all have. NCOs shagging recruits ... girls doing extras to get through their tests. But a recruit involved in stealing rifles? That I struggle with.'

'What kind of extras do you mean?' I said.

'How many kinds are there? I interviewed one girl after she was seen leaving an NCO's married quarter. It turned out she'd been to see him after a friend of hers failed her basic fitness test. He offered to fix the result if she would sleep with him.'

'Did she?'

'Yes, but she wouldn't make a statement. Her friend never found out what she did for her.'

'Back in my world, that would be rape.'

247

'You think I don't know what constitutes consent, Finlay? We study the same law as you do, you know?'

'You realise Davenport might also have been coerced into doing that video?'

'I'm not fuckin' stupid, sir. I was just saying I find it hard to believe a recruit would be part of a plot to steal rifles.' Floria's voice shot up several notches in both pitch and volume. Immediately, a window from the nearby building opened followed by a male voice enquiring if we were ok. Floria raised a hand apologetically, and the window closed. 'Sorry,' she continued, less angrily. 'I do realise that, yes.'

'I promised Angela Davenport's father I wouldn't let this video go public. We agreed I should only use it to establish what's been going on.'

'You want to see Davenport's file to try and work out who they are, I assume?'

'I've a mate tracing the phone used to send it,' I said. 'I'm hoping her file might help create a short-list.'

Floria nibbled at her bottom lip as she stood thinking. Finally, she seemed to make up her mind. 'You realise what will happen if I draw that file?'

'What?'

'If someone tips off the MOD, you and I will be for the high jump.'

'We'll just have to make sure that doesn't happen,' I said.

'So, you don't think it was suicide any more then?'

'Let's just say I've grown closer to your opinion than I was. I apologise ... like many others, I was too quick to assume the suicide verdict was the right one.'

Floria grinned. 'I'm not one to say I told you so, so apology accepted.'

'And there's something else,' I said. 'Something I probably should have told you about earlier.'

'Like what?'

'Last night, someone left a note on the windscreen of Wendy Russell's car. It was a threat aimed at me.'

'Really? Was this while you were asleep?'

'Just before we turned in.'

'What did it say?'

'To back off or my family would be at risk.'

'Nasty.' Floria's top lip turned up as she scowled.

'It's personal for me now, Floria,' I said. 'Nobody should get away with threatening a man's family.'

'Ok ... ok' she replied. 'You're angry, I can see that and I've heard enough. I'm persuaded. Carpe diem, as they say. I'll get you the Davenport file. If anyone's going to be hung out to dry, it may as well be us.'

***

With the office door closed, I took photographs of the Brecon AWOL files as quickly as I could, all the time listening out for the sound of Floria's return. I'd just finished when the sound of rapidly approaching footsteps in the corridor was followed by a younger, apologetic voice. I heard Floria laughing before what sounded like the body armour I'd seen earlier being moved. I shoved my phone back in my pocket just as the door swung open and Floria's face appeared. 'Got it,' she announced, with a grin.

I was immediately struck by the size of the box file in Floria's arms. It was large, clearly heavy, and as she kicked the door closed behind her and dumped it unceremoniously on the desk in front of me, I realised we were in for a long haul.

'Did you finish with those AWOL files?' she asked.

I nodded. 'Nothing of use, really,' I said. 'Did you notice anything?'

She grinned, a look that told me she was pleased with herself once more. 'I'd bet anything you like they went together.'

'Why's that?'

'Because one of them is Private Debbie Bishop.'

I flicked through the Bishop folder to reveal a picture of a pretty, dark-haired girl with deep brown eyes. I'd been so focussed on photographing the pages, I'd neglected to read them. 'Why does that mean they went together?'

'Bishop is what we call a cee-bee-bee.'

'A cee-bee-bee? Like the TV show?'

'Not really. It stands for Camp Bike Bitch. Basically, she was ...'

'I think I get the idea, Floria,' I said, as I read the file properly, this time noticing the coincidences in the dates and times. Not wishing to reveal the value of what Floria had just said, I shrugged, but no more. In truth, I realised I had just learned where Wendy might find her undercover cop. 'My hunch was no good,' I said. 'Neither Bishop or the male soldier have connections to the girls from Davenport's intake or the day the rifles went missing.'

'No dramas. I'll go get us a brew in a minute,' Floria said, pointing back to the large box file. 'This could take a while.'

Inside the box, a buff folder, similar in appearance to those belonging to the other recruits, sat on top of a thick bundle of papers tied with thin red tape. It was labelled 'Davenport, A C, 194/27'. Crow 27, intake 194, I surmised, as I recalled Floria's earlier explanation. I flicked it open. 'I'm amazed you were able to get this so easily,' I said.

'It's a copy. The original paperwork is with the MOD at Whitehall. It might be best if you keep quiet about this.'

I looked up, and guessed from Floria's 'you know what I mean' expression that she'd gone out on something of a limb. 'Does anyone know we are looking at this?' I asked.

She shook her head, just slightly, but enough to confirm my suspicions.

'How long do we have?'

'The CO is out for the day,' she replied. 'He keeps a spare key to his filing cabinet under a plant pot in his office. So long as we're not seen, we'll be ok for a while.'

'Provided nobody walks in here and catches us you mean?'

'I might have told the lads you'd arrest anyone who came in while we're working.'

'You actually said that?' I said, as we both began laughing.

As Floria then headed off to sort out some tea for us, I scanned through the list of contents to the file. I soon found what I was looking for; the statements taken from witnesses to Angela's death. As I read, I learned the official version of what had happened on the day she died.

I still had my head down when Floria returned. 'Do you worry about your family when you're working away,' she said, as she planted two steaming mugs of tea on the desk next to me.

'No more than anyone else,' I said. 'My wife can look after herself, believe me.'

'Find anything interesting?' she asked, as she pointed at the Davenport file.

'The post-mortem,' I replied. 'The way I understand it, one round killed her having entered through the eyebrow over her left eye.

'Kinda weird, shooting yourself in the eye, don't you think?' Floria replied. 'Like looking into the instrument of your death as you watch it all happen.'

'It's not something I've ever heard of before,' I said. 'It also says there was powder residue on both her hands consistent with having been wrapped around the end of the barrel at some point … and, specifically, her left first-finger had no residue on it. The pathologist's conclusion was she pulled the trigger with her left hand while she held the barrel against her eye with her right.'

'That's correct, yes.'

'Finding less residue on one finger of her left hand could simply mean it was further down the barrel than her right hand at the moment the weapon was fired.'

'Or her right hand was partially wrapped around her left, a bit like a golfing grip?' Floria replied. 'So, both sets of fingers were touching the barrel sufficient to be marked by residue but the deposits on the right hand were greater.'

I scowled. 'Makes you wonder why the scientists didn't explore that idea, doesn't it? People who use a rifle to commit suicide tend to shoot themselves from under the chin, or in the mouth. There's no comment in the file about a wound over the eye being unusual.' I leaned back in my chair. 'Davenport wasn't left-handed, was she?' I added, as I continued reading the post-mortem findings.

'No.'

'And, if you look at an SA80 from the barrel end, the slide mechanism to cock it is on the left?'

'Correct, assuming it's the right way up, of course. If you try and fire it left-handed, the slide mechanism will take lumps out of your face; that's why we all have to learn to be right-handed.'

'Ok,' I said. 'Now bear with me. Sit on the floor, imagine you are Angela Davenport and that you're about to shoot yourself. Hold an imaginary SA80 in front of you, with your right hand wrapped around the barrel.'

Floria sat cross-legged and held her arms up in front of her. As soon as she was in position, I asked her to go through the motion of

252

cocking her imaginary weapon, taking off the safety catch – which she did with her right hand – and then firing it. She moved slowly, deliberately, exaggerating each movement as she did so. I asked her to do it a second time and, at the point of reaching for the safety catch, I stopped her.

'Now use your left hand to release the safety,' I said.

She twisted her hand as she went through the motion. 'I wouldn't be able to reach,' she replied. 'Not in the normal way. I'd have to use the back of my finger or swap hands.'

'I agree,' I said. 'So, if Davenport used her right hand to release the safety, why would she swap to the hand around the barrel before pulling the trigger?'

'Her left hand, you mean?'

'Exactly. Both hands having had contact with the barrel might explain why she had powder residue on them but why swap? She could have simply kept her left hand around the barrel and then used her right hand to release the safety and pull the trigger.'

'But the Post Mortem concluded she had her right hand around the barrel?'

'I don't think she'd have racked the weapon with the barrel facing her,' I said, slowly, as I pictured the scene in my mind's eye. 'It's too difficult and not the way she would have been taught. Better if the weapon were facing away from you then you could rack it in the normal way with your left hand while you use your right to take the safety off.'

'And like you say, why then swap to pull the trigger with your other hand? Why not just keep holding it with your left hand and fire it with your right?'

'And it still doesn't explain why a right-handed person would use their left hand,' I mused as I flicked through the pages to one of the statements. 'Your idea about both hands being on the barrel at the time the weapon was fired makes better sense. But how then did she pull the trigger?'

'Maybe she didn't?' Floria said, raising her eyebrows.

'Perhaps we should talk to some of the witnesses at the scene?' I said, as I realised we were starting to develop a workable alternative theory that might support the notion Davenport hadn't shot herself.

'There's a key statement here from Sergeant Slater,' I added. 'Same bloke whose name came up the day the rifles were stolen. He describes himself here as her lead instructor. He says she was on gate duty … she went missing and while they were searching for her, he heard a shot. That was at about 7.30 in the morning, so he says.'

'He didn't find the body, though,' said Floria. 'That was some recruits on guard duty.'

'Who, presumably, are now posted overseas?'

'Correct, so we won't be talking to them anytime soon. But, to go back to what I said the other day, who kills themselves an hour after they've started their shift? Middle of the night, cold and feeling miserable, maybe? And Davenport was doing well in training. When you get to her progress reports you'll see that.'

Floria was right. As we moved on, I saw that Angela Davenport's reports were indeed good. She wasn't exceptional, but it was clear she wasn't struggling to reach the required standards. I kept reading but it was a huge file and, with time limited, I started to make do with looking for anomalies. I ignored routine and ordinary, and focussed on things that stood out.

'Did you know that, in the UK, men aged between twenty-five and fifty are more likely to die from suicide than any other reason?' I said, as I paused for a moment.

'Including car accidents?' Floria asked.

'And disease. But … and this is interesting, although more men actually die from suicide than women, more women attempt it.'

'So, we women are less good at killing ourselves?'

'Less successful, certainly,' I said. 'Men choose quick, violent methods and seem to care little about the effect on others. Women choose less messy ways like pills, possibly so whoever finds them won't see anything too unpleasant. And because they choose pills, they often get rescued in time.'

'So, Davenport chose what you'd describe as a male method?'

'It's another anomaly,' I said, as I tapped my fingers on the file in front of me before draining the cold dregs of my tea. 'Slater's a clear connection. I reckon we should prioritise speaking to him.'

Floria's eyebrows rose in unison. 'You want me to arrange an interview?' she said.

'Definitely,' I said. 'Remember when we saw Private Morgan's mother? She said Tom had been warned by his lead instructor not to snitch on his NCOs. Slater refers to himself in his statement as Angela Davenport's 'lead instructor', same expression.

'Ok ... but we tread carefully,' Floria replied, holding up a hand. 'You want I should arrange it for later today?'

'Not yet,' I said. 'Let's talk to him tomorrow morning. First we'll have a chat to the remaining girls from Davenport's intake to see what they can tell us about him. I wouldn't mind betting that whatever has been going on at this camp, Sergeant Slater either knows about it or is in it up to his neck.'

***

At Floria's suggestion, I waited outside the front of the RMP building while she returned the box files and personnel records to their rightful homes. Alone, and with time to spare, I sent a short text to Wendy warning her to expect some photographs. It took me a couple of minutes while I remembered her guidance but, as the first one came up 'sent', I soon became more proficient. I then sent another text to her, *Progress. Look at Bishop file. Fl thinks went together.*

255

I'd closed the phone and was about to put it away in my pocket when it started to ring. It was Wendy calling me back. 'That was quick,' she said. 'What progress? And who's Bishop? Is she connected, do you think?'

'I think I can save you some time,' I said, as I stepped further away from the nearby windows. I didn't want anyone to hear what I was about to say.

'Do you know where he is?' Wendy said. 'Is that what the final text meant?'

'I don't know where he is but I think I can point you in the right direction. If you look you'll see that Bishop went missing at the same time as your man. Floria seems to know Bishop and thinks the two of them probably went together.'

'Why does she think that?'

'Because the girl has a bit of a reputation,' I said. 'If she's right, your DC is having a little fun on the job's time while his wife thinks he's still undercover. If he and Bishop used cash they could be hard to locate but you might get lucky if you check her credit cards.'

'If you're right, I'll bloody kill him,' Wendy said, angrily. 'Our efforts have been focussed on the assumption he was either being prevented from contacting us or something unpleasant had happened to him.'

'Hopefully, the truth will prove rather less sinister,' I said. If Wendy could have seen the cynical look on my face, I don't believe it would have surprised her. It wouldn't be the first time an undercover operator had become involved with someone they shouldn't, and I was quite sure it wouldn't be the last.

'I also have some news for you,' Wendy said. 'I spoke to Bill first thing this morning and he's agreed to provide some short-term protection for your family. It's already in hand.'

'I haven't told Jenny yet,' I said. 'I'd best call her now.'

'Yes, best you do. Are you any closer to letting me have that video?'

'I've just been given access to Angela Davenport's file. It's thrown up a suspect, a Sergeant who I think may know more than he said in his statement.'

'What's his name?'

'Paul Slater. Can you see if he's been flagged up before?'

'Are you on to something?' Wendy replied, concern in her voice. 'Slater was one of the witnesses at the inquest. He was one of the first on scene after the recruits found Angela Davenport.'

'I know,' I said. 'What I'd also like to check is if anyone had previously flagged him as a suspect for anything, anything at all.'

Wendy ended the call with a thank-you for the information on her DC and a promise to run some checks for me. It was only as I returned my phone to my jacket pocket that I sensed someone approaching. It was Floria, and she was just a few metres away from me. She must have emerged from a side entrance when I'd been expecting her to use the main door. I wondered how much she'd heard.

Chapter 50

Jodie Baker waited in the darkness and listened. From behind the education block, a huge, glass-walled building about half way between the parade square and her accommodation block, she'd heard a cry. It sounded like someone in pain.

The noise came again. This time it was more of a stifled cry. Someone whimpering.

Quietly, she stepped off the path and onto the wet grass. It was difficult telling how far away the sound came from. At night, when all was quiet on the camp, voices carried surprising distances as they bounced off the building walls. It was easy to become confused. She held back, unsure whether to investigate or to simply mind her own business.

A deep, male voice penetrated the shadows. It sounded aggressive, menacing; an NCO, probably. A good reason not to stick my oar in, she thought. Silence followed, and then another sob. It was close. Perhaps she could call out, let them know they'd been heard. Then she could run away and whoever it was wouldn't even know who'd disturbed them.

The grassy area between the deserted teaching block and store was dark, like wet ink. Jodie crept forward, knowing she was being foolish but unable to stop herself. As her eyes adjusted to the gloom, she began to make out two shapes. One was small and huddled, back against the wall of the store. The second was much larger; a behemoth towering over a smaller, vulnerable figure. She could see the smaller shape was a girl who had one fist wrapped around the nozzle of a rifle, her other hand pushing helplessly against her tormentor as he jammed the barrel hard into her mouth.

'Tell me her name you fuckin' slag,' the man said. A pit formed in Jodie's stomach as she recognised the voice. It was Paul.

'No, please,' panted the girl, her desperate words distorted by the object between her lips.

'Go on then,' Paul hissed. 'Fuckin' do it. Shoot yourself and do us all a favour.'

'Please,' the girl said again, her distress evident as she struggled to speak. She mumbled something Jodie couldn't quite make out before wrenching her face away from the barrel towards where Jodie now stood transfixed. Their eyes locked.

Paul also looked across. He sneered. 'What are you lookin' at, Baker,' he called out, disdainfully, just loud enough for her to hear.

Jodie's legs felt weak as she remained motionless, unable to retreat or to run away. The female soldier said something quietly. Paul let go of the rifle, placed his hand on the girl's face and then viciously squeezed her cheeks. 'You'd better not be lying, Towler,' he said, his victim whimpering again.

As Paul threw her an angry glance, Jodie realised she knew the poor girl. Towler was the recruit who'd been caught sleeping in the room of another female soldier at the 25 Regiment accommodation block. Then, without uttering another word, Paul released his grip, turned quickly and strode away into a small copse behind the buildings where he disappeared out of sight. She turned to speak to Towler but she was also gone, her escape route hidden in the shadows cast by the buildings. There had been no departing 'thank-you', no expression of appreciation, nothing.

'Ungrateful bitch,' Jodie spat.

**

Jodie waited quietly in the shadows opposite the main entrance to Rowallan Block. She prayed Paul wouldn't be waiting for her. As she watched through the windows, she could see girls working on their kit, ironing, polishing boots and preparing their lockers ready for the morning inspection. Many were wandering around wearing nothing more than their underwear, all well aware they could be seen from outside. Occasionally, lads had been caught watching them. Not tonight, though. Everything looked as it should, with no sign of Paul or any other NCO doing one of their so-called inspection visits. It looked safe. With a nervous sigh, Jodie headed inside.

Opening the door to her shared room, she found the overhead light off, the only illumination coming from a small lamp one of the girls used to read by. As she stepped through the doorway she saw Naomi. Her friend had been waiting behind the door. Naomi grabbed the handle, before looking furtively up and down the corridor. 'Did you see him?' she hissed as she closed the door.

'See who?' Jodie said, nervously, half-expecting she knew the answer.

'Your fuckin' boyfriend, that's who. He's just been here with a message for you.'

Jodie felt the pit in her stomach form again. 'What did he want?' she asked.

'To speak to you, of course,' Naomi continued. 'He guessed you might not be here so he left a message … he said if you want to go to Leconfield, you're not to tell anyone. He said you'd know what he meant.'

'He was picking on Towler,' Jodie began. 'Did he …'

'He gave us a job too,' Naomi said. 'He says it's important, a real favour and, if we do it, we'll get posted to whatever Regiment we want as soon as we want it.'

Jodie frowned. 'He said that?' she replied.

'Don't you wanna know what the job is?' Naomi seemed perplexed by Jodie's low-key reaction. Finding a way to get posted from the camp was a dream, something the two girls had discussed many, many times.

'Ok, what is it?' Jodie asked.

'There's a lass over at 25 Reg'. He wants us to get her to deliver a message.'

25 Regiment, Jodie thought. The same place Towler had been caught sleeping over. It was too much of a coincidence. Perhaps Paul had got what he wanted from the girl after all. 'It that it?' she asked 'Just ask a girl to deliver a message and we get our postings? What's the catch?'

Naomi shook her head. 'Let's face it, Jo. They're bored with us now. They want the girls in the new intake. It suits them to have us do one last favour before they move us on.'

Jodie shrugged. 'So, what's the message, and who do we give it to?'

It's a Scots girl called Orr. She's dead friendly with a woman officer, apparently. They want her to pass the officer a message to come see us.'

Something didn't add up, Jodie thought. 'Why on earth would a 25 Regiment officer come here to see us?' she demanded. 'That's crazy.'

'Don't ask me,' said Naomi. 'I'm only telling you what Slater said. Obviously, he wants this officer to come and see him and, for some reason, he needs us to make it happen.'

'When is this meeting supposed to happen?'

'Tomorrow night.'

'Tomorrow night?' Jodie exclaimed. 'How the hell do we do that?'

'We'll have to think of something. As it's a woman officer, maybe we could tell her it's a welfare matter we can't discuss with our NCOs? That might work.'

'I could ask her to come to the Armoury,' Jodie said, stalling as she attempted to think things through. Naomi could be right; Paul and his mates might have tired of them. But she didn't trust Paul, and didn't imagine doing him a simple favour was going to undo what had happened. 'She might be more comfortable with that?' she added.

'But Slater wants her to come here,' Naomi persisted.

'Officers from outside never come here. We might have to come up with a better story.'

'How about we start with getting her to the Armoury,' Naomi said, excitedly. 'You can tell her a bit about the NCOs. Tell her what they get up to. She's bound to have heard the rumours, anyway. Then tell her there's another girl she can speak to here.'

'What other girl?'

'Me, you idiot.'

'And in return for doing this little favour, we get our postings?' Jodie shrugged. She didn't like it when her friend called her names. She wasn't as bright as Naomi or as attractive, but she wasn't an idiot, even though sometimes she did stupid things. 'It all sounds too good to be true,' she continued. 'But it doesn't give us much time to find Orr and persuade her to talk to this officer.'

'But we'll try won't we?' Naomi said, more urgently. 'You of all people must want away from here, surely?'

Jodie still felt unsure. Paul was never one to be trusted especially after what had happened to Davenport. She had nothing to lose, though. How could things get any worse than they already were? If there was a chance, they had to take it. All they had to do was deliver a simple message. What could be the harm in that? 'Ok, I'm in,' she said, finally. 'What's this officer's name?'

Naomi reached over to her bed and retrieved a small post-it note that had been resting on her duvet cover. 'Rodgers,' she read. 'Second Lieutenant Ellie Rodgers.'

Chapter 51

Before heading into the Mess for breakfast, Ellie gave herself a quick once-over in the ante-room mirror. She looked good, and the scratches on her neck were fading nicely. Her eyes were bright, something that particularly pleased her considering the tiny amount of sleep she'd had following the Regimental Dinner.

Ten such dinners took place each year and the CO expected every officer to be present. The President of the Mess Committee, Major Danvers, had organised an excellent event, with several local dignitaries present as guests. A series of toasts set the tone for the evening, the first being proposed by the Major when he stood and raised his glass to the longevity of the Queen, as Colonel-in-Chief to the Regiment. Normally, the newest junior officer present was then expected to respond by drinking a ghastly concoction created by the mess stewards. Having previously been through that initiation, Ellie was excused so, with no new officers due to arrive from Sandhurst for several months, they'd had to forego a traditional – if frequently messy – part of the evening. Only once the meal concluded and all dignitaries had departed, had the hard drinking really begun. And after that, with furniture safely cleared to one side, the games had also started. 'Boys will be boys' was something Ellie often heard quoted in the Mess as, with each bottle of champagne that popped, the behaviour of all present became more and more raucous.

Colonel Bullen had taken her to one side during a quieter moment while many of the officers were outside. They were cheering on two of the longer-serving members who were sprinting around the building in an attempt to settle a wager as to which of them was the most intoxicated. Bullen had been discreet and reassuring, advising her 'things had been taken care of' and there was no longer any cause for her to be concerned about Pemberton or the Sergeant. He'd also complimented her on her choice of an evening dress with matching scarf to hide her neck injury.

Ellie had been about to ask whether the two men had already left camp when an Orderly entered the mess to announce the arrival of the Colonel's car. At the same time, two of her fellow subalterns drunkenly proclaimed her 'election' as temporary President of the 'Subbies' Court'. Realising clarification on what Bullen had said would have to wait, she had joined her colleagues. The 'Subbies' Court' was an informal hearing where humorous 'charges' were laid by Subalterns – 2nd Lieutenants – against their senior officers in an attempt to bankroll the junior officers' champagne. Ellie threw herself into the role with great vigour. On her instructions, two Lieutenants were 'fined' for what the subalterns alleged to be '*over-zealous application of accurate parade times*' and a Captain – who had the temerity to plead not-guilty to a charge of '*conducting Company Officer Group meetings late on a Friday, thereby preventing his junior officers from fully exploiting the benefits of Mess Happy Hour*' – allowed Ellie to please her fellow junior officers by quadrupling his punishment. Sufficient funds had been generated to facilitate a very late finish.

There was just enough time for breakfast before morning parade. Ellie smiled at her reflection. Her tunic was neatly pressed, creases sharp, collar-dogs gleaming and Corps lanyard neatly in place. On her shoulders, the single pips of a Second Lieutenant were clean and polished. Her long skirt, flesh-coloured tights and beetle-crusher shoes were also immaculate. She was especially proud of the shoes; an hour spent bulling them the previous day had produced a shine even Sergeant-Major Holt would have been impressed with. She looked good, and a lot better than the image she'd seen in the NAAFI mirror a couple of days previously.

The high ceilings of the mess caused the rap of her heels on the wooden floor to echo as she walked briskly through to the dining room. Any evidence of the previous evening's activities had been spirited away by the stewards, to be replaced by a scrubbed floor, the aroma of hot food and the scent of freshly polished beeswax. The huge centre-piece dining table, now cleared of Regimental silverware, was gleaming. At one end, steel trays of sausages, bacon, scrambled egg and all the other requisites of a military hang-over cure, lay waiting; hot and ready to be consumed.

The room was quiet, with only one of the small tables laid out and occupied. Ian Wright, a Captain from her Regiment HQ Company was tucking in accompanied by one of his subordinates, a Lieutenant Ellie remembered was called Peter. His surname escaped her.

Her intention had been to eat alone but, as she headed toward the far side of the dining area, Ian beckoned her over. 'Join us, Miss Rodgers,' he called.

Ellie noticed a discreet nod of heads between the two men as she placed her breakfast plate on the table. Both had finished eating and had put their plates to one side ready for collection by a steward.

'Good effort with the Subbie's court last night,' Peter said, as he downed the last of his tea and then slid his chair away from the table. 'Duty calls, I'm afraid … hope to see you later.'

With only the two of them now present, Ian Wright made easy – if a little one-sided – conversation about the mess dinner as Ellie ate her breakfast. Once finished, she placed her knife and fork carefully on the empty plate in the '11 o'clock to 5 o'clock' position she'd been taught at Sandhurst. Ian politely asked if she'd like her tea topped up. Ellie nodded, and smiled to herself. On her last visit home, when she'd placed her cutlery so precisely, her mother had laughed out loud at her daughter's new-found standards of etiquette.

'You handled your first Court well, if you don't mind me saying,' Ian said, as a steward took Ellie's plate. 'The junior officers can be a raucous bunch.'

'I've had some things on my mind lately,' she replied. 'It was a timely distraction.'

'Yes … I've heard. I confess I asked Peter Donovan to leave to allow an opportunity for me to say something.'

Ellie bit her lip and paused for a moment. 'What might that be?' she said, cautiously. Ian Wright was HQ Company, closest of all to the rumour mill and, even though the Army was a small world, she was irritated to think word could have spread so quickly.

Ian breathed in. 'I'd just like to reassure you we're not all like Giles Pemberton,' he said.

'Probably just as well,' Ellie quipped. 'I'd be up on an assault charge in no time.'

If Ian understood her need to make light of the situation, he didn't show it. Neither did he laugh. 'The Army has some archaic attitudes to overcome,' he continued, with a straight face. 'We may not see it in our time but dinosaurs like Pemberton will be a thing of the past one day.'

'Colonel Bullen surprised me.'

'He's top drawer, Ellie, mark my words. You work hard for the boss and he'll have your back.'

'So I'm learning. Have you heard if anything's going to happen to Pemberton?'

'Already done, so I here. A quickly arranged deployment to Iraq for both him and that Fitzgerald chap.'

Ellie allowed herself a smile. 'That's something to be pleased about, I suppose,' she said, dryly. 'From what I'm told, it seems a lot of the men at the Training Regiment need to be kept away from female soldiers.'

'Indeed,' Ian replied. 'That entire place is best kept at arm's length, in my view.'

'Do you mind if I ask you a straight question?' Ellie said.

'Sure, we're all friends.'

'What do you think really happened to Private Davenport?'

Ian sat back in his chair as he looked at her, askance. 'What on earth brought that up?' he said.

'Somebody asked me that question at the dinner last night.'

'Did they really?' he replied. 'Well, whoever that was, they need to learn to curb their tongue. The inquest decided it was suicide.'

Ellie screwed up her face. 'I'm curious what those with experience think,' she said. 'I mean, what do *you* think happened to her? You said the Training Regiment should be kept at arm's length, so what does your gut tell you?'

Ian folded his newspaper, before tucking it under his arm. 'I think that people like you and I should be very grateful not to have been caught up in that mess and we'll leave it at that,' he said, as he stood ready to leave. 'And before I forget, one of the stewards left a message for you from one of your platoon … a Private Orr. She's asked if it might be possible to secure a few minutes of your time this morning.'

***

Following morning parade, two of Ellie's NCOs did the nitty-gritty, hands-on part of the room inspection; checking lockers, beds and kit, and shaking-up the girls who were found lacking. Ellie stood back and watched. The hour went quickly with only one room found to be in a poor state. Whilst the NCOs were reminding the occupants of their need to improve standards, she used the opportunity to instruct Private Orr to attend her office at nine-thirty.

Orr arrived exactly on time, and with some very interesting news.

'Why does she want to meet with me?' Ellie asked, with some trepidation.

'I told her about you, ma'am. Said you was up through the ranks and knew your stuff.'

'Is she the girl that was caught in your room?'

'No, ma'am, but she's a friend of that girl. She needs to talk to a woman officer and they don't have one over there.'

Ellie thought for a moment as she tried to reconcile the possibility of a genuine coincidence against her natural sense of suspicion. 'Did she say what about, exactly?' she asked.

'Not in so many words, ma'am,' Orr replied. 'But, I'd hazard a guess it's about the rape.'

'The rape?' said Ellie, as she felt her insides lurch.

'One of the girls got herself drunk at a pub, I was told. An NCO found her in the toilets and took advantage.'

Ellie sat back heavily in her chair. It had to be the same incident she had witnessed, the one involving Naomi's room-mate. 'Was it reported to the RMP?' she asked.

'Not so far as I know ma'am.'

'And why haven't they gone through their own chain of command?'

'Apparently they can't. It's one of their NCOs who done it.'

'Did this girl suggest a time or place for this meeting?

'Only that it needs to be real soon. Today, if possible, she asked. I said if you agreed I'd find out where and when.'

'Very well,' Ellie said, taking a pen from her drawer. Even before she posed her question or heard Orr's answer, she had a sense of foreboding. It was as if she knew what was coming. 'What is this soldier's name?'

'Private Baker, ma'am,' said Orr. 'Private Jodie Baker.'

Chapter 52

My evening telephone call to Jenny didn't go quite as I'd hoped.

Following a long afternoon in a water-park, the girls had been exhausted and after a mumbled, sleepy goodnight, her sister had taken them off to bed. That had left Jenny clear to give me both barrels. She immediately demanded I explain what the heck was going on. When I asked what had fired her up, I discovered she had arrived back at the cottage that evening to find two armed protection officers waiting for her and her sister. The outcome was an object lesson to me in getting my priorities right. I should have shared the details of the note with Jenny immediately and included her in the risk assessment. Eventually, after much back-tracking and apology, she forgave me and, although we agreed the threat was almost certainly an empty one, she accepted Bill's decision was a reasonable precaution. All things considered, I got off lightly.

***

Floria and I had arranged to start the morning by speaking with two of the girls we'd identified from Colonel Hine's lists – Privates Jodie Baker and Naomi Briscoe. After that, we would interview Sergeant Paul Slater. Prince Albert Barracks seemed, at least superficially, to be carrying on as normal now that news of Tom Morgan's death had filtered through every part of the camp. The decision to prevent soldiers talking to the press had also paid dividends, with the number of reporters at the main gate having dwindled considerably. We entered the camp without difficulty and parked near the main doors to Rowallan block, the female accommodation.

As we walked into the foyer area, I was struck by yet another wave of nostalgia. Ask any soldier, serving or retired, and they will tell you there is nothing quite like the aroma of military accommodation. It has a smell all of its own, impossible to fully describe yet easily remembered; a curious mixture of stale sweat, pine disinfectant, boot polish and the unidentified preservative it was said the MOD use on all uniform and equipment. Once in a while, other odours would dominate – such as when the toilets were backed up and a suitable 'volunteer' had yet to be found to clear them – but on most days, soldier accommodation all over the UK shared this particular smell.

I ran my eyes over a rather tired-looking notice board at the bottom of the stairs. It displayed a mixture of posters, adverts and what appeared to be standing instructions such as fire drills. Although the best part of twenty years had passed since I'd been in such a building, it was all very familiar. The room we were looking for was Number 7, situated on the first floor. Floria had arranged for Baker and Briscoe to be there to meet with us. I had a list of things I wanted to ask them; about the day of the theft, about Michael Davenport's claims and, if circumstances allowed, about Angela Davenport. With them, Floria said, would be a female Lance-Corporal, their Phase Two NCO. I'd expressed some surprise at being allowed such easy access without having to secure permission from Colonel Hine, but when Floria simply winked at me in response to my posing the question, I realised what had happened – she hadn't actually asked him.

The door to Room 7 was closed. Floria knocked once, opened the door and walked straight in. That she didn't wait struck me as deliberate – something RMP soldiers were probably in the habit of doing in the hope they may catch someone unawares. As it turned out, the three women were waiting for us; the recruits sat together on one of four beds, their NCO – Lance-Corporal Bevan – stood by the window. All three stood immediately to attention. Immediately, my eyes were drawn to the clerk from the Armoury, the soldier I'd seen watching us from the window before and after our visit with Sergeant Andrew Masters. Her name badge confirmed she was Jodie Baker.

At my suggestion, we all relaxed, sat on opposite beds and I began what I'd hoped would lean towards a friendly exchange rather than two cops asking questions of potential witnesses. Frustratingly, neither recruit was willing to engage in any form of meaningful conversation. Several times, I saw them glance in the direction of their Corporal before even responding to my warm-up, get-to-know-you type questions about life at the camp. Briscoe was the more talkative of the two but, as we slowly worked our way to the day the rifles were stolen and how well they had known Angela Davenport, even she began to clam up.

'Did you ever hear Private Davenport say it wasn't *her* rifle that was taken?' I asked, eventually. I was hoping to corroborate what Michael Davenport had said. If these were his daughter's mates, I thought, she may well have said something to them.

Briscoe looked confused. 'News to me, sir,' she said, rather abruptly.

Out of the corner of my eye, I saw a look of doubt flash across Jodie Baker's face. I turned to her. 'What about you, Jodie?' I said. 'Have you ever heard that claim?'

'I haven't, sir,' she replied, vehemently. 'To be honest, after it happened, Davenport kept herself to herself, mostly. We didn't see much of her.'

'What did she do with her time?' I asked. 'Was there a boyfriend?'

Briscoe took over again. 'She didn't have time for boys … too focussed on passing the course.'

I stood up to stretch my legs as Floria asked once more about possible boyfriends. Corporal Bevan chose that moment to interject, politely suggesting we might call the meeting to an end. I had no doubt it was an intentional move to prevent her charges from discussing the Davenport case any further and, when my attempts to negotiate a few more minutes were stonewalled, that suspicion was rather confirmed.

With the interview brought to a disappointing and premature conclusion, Floria and I headed down the stairs. I was deep in thought, knowing we were close to something but unsure how the various threads might tie up. As a result, I didn't react to the appearance of Naomi Briscoe behind us. It was only as Floria turned that I realised the young recruit was there.

Briscoe pointed towards the exit. 'Outside,' she said, as she glanced back over her shoulder. 'I've only got a second. Corporal Bevan thinks I'm having a pee.'

As the double doors closed behind us, Briscoe's eyes darted in all directions, scanning the windows of the building as well as the grassed areas outside. 'You didn't get these things from me, ok?' she said, as she leaned in close.

Floria and I nodded in unison.

'You've got the wrong end of the stick with Davenport's rifle. On the day, it *was* the rifle she used that was stolen but it wasn't *her* rifle, if you know what I mean.'

'I'm not sure,' I replied. 'Put it in simple terms even a civvie can understand.'

'Ok.' She paused for a moment, as if looking for the words to best explain what she wanted to say. 'Davenport was Crow number twenty-seven on our intake and when we first arrived here she noticed there was an SA80 with the same number painted on the stock. So, she always used that rifle, number twenty-seven; on the range, for drill, for everything. Someone else had taken it on the day of the parade. She was livid, made a real fuss. Everyone knew she wanted that rifle. She even accused one of the staff of doing it on purpose to wind her up.'

'So, if she told someone it wasn't *her* rifle stolen …' I said.

'She meant it wasn't her special rifle.'

'Who did she accuse?' Floria asked.

'I can't,' Briscoe said. 'You don't know this place. If I told you my life would be hell.'

'You said these *things*,' I said. 'Is there something else?'

Briscoe hesitated once more.

'Whatever you say will be between us,' I said, as I tried to reassure her.

'You might be barking up the wrong tree asking about Davenport's rifle,' she said. 'The boy they found dead on the mountain, Tom Morgan. He's the one you ought to look at. Sergeant Masters and Tom were good mates. It wasn't a coincidence the other rifle taken was Tom's.'

From inside the building, I heard a door bang. If she'd been nervous up to this point, Briscoe now appeared positively frightened. 'I've got to go,' she spluttered, as she turned and ran back inside.

As we stood looking back towards the door through which Naomi Briscoe had just disappeared, Floria turned to me. 'So, the second signature on the register was Tom Morgan's.'

'Makes sense doesn't it?' I said. 'Morgan and Davenport were the guards and those rifles are the ones stolen.'

'And now both are dead,' Floria replied.

'And we're supposed to accept both deaths were suicide.'

'Maybe the rifles weren't stolen from the lorry at all? I don't understand why you asked about Davenport having a favourite rifle. I thought we were trying to identify the men in the video? Where did this idea come from it might not have been her weapon that was stolen?'

'It's what she told her father,' I said.

'I don't remember that,' Floria replied.

'Let's move,' I said, as we began to walk along the path leading away from the block. Once we were a safe distance away, I explained what Michael Davenport had said to me. Floria didn't look at all happy.

'With respect, sir,' she said. 'You're doing it again. You need to stop holding out on me. Why didn't he say something at the inquest?'

'Apparently, he did but he was told that checks of the weapon registers confirmed his daughter signed for one of the stolen rifles. Nobody ever mentioned her having a favourite rifle.'

'What about Briscoe? Do you think she's right about Tom Morgan?'

'I think we should take another look at his statement and file,' I said. 'We also need to go through all the old Armoury registers,' I said.

'You have an idea?' Floria asked.

'I think they might support a idea that keeps popping into my mind. Tell me, how we know for certain it was the weapon she signed for that was stolen?'

'Like I told you ... it was one of my team who checked the registers before the pages went missing. He remembered seeing Davenport's signature against one of the two rifles that had gone. He said the second signature was just a scribble he couldn't read.'

'And Private Briscoe now says that scribble was Tom Morgan's. She also confirmed Davenport had a favourite rifle. So, everyone would have known she'd want it for the parade.'

'Makes sense. And it's also possible someone would take it to wind her up. That's the kind of thing soldiers do.'

'And with the Register pages missing, we can't know who actually took rifle twenty-seven that day?'

Floria became quiet for a moment. 'I'm pretty sure that rifle was the one found next to her body a month later,' she said, as she stopped walking and held her arm across my chest. 'Are you suggesting Davenport may have arranged for her favourite rifle to be used by someone else because she knew in advance the weapon she was using was going to be stolen?'

'I'm not sure ... but the only alternative explanation I can come up with at the moment is someone unexpectedly took her favourite rifle to stop her using it, and why would they do that? Do we know for certain it was rifle twenty-seven found next to her body?'

'I'm as sure as I can be but we could check the report again?'

'Can we do that safely?' I asked.

Floria's eyes lit up as she grinned. 'Just watch me.'

Chapter 53

While Floria went off to grab the Davenport file, I made myself comfortable in the back office of the RMP HQ building. I was re-reading Tom Morgan's AWOL report when she re-appeared.

'You'll need to be quick,' she said, as the door swung open and she placed the now familiar box on the table in front of me. 'If someone clocks I've taken this again, they'll definitely think we're onto something.'

'I spotted something in the Morgan report,' I said.

'Something we missed?'

'It didn't appear significant at the time. The date he went missing. It was the day after Angela Davenport died.'

'I never made that connection,' Floria said, apologetically.

I opened the box, thumbing through the pages as quickly as I could. Floria left me to it again while she headed off to retrieve the Armoury registers. It didn't take me long to find what I was looking for mentioned on the initial report from the RMP Duty Officer. It was also in the statement of Sergeant Slater, the NCO whose name kept cropping up. The serial number of the SA80 was referenced in the RMP report but not in Slater's statement. That wasn't a surprise. In the circumstances, I wouldn't have expected Slater to note such a detail. What did appear in both sets of paperwork, though, was the digits painted in white on the base of the rifle found lying next to the body. Floria had remembered correctly, it was number 27.

I had the file closed and ready to be returned as Floria appeared once more. I confirmed her memory had been correct before we swapped paperwork and she headed back to the CO's office. I then began the laborious job of scanning the numbers and columns in the registers, being careful to keep them in date order. It was slow going and by the time Floria appeared once more, this time bearing two mugs of tea, I'd only made a small impression on the pile.

'Colonel Hine wants to see us,' Floria said, as she rested one of the mugs on the table near to me.

'Both of us?' I asked.

'Apparently, yes. He left a message earlier this morning ordering us to call in without delay.'

'*Ordering* us eh? Well, at least I'll have some news for him. I've arranged for that speeding notice to be killed off.'

'Colonels don't do requests, Finlay, as I'm sure you remember. He won't know what time his message was delivered, though.' Floria took a sip from her tea as she ran her eyes over the documents in front of me. 'Would you like some more help?' she said with a grin.

I smiled, and pushed half the forms in her direction. 'Rifle twenty-seven. See if you can find it.'

It took us nearly an hour, a period during which we checked and then re-checked. I wanted to be sure. By the time we'd finished pouring over the columns of dates and numbers, my torso was aching even more than my eyes. I leaned back in my chair, stretched my arms and shoulders and, as I rubbed away the stiffness forming in my neck, I turned to Floria. 'It's not there is it?' I said.

'No,' she replied. 'From the day of the parade through to the day Davenport died over a month later, not one soldier signed out rifle twenty-seven.'

'Making it unlikely Davenport hid her favourite rifle on the day of the parade knowing hers was due to be stolen?'

'If she'd done that, she'd have resumed using it immediately afterwards. But nobody used it at all.'

'Until the day it appeared next to her body, having been used to put a bullet through her brain.'

Floria stared blankly out of the window. She looked shocked, and, as she spoke, I was a little non-plussed when I saw she was on the verge of tears.

'I thought we'd stumbled across something with the Morgan connection,' she said. 'But this is better. This is it. It's what we've been hoping for. You've no idea how important this is. Not just to me … to every woman on this camp. Someone hid Davenport's rifle and then used it to kill her.'

'We're close, Floria,' I replied. 'But we're not there yet.'

'We've always been puzzled why anyone would remove the register after we'd looked at it. It didn't make sense … until now. You've fuckin' cracked it.'

I smiled, reassuringly. 'Everyone assumed the theft of the rifles and the missing register page had to be connected. I think someone wanted to hide the fact that on the day of the theft, nobody signed out Davenport's favourite weapon. I think someone had that rifle hidden away on the day of the parade and ...'

'… he used it to kill her because everyone knew it was her rifle and would assume she'd killed herself. Damn it.' Floria slammed a fist on the table, causing the papers to jump into the air. 'I knew it, I bloody knew it. She *was* killed.'

'It certainly looks possible,' I said, cautiously.

'It has to be Masters.'

Floria's assertion surprised me. 'Why him?'

'Because he has to do audits of the weapons. If number twenty-seven was missing, even for a short time, he would know and he should have reported it.'

'Let's keep an open mind, shall we?' I said.

'But why kill her?' said Floria, excitedly. 'I don't understand why?'

'For my money, it has to be linked to that video and text threats,' I replied. 'She was being pressured into keeping quiet about something but we're still a long way from proving someone *deliberately* killed her; it could even have been an accident.'

'If she was involved in stealing the rifles, maybe she was going to blow the whistle?'

'I can't see it. She was a good recruit from a decent family. Why would she get involved in stealing guns?'

'Like I said before,' said Floria. 'Recruits will do unbelievable things to get through their Phase Two. One thing is certain. If we can show this is the motive behind the texts, we're close. If we can prove Masters sent the messages, we've got him.'

'We may also be getting close enough to scare people into doing silly things,' I said.

Floria hesitated as she took in the implication of what I'd said. 'You mean like breaking into the home of an Assistant Chief Constable?'

'Exactly. Maybe it wasn't the MOD keeping tabs on me after all?'

'Maybe it was whoever killed Davenport?'

'And maybe you were right to say there's more to her death than the inquest knew about. I was wrong. I can only apologise.'

Floria smiled and reached out a hand to shake mine. 'Apology accepted,' she said. 'Now, let's go catch a killer.'

***

'I've *got* to report it,' Floria panted. Like me, she was breathing heavily following our fast, uphill walk to the Training Regiment Headquarters. 'When you add it all up; the video, the text threats, your theory on residue and the mystery of her favourite rifle … the more I think about it, the more it makes sense.'

My walking pace slowed as I thought how best to keep my young companion in check whilst, at the same time, harnessing her enthusiasm. I understood how she felt. Having seen the failings of the Davenport investigation from the beginning, she was excited. She also knew how tough it was for young women to succeed in the Army. To be judged equal to the men, they had to be better. Everything was stacked against them; the physical requirements, the

279

culture and, perhaps most significantly, the attitudes of the soldiers who trained and assessed them. Watching the Davenport video had been tough enough for me. As a woman soldier, the experience had been doubly hard for her.

Up to this point, I'd let Floria express her opinions unopposed. I knew we were building a picture of what *may* have happened to Angela Davenport, though, no more. What we had was supposition, not evidence. I needed her to be patient.

I stopped walking just as a group of recruits in PT kit ran past us. They were in formation, three abreast and six or seven-deep, with a white-vested PTI jogging alongside them. 'We're taught something on detective courses, Floria,' I said, once the recruits were a safe distance away. 'Coincidence is not causality. At the moment, we're missing some key parts to the jigsaw. First, there's nothing to directly connect the video and text messages to her death. Second, we don't know why the texts were sent and third, if you think about it, the absence of that rifle from the register could easily be explained by it being in for repair work or something similar.'

'That's bollocks,' Floria said, her frustration clear. 'How do you explain the residue on both hands, then? Someone, probably Masters, used her favourite rifle to kill her and make it look like suicide.'

I held up a hand. 'Take it easy,' I said. 'Save that anger for whoever killed her. We'll give Hine the news he wants to hear about the traffic summons and then we'll go find this Slater character. If Masters is a killer, I'm convinced Slater is the key to proving it.'

'Is Slater also a suspect?' Floria asked.

'His name keeps cropping up … but remember what I said about coincidence?'

'Get his kit off and see if he has a tattoo of a snake disappearing up his arse.'

I laughed, even though Floria had a point. 'And how would you suggest we do that?' I said. 'When we get back from seeing Hine, I think we also need to go through the Armoury register again.'

'Again? To what end, exactly?'

'To look back at the entries for the other rifle that was stolen. Maybe it was also someone's favourite.'

Floria didn't reply. She seemed to be looking past me towards the HQ building we were heading for. I turned to follow her line of sight and, in one of the office windows, I saw the outline of a figure stood watching us.

'We need hard evidence, Floria,' I said, as the figure disappeared from view. 'With all the shitstorm that blew up after Deepcut, we can't simply take circumstantial evidence as proof something happened without even knowing why or who was responsible. And, if we went public with it now, it would give those involved a chance to destroy or hide any physical evidence we might yet find.'

'So, how do we get people to talk?' Floria asked, as we approached the HQ entrance. 'Someone on this camp, maybe several people … they know things. But they'll never talk, not unless you know a way to force them.'

Chapter 54

Ellie froze, stood still and then reverse-stepped quietly along the path until she was hidden behind some shrubs. It was only by good fortune she'd not walked straight into Floria, standing on the path to the RMP Headquarters. Her friend was with Finlay, the detective, and both seemed so absorbed in conversation they hadn't looked up. She checked her wristwatch and cursed under her breath. In a few minutes she was due at the Armoury. If they didn't move soon she would be late.

The last thing she needed would be to have to explain what she was doing in this part of the camp. Leaning forward, she chanced another glimpse through the shrubs. Floria had turned towards the RMP building, the detective close behind. It looked like they were heading back indoors.

She stepped into the open, the soft soles of her desert boots hardly producing a sound on the worn tarmac. With heart racing, she quickened her pace, keeping her face turned away, hoping she would look like any other soldier going about their business. There was no yell, no call. They hadn't seen her.

The Armoury was adjacent to one of the recruit parade squares and, as Ellie approached, the loud voice of a PTI putting young soldiers through their paces filled the air. The training instructor was giving his unhappy victims a real beasting. As he screamed, the unfortunate Crows lay face down on the tarmac, doing press-ups as fast as they were physically able. There was one exception, a male recruit stood to attention who, Ellie surmised, had probably committed some form of misdemeanour. His mates were suffering the consequences of whatever he had or hadn't done. Two other NCOs walked among the prone recruits. One of them dug his boot hard into the ribs of a soldier before leaning down to the young man and shouting something in his ear.

As she turned onto the path leading to the Armoury, a face briefly appeared at a window to the left of the entrance. Her arrival had been noticed. The outer security door to the building was ajar, the padlock resting in its clasp. Ellie pulled it back toward her and, as the second, inner door swung open on its hinges, she saw a young woman with tied-back mousey blond hair dressed in shirt and camouflage trousers. She was standing just inside the entrance and looked nervous. Ellie glanced down at her name badge – Private Jodie Baker.

'Lieutenant Rodgers,' Ellie announced. 'I believe you want to speak to a female officer.'

***

When she'd first heard Orr say the name of the recruit she wanted her to meet, Ellie couldn't believe her luck. Even if it meant running the risk of bumping into Mick Fitzgerald, it was manna from heaven, a golden opportunity to identify the soldier in the respirator. Now, she wasn't so certain. She wondered how much she would be able to get from Jodie Baker.

As she led the way armoury, Baker had the look of a startled rabbit caught in headlights. Inside the building, away from prying eyes, everything about the girl oozed fear. 'We only have a few minutes', she said, hastily. 'I can watch him on the parade square from here.' She pointed at a register open on the desk in front of her. 'If he catches you here just say you were looking to book some weapons for range practice tomorrow, or something.'

'Who is *he*?' Ellie asked.

Baker stepped gingerly towards a large window overlooking where the recruits were now doing sit-ups. As Ellie followed her gaze, she noticed there was no sign of the recruit who'd been stood to attention. All three physical training staff were present and a fourth man had joined them. It was an officer by the look, standing with his back to the Armoury window. Unlike the NCOs who were dressed for PT, he was in full desert kit, including boots. As he walked on to

283

the parade square, one of the NCOs spoke to him. He didn't salute though, something Ellie would have expected, especially with recruits watching on.

'Are you referring to one of those NCOs?' Ellie said, as she watched the officer continue what appeared to be a rather heated conversation.

'He's my Sergeant, ma'am … Andy Masters,' Baker replied, pointing to the PTI standing talking with the officer. 'He's a big part of the problem I want to talk to you about.'

Ellie barely heard the words. Her heart had begun to pound the moment Giles Pemberton turned sideways and she caught sight of his face.

***

Fortunately for Ellie, Pemberton concluded his conversation with Sergeant Masters quite quickly before striding off in the direction from whence he'd appeared.

Jodie Baker was hard work as, every few seconds, she stopped talking to glance through the window before continuing. It proved to be worth the wait. Her story was even more incredible than Orr's. Eventually, as she finished, Ellie sat down at what she now knew was Masters' desk. 'So, you're saying Masters is just one of several NCOs who pick a favourite from each intake?' she said.

'A victim,' Baker replied. 'They're victims … not favourites. And now he wants me to do extra favours for him.'

'Just to be clear, you mean sexual favours?'

'He's a bloke. What other kind would there be?'

Ellie nodded. In the few minutes they'd been together, she'd already begun to understand better how the NCOs in the Training Regiment were operating. They'd been exploiting their power over the Crows. Although their methods varied – from threats of assault through to favouritism and grooming – the goal was always the same; sex with young, female soldiers. Jodie Baker was pretty but, despite her womanly appearance, Ellie could see she was vulnerable, and still displayed many child-like qualities. It was clear she was petrified of the NCOs and it came as no surprise that she'd become one of their targets. 'How old are you, Baker?' she asked.

'Seventeen, ma'am.'

'Left school this Summer?'

'I left early … school wasn't my thing.'

'Do you have a boyfriend?'

'Not while I'm seeing one of the Training Staff. He wouldn't like it.'

Ellie felt a rush as she realised Baker may have bought the aftershave for a specific NCO. 'Does he buy you presents?' she asked, sensing an opportunity.

'Sometimes. At least he did in the beginning when I was flavour of the month.'

'Not any more then?' Even as her heart raced, Ellie felt it best to move slowly. She might not have a better chance. 'Have you tried buying him things?' she asked.

Baker sneered in reply. 'Not that it did any good.'

'Typical men stuff?'

'You got it.'

'Like what?' Ellie was so close now she could almost feel it.

'Usual stuff you buy a bloke,' said Baker.

'Like cologne maybe … or aftershave?'

'He gave it away. It cost me a bloody fortune from a posh place in town and he gave it away.'

'That was thoughtless.' Ellie said, as she cursed under her breath. If she now asked Baker who the aftershave had been given to it could reveal her agenda. It would have to wait.

'There are others who want to speak to you,' Baker said. 'Naomi … she's my mate … she's had it much worse than me.'

Ellie swallowed hard as she remembered the girl from the NAAFI. There can't be too many recruits called Naomi. 'In what way?' she asked.

'She's been made to sleep with a couple of them.'

'You said earlier a girl had been raped.'

'That's my other friend Amy. We'll try and get her there as well.'

'Jesus. Are there any young women on your intake who haven't been abused?'

Jodie shrugged, but didn't reply.

'Does this Naomi have a surname?' Ellie asked.

'Briscoe. Naomi Briscoe,' said Baker.

Ellie took a deep breath. Naomi and Amy. It was the same girls. Meeting them in her official capacity was going to be a problem. Makeup and a tidy dress might change appearances superficially but she was certain to be recognised.

Baker pulled away from the window, her facial expression anxious once more. 'He's coming back,' she announced.

'Sergeant Masters?'

'Yes. Come back later, will you? Ten o'clock, Rowallan block. We're on the first floor, room seven.'

Ellie remembered the room from when she'd helped the bedraggled and drunken Amy get back there. Four beds. One unused and formerly occupied by a now-dead recruit, another belonging to a girl staying out with her boyfriend. Baker must have been the absent girl.

'I'll be there,' she said as the sound of the main entrance door swinging open reached her ears.

'Baker, where the fuck are you?' A male voice roared from the Armoury entrance.

Ellie opened the office door. An NCO – the one she'd seen talking to Pemberton – stood at the far end of the corridor. It was Sergeant Masters. He was slim, fit-looking, and wearing a sweat-soaked PTI vest. An angry snarl crossed his face before his eyes saw the rank insignia on the chest of Ellie's camouflage jacket. In an instant, his composure changed. 'Apologies, ma'am,' he said, politely. 'Is Private Baker with you?'

'She is,' Ellie replied. 'I was hoping to book a Browning to use on the range tomorrow. I'm told it should be no problem.'

'No problem at all, ma'am.'

Ellie's heart pounded as Masters approached. She could see sweat was trickling down his neck and shoulders from the effort he'd been putting in on the parade square. He looked warm, glowing, and as he drew closer she felt the heat emanating from his skin. Without thinking, she felt her hand reach towards her neck, the tips of her fingers gently touching the now fading bruises.

And then a smell reached her nostrils. At first, it was just a vague hint, sweet and familiar. Then, as they met in the doorway, there was no mistake. Outside the NAAFI. The soldier in the respirator. The smell of aftershave now so firmly recorded in her memory. It was him.

Chapter 55

Colonel Hine was waiting for us. Of his Adjutant, the aloof note-taker Giles Pemberton, there was no sign. A Captain I hadn't seen before greeted us in the HQ Reception area before showing us through to his CO's office.

As we stood expectantly in front of the Colonel's desk, my phone beeped twice in my pocket. I ignored it but I saw the Colonel scowl at me before telling the captain to leave us and close the door behind him.

'Sit,' said Hine, the moment the latch clicked home. 'How well do you know Inspector Finlay?' he immediately asked, before we'd even sat down. The question was addressed to Floria and seemed to take her as much by surprise as it did me.

'I'm not sure I understand the question, sir,' she replied, before glancing across at me, a confused frown on her face.

Hine leaned forward on his elbows, his gaze focussed on Floria, chin resting on clasped hands. 'Would you describe your relationship as entirely professional?' he said, slowly.

'One hundred percent, sir.' Floria sounded offended and I was now doubly bemused. I also wondered if, as was often the case in the services, rumour had grown on the back of two people spending a lot of time together.

'Then why do you address the Inspector by name rather than rank, Sergeant?' Hine continued. The Colonel's tone had become quite accusatory and, anticipating he was about to suggest Floria and I had started some form of relationship, I decided this was the time to stop him in his tracks.

'Sergeant McLaren was following my instruction,' I said, as assertively as I dared without sounding rude. 'I instructed her not to call me sir but to use a name I'm more comfortable with.'

Hine didn't allow me to distract him. With his eyes still glued to Floria, he addressed her again. 'What do you know of Inspector Finlay's military background, Sergeant?' he asked.

Floria now looked distinctly uncomfortable. Although I could say nothing to help her, I silently urged her to be honest and not to hide what I'd revealed on the mountain. I didn't want her to lie as I had a feeling Hine already knew the answer to his question.

She didn't lie. With just a cursory glance toward me, she replied honestly. 'Mr Finlay did mention he'd served many years ago, sir. We were searching the area near where Private Morgan's body was found and I thought he looked like a soldier, like he knew what he was doing.'

'So, you challenged him?' Hine demanded.

'I did, sir. It was then he mentioned his service.'

'Did he go into any detail?'

'Not much as I recall, sir. He was an officer, he did mention that. He served with the Royal Artillery.'

Hine leaned back in his chair and breathed in deeply. 'Thank you for your honesty, Sergeant. You never thought to report this?'

'I did report it, sir. That same day I followed correct protocol and reported it through my chain of command.' This time, Floria didn't look across at me. That she'd relayed our conversation to her seniors was unexpected but not surprising.

Hine turned his gaze to me. 'I've had the Ministry of Defence on the telephone this morning, Inspector … or should I say … Captain.'

Although I was careful not to show any signs of reacting, I was swearing under my breath. I still needed time if Floria and I were going to put the pieces of the puzzle together and discover what had really happened to Angela Davenport. For that, I might need the Colonel's help. Bill's idea of concealing my military past had backfired and now I'd been shown to be less than entirely honest with my hosts. Hine would be angry, and rightly so.

'What did the MOD say? I asked, as I stalled for thinking time.

'That you're ex Hereford and you're here to dig into the Davenport case.'

I swore under my breath. If someone had played a trump card aimed at having me returned to London, now was going to be the moment I learned whether it had worked. 'Right on one count, Colonel,' I said. 'Not on the other. My brief is simply to find the link between London and the rifles. My boss decided my background was best not mentioned in the hope soldiers might say something they'd assume I wouldn't understand.'

Hine was silent for a few seconds, as if he were making his mind up how to respond or what to do next. I had the feeling he hadn't expected me to be quite so open with him. 'Quite so,' he said, and I was left wondering for a moment if we'd gotten away with it. We hadn't.

'The MOD doesn't like spies operating within barracks, Inspector,' he continued. 'You really should have been more upfront from the beginning. In different circumstances …'

'You would have helped me?' I said, interrupting him and hoping I might be able to rescue an impossible situation. I was wrong.

'Quite possibly,' Hine said, as he continued. 'The theft and the suicide happened before I arrived here. If you'd found evidence of malpractice or criminality I would have been the first to support you. Now, it's too late. My orders are to have you escorted off base immediately with no return under any circumstances. I'm sorry, Inspector. Your time here is at an end.'

Chapter 56

Floria looked dispirited as she listened attentively to Hine's instructions. At appropriate points, she nodded or responded with a deferential 'yes, sir'. Not once did she so much as a glance in my direction.

The Colonel instructed her I was to be considered PNG – persona-non-grata. The fact he didn't explain the expression to me came as no surprise. He knew I wouldn't need clarification. I was an 'unwelcome person', barred from the entire barracks and, only in the unlikely event someone in London could persuade the MOD otherwise, would I avoid being on the next train home.

As we left the HQ building I went to speak to Floria. She held up a hand to silence me. 'How many times in the last couple of days have I asked you not to keep things from me?' she said.

We walked on in stony silence and it was only as we reached the path leading to the RMP offices that I decided it was time to attempt an apology. 'Don't … just don't,' she said. 'We were so fuckin' close. Wait here. I'll just be a minute and then I'll drive you back to your quarters.'

As she strode away, I waited. Fully twenty minutes went by, during which time I thought things through. Floria was right. I really should have taken her into my confidence more. As Floria returned and closed the door behind her, she looked me up and down, icily. 'Best we get this over with,' she said, jingling the car keys in her hand.

We turned and walked toward the car. 'You didn't tell him about killing off that speeding ticket,' she said, as she opened the driver's door.

'Let him sweat,' I said. 'I'm sorry I did it now.'

Floria shrugged as if to indicate her indifference. I had a feeling it was going to be a long and rather uncomfortable drive to Wendy's.

We drove north out of Cwmbran, onto the dual carriageway and, then along the straight but undulating road to Usk. No words were spoken and Floria gave me no indication we were to go anywhere other than Wendy's. On the outskirts of the town, she unexpectedly slowed the car and turned hard left into a small car park. We pulled up overlooking the River Usk and, as she killed the engine, I guessed it was here we were going to talk.

'Why didn't you tell me?' Floria said, as she stared across the water.

The car park was deserted; the only activity I could see being on the far side of the river, on a path that sat between the town and the water's edge where a woman was walking a small dog. 'If you're referring to my time at Hereford, would it have made any difference?' I said.

'Jesus … you told me you were a bog-standard artillery officer. You were Special Air Service, for Christ sake. You guys are nails. The prats on this camp would have respected you.'

'Or they would have clammed up. Besides, it was a long time ago.'

'So, what are you now, MI5? Is that why you're so bloody secretive?' She slammed her hands on the steering wheel. 'That's it, isn't it? God, I'm such an idiot … I knew I was right the first time I asked you. Ordinary cops don't get their Army records redacted.'

'I'm sorry Floria,' I said. 'Truly I am. I'm not MI5 and it is true my boss decided my presence here would create enough waves without throwing in the fact I'm ex-regiment.'

'If you were MI5, would you admit it?'

'Probably not,' I said, conceding the point.

My companion's expression softened slightly. 'So, how long were you SAS?' she asked.

'I did two back-to-back tours, six years altogether.'

'I knew it. It's the way you move, the way you look at things. You have the memory of military tradecraft in your bones.'

'A cop can always spot another cop. Same with soldiers, I guess.'

Floria shook her head from side to side. 'You should have said.'

'I find it's a part of my life best kept to myself.'

'But why?'

'For a number of reasons. From local hard-nuts trying to pick fights to prove how tough they are, through to people accusing you of being a Walter Mitty, a fake. It's less hassle to keep it quiet, in my experience.'

'Those concerns don't apply here, though?'

'Here? No. Here, it was simply what my boss decided.'

Floria shook her head in apparent frustration. 'I am so … so …'

'Angry with me?' I said.

She turned to me and glared. 'I'm angry with myself, Finlay … you don't seem to understand. I'm disappointed, more than you can imagine. After the mess at Deepcut, it's become even worse for us women. The predators seem to think they've been given a free rein now, they think they're untouchable. This could have been our best chance to strike back.'

I sat in silence for several moments as I let Floria's words sink in. So much more seemed to be resting on exposing the truth behind Angela Davenport's death than I'd realised. The decision to hide my military background had given those within the MOD who wanted things swept under the carpet a perfect reason to squeeze me out.

'I did the check you wanted,' Floria said, before I could speak.

'How do you mean?' I asked.

'While I was in the office just now, I checked the register for the second rifle like you suggested … to see if anyone favoured it. I only found a few entries before I stopped because the same name came up each time ... it was Tom Morgan.'

'I had a feeling it might be,' I said.

'Ellie Rodgers rang me as well.'

'What did she want?'

'She has to come over to the Training Regiment this evening, for some reason. She wanted to confirm Mick Fitzgerald had left the base.'

'And has he?'

'I don't know,' she replied. 'I asked her to wait until I could find out but, like I said before, Ellie can be impulsive. How did you know it was going to be Morgan's name on the register?'

I opened the car door. 'I suspected Morgan's rifle was stolen because the thieves knew they could rely on him to keep quiet. Come on ... let's walk.'

As we joined the path running alongside the river, I noticed the power with which it flowed. The water was also a deep, reddish-brown, the result, I imagined, of heavy rain further upriver in the Black Mountains. Near the bank, where the water slowed in tranquil pools, flies flitted across the surface. Beside me, Floria kicked her feet angrily as she walked. An idea had begun forming in my brain as I'd waited for her outside the RMP building. It was our outstanding lead, and possibly our best one. Paul Slater. We were about a hundred metres from the car before I decided this was the time to raise it. 'Is the car bugged?' I asked.

'Are you serious?' Floria threw her head back, her laugh almost mocking as she turned to face me.

'Can't be too careful,' I said. 'We're very close ... you know that don't you?'

'Why do you think I pulled in?' she answered. 'Like I said just now, this was the best chance we've ever had to crack this case. You've been here no time at all and you've already unearthed things nobody else has. Now … we're stuffed.'

As Floria stared out over the water, kicking at the long grass near her feet, I scanned the path to confirm nobody had appeared. At the far edge of my vision, I caught sight of a small splash in the water – a trout rising to seize one of the flies I had noticed earlier. 'I've been thinking,' I said, as I satisfied myself we were alone. 'Slater is our best lead. And the way I see it, we've got two choices. Either you take our suspicions through your chain of command …'

'Or you hand that phone in. Either way, we're back with the same people who messed up the original investigation.' Floria sounded defeated as she cut across me.

'Do your people know we're getting somewhere?' I asked.

'You know how things work in the Army, Finlay. I have to report to my boss and he reports to his boss. What's your second choice?'

I smiled. 'We give Sergeant Slater a shot.'

'You're wasting your time and mine,' Floria replied. 'If you put one foot inside the camp, you'll be thrown in the guardhouse.'

'Does Slater live inside or outside the perimeter?'

'Outside. He still has a married quarter even though his wife walked out some while ago. You're not thinking …' she said, slowly.

'That we could pay him a little visit?'

'You have to be kidding,' she replied, rounding on me. 'Are you asking me to do something off the radar with a PNG? They'd hang me.'

Before I could reply, the telephone in my jacket began to vibrate. Apologising to Floria for the interruption, I pulled it from my pocket.

It was Wendy. 'Have you seen the messages from Bill and me?' she said, as soon as I held the phone to my ear. It was only then I remembered the texts that had arrived as Floria and I were about to speak to Colonel Hine. With everything that had happened since, it had slipped my mind to read them.

'Not yet,' I replied. 'What's up?' There was a pause before Wendy replied.

'Well,' she said. 'I hope you're sat comfortably. This could take a while.'

Chapter 57

'So, you've already been thrown out?' Wendy said, once she'd finished telling me how the top brass at the MOD had also been leaning on her Chief Constable and I'd explained what had happened during the meeting with Colonel Hine.

'We're on our way to your place to collect my stuff,' I replied.

'I see. That's not entirely surprising. Bill has been told in no uncertain terms to have you brought back to London.'

'Did he say what happened?'

'I guess you haven't spoken to Harry?' Wendy said.

'I haven't. Can you speak freely?' I replied, hoping my friend would be alone.

'I'm in my office. I'll switch to my mobile but before I do that, I have news on DC Liverick.'

'You found him?'

'In a bed and breakfast in Tenby, of all places. He was with that girl, just like you predicted.'

'That was bloody quick. I suppose I should be thankful we got one decent result.'

'At the cost of a marriage, Finlay, don't forget that.'

Wendy ended the call and as I waited for her to call back, I saw Floria edging closer to me. 'Was it Miss Russell you were talking to earlier, outside our HQ?' she said, inquisitively.

I nodded as I checked the phone screen to see what the second message had been. As Wendy had predicted, it was from Bill Grahamslaw, asking me to contact him urgently. 'Yes, it was,' I said, as I returned the phone to my pocket.

'I heard you telling her about Private Bishop and to look for her credit card usage.'

'It's a lead they were following up.'

Floria hesitated for a moment. 'You know we've often wondered whether the civvie police would ever place an undercover operator in the Army. That's the real reason you were here, isn't it? You were here to find him.'

Whether I confirmed or denied Floria's conclusion made little difference now. 'My original job was the rifles,' I said. 'Things evolved and I was kept on to help locate him.'

'Did the police think he'd been killed or something?'

'He was overdue contacting his handler and they had no idea where he was. Your tip about Bishop proved to be right.'

'So, now you've located him, are you still serious about finding out the truth ... about Davenport, I mean?'

'Absolutely. That's why I want us to speak to Sergeant Slater,' I answered.

Floria looked down at her feet. 'And you're convinced Slater is connected to that video?' she said.

'He seems to have his sticky little fingers on everything that goes on around here. If he wasn't involved himself, he'll know who was.'

My phone began ringing once more. It was Wendy calling back. She apologised for the delay and when I asked about the withheld number showing on the screen, she explained.

'You're not the only one to use a burner phone occasionally, Finlay. And, just to make you laugh in the face of all this shit-storm, I'm currently sitting in a cubicle in the senior officers' toilet so nobody hears us talking.'

'Do you think your land-line is monitored?' I said, as I laughed at the image her remark had generated.

'I really don't know anything anymore, Finlay. All I'm sure of is we've rattled a cage at the MOD and the monster inside is angry. I'm not taking any more chances and time is pressing. I want that video.'

'You'll have it today,' I said. 'And, to go back to your question, I've not heard from Harry since I followed your advice about doing a phone trace.'

'Call him this evening at nine,' Wendy said.

'I'll most likely be on my way home then.'

'Don't be in such a rush. We still need to get that phone from you and do a proper de-brief. Harry will be at work this evening and expecting your call. He rang me earlier while the Chief was on one of his phone calls with the Ministry. It seems he ran the number of the phone used to send the texts to Davenport through the MI5 system. His check triggered an alert at GCHQ. He was hauled in and asked to explain why he was doing it.'

'Someone had the number registered?' I said, as my mind began racing. GCHQ, the Government Communications Headquarters at Cheltenham, didn't monitor any old mobile telephone number. Someone had to have asked them to do so.

'Exactly,' said Wendy. 'And, given your long-standing history together, there was no way Harry could prevent them realising his unofficial check was linked to you.'

'So, if it's someone at the MOD who knows about the number, they may know the phone was also used to send the video and it's connection to this place,' I said.

Wendy lowered her voice. 'That's a lot of ifs, Finlay. You need to get a grip of yourself. A GCHQ log request could have been made by anyone from the Secret Service to the Military Police.''

Turn over the right stone and the bugs will appear, I thought. 'Can you buy me a little time?' I said.

'How much? The Chief can't even justify keeping you here as a witness in the death of Private Morgan now.'

'How's that?'

'The SIO hasn't called you?'

'What is it with this place?' I said. 'Nobody tells me anything.'

'Probably the network,' Wendy said, in a matter-of-fact tone. 'The post-mortem toxicology result came through on Morgan. He took a little too much ecstasy and had no water with him to re-hydrate. It looks like his death was accidental.'

It was disappointing news. 'No evidence of foul play?' I said. 'I was convinced he'd been got at to stop him talking to us.'

'No evidence at all and the best I can offer you is one more day,' Wendy said. 'You can stay at mine tonight and head home tomorrow. I'll square it with Bill.'

'I might need less,' I said, hopefully. Truth was, I knew I was only going to have one chance and, if that worked, I might have an answer that evening.

'Ok … just don't show your face here at Police HQ. If Bill calls you, it'll be to order you back to London, so don't pick up.'

I said thanks and hung up the phone.

'Do you have a plan?' Floria asked.

'Not one I can deliver on my own,' I said.

She took a deep breath and then smiled. 'Even if I live to regret this, at least I'll have a clear conscience.'

'You're in then?' I said, just as my phone began to ring once more.

I checked the screen. Thankfully, it was Wendy again and not Bill. 'Three times in as many minutes,' I said, as I answered. 'Are you still on the loo?'

Wendy laughed. 'I'm back in my office,' she said. 'I've just looked at the post-mortem photographs for Private Morgan. You're not going to believe what's on his lower back.'

A pit formed in my stomach as I realised why my friend had called back so quickly. 'Don't tell me?' I said.

'You guessed. A snake tattoo that looks exactly like the one in that video.'

'So, Morgan was one of them?'

'No doubt.'

Floria looked me hard in the eyes as I ended the call. 'Did you hear that?' I asked.

'I did,' she replied. 'And if I had any doubts before, I don't now. I'm in.'

Chapter 58

Police officers tend to smile wryly at an oft-repeated scene in films where two cops are seen sitting casually in a car, windows steamed up, takeaway coffees and doughnuts to hand, as they keep watch on somebody. Reality, not too surprisingly, is nothing like that. And yet, here we now were, Floria and me, sat in her official – if unmarked – military police car in a communal car park opposite Paul Slater's house doing just that, even down to the doughnuts. We were one among many cars though, which helped, and although I'm not an expert in surveillance, there's one thing I have learned; it's not so much a case of being hidden, more about not being noticed. I hoped my tutors had been right.

That afternoon, Floria had left me in her car while she went to check the Training Regiment duty roster. I took advantage of the opportunity to make another call to Wendy. As I outlined a plan I had been formulating, she was sceptical at first but eventually accepted it was worth a try. If Slater was the link, we needed to shake him up to see what it produced. Wendy also agreed to speak to Harry, and to explain what I would need from him if my idea worked. I could have done it myself except for the fact Floria might have returned at any moment and, for my idea to work, I needed it to be as much a surprise to her as it might be to Slater.

As it transpired, I would have had time to call Harry. After talking to Wendy, I waited on my own for nearly an hour and, with each passing minute, I'd become increasingly anxious, fearing Floria had been rumbled and our last-ditch effort had been compromised. In the event, I needn't have worried. She returned to the car safe and sound, carrying doughnuts, coffees and, in her pocket, a photo-copied page with the names and contact details of all the Training Regiment NCOs. She also reported that Slater was due to finish work around 9pm.

'Sorry I took so long. I had another call from Ellie while I was in the HQ building,' Floria said, as we began our watch.

'What did she want?' I asked.

'She told me the reason she needed to go to the Training Regiment is because she's been dealing with a complaint of sexual harassment. She spoke to the victim this morning. It was Jodie Baker.'

'Bugger me,' I said. 'Now, that is a coincidence. Did she give you any detail?'

'Baker wants help. She claims Masters and Slater are keeping her at the camp as a plaything. Apparently, Slater signs the authorities for courses and transfers and he won't sign hers.'

'Did she give you any detail?'

'According to Ellie, Slater beasts each intake until the weak ones think they're not going to make the grade. Then he offers them help, individual attention. He becomes the caring, supportive Sergeant who recognises their abilities when nobody else seems to care. He persuades them only he can help them pass the course.'

'And then they discover the price, I guess? Did Baker happen to say whether Angela Davenport was also one of Slater's conquests?' I asked.

'Not that Ellie mentioned. She only rang so I wouldn't think she was going after Mick Fitzpatrick.'

'Why would you think that?' I said. I shifted in my seat to try and regain some comfort and then quietly eased the passenger window down an inch to reduce the condensation building up on the inside of the windscreen.

'Because of their history,' said Floria. 'Because he raped her and got away with it.'

'Let's hope she keeps her word, I said. 'In any event, what she said will help us put pressure on Slater.'

The contact list Floria had copied bore the names of NCOs from Lance Corporals through to a Regimental Sergeant-Major. Slater was on it, of course, as was Andrew Masters. More in hope than in expectation, I scanned it for the telephone number used by the sender of the video. It wasn't there. Frustrated, I took out Angela Davenport's phone and we watched the video again, looking for anything that might help with identifying the second man. Nothing jumped out at us. We then sat in silence for about twenty minutes, watching and waiting, until Floria suddenly spoke.

'His hands,' she said.

'Who's hands?' I asked.

'The second man in the video … the one without the tattoo. The insides of his hands were callused. Soldiers have rough skin, for sure, but I've only ever seen a few recruits with hands like that and that's because they'd been farmers or suchlike before starting training. Callused hands … rough skin. And an older man, definitely an older man.'

'Maybe someone who does a lot of manual work? An engineer, perhaps?'

'That's my bet,' she said. 'And not just any NCO. Those hands belong to someone who works outside.'

'Like most soldiers do,' I said, bleakly.

'Not those in admin jobs. Clerks always have soft hands.'

I held up the palms of my hands to show her. 'It's been a long time since these had calluses.'

'What used to cause them?'

'Rope climbs, abseiling … weapon handling. They just seemed to appear.'

'Maybe our man does similar? My money's still on Masters.'

'If we get the chance, we'll have a good look,' I said. 'And we'll check Slater too.'

'So, what did you actually do in the SAS?' Floria asked.

'I was a troop commander.'

'No, I mean what did you *do*?' she said. 'Like where did they send you? Did you do some good stuff?'

'We all sign an undertaking not to talk about it, Floria, and with good reason. As soon as people know your ex-22, they want to know what secret ops you've been on, if you've killed anyone or what's the trick to getting in. It can get a bit tedious, to be honest.'

'You must have learned some cool things though?'

'I learned how to break into people's houses for one thing,' I said, as I reached for the passenger door-handle. I was about to open the door when the phone in my jacket pocket started to buzz. I held my hand over the screen to stop the light being seen from outside the car and glanced down to see who wanted me. The name Bill Grahamslaw was showing.

For a moment, I thought about not answering as Wendy had advised, but I decided against it. Bill would no doubt keep trying until I eventually picked up.

'Where are you?' he asked, again without so much as a hello.

'On a road between the barracks and Wendy's house,' I answered, not entirely dishonestly.

'She tells me you've already been thrown off the camp.'

'Escorted past the gates and told not to come back, yes. I think I may have asked questions the MOD preferred I hadn't.'

'My fault. They were hacked off to discover we'd hidden your SF background. To stop you, they went right to the top.'

'To the Commissioner?'

'To the bloody Home Secretary, Finlay. They spoke to him personally.'

'No mention for me in the New Year's honours then?' I said.

Bill ignored my jibe and simply asked if I would be heading back to London that evening.

'In the morning, if that's ok?' I said. 'I thought I'd take Wendy out for a meal as a thanks for her help.'

'You sure that's all you're planning on doing?' he said, with some scepticism. 'It's not like you to back off so easily, Finlay.' Sat beside me in the driving seat, Floria had begun tapping her fingers on the steering wheel.

'I have one loose end to tie up that won't involve going to the barracks,' I said.

Bill huffed slightly and I imagined him sitting at his desk, coffee in one hand, phone in the other, and all the time knowing damn well I was up to something. 'No stupid tricks,' he said, firmly. I agreed and ended the call.

'I think it's time to have a little look inside Slater's house,' I said, turning to Floria.

'I thought we'd agreed to wait? He's due to finish work fairly soon.'

I opened the passenger door, confirmed the ring setting of my phone was on vibrate, and then stepped out. 'We've got one chance and I don't want to blow it if he decides to head elsewhere,' I said. 'If he shows, call me.'

I eased the car door closed. It was time to start the ball rolling.

Chapter 59

Within a few seconds I was across the car park and in the shadow of a narrow alleyway behind the houses.

The local properties were all typical MOD style; semi-detached and terraced, white UPVC windows and with small, unkempt gardens to front and rear. I found my way to the rear gate of Paul Slater's home and, after checking there was no security lighting or alarm, walked up the path to his back door. A possible entry point through an open window into the downstairs toilet presented a decent opportunity but a quick search revealed something better, a key. It lay hidden beneath a pot containing a rather desiccated looking tomato plant. I unlocked the door and then returned the key to its hiding place.

Inside, the house was in darkness. As soon as I entered, I was struck by the smell of stale sweat coming from a pile of dirty clothes lying on the floor in the kitchen, next to a washing machine. I moved on, treading carefully but as quickly as I could as I made for the living room. Once there, I closed the curtains. Next stop was the front door which I also unlocked so that both front and rear exits were open. It's a golden rule in surveillance – make sure to set up your escape, that way you're unlikely to need it. Next, I crept upstairs where I also shut the curtains in the two bedrooms. Satisfied I couldn't be seen from outside, I then turned on the first of the bedroom lights.

To a neighbour or a passerby, the sight of someone creeping around in the dark or using any kind of torchlight in an empty house means just one thing, an intruder. Draw the curtains, turn on the lights, and the assumption is the occupier is at home. A method adopted by burglars, it was a technique that had become part of both security service and military training when searching unattended premises – ok to be seen, make sure you're not noticed.

I started my search in the main bedroom. There's something about the human psyche that causes people to hide things they wish kept secret as close to their nest as possible. Although not foolproof, it had certainly been my experience that bedrooms tended to reveal the most interesting things about people. I worked quickly, anxious to look in as many places as I could in the time I had available. Rummaging beneath the bed, I found only dust bunnies and a small bergen containing a new pair of boots and some camouflage kit. The bedside drawers proved more interesting. It looked like someone else had been staying. The first clue was a woman's hairbrush and then I found a letter addressed to Jodie Baker, with an address in the main barracks. The envelope had been torn open and contained a letter from her family together with a small photograph of a man and woman standing in the rear garden of a house – her parents, I guessed. An open packet of condoms provided some confirmation of what Baker had said to Ellie Rodgers, a supposition that was backed up when I found woman's underwear lying in one of the corners.

I desperately wanted to find either the room used to film the video of Angela Davenport or the phone used to send it. If not, if I could just find something to link Slater to her, I'd have some significant leverage to use when Floria and I began talking to him. I looked everywhere obvious I could think might be used to hide evidence. But, as I finished in a bathroom that contained nothing apart from some deodorant and a shaving kit, I became increasingly frustrated. My next target was the second bedroom. I was just beginning a search when the phone in my pocket began to vibrate. I checked the screen and saw Floria's name.

Pressing the answer button, I held the phone tight against my ear. 'He's here,' she whispered. 'And not only that … he's driving a car like the one I saw on the mountain.'

'How long do I have?' I asked as I stepped away from the window.

'Maybe a minute or so. He's just opened his car door. Did you find anything?'

I headed onto the landing and began taking the stairs, two at a time. 'Not much,' I replied. 'But it looks like Jodie Baker stays here. There's a letter to her and what looks like her underwear.'

'He's clocked the lights,' Floria said, hurriedly. 'You'd better move.'

My luck had run out.

***

Cops excluded, not many people assume the worst on finding a window of their home open, a light on, or even their front door unlocked. It takes a certain mind-set to immediately conclude there may be an intruder in your home. Most people assume the error is their own. That gives a burglar – or a cop in this case – the advantage. I've nearly been caught on several occasions, the closest in Northern Ireland in the late seventies when a team I was with were compromised placing recording devices in the home of a known IRA member. A tough republican with a fearsome reputation, even he had called out in the apparent belief one of his family had turned up without warning. As we made our escape through the rear windows, one of our lads had the presence of mind to shout a warning using an assumed Belfast accent, making it appear a team of local burglars had been caught in the act.

Not knowing which door Slater would use to enter the house, I walked as quickly as I could through the hallway and into the darkness of the living room. I'd made a mistake allowing a sense of urgency to override patience. We should have watched for him to return, waited until he'd settled in and then knocked on his door. We could have searched his home while talking to him. My best option now was to hide, hope he would react to the bedroom lights and then trust he'd think he'd either left them on or his girlfriend was in the house. Most people in his position would first call out and then go upstairs to investigate. As he did that, I'd be away through the nearest open door.

The sound of a key sliding into the lock of the front door caused my heart to pump wild and fast.

'That you, Jo?' a male voice called from the hallway. I moved back into the shadows and tucked myself behind a settee. It wasn't

309

perfect. If Slater opened the living-room door, turned on the light and started looking around, he would spot me within seconds.

'You upstairs?' he called again.

The sound of a set of keys being dropped onto the hallway table was followed by footsteps, moving slowly in my direction. The living-room door creaked open.

'Sergeant Slater?' It was Floria's voice, and from further away, near the front door.

'Who's asking,' he replied. The door stopped moving.

'Sergeant McLaren, SIB,' said Floria. 'Would you mind if we stepped into your kitchen for a moment?'

'What do you want with me, love?' Slater's voice now came from further along the hall, as if he'd taken a couple of steps towards where I assumed Floria was standing.

'My colleague and I just want to ask you a few questions,' she continued. 'If we could just take a seat in your kitchen, he'll be along in a few seconds.'

Clever, I thought. She thinks I'm upstairs so she's taking him to a room from where he won't be able to see me appear. And, not only that, she's telling him she isn't alone – so don't go thinking about doing a runner or turning nasty.

In the seconds that followed, as I listened hard for any further sound of conversation, I heard just two things; the kitchen door closing and the thumping of my heart as it forced blood through the narrow vessels near my eardrum. When it eased and I entered the hallway, I found the front door left open. I closed it firmly so the sound could be heard before opening the kitchen door.

Floria and Sergeant Slater were sitting at opposing ends of the table. Slater was in desert camouflage kit with a green, wax-cotton jacket over the top. Hair cropped short, he looked fit if a little overweight. He scowled at me, a challenging look that seemed intended to intimidate. I ignored him and as Floria's gaze shifted to me I winked at her – a thank you for her skill in rescuing me from potential disaster. She smiled in response.

'Sergeant Slater, meet Detective Inspector Finlay from the Met,' Floria said.

'An Inspector calls,' Slater said, a hint of irony in his voice. 'I was wondering when I'd be seeing you.'

'Word spreads quickly,' I said. 'You're aware why I'm here on camp, then?'

'*Were* on camp,' he smirked. 'I also heard you've been barred.'

'Who's Jo, Sergeant Slater?' I said, ignoring the jibe. Floria frowned at the question. It seemed she hadn't heard Slater's calls as he entered the house.

'No idea,' he replied.

'I was in the street when I heard you call out that name,' I said. 'Were you expecting someone to be here waiting for you?'

'Ah … yes, he's a mate. Sometimes stops over with me.' Slater smiled brazenly, a look I suspected might change when I retrieved Jodie Baker's letter from his bedside cabinet. For now, it was time to see if my plan was going to work.

I sat down at the kitchen table and began with some routine questions; asking Slater about the Army, about training, about his career to date, anything I felt would get him talking. I wanted him relaxed and confident he had things under control before we moved on to the more challenging stuff. It worked; he was talkative and seemed quite fond of the sound of his own voice. He also seemed keen to explain to me, a civvie, how little people like me understood Army life and how he was possibly one of the best NCOs the young recruits had. As we chatted, Floria's eyes glanced scornfully toward the ceiling several times. It was clear she didn't share Sergeant Slater's assessment of his abilities. Finally, we reached a point where I felt confident enough to ask about the stolen rifles.

'So, they turned up in London?' he said, in response to my question.

'Yes. And, as you will no doubt know, the register they were booked out on has gone missing.'

'I was aware of that.'

Floria looked at him quizzically. 'Are you sure there's nobody else in the house?' she asked.

For a split-second, a look of uncertainty crossed Slater's face. 'Not so far as I know,' he replied.

'The lights are on upstairs,' I said. 'Did you leave them on?'

'Must have done.'

'I'll check,' Floria said, as she pushed her chair back across the kitchen floor and stood up. 'I need to use your toilet, anyway. I'll just have a quick look around at the same time.'

'You have a warrant, I assume?' Slater replied, his earlier humour now replaced by a hint of resentment.

'We don't need one,' I said. 'We're making sure there isn't a burglar hiding upstairs.'

The Sergeant waved his hand dismissively as Floria disappeared into the hallway.

'Do you have a mobile phone?' I asked. Slater looked at me quizzically for a moment before casually tapping the breast pocket of his camouflage jacket. 'May I?' I said, holding out my hand.

He reached into his pocket, placed a modern-looking phone on the table and then slid it gently across to me. I recognised it as identical to the model used by Angela Davenport. 'It's an N-90,' he said, loftily.

'Means nothing to me,' I said, although I was wondering if we'd struck gold. 'A phone's a phone in my book.'

He sneered, as if dismissive of my ignorance. 'It's the latest model; set me back a few quid I can tell you.'

I reached into my pocket for my notebook, found the telephone number I wanted to check and typed the numbers onto the phone's contact list. It didn't register. Then, just to be sure, I typed in my own number and pressed the green 'call' button. My phone buzzed immediately and when I checked the incoming number it was very different to the one we were looking for. As I glanced across at Slater, I had a sense he had registered my disappointment. 'So, what are the unofficial theories on what happened to Davenport?' I said, as I passed the phone back to him.

He held out a hand, as I'd hoped he would, and I took the opportunity to look at it. It was smooth, even a little podgy, the nails hard-bitten and broken. There were no calluses I could see. He looked away from me and towards the hallway door. 'With no disrespect, sir,' he said. 'I thought you said you were here to talk about the SA80s that went, not go through something that's done and dusted? The inquest said it was suicide, end of.'

'Humour me. Soldiers talk, don't they? Do they think Davenport's death was connected to the theft?'

He shrugged, dismissively. 'If you listen to some of the Crows, they reckon it was because of an ex-boyfriend she got into an argument with.' He placed the phone carefully back in his pocket.

'At 7.30 in the morning?'

'They rise early here, sir. As for me, I've heard nothing to question the conclusion that she done herself in. She had powder burns on her hand ...'

'Both hands,' I said. 'As if her fingers were wrapped around a rifle barrel she was trying to push away from her face?'

Slater shrugged. 'I think the inquest got it right. She didn't have any real beef with anyone, she was a popular girl. The jealous ex-boyfriend theory had some legs except there wasn't an ex-boyfriend anyone knew of.' He slid back his seat and turned toward the door. 'Is your pet monkey going to ...' He stopped mid-sentence as Floria re-appeared in the doorway, the letter addressed to Jodie Baker held triumphantly in her hand.

'Thought you said Jo was a bloke, Sergeant Slater?' she said, as she dropped the letter on the table in front of me.

Slater leapt to his feet, the chair he'd been sitting on clattering onto the tiled floor. 'You're out of order McLaren,' he replied, angrily. 'What gives you monkeys the right to go nosing through people's private property?'

For a moment, Floria didn't respond. I sat still as I watched beads of perspiration appearing on the top lip of the training Sergeant's face. Gone was the benign, accommodating man we'd been speaking to a few moments earlier.

'Why don't we sit down and relax?' I suggested, calmly. Beneath the table though, I'd prepared. Moving my feet slightly, I braced myself in case things were about to kick-off.

Slater reached sullenly behind him, lifted the wooden chair from the floor and sat down again. His face had become flushed, sweat now clearly visible through the cropped, spiky hair that covered his scalp.

'Does Private Baker make a habit of leaving her personal corres' in your bedroom?' Floria asked. Her tone was scornful, taunting, as if she wanted to knock Slater off balance and increase the likelihood of him saying something that would help us.

It failed. In an instant, a virtual wiper-blade appeared, passing across the surface of Slater's face. His red-mist phase was gone, his composure and self-control returned. Only the sweat remained. He smiled, but his lips were thin and unpleasant. There was no warmth behind them.

'We met Private Baker in the Armoury,' I said, as I watched him. 'I take it she's a friend of yours?'

'Not a friend,' he replied. 'She's a Crow and it's my job to look after my flock.'

'It's a murder of Crows,' I said.

'And what do you mean by that?' Slater leaned forward over the table, fixing me hard with his gaze.

I kept still. 'The collective name for Crows ... it's a murder, not a flock.'

Slater's thin smile returned as he relaxed again. 'Ah ... ok,' he said. 'I thought you were being clever.'

'Like Angela Davenport's death?' I said, and again I braced myself in case the question triggered another angry response. 'Was that a murder?'

If the question got beneath his skin, Slater didn't show it. Instead, he ignored me and switched his gaze to the letter now sat on the table in front of Floria. 'That's from her parents,' he said, as he pointed at it. 'She asked me to read it because she needs advice on how to handle them wanting her to leave the Army.'

'Why is it in your bedroom?' Floria asked.

'Because it's bloody private,' he snapped. 'She gave it to me to read and I said I'd help draft a reply for her. It's the kind of thing a decent NCO does for his soldiers.'

'Did you provide the same kind of support to Tom Morgan?' I said.

Slater showed no reaction to the mention of the name. 'Morgan was a good lad,' he said, coolly. 'Sailed through training. We had a drink to his memory in the Sergeants' Mess this evening.'

'He didn't need extra help then?'

'We ... and by that, I mean *all* the NCOs ... we liked Morgan. One of the lads even invited him to join us in the Mess on his last night here.'

'Was that Sergeant Masters who invited him?' I asked.

315

'I don't recall.'

'It's unusual though. Allowing a Crow in the Sergeants Mess?'

'Like I said, Morgan was a good lad.'

'Do you recall if Masters signed him in?' I asked.

'No idea.' Slater looked at me with curiosity. 'You ex green Army yourself, Inspector?'

I'd made a small slip, of the kind Floria had previously picked up on. Not everyone, and particularly not a civvie, knew a guest had to be signed in to the Sergeants' Mess. 'Just a family connection,' I said. 'Father was a fusilier in the war. I paused for a second and then stood up. 'Ok, we're done here,' I said.

From the look Floria gave me, I could see she didn't agree. That was good, because I wanted her to feel frustrated.

'Were you at Deepcut when any of the deaths happened there?' Floria said, unexpectedly.

I saw real venom in Slater's eyes as he turned away and ignored her.

'Were you?' I asked him.

Slowly, the Sergeant faced off to me, a look of contempt on his face. 'I was not,' he said. 'And I think you should leave.'

Chapter 60

'You gave up too easy,' Floria said, angrily, as we climbed back into the car. 'I thought you'd know a way to *make* him talk.'

'You assume I've given up, Floria,' I replied.

'You need to understand what's at stake here,' she continued, seemingly having either not listened to or not heeded what I'd said. 'Hundreds of women in the Army have suffered at the hands of people like that pervert. Just think about that for a minute because I'm telling you there are very few exceptions and those that haven't been through it have witnessed it. Ask any woman who's served and she'll tell you. These monsters are everywhere.'

'So, what are you suggesting we do?' I asked.

'Beat it out of him.'

'Forcing a confession out of him is worthless. It won't stand up in court.'

'I'm beyond caring, frankly. We need to loosen his tongue, if only to find out who else is involved. People like Slater need to learn they aren't immune from justice and however long it takes, we'll come after them. Only once they see their kind behind bars will we ever begin to put a stop to it.'

'Retribution isn't justice, Floria. And like I said a moment ago, what makes you think we're finished. The night is young. Give it twenty minutes and we'll shake him down again. I've interviewed a lot of men like Slater. His kind don't admit anything, even when the evidence is staring them in the face.'

Floria turned to me and smiled, expectantly. 'We're gonna go back for another pop at him?'

I nodded. 'In a moment, just as soon as I've checked something. Slater's involved, I'm sure of it. He had the same model phone as

Angela Davenport in his pocket. Even boasted how much it was worth. How many of those do you think we'd find on this camp?'

'Maybe someone here bought a job lot?' she replied. 'Knowing how tight squaddies are, it could be someone dealing in cheap black-market ones. Did you check it?'

'I did. It wasn't the one we're looking for.'

'But we're so close,' she said, slamming a fist into the palm of her hand. 'I should have pummelled the fucker until he told us what we want to know.'

'I glanced at my watch. I was almost forty minutes late for the call to Harry. 'I need to call a friend,' I said. Reaching into my pocket for my phone, I soon found the number for Harry's work line. 'You can do what you like after I'm gone,' I said as I keyed it in. 'Don't rely on it working, though. Torture victims spill what they think you want to hear, whatever will make the violence stop. Finding out what they're hiding takes more guile.'

'Surely you must know a couple of tricks to get him talking?' Floria replied. 'Christ sake, he was sweating like a marine on a spelling test when I showed him that letter belonging to Baker.'

'You got under his skin.'

'Did you look under his bed?'

'At the bergen you mean?'

'Did you see the duct tape hidden in one of the boots? Who the hell keeps duct tape under their bed?'

I frowned, thinking for a moment before I pressed the call button to reach Harry. I'd missed the tape, and Floria was right, it was an unusual thing to do. 'Baker is sleeping there,' I said. 'I'd be certain of it. But Slater isn't the first NCO to have a relationship with a recruit and he won't be the last. Did you look at his hands?'

'Damn … I forgot.'

318

'I didn't. They were smooth, no calluses. He wasn't the second man in the video.' As my call connected, I held up my hand to pause our conversation.

Harry answered immediately. 'You took your time,' he said. His voice was warm, relaxed. Good news, I figured. Hopefully, it meant my request to trace the phone used to send the video hadn't got him into too much hot water.

'I had the impression it was all fairly routine,' he said, after I asked what had happened when he searched on the number. 'The boss called me upstairs … told me it was flagged, and that I was to keep an eye on it.'

'You weren't warned off?' I said.

'Not at all. But she knows our connection and, given what's happened since, I've no doubt she told the MOD. Perhaps they decided you were getting too close and had you pulled.'

'So, who set up the flag?'

'Special Investigation Branch. But knowing that won't help you. It could be anyone in the RMP from the Provost Marshal through to a local investigator somewhere.'

'But, it's a burner phone though?' I queried.

'It's an unregistered sim card, yes, and it's still in use. I got your message from Wendy so we've been monitoring it. It's turned on right now.'

'That's just what I was hoping for,' I said. 'How quick to get a fix on the user?'

'I can tell you right now. It's located in the area of Prince Albert Barracks.'

'Can you be more specific?'

'Sorry. We've triangulated it from local masts but the camp area is the best we can say.'

Floria tapped me hard on the arm. As I turned towards her, I could see she was pointing towards Slater's house. I looked across to see the curtains twitch before the living-room light was extinguished. We were being watched.

'Hold on a minute,' Harry said, excitedly.

'What's up?'

There was no response for a few seconds. In the background, I could hear the sound of someone using a keyboard. Then a second voice cut in, female and quietly spoken, saying the words '*incoming call*'.

'You there, boss?' Harry said, as he came back on the line.

'What's happening?'

'The burner phone, it's live. Someone is using it right now.'

Floria had the driver's door open before I could react. I dropped my phone, pulled her back in the car and held her arm tight. 'Wait,' I said. 'Slater is doing what I'd hoped. He knows we're close so he's warning his mates. He also knows I can check on the Nokia he had in his pocket so he's using another phone he thinks we don't know about. That will be the phone we're looking for.'

'I heard what your friend said,' Floria replied, excitedly. 'Why didn't you tell me what you were up to?'

'I needed you to act naturally. If you'd known it was a trick, you might have behaved differently.'

'If we're quick, we'll catch him with it.'

'He's watching us from behind the curtains right now,' I said, firmly. 'By the time we get to the front door of his house he'll be out the back and the phone will be gone with him. Just start the engine … and don't look at the house.'

'But what are you planning?' Floria said, as she turned the key in the ignition. 'We can't just leave him there.'

'Drive off nice and slow. Make it look normal, no rushing. Stop when we're in the next side street.'

As I picked up the phone from the floor of the car, Floria put the car into gear. The call had disconnected. I rang Harry back.

'What the hell happened there?' he said.

'Youthful enthusiasm,' I replied. 'Is he still on the phone?'

'Yes, it's connected now … an incoming call. If he's close to you, you'd best move quickly.'

Floria did as I'd asked her, parked the car around the corner out of sight of the house and switched off the engine.

'Ready?' I said.

'Damn right,' she said, as she reached for the door handle once more.

'Follow me, then.'

We moved quickly, into the alley-way and from there into Slater's garden. With Floria at my shoulder, I checked the rear door leading to his kitchen. Quietly, slowly, I eased down the handle. The latch disengaged with a gentle click. It was still unlocked, just as I had left it. I turned to Floria and held a single finger to my lips before stepping into the darkness.

Chapter 61

Slater's raised voice was coming from deeper inside the house. 'No way, mate,' he said. 'This time you're on your own.' He was still on the phone. I moved quietly across the kitchen. In the hallway, I could hear footsteps coming towards us. The door to the kitchen opened.

Slater ran as soon as he saw me but he then faced the impossible task of unlocking his front door before I caught up. In his left hand he was holding a small Nokia type phone, a much older and less flashy device than the model he'd produced earlier. He turned as I came up behind him, raised his arm, and moved as if to smash it on the wall. I dived forward, managing to deflect most of the force and then wrestled it from his grip. He continued to resist but my knee slamming into his groin was immediately followed by Floria's forearm connecting with his chin. It ended the fight.

'Kitchen, now,' I said.

***

'It's working fine,' said Floria, as she checked Slater's second phone. Once again, we were sat around his kitchen table. This time though, the subject of our questioning was looking a lot sorrier for himself than he had a few minutes previously. On the table sat the N-90 he'd had in his jacket, some keys, a few coins and a scrunched-up piece of paper; the entire contents of his pockets.

'Who were you talking to, Paul?' I said. My question was met by silence and only the briefest of scowls.

'Ring the number,' Floria said. 'We need to confirm this is the right phone.'

'It looks too old,' I replied, as I reached in my pocket for my notebook and phone, located the number we were hoping to trace, and called it. The connection was unobtainable – phone switched off. 'You sure it's on and working?' I said to her.

'Definite,' she said, checking the screen. 'Full signal showing.'

'Hang on a minute.' I watched Slater carefully as I then dialled Harry again.

'This is getting to be a habit,' he said, as he answered. 'Did you get your man?'

'We think so. Is the device still on?'

'Negative. It disconnected from the network a couple of minutes ago.'

'You're sure? The phone we've recovered is on and connected.'

'Then it's not the one you're looking for,' he said.

'It's not it,' I said to Floria. 'Try looking at who he called.'

I had a horrible feeling of déjà vu as I recalled Harry saying the call had been incoming to the suspect phone. Slater hadn't been receiving a call on the suspect device, he'd *called* it. Our only hope now lay with his phone log.

Floria tapped the tiny keys. All the time, I kept my eyes on Slater, watching for a reaction. He turned to sit across the chair, his legs crossed, his arms and head hung low on his chest.

'Shit,' Floria exclaimed.

'It's not logged?' I said.

'Quite the opposite. Look.' She slid the phone across the table towards me and, as I looked at the screen I noticed she was standing up. I read the name.

Pemberton.

***

'Why did you call Captain Pemberton, Paul?' I said, as I returned the phone to Floria. She had just re-appeared having had another look around the upstairs rooms. The concerned look on her face told me something was awry.

323

'It's not a crime to call someone is it?' Slater replied, venomously.

'Ask him straight,' said Floria, looking at me. 'Give him a chance to redeem himself.'

A moment of uncertainty crossed the Sergeant's face. 'What do you mean by that?' he demanded.

'I mean how do you explain these?' Floria said as, from her pocket, she pulled what I first took to be three or four playing cards. It was only as she spread them out on the table that I saw they were photographs. 'Not exactly what you'd call family snaps are they?'

I leaned forward for a closer look. The photos were all of young women in varied states of undress. I remembered Michael Davenport's words. Only a father would really understand. Slater was clearly the kind of man every father dreads his daughter meeting. 'Where did you get those?' I said to Floria.

'Upstairs. They were in a cupboard in the second bedroom. I know a couple of them.'

'Are they Crows?'

'Yes. I found a ski mask as well.'

'A black one?'

Floria nodded as I turned to face Slater. 'It was you left the note, wasn't it?' I said.

He stared at me, a blank expression on his face. There was no denial, no attempt to ask me to explain. He knew. It was Slater who'd tried to warn me off.

I held one of the photographs up in front of him. 'Are these all recruits, Paul?' I demanded, as he continued to look at me with disdain. 'These are kids, barely out of school. You've been taking pictures while you have sex with them?'

'Consenting adults, Inspector.'

I took a breath and composed myself. 'Ok … enough's enough. Let's cut to the chase. We've evidence implicating you in the murder of Private Angela Davenport. When we leave here tonight, you're coming with us.'

'You're nicking me?'

'The evidence we have puts you on a fine-line between being involved or simply knowing what happened?'

'Which means exactly what?' he answered. 'She killed herself, everyone knows that.'

'We know different, Paul. What do you want to be? A witness or the accused.'

'Sounds complete bollocks to me, you've got nothing.'

In for a penny, in for a pound, I thought. Floria had sat back down now and was staring aggressively at Slater. As she'd suggested, it was time to ask the questions we both wanted answered. 'What do you know about the video Captain Pemberton sent to Davenport?' I said.

'What video?' he replied. 'What is this bullshit?'

'Pemberton was blackmailing her, sending her messages from his phone, the phone you just rang … he made a film and then used it to threaten her.' I watched Slater as we talked and saw how his body language was now changing. Contrary to my expectations, he seemed to be growing in confidence, his shoulders becoming straight, his eyes studying me and Floria. He shook his head. 'News to me, and I don't know what you think you have but it's bollocks. The inquest verdict was suicide.'

'We've been told it was *you* who hid Davenport's favourite rifle on the day of the parade,' I said. 'And then *you* used it a month later to shoot her before faking her suicide.'

'What?' Slater's demeanour changed in an instant as he slammed a fist down on the table. The transformation from arrogance to anger was so profound it was as if a switch had clicked and an intense, angry and violent twin who'd been lying dormant beneath the surface had emerged. 'Who told you that?' he spat.

'It all adds up,' I said, leaning close into his face. 'Unless you know better?'

'What would I know? Is one of them bastards fitting me up?'

'All I know is when we leave here tonight it will either be with you in handcuffs or us knowing what really happened to Davenport.'

'So, you don't believe it either?'

'I'm keeping an open mind.'

As I stepped back, Slater hesitated for a few moments. It looked like he was weighing me up. Trying to decide whether to speak or remain silent. Finally, he spoke. 'Don't treat me like a fucking idiot,' he said.

'From where I'm looking, I see a faked suicide put together by a killer covering his tracks,' I replied. I wanted to push Slater hard now. If I could convince him someone was putting him in the frame, he might be prepared to open up. I wanted to know if he would be prepared to name names to get off the hook.

It didn't work. He leaned back in his chair and, almost as if another wiper had been drawn across his face, he was back in control. 'I'm saying nothing more, not a thing,' he said, calmly. 'And you've got nothing, you're bluffing.'

Floria and I continued for several more minutes as we worked together to try and put Slater under pressure but we got nowhere. In the end, he turned to face away from us, ignoring us completely.

As we sat in silence for a moment, Slater raised his head to watch what Floria was doing at the opposite end of the table. She'd been reading the tiny piece of paper she'd found earlier in his trouser pocket. Suddenly, and quite unexpectedly, she leapt from her seat and went back upstairs. A few seconds later I heard her on the telephone.

'What's she up to?' Slater said.

Although I had no idea, I decided to bluff him. 'She's talking to some other officers to see if their suspect will tell us any more about you.'

'You've got someone else as well?'

'Someone who seems keen to put you in the frame.'

'Fuck off, you're bluffing.'

'Do you know what they do to nonces in prison, Paul? Do you want me to tell you?'

'I'm saying nothing.'

And there we sat, listening to Floria talking frantically on her phone, both of us wondering what she was doing.

A moment later, she burst back into the kitchen. She was pulling at something in her inside pocket, something with attached wiring. My jaw must have dropped as I recognised what I was looking at – it was a bug, a listening device.

I frowned at her. 'You're wired?'

'What did you expect? That we would be interviewing the one person who can expose the whole rotten barrel and I wouldn't be recording it?'

Floria moved closer to where Slater sat, his face turned now away from us. 'I was right about your car then?' I said, as she dropped the note on the table in front of me.

'No,' she replied, as she stared, venomously at Slater. 'As it happens, you were wrong. And you can blame yourself. When I reported back to my office that you'd asked if the car was bugged, they thought it was funny. They stopped laughing when I suggested it was actually a good idea.'

'So, what happens now?' I demanded, half expecting the rear door to the house to burst open and several military police officers to come barging in.

With her left hand indicating the note on the table, Floria moved closer to Slater. 'When and where are you meeting Mick Fitzgerald?' she said to him, angrily.

Slater sneered and then stared hard at me, his lip raised in a snarl. 'I have no idea what she's talking about … Robert,' he said, slowly.

My stomach tightened as I recalled the words in the note left on Wendy's car. Slater had paused deliberately before using my name. He knew what was on the note left on Wendy's car and he was now threatening me again.

What happened next took me as much by surprise as it did Paul Slater. From her jacket pocket, Floria pulled a small, telescopic baton which she racked with a flick of her wrist and then swung down hard on Slater's head. There was a crack as the steel struck home. The effect was instant; he folded to the floor in a heap.

'What the …' I stood, leaning in towards the Sergeant's now semi-conscious form, holding out my arm in a vain attempt to protect him. 'What are you playing at, Floria?' I exclaimed. 'I said we'd put him under pressure, not beat him senseless.'

'The bug is off, Finlay,' Floria spat as she rounded on me. 'You said yourself he's the kind that won't talk and we're getting nowhere.'

'You should have trusted me,' I said.

'We're out of options. I'm gonna bring him round then we'll see if he wants a little more before he talks.'

'That won't work,' I said.

'This is on me, not you,' she replied, angrily. 'Look at the note … look at the bloody note. This bastard isn't gonna talk unless he's persuaded and we haven't got all night. Read it!'

I did as Floria asked. In the half-light of the kitchen and with my fingers trembling at the rush of adrenalin, I strained to read the scribble. When I did, the message was clear.

Copper gone. Room ready. Rogers due 2200hrs.

'Who's it from?' I said to Slater. It was a pointless question as he was still too stunned to respond.

'It has to be Fitzgerald,' Floria said from behind me. 'They're planning something to do with Ellie.'

'How do you know it's from him?'

'Because of how he spelled her name. At the court martial, Fitzgerald could never get his head around her surname having a D in it.'

'That's why he was on the phone,' I said. 'He was telling them he wouldn't be joining them.'

'Exactly,' Floria said, throwing a saucepan of water over Slater's face before checking to see if he was coming around. 'Ellie said she was due to meet some recruits. It has to be a trap. Fitzgerald wants retribution and they plan to do it tonight before he gets transferred off the base.'

'Room ready … what the fuck does that mean?' My stomach felt hollow. I thought of Angela Davenport, drugged and vulnerable, in a room with three men. 'Ring her,' I said. 'Warn her off.'

'That's what I was trying to do while I was upstairs. Her mobile is turned off.'

'Ring the Officers' Mess.'

'I called them too.' Floria said, as she began to remove her jacket. 'She went out around nine o'clock.'

'Ok,' I said, as I thought things through. There was one last trick up my sleeve to persuade Slater to talk. 'Do you remember what I said in the car?'

Floria nodded, confirming she understood although looking slightly confused. It was time for my final play.

As Slater became more alert, I knelt down, got my face close to his and put it to him straight. 'What does 'the room's set up' mean?' I demanded.

Slater raised his top lip and scowled.

'Where's Rodgers due to be at ten?'

Again, he didn't reply. As expected, we were getting nowhere.

'Either you tell us now what's going on, Sergeant Slater, or you'll tell us after my friend has finished with you … your choice.' I nodded at Floria, hoping she would follow my lead.

Slater laughed in my face. 'You can't fuckin' touch me, I've got rights. You lay another finger on me and you'll both be in the Guardhouse.'

'If you don't want to watch, go sit in the car,' Floria said to me. 'I've had to put up with arseholes like this my entire time in the Army. They only understand one thing. A bit of summary justice … that's what you Met boys call it, I believe? How would you feel if it were one of *your* daughters those men had filmed themselves raping?'

Slater shakily raised himself onto his elbows. He was a predator, one who exploited vulnerable young recruits to fulfil his warped sexual pleasure and this was our final chance to discover what he knew. Floria's methods were never going to work and would end up with us both in the dock. I knew a better way. I'd read Slater's file and had an idea I thought might break him.

'Ok,' I said, as I looked down at Slater's prostrate form. 'Go get the duct tape from upstairs.' I pulled the curtains of the kitchen window together and began pushing the chairs clear of the table.

Floria hesitated. 'What for?' she asked, as she glanced toward the hallway door.

'When you get back, tape his legs together and put him face-up on the table. I'll show you a little trick to loosen his tongue.'

Once Floria had left us, I leaned over Slater to discourage any thought he might have of trying to escape. 'What are you gonna do?' he asked, a first flicker of doubt appearing in his eyes.

'I'm going to make you wish you'd been more honest, Paul,' I said.

'But you're a cop,' he said. 'You follow the rules.'

'Maybe I am,' I replied, as I stared hard at him. 'And maybe I'm not. The only thing certain now is you're going to tell us what we need to know, the easy way, or the painful way.'

'You can go to hell,' he replied, angrily.

Floria returned quickly with what we needed. I put a section of the duct tape over Slater's mouth and, as we worked to bind his legs and arms, I said nothing until the remaining tape was in place and he was lying prone on the kitchen table. I then put two saucepans under the table legs to raise the feet. It was important his head was lower than his body. I wanted him to understand I knew what I was doing.

'Fill two large saucepans with water,' I ordered Floria. I pulled a small towel from a kitchen drawer and held it in the air, making a point of stretching it out and testing it for strength where I knew Slater would be able to see what I was doing. All the time, I watched his eyes. He was studying me.

***

Of all the experiences I went through during SAS selection and training, I would have no hesitation in saying the prisoner interrogation phase was, by far, the worst. Some candidates, myself included, started out with the naive belief that, if you successfully evaded being captured by the 'hunters', you would avoid being thrown blindfolded into the tank – the softening-up room – from where, one by one, you would be taken for questioning. Others deemed it pragmatic to be caught early in the belief it was better to face interrogation on a full belly and with your energy reserves intact. The reality was nobody ever escaped interrogation and there was no 'best way' to prepare for it. It was part of the test, and no matter how long you kept the directing staff waiting, your turn would come.

When you are undergoing enhanced interrogation – water-boarding as it's so often called – nothing else in your life has any relevance whatsoever. The only thoughts in your mind revolve around survival. On your back, head below your feet and strapped to a board with a wet towel draped over your face is disorienting, even by itself. You feel vulnerable but you've been trained, and you're expecting it. As the water starts to enter your nose and mouth you think, as many others before you have, 'I can beat this, I can breathe through my mouth, use my tongue, spit the water out and take quick breaths.' For a few seconds, you might even convince yourself it's working, but then the water keeps flowing, and your nose, your mouth and your throat fill with water and panic starts to take over. You feel you are drowning and so you fight, and you strike out with all the strength your adrenalin-fuelled body can muster. In those moments though, it's not fellow human beings your limbs are competing with, it's restraints like duct tape or ropes, something you will never beat.

My sole experience on the board still haunts me. After the water stopped, the questions began. What is your real name? What is your mission? What unit are you from? All the usual things a captured soldier is supposed to resist. Disoriented and in a state of panic, it's almost impossible to resist. You try though, because you are determined, and because you want to be a part of a unique band of brothers called the 'Special Air Service'. You're convinced you must hold out to achieve that. Then, just when you think you've passed the test and it's all over, the experience is repeated. And this time, you *know* what it's going to feel like.

As a technique, enhanced interrogation trumps almost all methods of physical torture – and torture is most certainly what it is – as there are no visible scars and no wounds. At the end of my second session under the towel – which I was told later lasted just sixteen seconds –

I was convinced something had gone wrong and I was about to drown. Terminal hypoxia they call it. In my panic, I willingly confessed to being a Russian spy attempting to infiltrate the Special Air Service as part of a plot to assassinate Andy Pandy. Yes, Andy Pandy, an idea the interrogators found to be particularly amusing when it came to questioning 'Ruperts' – the officer candidates.

***

I ripped the tape away from Slater's mouth. 'Are you ready for this, Paul?'

'You're fuckin' bluffing,' he said. His confidence had slipped though. There was less anger in his voice, less arrogance. The doubt was creeping in.

'I don't know if you're familiar with the technique, Paul,' I continued. 'So, we'll begin with a little explanation. I'm going to place this cloth over your face. When I give the command, my friend will begin pouring water in your nose and mouth. You will struggle to breathe …'

'I know what it is,' Slater interrupted. 'What kind of a fuckin' cop are you?'

I leaned over his face and smiled as sadistically as I could. 'One with the brakes off. I'm sure you know all about the board, Paul. But, I'd be surprised if you've experienced it. Humour me as I explain what's going to happen. This is going to hurt … a lot. At first, you'll think it's nothing but in a few seconds your throat and lungs will start burning to the point where you begin to wonder if it is actually acid being poured into you.'

I brushed the cloth gently over Slater's cheeks and nose. I was tormenting him. I knew the more he feared what was about to happen, the less he'd be able to resist and the sooner we'd have some answers. 'Try not to fight,' I said. 'It only makes things worse as your muscles demand oxygen and your lungs fill with water.'

I glanced across at Floria. She looked scared. In her hand she held one of the saucepans. He hands trembled. For a moment, I thought she may lose her nerve. 'Ready?' I said to her. She nodded.

I laid the cloth over Slater's face. 'Pour,' I said. 'And keep pouring until I tell you to stop.'

Chapter 62

Jodie darted back and forth, using the shadows cast by the estate street lights to hide. It was just like the days when, as kids, she and her mates had broken into the rear of the local shops and were hurrying home, dodging the cops looking for them. Only this time she was on her own, and in a hole so deep her whole body shook with fear.

In her hand, she still held her key to Paul's door. It was only luck she'd not walked in on what had been happening. A cautionary habit of checking through the front window to see what Paul was doing had saved her. If he was in front of the television, watching porn with a pile of empty cans beside him, that was a bad time to call. Full of beer and horny, Paul was a man best avoided.

With the sofa empty and television turned off, she'd spotted a light coming from the kitchen. Presuming Paul was about to head off to join his mates at the motorpool, she'd put her key in the lock of the front door and had just been about to turn it when she'd heard what sounded like a muffled scream coming from the kitchen. At first, she'd wondered if it was a radio but then it repeated, and this time louder. Not knowing what she might walk into, but aware she could be in big trouble with Paul if she didn't show, she'd walked around to the rear alley and into the back garden to check.

What she'd seen through a gap in the curtains had frozen her to the spot. Paul was taped down on the kitchen table while the military policewoman held a saucepan of water over his face. The detective was standing to one side, writing in a small notebook. Paul was doing nearly all the talking and his voice, it was so high-pitched and trembling, unlike anything she'd ever heard before. And every time he stopped talking, the policewoman would make as if she were going to pour more water over him. Paul would squeal like a stuck pig, 'no ... no, please no,' as he begged to them to stop before starting talking again.

Jodie recognised what was happening immediately. She'd seen it on the news and read about it in magazines. Water-boarding they called it, an interrogation technique the Americans were said to use. It was horrific. The cops wanted answers and were now prepared to do whatever it took to get them. Paul was telling them everything and that meant one thing. They would be coming for her too.

She'd retreated to the shadows. She had to run ... somewhere. Her immediate thoughts had been to go home to her family. She could get a cab, get to the train station, then phone mum to see if she'd come and pick her up. No use asking her step-dad, he wouldn't shift his lazy, fat frame from the settee to help anyone, least of all her. After a few moments, though, she'd changed her mind. It wouldn't work. After the barracks, her home would be the first place the cops would look.

For the third time in as many minutes, she reached into her jacket pocket, pulled her mobile out and, using her body to hide the light from the screen, called Naomi's number. Paul had been wrong, so wrong. 'Don't worry,' he'd said, and so many times she'd lost count. 'As soon as the inquest is over, the police will lose interest.' Again, the call cut through to an answer-phone. Where was her friend, she fretted? Surely, she'd have finished with that officer by now?

Getting back to the camp now seemed the only sensible thing to do. She'd head to the block and find her friend. They could go together to tell Sergeant Masters what she'd seen at Paul's house. He'd know what to do.

Chapter 63

The smell of takeout pizza drifting from an open window reminded Ellie she hadn't yet eaten. She checked her watch. It was time to make a move and, from her position in the shadows behind Rowallan block, she'd seen nothing to cause concern.

First floor, Room 7, Baker had said. Ellie had been watching the comings and goings just to be sure. Room 7 was lit but she saw no sign of occupants. In other rooms she'd seen young women in various states of dress, some doing ironing or cleaning kit, others sitting around chatting. Three windows were unlit, possibly where young soldiers were on a guard shift or the room was unoccupied. Nobody seemed to bother drawing curtains.

The call to Floria had been a wise move. She'd been in need of a sounding board and her friend had been the perfect choice. Floria had been cautious, even a little fearful, and had initially counselled against attending the meeting. She had a promising enquiry underway and thought Ellie might be best waiting until someone from the RMP was available to go with her. Ellie hadn't been convinced, even though she'd agreed with her friend it would be best to avoid bumping into Mick Fitzgerald. 'These girls could easily change their minds,' Ellie had said. Floria had eventually conceded the point, and although she'd warned to be careful, she'd agreed a meeting with girls who were willing to talk wasn't an opportunity that would come again soon.

How Naomi would react when they met had also caused Ellie some disquiet. Would she be hostile as she recognised the girl who'd befriended her, especially when she discovered Ellie was an officer? Might she Naomi duped, or would she be relieved on seeing a familiar face? Ellie hoped them both being scousers would help swing it. That shared background might just be enough to overcome any sense of betrayal.

***

Ellie stepped out of the shadows and walked purposefully around the side of the building towards the main entrance. In the quiet of the hallway, two young soldiers were lent against a wall in a tight embrace. Neither reacted as she marched past and up the stairway. At the first floor landing she turned left into the corridor, counted past three closed doors on the right, and then stopped to check the door sign. It was number 7. She knocked on the door twice, and not too hard. Announce presence, don't make it sound official, she thought. After two or three seconds, the door swung open.

She recognised Naomi immediately, but she had the advantage of expectation. Perhaps it was stepping in from the poorly lit landing or the combination of uniform and lack of make-up, but Naomi showed no immediate sign of knowing her. That changed though, the moment she spotted the fading marks on Ellie's neck. 'It's you,' she said, her mouth open, her eyes wide with surprise.

'The very same,' Ellie replied, as she scanned the room. There was a smell of sweat but they were alone. From the outline of a figure on one of three duvet-covered beds, it looked like Naomi had been lying down waiting for her visitor to arrive. On the pillow of another bed lay the base and tip of a pool cue, unscrewed and presumably belonging to one of the occupants of the room. 'Where's Jodie?' she asked.

'Er ... she ... oh, fuck, this wasn't meant to happen,' said Naomi.

The response wasn't as Ellie expected. 'I don't follow,' she asked. 'I thought she was supposed to be here with you?'

'It wasn't supposed to be you, I mean,' Naomi blurted. 'You're a mate ... sort of. I was expecting some random officer I'd never heard of.'

'Well, it's me. And yes, I'm guilty of putting some slap on so I could mix in the bar.'

'You were spying on us?'

'I was following up on a complaint alleging women in my Company were having problems with the training staff.'

'Well, you certainly got an eyeful, didn't you? Corporal West groping Amy in the toilets saw to that, didn't it?'

'Jodie tells me you want to talk about your NCOs?'

Naomi had begun to pace up and down the small room, her eyes darting from side to side and then to Ellie, to her face and to the bruises on Ellie's neck. 'I don't believe this,' she repeated several times. 'I don't fuckin' believe this.'

Ellie stood with her back to the door, watching Naomi but confused by her behaviour. 'What don't you believe?' she asked.

'I don't believe what's happening,' Naomi said. 'This was supposed to be a little errand, a favour to make sure we got the postings we wanted.'

'What kind of favour?'

Naomi stopped pacing and turned to confront her visitor. 'Who are you?' she demanded. 'I mean, who are you really?'

'I'm someone who wants to help,' Ellie replied. 'I came up through the ranks and I've been where you are now. I've only been an officer for a couple of months.'

'You made it to Sandhurst from the likes of this place?'

'It can happen. It was graft all the way, I can tell you.'

Naomi breathed deeply. 'I believe you. I guess you want an explanation?'

'That would be a start.'

'You remember that man in the respirator outside the NAAFI?'

'Sergeant Masters.'

'You know his name?' Naomi replied, hesitantly. 'How can that be ... I mean, how could you? He's one of them, the Respirator Gang. They rule this place.'

'I recognised him when I saw him at the Armoury earlier today. The next time we meet will be a day he regrets.'

'You'll be wasting your time. He's untouchable.'

'We'll see,' Ellie said. 'So, how many are there in this gang?'

'Four or five hardcore, we reckon. But they bring in the odd recruit they take a shine to, to make up their numbers. Tom Morgan, the lad they found up the mountain, he was one of 'em.'

'What do they get up to ... apart from raping drunken women, of course?'

'What don't they do? Mostly it's about having sex with the girls, yes ... but they're into other things as well. They took the rifles that copper's been asking about. Do you know Sergeant Slater?'

'Why, was he also involved in stealing them?'

'He made sure Morgan and Davenport were posted to sit in the cab of the lorry so it would be easy for Masters to take their rifles.'

'So, it was Masters who took the rifles?'

'He was in on it, definite,' Naomi said. 'I reckon if things had gone to plan you would be talking to their little gang right now.'

'Gone to plan? What kind of plan?'

'That's why you're here. This was set up by Slater to get you to the motorpool. What Jodie told you was just a story to get you here ...'

'But it sounded true.'

'It is true, everything she said. Only ... we don't actually want it going no further. We just want our transfers.'

'So, what was supposed to happen?'

'I was supposed to meet you here and then take you to meet some other girls. Only there wouldn't be any other girls … just Slater and his mates.'

'It was a trap?' Ellie said, as she sat on the nearest bed. 'How on earth did they make you do this?'

'They've got stuff on us, things they would use if we crossed them.'

'What kind of stuff?'

Naomi paused and turned to look at her reflection in the window. 'The motorpool is where they take their girls,' she said, without answering the question. 'They've got a room they use.'

'Who is they?' Ellie pressed. 'Can you give me names?'

'Slater, Masters, Doug West and one or two others we're not sure of. Their victims don't exactly talk about it.'

'And you?'

Naomi lowered her gaze to stare at the floor. 'Jodie failed her fitness test. They said if I did it for one of them then she wouldn't get kicked out. I didn't know they were filming it.'

'They filmed it?'

'That's what they do. It's their clever trick. They record themselves having sex with you and then use it to control you.'

Ellie felt queasy as the implications of what Naomi was saying sank in. Assuming it was all true, and she had no reason to think otherwise, what was going on in the Training Regiment was far worse than she could have imagined. 'And knowing that's the kind of thing they do,' she said. 'You still went along with fooling me into going there?'

'We figured they wouldn't touch an officer … and they said they only wanted to discuss something with you. But we weren't to tell you, we had to stick to their story and, if we did as they said, we'd both get our transfers.'

'What time were they expecting you at the motorpool?'

'Just after ten. We should have been on our way by now. Christ, this really is a mess.'

'How many of them are going to be there?'

'Like I said, we don't really know. Masters and Slater will be there, probably … and maybe that new Sergeant. He seems to be well in with them already.'

'The new Sergeant?' Ellie asked, as the hairs on her neck stood up.

'Fitzgerald,' said Naomi.

Ellie reached out a hand to Naomi but held back when she saw how much her fingers were trembling. 'Best you sit down,' she said, as reassuringly as she could manage. Her heart had begun pounding so hard it seemed fit to burst from her chest. 'I think I know what's going on and, if I'm right, we're going to need a plan to stop this evening ending very badly for both of us.'

Chapter 64

Aware of the ticking clock, the two women quickly discussed their options. Naomi felt constrained by fear whereas Ellie wanted Fitzgerald caught bang to rights. It was a quarter past ten by the time they'd agreed a strategy they both felt comfortable with.

The plan was for Naomi to head to the motorpool on her own and report that, although she'd done her best, Lieutenant Rodgers had refused to accompany her to an isolated part of the camp at such a late hour. Although worried the NCOs would be angry, Naomi accepted there was little choice. Ellie would wait in the shadows, ready to call the MPs if anything should kick-off. If it didn't, Ellie would deal with the NCOs in the coming days.

At least that's how Ellie sold it to Naomi. In truth, she had other ideas, more immediate and more effective. 'I'll leave first,' she said, as she stood up from the bed. 'Give me a couple of minutes head-start.'

She stepped away from Naomi and reached for the door handle. Two minutes, she calculated, would be more than enough to find a spot somewhere between Rowallan Block and the motorpool where she could wait in the shadows ready to follow the young recruit. Then she would call Floria. Fitzgerald was behind this, she was certain. Slater was just a messenger. Mick Fitzgerald arrives at the barracks and, within a couple of days, two recruits have attempted to deliver a fake message that should have taken her at night to a remote part of the base. It was too much of a coincidence. It was time to turn the tables on him.

A dull sound from the corridor alerted Ellie to the presence of someone outside. She turned to Naomi and raised a finger to her lips before turning off the overhead light prior to opening the door. Her eyes were still adjusting to the darkness as the handle twisted in her hand. Someone was turning it from the opposite side. 'My office tomorrow, Briscoe,' she said, in as official a voice as she could muster. 'And don't keep me waiting.'

The door burst open. Startled by the sudden movement, Ellie stepped back as a dark figure flew headlong towards her. She scrabbled to turn the light back on but everything was happening too fast. A shoulder charge caught her hard on the chest, knocking her across the room and onto the floor. Naomi screamed.

Disoriented and with the wind knocked out of her, Ellie lay stunned for a moment.

'Thought you'd got away from me did you, Ellie?' a voice said. The tone was menacing, and muffled in a way she'd heard before, in Germany. He'd been wearing a balaclava that night as well.

It was Fitzgerald.

***

The door slammed as Fitzgerald aimed a kick at Ellie's exposed shin. His boot connected and a sharp, burning sensation ran up her leg.

A shadow moved fast across the room and towards the door. It was Naomi, trying to escape. Fitzgerald blocked her, and then swung a series of punches at her head and upper body. The sound of fists striking home and Naomi's pitiful cries of pain bought Ellie a fleeting moment to think. An idea formed. The pool cue … on the pillow. She had once one chance.

Quickly, she lunged in the direction of the empty bed. She fell short, but only just. Without standing she threw her arm up onto the pillow, groping in the half-light for the heavier of the two cue parts. On the first attempt, her hand found empty space but she was in luck; as she desperately searched, her fingers wrapped around the steel screw of the cue base.

The light flickered on to reveal Fitzgerald standing by the door. He was wearing a tatty set of mechanic's overalls, heavily marked with oil and other stains. Pulled over his head, as Ellie had guessed, was a woollen balaclava showing just his eyes. He roared angrily, moved forward a step, and then swung back his leg as if he were about to kick a rugby ball over a set of posts. His right boot was aimed at Ellie's head and would surely have sent her into oblivion had she not seen it coming. She rolled away at the last moment and, as the boot struck thin air, seized her chance. As hard as she could, she swung the cue around and into the knee of Fitzgerald's supporting leg.

There was a crack, the sickening sound of wood striking a joint lacking protective soft tissue. Fitzgerald roared again but this time it was in pain. He kicked out. This time though, he was slower and off-balance, and Ellie was already moving. She leapt forward and brought the back of her skull up, hard against his chin. The effect was instant from the moment she connected. Fitzgerald staggered and fell backwards.

'Bastard,' Ellie screamed, as eighteen months of pent-up rage lent strength to her arm. She brought the cue down time and again. The more her stunned attacker fought back, the more he resisted, the harder she hit him. Elbows, shin bones, knees and forearms, all bore the brunt of her wrath. Finally, he gave up and lay still, his hands held across his balaclava-covered face in surrender, his fingers bloodied and trembling.

Ellie was also shaking as she stood and looked over to where Naomi sat on the floor, watching her. The young soldier's eyes were wide and staring. A thin track of blood trickled down her chin from what looked like a split lip. 'You ok?' Ellie asked, between panting breaths.

'I thought you were gonna kill him,' Naomi said.

'I probably should have.'

'Who is he?'

'A piece o' shit who forgot women can fight. He's the new Sergeant you mentioned.'

'So, why did he attack us ... what do we do now?'

'We call the MPs,' Ellie replied. 'With this bastard's history, he'll go down this time.'

345

'This time?' Naomi said, as she attempted to stand. She grimaced at the effort, her movements laboured and unsteady. 'He's done this before?'

Ellie leaned forward, pushed away the hands of the figure lying prostrate in front of her and pulled up the balaclava. 'Naomi Briscoe, meet Sergeant Mick Fitzgerald.'

'You won't get away with this, Ellie,' Fitzgerald said, weakly.

'What's he mean by that?' said Naomi.

Ellie dropped the pool cue onto the bed next to her, close enough she could reach it quickly if needed. She leaned against the wall, took a deep breath and then opened the nearest locker. She took two neck-ties from inside and began securing Fitzgerald's feet and wrists.

Only when she'd finished did she begin her explanation. To an increasingly horrified young soldier she explained how, on a gloomy night in Germany, soaked to the skin by the rain and much the worse for drink, she'd been alone and sleeping on her bed when she'd been woken by a man in a balaclava climbing on top of her. That had been Mick Fitzgerald. He'd been waiting for her, knowing she'd be drunk, because in those days, she often was.

She described how she'd been pinned down by a man she feared may end her life. And how, afterwards, her attacker had warned her, if she ever reported what had happened, he would find her again, and the next time it would be worse.

'So, this was him carrying out his threat?'Naomi asked.

'He didn't know me,' Ellie said. 'I reported it. In some ways I wish I hadn't because he managed to convince a Court Martial he was innocent.'

'How could he do that?'

Ellie scowled. 'Every officer and Senior NCO on the jury was male. He told them I consented when we were both drunk, and how the injuries I got were rough sex.'

'So, him and his sick mates were planning to have you again?'

'He warned me this day would come, Naomi. I didn't take it seriously enough. For men like this, it's about power, not sex. He wanted to show me who was boss.'

'It'll be different now you're an officer. The bizzies will believe you.'

Ellie understood the point. A military court might well take her more seriously this time. This time it would be an officer's word against that of a soldier. Carefully, and with her legs shaking, she sat down on the edge of one of the beds. 'He'll claim we attacked *him*, you know that don't you?' she said.

'As revenge, you mean? For him raping you?'

'That's how he'll try and make it look. It's still a man's army. We women have to stick together or people like him will always be believed. I'm going to call the MPs now so, before they get here, I want to be sure I can count on you?'

'Whatever it takes,' Naomi said as she sat down heavily on the unmade bed. 'This bastard deserves whatever's coming to him.'

Ellie nodded her thanks, just as there was a knock at the door. Someone nearby had been concerned at the noise and they'd come to find out what had happened. She stood up, walked to the door and turned the handle. As it opened, she breathed in deeply. From this moment on, the inquisition would start.

As the door swung towards her and the light from the room reached the now darkened corridor, Ellie reeled back, her eyes focussing on just two things. The first was another man in dark clothing, his face concealed behind a black, rubberised respirator. The second was the pistol held firmly in his hand, the barrel pointed straight at her chest.

And then she noticed something else, something so dreadful it struck like shards of ice into her bones as it penetrated and overcame every part of her being. It was a familiar smell, spiced and woody. The smell of expensive Italian cologne.

Chapter 65

Floria summoned two burly MPs to stand over Slater. I explained he was a key witness and they should go easy on him, before joining Floria outside the house. As we walked towards her car, she was on the phone, talking to her Headquarters about the search for Ellie. 'I can't believe what I'm hearing,' she said to me, angrily. 'They're still getting into fuckin' position ready to make the arrests.'

'They need to get a move on.'

'I know, I know,' she snapped, as she ended the call. 'Tell me something, would you have gone through with it? Would you have told me to keep going if he hadn't opened up so quick?'

'It was a bluff,' I said, with a grin. 'In his personnel file, there was a reference to him having been a guard at Abu Hag, the American prison camp. I figured he may have seen enhanced interrogation being used so he'd know what was coming. That's the reason for the psychological stuff before the towel went over his face.'

'I really thought we were going to water-board him.'

'I wanted you to believe it. That's why I didn't tell you beforehand. I wanted you to think it was going to happen it as much as he did. I don't imagine you'll ever find yourself in a similar situation, but take it from me, the best interrogators don't need to beat things out of people.'

'Something you learned in the SAS, I suppose?'

'They taught me some very clever tricks, yes.'

'Slater was pathetic, as much resistance as a chocolate teapot. '

Floria was right. Slater had given up what he knew very quickly once he understood – or thought he understood – what was about to happen to him. He told us Ellie Rodgers would almost certainly be in the Armoury, where Fitzgerald and Masters were planning to take her. She's been tricked into attending Rowallan accommodation block where she would be expecting to meet a recruit with some information. Only it wouldn't be a recruit, it would be Mick Fitzgerald.

We also learned about Slater's role in Masters' gang. In return for them turning a blind eye to his penchant for young girls, he did jobs for them. He'd been told to watch me from the field behind Wendy's home and he'd also been at the wheel of the car that nearly ran Floria over. Masters gave the orders, he said. Pemberton, despite his rank, did exactly as he was told. It was Masters who'd ordered him to break into Wendy's house to search my room and then, when Pemberton told him I had a young family in London, to leave me the warning note.

We also learned how the rifles had been stolen. It had been a simple plan, surprisingly so. With the recruit rifles sealed in the back of a transport lorry, Masters had instructed Slater to assign Morgan and Davenport as guards. Morgan, because he'd borrowed money from Masters and needed a way to repay the debt; Davenport, because the Armoury Sergeant had a bit of a thing for her. Morgan had been briefed to leave both their rifles in the cab rather than placing them – as the RMP were told – with the other weapons in the rear. After Davenport and Morgan were relieved, Slater's role had been to drive the lorry to the armoury. Instead of going directly there, he'd diverted via the motorpool where, inside the privacy of the hangar, it had been simple to hand the two rifles to Masters without anyone seeing them. The lorry arrived at the armoury, seemingly on schedule, and with the rear section still intact, thereby creating the suspicion the theft must have occurred at the parade ground. Masters hid the stolen weapons in the motorpool until the heat died down and then moved them to London with a consignment of stolen mobile telephones.

It was later when things began to go wrong. Having learned it was hers and Morgan's rifles that had been taken, Davenport worked out Slater knew more than he'd told the Military Police. She'd confronted him and challenged him with her suspicions. Slater had reported this to Masters who'd decided the young recruit needed to be kept quiet.

Their chosen method was the tried and tested sex video they'd used on other women recruits. They would get her drunk or drugged and then film her. Later, once she was sober, they would show her the video and warn of the consequences should she ever threaten them again. Tom Morgan had been key to their plan. Davenport considered her fellow Crow to be a friend and, one night in the NAAFI bar he'd sat with her while they discussed whether she was going to report her suspicions to the military police. Acting on instructions from Masters, Morgan used the opportunity to slip a pill into her drink. The moment the drug entered her stomach, her fate had been sealed.

But the blackmail had backfired. When Masters sent Davenport the video, she reacted angrily and, rather than ensuring her silence, she'd told him she intended exposing all three of the men. For Masters, this had been too great a risk so he'd decided to confront her. According to what he'd later told Slater, they had argued, Davenport had struggled and the weapon Masters had used to threaten her – rifle number 27 – had gone off in her face, killing her instantly. Knowing rifle 27 was Davenport's favourite, and to make it look like suicide, Masters had rubbed her hands on the weapon before placing it on the ground next to her. Forgetting the issuing register showed Davenport booked out a different rifle that day had been an oversight and it had only been when the RMP had telephoned saying they wanted to seize it that Masters realised its significance and destroyed it.

'Why have Pemberton listed for that number, if it was Masters who sent the video?' Floria asked as she started the engine.

'I don't know. Maybe they both use it?' I said.

'If we catch Pemberton with the phone used to send it, we'll have him too.'

Floria's phone began to ring. As she answered the call and I listened in, I realised it was bad news. Room 7 of Rowallan Block was unoccupied but was showing signs of a recent struggle. The Armoury was deserted. She hung up and slammed the car into gear.

'Colonel Bullen from the Signals depot has organised a search but Masters' house is outside the camp and we're the closest,' she shouted, above the roar of the car engine. 'Hold on tight.'

Chapter 66

Jodie ducked out of sight as another car drove past. Hiding in the trees from every set of headlights made for slow progress. Only one driver saw her, even gave her a wave, but he was a squaddie, young and on his own. He didn't stop.

Eventually, she made it to the side gate of the camp. A soldier she recognised from the NAAFI was manning the post. He was one of the new intake, the latest to discover just how tedious guard duties were. Jodie ducked her head and waved as she approached the tiny hut next to the barrier where he was sheltering. He gave her a relaxed smile, waved her through, and gave no indication at all he'd been told to keep an eye out for anyone.

The camp was quiet. As she turned onto the main road leading toward the female block, she slowed her pace. Two lads in short-sleeved shirts and jeans appeared from some bushes alongside the opposite footway. They were heading in her direction and were half-leading, half-carrying a third recruit who'd had far too much to drink. She was relieved to see them, and for good reason. If one of the late shift NCOs should appear, they would immediately be the focus of his attention. Normally, the male staff would stop any female recruit they caught moving around the camp. Often it would be for a bit of banter, to alleviate boredom or – as they put it – keep the Crows on their toes. Once in a while though, there would be an unpleasant edge to the meeting such as an opportunity to bully or even to exploit the situation to see if a lone woman might be up for a little fun. A group of drunken soldiers struggling to get back to their accommodation couldn't be ignored and would leave Jodie free to continue on her way.

The drunken recruits turned off towards the male block without meeting an NCO. Lucky them, Jodie thought. Arriving at Rowallan block, she stopped, looked around and listened. Except for some distant laughter coming from the direction of the NAAFI, there was no sound. She walked briskly towards the entrance when a movement in her peripheral vision caused her to stop. What she saw almost made her faint. Emerging from the darkness were the two people she wanted most to avoid. It was the cops, the ones who'd been torturing Paul. They were standing at the end of the path, waiting, just staring at her.

Chapter 67

'It's Jodie Baker,' Floria whispered to me.

I didn't need to be told. I'd also recognised the young recruit stood outside the accommodation block. After finding Sergeant Masters' home deserted, Floria and I had been en-route to the RMP building to meet the search party when we'd decided to take a look at Rowallan Block for ourselves. Spotting Jodie Baker was a bonus I hadn't expected. She started at us silently, her eyes wide, mouth open. She looked petrified.

'Wait there, please,' I called out. 'We just need a word.'

My gentle approach proved futile as Jodie turned away from us and sprinted into the darkness. Next to me, Floria exploded into movement and, as she raced across the grass, Jodie slipped and fell on the damp surface. She rolled over and attempted to stand again, but it was too late. Floria had made up the ground and was on her.

Anyone who has ever tried to restrain a frightened cat will be able to picture the scene as Floria and I attempted to hold on to Jodie Baker without causing her any serious injury. She spat, screamed, bit and scratched with a strength that belied her small frame, seemingly convinced we were trying to murder her. Fortunately for us, the commotion drew the attention of a couple of Military Police searchers. They came running over and, with each of us pinning a limb, we managed to restrain Jodie face-down on the ground. 'Don't hurt me,' she begged, as she stopped struggling.

Floria was holding her left arm. 'What are you doing here, Baker?' she said, leaning close to the girl's ear. 'Why did you run?'

'I saw what you did to Paul,' Jodie yelled as she made one last and rather half-hearted attempt to throw us off.

Floria's eyes flared as she turned to me. I didn't say anything, I was too busy trying to hold on to Jodie's arm. I was also thinking how we could have missed finding her hiding in Slater's house and how we were going to prevent her saying anything more in front of the two MPs. There was also another problem looming. Figures were appearing at the windows of the accommodation block overlooking us. Recruit soldiers, attracted by the commotion, were beginning to take an interest. It wouldn't be long before one or two of them appeared to investigate what was going on.

'Where are the others?' Floria hissed, as she twisted Jodie's arm.

'What others?'

'We need to know what's going on, Jodie,' I said, firmly. 'We don't have time to mess about, so tell us where they are.'

Jodie twisted her head around. She had tears in her eyes and looked like a frightened child. 'Don't hurt me … please,' she begged once more. 'I thought you were after me.'

I eased off my grip just as Floria leaned back onto her haunches and lowered her voice. 'You listen to me,' she said, her voice calm but menacing. 'We know Masters is planning to meet a female officer tonight. That officer is missing and if she comes to any harm, you're involved. Do you hear me? Help us now or it will be you we're after.'

Jodie looked confused. 'I was only doing as I was told,' she said, after a pause. 'You don't know what they're like.'

'What were you told?' I asked.

'To get Lieutenant Rodgers to the motorpool hangar at 2200 hours.'

'To the motorpool?'

'Yes, I'm telling the truth, I promise.'

'And how was that supposed to happen?'

'She was coming to our room. My friend Naomi would then take her to the hangar.'

'It never occurred to you it might be a trap?'

'They just want to talk to her, they said.'

I turned to look at Floria. Her eyes were open in alarm. The motorpool hangar was quiet and deserted. It was a part of the camp you wouldn't normally go unless you had business there.

From the direction of the main door to the block, I heard a door open. A female voice called out. Floria sent one of the MPs to check the motorpool hangar while the other broke off to intercept the growing number of recruits gathering by the main door to Rowallan block. One or two, possibly the bravest amongst them, were getting uncomfortably close. As soon as the MPs were far enough away, Floria leaned once more into Jodie's face. 'How did you see us at Paul Slater's house?' she said.

'I was in the garden,' Jodie replied. 'I saw you through a gap in the curtains.'

'What was it you think you saw?'

'You guys … you were water-boarding Paul.'

Floria glanced across at me, her look a mixture of anger and concern. 'What you saw wasn't what you think, Baker,' she said, as she squeezed Jodie's arm. 'It was a trick to get him to talk, no more.'

I now realised why Jodie had appeared so petrified when she'd seen us approaching. She wasn't simply afraid of being caught doing something wrong. She had been terrified of us, and what we might intend doing to her.

'You're messing with forces way out of your league, Baker,' Floria added, before loosening her grip on Jodie's arm.

Jodie breathed deeply, her chest and arms shaking with emotion. 'I understand … I do. And I won't say anything, I promise. Just get me away from this place is all I ask.'

'Do what we ask and you have my word on that,' said Floria. 'Break your promise and you'll be sorry.'

As I stood, I looked up. The recruits were on us. We were surrounded.

'Leave her be,' said a small female soldier at the front of the group. Despite the girl's stature, it was clear she meant business and was prepared to speak for the others. In her hand I picked out the familiar shape of a half snooker cue. The second MP was near the block entrance arguing with two male recruits.

Stood next to me, Floria took hold of Jodie's arm and then held up her free hand towards the crowd. 'Unless you all want to end up in the Guardhouse, I suggest you back off,' she shouted.

'Do what she says, Amy,' said Jodie. 'I'm ok; I don't need your help.'

'That's not how it looks from where I'm standing,' Amy answered.

I stepped in front of Floria and held up my hands. 'Keep back, I'm a police officer,' I said. 'Please return to your rooms.'

'What have you nicked her for?' a male voice called out. 'You should be nicking the fuckin' staff, not us Crows.'

The group had stopped advancing but a few of them, including the woman called Amy, appeared extremely wound up. I knew it would only take the reckless actions of one recruit or a careless word from me or Floria to ignite them. I'd been in similar situations many times before on the streets of London when the woodwork – as we called them – would appear from every nearby nook and cranny to see what the cops were doing and to give us a hard time. To the woodwork it was a sport, an opportunity to see how far they could push things without getting arrested themselves. More often than not, the situation would end peacefully but there were times when it could turn really ugly.

We didn't have time to waste negotiating so I decided to be as honest with the growing crowd as I could. 'We're on your side,' I said. 'We know about the respirator gang and what they've been doing. We will deal with them.'

'How can we be sure you ain't lying like they do?' said Amy.

'You'll never prove anything,' said another female voice near the back. 'They're untouchable.'

Despite the scepticism of Amy and the second girl, I noticed mutterings of approval from within the group. 'Why beat up Jodie, then?' Amy said, as she stepped forward to within striking range of the snooker cue.

'It was my fault,' Jodie said. 'And if you know what's good for you, you'll go back to your rooms and leave it to the monkeys.'

Jodie's plea did the trick. There were a few comments that I couldn't quite make out but within seconds the group began to disperse. Within a couple of minutes, only the recruit called Amy remained at the door to the accommodation block.

'Thanks,' I said to Jodie.

She didn't reply. With her arm still held firmly by Floria, we then set off towards the motorpool. We walked quickly, covering the distance in just a few minutes. As we approached, I saw movement in the darkness ahead of us. Three shadowy figures appeared. It was the MPs.

'Regimental Sergeant-Major Collins,' Floria said, indicating the tallest figure in the centre of the three. 'My boss.'

'We're about to go in,' Collins said. The RSM was a huge man, easily six foot seven, with broad shoulders and a bull-like neck. Add to that a nose that looked like it had seen many a bar-room brawl and hands the size of shovels and I could see what we lacked in numbers would be more than counter-balanced by having him in the lead. 'What's she doing here?' he continued, pointing to Jodie Baker.

'She told us where to find Lieutenant Rodgers,' I replied.

Collins scowled and then spoke to one of the MPs we'd met outside Rowallan Block. 'Ed, you bring her inside but keep her out of the way in case things kick off.'

'When we got here there was a light inside and the sound of music,' Collins said. 'Everything went off about a minute ago.'

'Someone tipped them off, do you think?' Floria said to me.

'Maybe a look out?'

'One of the Crows more like. Someone earning some brownie points.'

'Makes no difference,' said Collins. 'They've no place to run.'

'Are you aware one of the men inside might be Captain Pemberton, sir?' Floria said.

The Sergeant-Major frowned. 'Not likely,' he said, his tone matter-of-fact and authoritative. 'Mr Pemberton is on his way to Iraq. His flight took off about three hours ago.'

Floria looked askance as she turned to me. I had no answer for her. The timing of the Adjutant's departure meant he would have been several thousand feet about the Mediterranean when Slater made his call. Pemberton couldn't have answered it. So, who had Slater been talking to?

Chapter 68

The huge former-aircraft hangar was eerily quiet, the only sound coming from our footsteps on the concrete floor. Silent and ominous in the darkness, a line of sand-coloured Warrior personnel carriers stood silhouetted against the wall on our left. There was no look-out, at least none that we could detect.

We were six against I hoped two, maybe three. Masters would be here certainly, and the new guy, Fitzgerald. Maybe one more. Even with a giant of a Sergeant-Major on point, the last thing we'd want would a fist-fight in which we were outnumbered. Jodie Baker's friend, Naomi, was also unaccounted for, so I was half-expecting to find her as well. At the opposite end to the main entrance, I picked out two doors about fifteen feet apart. One was slightly ajar. It moved slightly, exposing a crack of light.

For a big man, Collins moved very quickly. A male voice inside called out just as he hit the closing door like a battering ram, his right foot crashing hard against the flimsy timber. It burst open, the redundant catch flying away across the floor. An MP flicked on a torch, the light illuminating the hangar, the beam dancing around the walls as Floria followed her boss through the door. I saw a melee of movement in front of them followed by shouts and then a scream. In the torch light, I spotted what looked like a side-board with cans of beer atop of it before I was unceremoniously barged to one side. The remaining MP sprinted past me to pile in and, as he disappeared, the door further along the wall opened.

I found myself facing a stocky, bare-chested figure in a respirator with me as the only obstacle between him and escape. A clenched fist holding a huge, adjustable wrench swung through the air in front of me.

Heavy and unwieldy, a wrench wasn't an ideal weapon but it was still perfectly capable of caving my skull in. And the message it conveyed was clear. Get out of my way. I held out an open hand and stepped to one side, as if inviting my opponent to pass unchallenged. It didn't convince. Next thing, he came at me, the wrench swinging down towards my head. I stepped back out of range, making sure he swung through empty air and creating an opportunity to strike back.

My attacker wasn't so easily fooled. As the wrench failed to connect, he too drew himself back, regained his balance and prepared to try again. This time he was less reckless. He jabbed twice, then again with more aggression, forcing me back into the darkness as I kept space between us.

'Put it down,' I said, trying to sound confident. 'There's only one way out of here and that's covered.' My attacker clearly wasn't in the mood to be bargained with. He roared and lunged again. He was agile, and had the clear benefit of youth, but I had the benefit of time. He knew help would soon reach me and that added an element of desperation to his decision-making.

As we continued our little dance, I began to see another advantage appearing. With his vision restricted by the respirator, my adversary couldn't see my feet. I tried shifting my balance once and then again. He didn't react. I feinted to sweep his leg with my foot and he was slow to see it coming. He laughed though, the filter of the mask muffling his voice and emitting a metallic sound. It was dismissive, even a little arrogant and told me he didn't consider me a significant threat. He was ripe for a shock.

My opportunity came unexpectedly. The door to the small room swung open and crashed loudly into its frame. It was the distraction I needed. As he glanced over his shoulder, ready to meet any additional threat, I ducked down and kicked hard at his nearest leg. He was well-balanced but surprise was on my side and as my shoe struck his shin I followed up with a straight punch hard into his groin. My fist was tight, my knuckles proud, and I was targeting soft flesh in a way I knew would hurt.

I connected, and he roared with pain. He raised the wrench again, going for the killer blow but, as his head came down to pick a spot to aim at, his chin met my rapidly ascending skull. The respirator gave him some protection but it was enough to stun him. He staggered, just for a moment, but it was enough. I reached under his thigh, tipped him up and spear-tackled him down onto the floor. His skull hit the concrete with a dull thud. As the wrench fell harmlessly from his grip, he groaned and lay still.

'Never under estimate a determined old man,' I said as I pulled the respirator away to reveal his face.

The sensation of someone striking the back of your head with an iron bar is one you never forget. Sound, pain and pressure waves hit at exactly the same time. You hear the crack, feel the hurt and experience the roar as a hot rush surges through your skull. I had just enough time to recognise Mick Fitzgerald before my limbs lost all strength and I went down like a broken marionette.

Chapter 69

When I came too, I was face down, the cold surface of the hangar floor pressed hard against my cheek. Nearby, I could hear low voices and had a sense of figures moving around me. I opened my eyes for just a moment, sufficient to catch a glimpse of a booted foot before the picture was replaced by blurred, stroboscopic stars. My head was throbbing, a dull ache that seemed to begin at my neck before crashing forwards in painful waves that smashed into the bone surrounding my eye sockets. I breathed in and, ever so gently, moved my feet, limbs and hands. My arms were behind my back, my wrists tied, but everything else seemed intact.

A male voice, harsh and angry, spoke above the others. The voice was raspy, reverberating like that of the film character, Darth Vader. 'On the floor, all of you,' it said.

Again, I eased my eyes open. My vision had improved and I could see a figure in dark overalls looming over me, the face covered, as Fitzgerald's had been, by a black, rubberised respirator. A black, 9mm pistol was pointing directly at my head, the tip of the barrel steady and unwavering.

'Are you ok?' It was Floria. She was lying beside me, her wrists bound by what looked like a cable tie.

I nodded, just gently, stopping immediately when a spasm of pain rippled down the muscles of my neck.

In the light from the storeroom, I could see Ellie Rodgers, also sat on the floor. She was licking at a heavily swollen upper lip. 'Where are the others?' I whispered to Floria.

'Fuckin' shut it,' said the voice.

'We meet again, Sergeant Masters,' I said, croakily. I'd guessed the likely identity of our captor and, as I focussed on Floria, I saw her nod, just gently. I was right.

'You're coming with me, Baker,' Masters said, from somewhere close behind me. 'Now put these around their ankles'

The clicking sound of cable ties followed Masters' instruction as someone I assumed to be Jodie, worked their way along the line of prostrate figures. I counted eight ties being applied before a small pair of hands pushed my lower legs together and I felt the plastic grip around my angles. Nine captives. Collins, Floria, Ellie Rodgers, Naomi, the three MPs and me made eight. For a moment I wondered who number nine was and then I realised. It was Fitzgerald. Masters was leaving him with us knowing we'd eventually escape but we'd then have to focus on guarding him before organising a pursuit. He was buying time.

Several seconds went by before I heard the door we'd used to enter the hangar slammed shut. We were alone.

***

Over the years, cable ties have become a very popular way to restrict the movements of detained people, to render them less of an escape risk, and to keep them that way until they can be secured in a cell or vehicle. Newsreels and television shows often show detainees with their wrists tied together in a way that looks both effective and secure. The reality, in fact, is quite the opposite. Get your hands in front, pull the ties very tight with your teeth, raise your arms above your head and then bring them down hard with your arms flared out like chicken-wings, and even the strongest ties snap at the locking point.

As I tightened the ties around my wrists and raised my arms I saw Floria, Collins and two of the three MPs were doing just the same. Inside of a minute, we had our restraints broken and were working together to free Naomi, Ellie and the third MP. Fitzgerald, we left.

As I ran to the hangar door, Collins followed close behind. The was no sign of Masters or Jodie. 'What the hell happened in there?' I demanded, as we stopped.

'He had a Glock hidden under a bed,' he replied. 'As we were releasing Lieutenant Rodgers, he got the drop on us.'

'So, is Baker a hostage or an accomplice?' I said.

'No way is she working for him,' said Naomi, from the doorway behind. 'She hates him.' I could see the others just behind her.

'I'll ring Colonel Bullen,' Floria said. 'Masters will be heading home to gather some things, I reckon.'

'How did you know where to find us?' Naomi continued.

'One of Masters' so-called mates told us,' I replied.

'Masters killed Davenport,' Floria added. 'That's why he's so desperate to get away.'

Naomi didn't respond although I caught a flicker of confusion crossed her face. I wondered if she also knew more than she'd first told us.

'He'll need money,' Floria said, turning to me with her phone to her ear. 'He wasn't planning this so he'll have to think quickly.'

'He'll want his stash,' said Naomi. 'Was it Sergeant Slater who said Master's killed Davenport?'

'Possibly, why do you ask?' I said.

'Nothing ... I just wondered.'

I saw Fitzgerald glaring at the young recruit as she spoke. 'Speak up, Briscoe,' said Collins. 'Do you know something?'

'He has a safe in the Armoury and a store room in the Sergeants' Mess. Jodie reckons it's stuffed with all kinds of things.'

'He'll want to get off the base quickly,' the RSM replied. 'My guess is he'll head to his quarters.'

'You cover the Mess and his home,' I replied. 'Floria and I will head over to the Armoury. We'll call you if we spot him.'

Floria nodded in agreement before lowering her phone and dialling in another number. 'Did they receive a mobile phone call after they grabbed you?' she said, to Ellie.

No, they didn't,' Ellie answered.

'Really? No call from someone saying they couldn't make it?'

'Nothing.'

Floria eyes flared as she stared hard at me. It was clear she was thinking the same as I was. We'd heard Slater talking to someone on the number used to send the Davenport video. Pemberton was in the air and couldn't have been the recipient. 'Who the hell did he call?' she asked me.

'We're missing someone or something,' I said, but Colonel Bullen answered her call before she could reply. It was going to have to wait.

***

With Fitzgerald secure in the rear seat of an RMP car, Ellie Rodgers confirmed Naomi wasn't a suspect. Collins then instructed Naomi to head back to her accommodation and await further instructions. Floria checked the back of my head and reported a lump the size of a small egg. 'He hit you with the Glock,' she said, as I winced.

Floria and I then set off, marching across the camp towards the Armoury. As quietly as we were able, we talked through the conundrum of Slater's mobile phone. She came up with a rather far-flung theory that he may have been calling Jodie Baker, but, apart from that, we failed to come with a solution. Eventually, we had to stop speaking as we approached the rear of the Armoury. I steered us into the cover of a small copse. The lights in the building were on.

With no windows other than at the front, the only way to discover what was happening inside was to approach the spot from where I'd first noticed Jodie Baker watching us when we'd called to speak to Masters. It was close to the front door and, as the lights from inside were penetrating the darkness for some distance, there was a danger Masters – if he were inside – would see us first.

We needed a plan, something that would keep Masters inside until help arrived. I whispered to Floria to wait in the shadow of the building and then I crept forward, keeping low behind a solitary car parked near the entrance. I wondered if it belonged to Masters and, more in hope than expectation, I checked to see if it was open. It was, but there were no keys in the ignition. Inside the Armoury office, I could hear someone moving around and the sound of a door opening and closing. I chanced a quick glimpse through the window. Jodie Baker was in view, sat in the same place she'd been when Floria and I had first met her. This time though, she was hunched up, her hands over her head as if trying to protect herself from something. I saw no sign of Masters until a noise behind the main door caused me to dart back quickly into the shadows. The door opened and he appeared carrying a holdall over his shoulder. He approached the car, opened the boot and, with a heavy thump, dropped the bag inside before leaving the boot lid open and returning to the Armoury.

The opportunity was too good to miss. I would grab the bag, remove it from the boot and put it somewhere out of sight. Masters, on returning to finish loading up, would know he wasn't alone and might waste time either looking for the bag or trying to discover who was watching from the darkness. Either way, it could buy us enough time to allow Collins and the others to join us.

Keeping low, I moved quickly back to Floria where I was surprised to discover Naomi Briscoe had joined her. With no time to ascertain how or why she had parted company with the others, I relayed my plan and asked Floria to get on the phone to summons help and request all the camp gates be closed. She raised a thumb to indicate she understood and I headed back to grab the bag. I had my hand on it when a now familiar voice made it clear my plan hadn't worked.

'This is getting to be a habit,' Masters said, his voice a mix of anger and frustration.

'I'd quit now, if I were you,' I said. 'The camp's on lockdown and there's a team of MPs in the trees behind us. No way out.'

'You really are quite something,' he replied. 'Get in.' I saw the barrel of the Glock in his hand flick towards the boot of the car.

My bluff having failed, I was weighing up my options, trying to decide how much time I could waste whilst appearing to be cooperative when a loud female voice called out from the darkness.

'Lay down the weapon!'

Chapter 70

Floria picked up the Glock and tucked it safely in her pocket. 'Brains over brawn,' she said, grinning at me. 'Never underestimate a determined young woman, Finlay.'

I smiled at her humorous reference to the comment I'd made in the hangar. She had a point, though. The unexpected and authoritative tone with which Naomi Briscoe called out had even convinced me a team of MPs were waiting in the darkness, having appeared in the nick of time. Before Masters had the time to react, I'd twisted the pistol from his hand. Thirty seconds later, Floria had him cuffed and face-down on the ground.

Sergeant-Major Collins pulled up in a car with two MPs a couple of minutes later just as Naomi appeared from the Armoury with her arm around Jodie.

'Let's ring the number of the phone again,' Floria said. 'It might be in the car?'

'It might even be in her pocket?' I whispered, tilting my head towards Jodie.

'What are you doing?' Naomi asked as Floria handed me her phone and opened the passenger door to Masters' car.

'Confirming something,' I said. On the screen, I could see the all-important number was programmed ready to go. Floria was looking at Masters' hands. They were heavily callused. She turned to me and nodded. We had him.

'Andrew Masters, you're under arrest for the murder of Private Angela Davenport,' Floria said, unexpectedly.

I frowned as she began cautioning him. I would have preferred to locate the phone first. 'It's ringing,' I said, as the call connected. We all stood in silence as the ring tone continued, unanswered. From Masters' car there was no sound, not even a hum. 'There's no reply,'

I said, as I ended the call. Masters hadn't reacted at all and neither had Jodie. 'You've got the wrong man,' Naomi exclaimed.

'What did you say?' I asked her.

'I said you've got the wrong man.' Floria and I turned towards her. Jodie, I noticed, had turned away, hiding her face in her hands.

'What do you mean?' I said. 'For killing Angela Davenport?'

'Yes ... that's what I mean,' she said, turning towards Jodie. 'Tell them Jodie, or I will.'

As Jodie pulled her hands away, I saw a trail of tears had formed on her cheeks. 'I can't,' she said. 'I can't.'

'Just tell them the truth,' said Naomi. 'Tell them who really did it and he won't have a hold on you anymore.'

Masters struggled beneath me and tried to speak but I had his face buried hard into the ground.

'Oh God ... I'm so sorry, Nem.' Jodie blurted, her voice subdued and trembling. 'It wasn't Sergeant Masters ... he didn't kill Davenport.' Her voice trailed off, her head lowered. She looked defeated.

'If he didn't kill Davenport, who did?' said Floria.

Jodie lowered her head again as she began to sob. Tears ran down her cheeks landing on the concrete in tiny, dark puddles. She sank to her knees, her chest heaving. 'Ok, ok,' she said. 'You're right, Naomi, I've had enough. It wasn't Masters, it was me. I did it. I shot Davenport.'

***

'What do you mean, you did it?' said Naomi, as she rounded on your friend. 'You told me Slater killed her.'

Jodie sank to the floor. Floria stared at me. I could sense her confusion and, as Naomi started becoming increasingly agitated, I realised the only way we were going to find out what was behind

Jodie's admission was to obtain some privacy. 'Can you get these two out of here?' I said to Collins.

The Sergeant-Major lifted Masters to his feet and, with the second MP helping, began marching him towards the waiting cars. The third MP took an increasingly upset Naomi by the arm as she continued to swear at her friend. Eventually, he was able to manhandle her away.

'Do you want to explain?' I asked Jodie, once things had settled down.

'Just don't do to me what you did to Paul,' she said, looking up at me.

'We told you before,' said Floria. 'It wasn't how it looked. What you saw was a trick to get him to talk.'

'If you say so. I won't tell no-one, I promise,' Jodie said. She was trembling but she'd stopped crying.

'What did Naomi mean about someone having a hold over you?' I asked.

'You've got no idea what it's been like seeing her lying with her brains all over the grass every time I close my eyes. I wish I'd told the truth at the time then none of this would have happened.'

'So, what did happen?' I said, crouching down and placing a hand on Jodie's shoulder. Floria had stepped closer but seemed to be content to allow me to do the talking.

'It was all because of that bloody rifle. Paul hid it on the day of the parade so it wouldn't get stolen. I thought he was just being kind but I should have known. He never does anything unless it's going to benefit him in some way. He gave it back to Davenport once all the fuss had died down. Said it was to keep her sweet, to stop her saying anything about the theft, but she told me the truth. He wanted to fuck her and saving her favourite rifle was part of his plan.'

'Sergeant Slater told us it was Masters who kept the rifle hidden and used it to threaten her,' I said.

'That's not true,' she said. 'He was covering for me ... he said whatever anyone said I was to leave the talking to him.'

'So what happened on the day she died?'

'She'd worked out it had to have been Paul and Sergeant Masters who stole the rifles. She told Paul if he didn't stop pestering her, she was going to report him.'

'So, you confronted her?' I said.

'I was so angry with her. She would have ruined everything. I wanted to warn her off, to stop her being a grass and to keep her away from Paul.' Jodie looked desperately at Floria, as if in need of her understanding. Tears formed once more on her cheeks.

'What happened?'

'She was really wound up. They'd got her drunk and made one of their sick videos. They do it to girls they want to control. They pop something in your drink and you haven't a clue what's going on. Paul said, in her case, they needed it as insurance to stop her talking to anyone about the rifles. Anyway, I figure Paul liked what he saw and wanted more. She was having none of it, not the black mail, not Paul. The night before, we were all in our room doing our kit when she told us she was going to the monkeys. There was no time, I knew I had to do something. We were both on guard duty in the morning so I went and found her ... told her that if she grassed I would tell everyone she knew about the plan to steal the rifles and that she was part of it. She hit the roof, called me all kinds of names. We ended up fighting. I'd put my rifle down but she hadn't. She tried to hit me with it and I grabbed it. As we struggled it went off. I didn't mean to kill her, I swear.'

'So why didn't you tell the truth straight away?'

'Paul came looking for me after Tom Morgan called him to say I was planning to have it out with Davenport. I reckon he wanted to stop me but it was too late. By the time he got there, Davenport was dead and I was in a real mess. I was panicking; I didn't know what to do.

372

He said it would look like I'd done it deliberate, like I'd intended to kill her. He said nobody would believe I hadn't done it out of jealousy.'

'So you covered it up? Made it look like suicide?'

'I wasn't capable of doing anything. Paul did all that. He said we had to move quickly before anyone came looking to find out who'd fired their weapon. He lay her on her back so it would look like she'd shot herself.'

'Who removed the register?'

'Paul. He scrubbed my name off the rota and destroyed the register so nobody would know I'd been on guard with her that day.'

'And what happened after that?' I said.

'He took my rifle back to the armoury and sent me to his house. I snuck out the side gate so there'd be no record of me leaving the camp.'

'Who sent the video to Davenport? Was that Pemberton? Is he involved in all this as well?'

Jodie half-laughed. 'Pemberton? He couldn't organise a piss-up in a brewery. Paul would only speak to Pemberton if they needed him to turn a blind eye to something.'

Pieces of the jigsaw were coming together. It was Pemberton who'd reported being unable to ascertain who'd been driving the lorry when it tripped a speed camera. Pemberton had been responsible for changing Andrew Masters' duties when we'd been trying to interview him. But Pemberton clearly wasn't the leader of the gang, and I was now less certain it was Masters. That left us with just one possibility. 'Do they use a lorry from the motorpool to send things up to London?' I asked.

'Phones,' Jodie said. 'They send nicked phones to a dealer.'

'Is *they* the respirator gang?' I asked.

'Of course.'

I was time for the all-important question. 'Who runs the gang, Jodie? Who gives the orders?'

'Paul,' she replied, without so much as a pause for breath.

'So, who has the phone that was used to send the video to Davenport?' I asked.

'It's Paul's. He keeps it hidden in his kitchen cupboard … behind the tins of food.'

'Shit,' Floria exclaimed, her scowl mirroring mine.

Paul Slater had called a telephone hidden in a cupboard not six feet from where we'd been questioning him. We'd been duped.

Chapter 71

Floria made a call to the MPs looking after Slater and was able to confirm they were still with him at his house. I could see the relief on her face as she gave them instructions to keep him there and wait for us. We walked back to her car, dropped Jodie off at the RMP Headquarters building and then headed to Slater's house.

'The bastard fooled us,' she said as we approached the main gate. 'All that stuff he said was bullshit.'

'Shifting the blame to the others,' I said. 'If Naomi hadn't prompted Jodie to confess, we would have been none the wiser.'

'He might have intended Masters should take the blame but it would never have worked. Masters wouldn't have admitted it, not in a million years.'

'At a guess, Slater was planning to put the phone somewhere to incriminate him. That would have given us a direct link to the blackmail, a motive and Slater's explanation of what had happened. Masters would have been toast.'

'He's a complete bastard dropping his mate in it,' Floria said. 'Do you mind if I have the pleasure of finding the phone in his cupboard? I want to see his face when I hold it out in front of him.'

'Be my guest. I'm looking forward to seeing it too.'

At the main gate, a female soldier appeared from inside the nearby booth. She looked apprehensive and had her rifle barrel pointed directly at our car. Floria rested her hand on my arm. 'Be cool,' she said. 'The guards are on alert. They don't know Masters has been caught.'

She eased off on the accelerator and opened the car window. The guard responded in exactly the way recruits were taught. She took the number of our car, Floria's and my name and then phoned the Guardroom to confirm she could now allow people to leave the camp. It took a couple of minutes but the barrier was soon up and we were away onto the main road. Floria drove quickly and, within a couple of minutes, we were back on the small housing estate where Slater lived. The streets were deserted with very few lights showing in any windows. Soon, I saw the parking area where we'd sat keeping watch earlier in the evening.

'That looks like Slater,' Floria said suddenly, pointing towards a line of parked cars in front of the houses.

I leaned forward to try and get a better look when I was thrown forward in my seat as Floria jammed on the brakes and the windscreen of our car shattered. We were blinded and, next thing, we must have struck the kerb hard, as the passenger side of the car bounced high into the air and tipped onto its side. Papers flew around me. Floria screamed. The sound of glass smashing into fragments and screeching metal filled the air as the car slid along the road on its roof. We then hit something solid and the car rolled. I experienced something like the sensation of being inside a washing machine as we tumbled over and over.

As the car came to a rest, I found myself lying on the internal roof lining, surrounded by debris. We were upside down, the engine stalled. The single streetlight we'd parked near earlier cast a dark shadow over us.

'I think I've been shot,' Floria said, weakly.

I reached across and unclipped her seatbelt. She crumpled into a heap beside me. 'Where are you hit?' I said.

'My arm,' she groaned. 'Christ, it hurts. I can't feel my hand. He must have got away from our lads. Can you get after him?'

I groped in the dark to find Floria's jacket pocket. Tiny pieces of safety glass scratched at my hands as my fingers finally located the outline of the Glock. Nearby, I heard the sound of a car door slam.

'Take it,' Floria said, as she eased the pistol from her pocket and pushed it firmly into my hand. 'It's still loaded. Be quick.'

I racked the slide of the Glock and heard a round ease into the chamber. Feeling around in the dark, it took me a couple of seconds to locate the release to the passenger door. Then, as it opened, I half-rolled, half-fell onto the tarmac surface of the car park. Nearby, an engine roared and, from the darkness, I saw a grey shape of a car bearing down on us. I had to move fast. I knelt, raised the Glock and pointed it at the windscreen. The car veered away from me. In the half-light, I couldn't confirm it was Slater so I switched my aim to the nearest front wheel, squeezing off two rounds, and then a third.

My head was still hurting, there were fragments of glass in my hair, my fingers stung and I could see blood trickling from several tiny cuts on my hands. My shoulders ached, my knees were sore and my left eye was half-closed due to the sweat that had run into it. None of that mattered, though. I could still shoot. As a soldier, I'd spent many hundreds of hours on the range, on training drills and exercises, perfecting my skills. Using a pistol was like second nature. I didn't have to think, didn't have to decide where to aim or assess how many rounds I needed. Like a musician who picks up his instrument after a period of abstinence, it was second nature, a muscle memory, something you never forget.

The bullets struck home and, as the tyre burst and the car slewed to a halt, I moved forward to cover the driver's door. Slater was quick though, and before I could get close enough, he was out of the passenger door and on his toes. I shouted after him but he kept going, across the car park and into the alley that ran behind his house. I half ran, half hobbled in pursuit.

Chapter 72

As I reached the alley, a bullet zipped past my left ear before thumping into a tree not six feet behind me.

I stopped, ducked beside a wall, and swore at myself. If Slater had been a better shot, if the light had been better, if I'd been moving slightly faster or if luck hadn't been on my side, my life may have ended right there at the entrance to the alleyway. Fortunately for me, one of those factors came down in my favour. My skill with a pistol remained but, in my haste to run him down, I'd forgotten some basic drills. They were the kind of all-important close-quarter battle skills that kept you alive. They made sure you used hard cover, stuck to the shadows and didn't allow an enemy to see your silhouette. I reached for my phone. It was time to stop being an idiot, remember my age, and call the cavalry.

This time I didn't hold back. 'Police officer requires urgent armed assistance,' I explained, as soon as the emergency operator picked up. I then gave my name, where I was, reported 'shots fired' and added, as calmly as I could, that I was also armed. I didn't want the first armed response team arriving to leap out of their car, guns at the ready, assuming the first weapon they saw was in the hands of a bad guy. As I ended the call, I stayed hidden, my eyes on the alley, looking for movement. There was none, and no further sound. Slater had either gone to ground or made good his escape.

I sat back to keep watch and let my eyes adjust to the darkness. About thirty to forty metres along the alleyway, a dark shape began to emerge. I looked hard at it and realised it was human, a figure lying prone in the dirt. I feared it was one of the MPs.

I called out. 'Armed police, if you can move, wave a hand to me.'

'It's me, you bastard,' Slater shouted back. 'I want to surrender.'

'Throw your weapon towards me,' I said.

'I dropped it.'

'Stand up and walk towards me keeping your hands in the air where I can see them.'

He didn't move. 'I'm hurt,' he said after several seconds, and in a weak voice that made me immediately suspicious.

I wasn't buying it, and I could afford to wait. With help on its way, Slater would seen be surrounded. Just then, I smelled burning, the familiar acrid smell of plastic. I looked back towards the car. There was smoke coming from the engine bay, a thin tongue of yellow flame near an upturned wheel was growing even as I watched.

Floria was in trouble. She was on her back, half out of the car but with her legs inside. I couldn't decide if she was exhausted or trapped. I was going to have to take a chance on Slater to pull her to safety.

As quietly as I dared, I stepped away from the alleyway and then sprinted over to her. I grabbed her by the shoulders and unceremoniously dragged her across the car park.

'I'm ok,' she yelled as I stopped and released my grip. I looked back to see the engine bay of the car was now well alight. Flames licked high around the tyres and were spreading.

Looking back towards the alley, I realised the diversion had created an opportunity. If Slater had been distracted by the car bursting into flames I could get behind him.

I checked Floria was ok, patted her gently on the head and then walked quickly around the houses to the far end of the alley, using the buildings to hide my movements. Around me, curtains were twitching. It wouldn't be long before people began emerging from their homes to find out what the commotion was.

I was in luck. As I tracked silently, back along the alley, using the shadows cast by trees and high fences, I soon found myself a few feet behind Slater's last-known position. He was still there, breathing heavily and facing away from me, his elbows resting on the ground to steady his aim. In his right hand, he still held the pistol. I moved silently until I was right above him, raised the Glock and aimed at the back of his head. 'Put ... it ... down,' I said, slowly.

I heard Slater swear before his head dropped forward onto his hands. 'Don't shoot,' he said, almost pitifully.

I stepped over him and twisted the pistol from his hand. It was a Makarov, the same type we'd discovered in London.

'Where did you get this?' I asked, slipping the magazine from the handgrip and placing it in my jacket pocket.

Slater ignored the question. 'So, what happens now?' he asked.

I didn't answer immediately. In truth, I hadn't thought that far ahead. I had Floria lying injured near a burning car and two MPs unaccounted for. I was alone, bleeding and bruised from the effects of a car crash, and standing over a killer who, a moment before, had been intent on me becoming his next victim. I'd been in better situations.

'You should have kept running,' I said.

'Not easy with a busted ankle.'

I glanced down at his feet. From what I could tell, his ankles looked fine. Carefully, I knelt, ran my hands down his torso to check for any concealed weapon and, finally, squeezed his lower legs. As I gripped the right leg, he winced in pain.

'Your little trick to stitch up Masters didn't work,' I said.

'I knew that as soon as you rang to say you were coming back. Which one of 'em grassed me?'

'All in good time.'

'It was Baker wasn't it? I knew it. I should've moved that slag on weeks ago.' Slater rolled painfully onto his back to face me, and I could see he was smiling. 'On your own?' he said, as he looked past me.

'Where are the MPs who were guarding you?' I asked.

'In my kitchen nursing sore heads,' he sneered. 'Don't worry … they'll live.'

I hoped it was the truth. 'We know everything, Paul,' I said. 'We know how the rifles were stolen. We know about your little gang and we know about the phone racket. We know what really happened to Davenport.'

'My, my. You have been busy,' he replied, with a smirk.

From the car park, I could hear shouting. It sounded like a neighbour had emerged from their home and was calling out to Floria. 'Want to tell me what happened?' I said.

'Without a brief? You must think I was born yesterday.'

'Jodie says *you* killed Davenport,' I lied. 'Cold blood to stop her from turning you in to the MPs, apparently.'

Slater snarled. 'That lying fucking cow. I saved her bacon. She's the one who shot Davenport. All I did was help her cover it up.'

'You made the video as well, she told us. It's you who likes to drug and rape recruits. It was your idea to record one to blackmail Davenport.'

Slater pulled himself up onto his elbows. 'I'll deny saying this but that stuck-up bitch had to understand we weren't playing games.'

'Why do you call her that?' I said.

'She thought she was better than us, better than me, even. She was going to take the video to the monkeys and she reckoned they'd believe her over me. She said I'd do time for rape. Her and her airs and graces … no discipline.'

'So, you filmed her to control her?'

'They have to learn … inside the wire, we make the rules. If they don't respect us, we lose control. I might have to send someone like her over the top to her death. If they don't obey without question, they'll never make it as a soldier.'

'That's first world war thinking, Paul.'

Slater laughed. 'Wherever did you read that? In The Times colour supplement or some such place? It's bollocks. In Iraq, we fight from trenches and fox-holes where we get up close to the enemy and it'll be the same in Afghan. A soldier has to able to kill, and to do it without challenging them that gives the orders.'

'So, that was enough to make you shoot her?' I said.

'I bloody told you. I didn't shoot her. I might have thought about it … but I didn't. Baker said it was an accident but who can tell. I won't do time, you know that don't you? I'll deny everything. It'll be my word against hers.'

'You'll go down, that's a promise.'

'You ought to kill me now,' he said, his tone hard and unemotional. 'Squeeze the trigger. Job done. Problem solved.'

'What about Tom Morgan?' I asked. Slater seemed willing to talk and I wanted to keep it that way until I was sure back-up had arrived.

He threw his head back and laughed. 'Morgan was his own worst enemy. Before he spiked Davenport's drink, he showed me how to crush pills into powder to get a faster reaction. I did the same for him, gave him a few more than he was expecting, and let nature take its course.'

'It was you we saw on the moor?'

'I wish I'd run your friend over now. She's another bitch who needs sorting.'

The sound of a distant siren reached my ears. 'You'll be behind bars for a long time, Paul,' I said. I'd heard enough and stepped back away from him. 'Time to stand up. Let's head back to the car park, shall we?'

'I'm going nowhere,' he said, with unexpected belligerence. 'And I'll need help to stand. You know what they do to men like me in prison, don't you?'

'No less than you deserve.'

'And what if I get off, could you live with that? I meant what I said in my kitchen about your family. I'll find them.'

'You won't get off,' I said. 'Now, let's go.'

'This won't stand up in court,' he replied, loftily, and without moving. 'I've no idea what the Inspector is talking about, Your Honour. I never said any such thing.'

'You'll go down, that's a promise,' I said.

He shrugged. 'Maybe … maybe not? Are you willing to take the chance? How old are your kids, Inspector?'

A knot formed in my stomach as again I recalled the note left on Wendy's car. 'I don't have kids,' I said.

Slater sneered. 'It matters not. Davenport was still alive when I got to her, you know. I watched her last breath, saw everything she ever had disappear in front of my eyes. Hell of a feeling I can tell you … gave me a real thrill. In twenty years, when they let me out, I may decide to go looking for another woman to have some similar fun with. I might pick your wife, if she's a looker. Do you want to take the risk, Inspector?'

I felt sick. My hands had started to sweat and I could feel my grip on the Glock had become slippery. Slater turned his face towards mine and sneered. 'I'll bet old man Davenport loved seeing the kind of things his daughter got up to.'

The approaching siren was closer now, the cavalry almost here. 'Death is too easy for you,' I said, as I looked around. The alleyway was still deserted but it wouldn't be long now.

'One round, Inspector … if that's what you really are,' he said. 'That's all I ask. Make it look like suicide.'

'Sorry, Paul. You're winding up the wrong bloke.'

'Not got the guts eh?' Slater said, with a smirk. 'You bottled it in my kitchen as well. You were never going to use that water on me. You knew it, I knew it. I've seen interrogators use that trick loads of times.'

'I'm a cop, Paul,' I replied. 'And, as someone reminded me recently, that comes with responsibilities.'

'Fine words,' he replied, as he rolled onto his knees, grimaced with pain and began to stand.

I took another step back, enough to create a safe space between us, just in case. Above and around us, a blue-flashing light illuminated the rooftops and the higher branches of the surrounding trees. 'Ending your life would only do you a favour,' I replied. 'Better you should rot in prison.'

'Sorry mate,' he said, standing on one leg and grinning at me as he did so. 'That ain't gonna happen.'

And with that, Paul Slater was gone. Faster than I could react, and perhaps now confident I wouldn't send a 9mm lead policeman to bring him down, he half ran, half limped down the alley. I thought about it, even raised the Glock and had the sights lined up between his shoulder blades. But, as I watched him go, I shrugged to myself and lowered the gun as I realised he hadn't thought his escape plan through. He was heading straight towards the approaching blue lights.

***

I've played and re-played what happened in the next few seconds through my mind a great many times and still not come up with an answer. What Paul Slater was thinking when he ran out into the road, I will never know. All I can say with certainty is that as the first police car arrived, he reached the end of the alleyway, looked to his right, hesitated for a moment, and then ran. I saw the danger and called out to him to stop. Whether he didn't hear me, decided to ignore my warning or really thought he could make it, I don't know.

Slowed by his injury, Slater didn't get far. The bonnet of the police car dipped savagely as the driver hit the brakes. I heard the machine-gun thud of the car's anti-lock brake system as it cut in and then the sound of tyres trying to grip on the desperately short length of tarmac that stood between half a ton of fast-moving metal and a soft human body. Then came the inevitable, the grimacing sound of bones snapping and the crunch of shattering headlamp glass.

As Paul Slater flew high into the air, spinning over and over before reaching the highest arc of his flight, some twenty feet up, I stood powerless and in awe. That moment seemed to last an eternity yet all I really recall now is how quiet and strangely peaceful the alleyway became for those few seconds.

He was dead before he hit the ground.

Chapter 73

Although the local hospital staff were quite used to dealing with soldiers injured on exercises in the nearby mountain ranges, it's not every day three injured Military Police are wheeled into A and E alongside a recently-abducted female officer with head injuries, and all under armed guard.

Floria had been lucky, although painful and debilitating, the injury wasn't a life-changer. The bullet had struck the muscle of her fore arm causing only soft-tissue damage. She was scheduled to have surgery later that night. The two missing MPs had been located, semi-conscious, in the kitchen of Paul Slater's house. Believing their prisoner to be co-operative, they hadn't handcuffed him. Slater had used that advantage to good effect. Both were suffering concussion to add to a major case of dented pride.

After some minor first-aid to my cuts and bumps, I went to see Floria. I found her in a private room, arm in a sling, waiting to be taken to theatre. A very pale Ellie Rodgers was sitting on a chair next to the bed, talking with her.

Floria looked around and smiled broadly, as I appeared in the door. 'Did Mr Collins say it was ok to come and see me?' she said, reaching a hand out to greet me.

'Wild horses wouldn't have stopped me, Floria,' I said, with mock gallantry, before brushing her hand to one side and giving her a peck on the cheek.

'Shall I leave?' Ellie said, with an attempt at a laugh that caused her to wince in pain.

Floria looked slightly embarrassed as she wagged a scolding finger at me. 'Now, now, Inspector,' she said. 'Be serious for a minute. I was really scared when the car rolled and I thought we were trapped ... I thought Slater might ram us. And then I saw what you did. You were … amazing. The way you shot the tyres of his car, it was incredible.'

'You can take the man out of the Army,' I replied.

'But you'll never take the Army out of the man. When I heard another shot after you'd run into the alley. I was afraid he'd killed you.'

'Well, clearly he hadn't,' I said.

'Let me finish. When you re-appeared, I could have kissed you … really.'

'Now, I'm definitely leaving,' Ellie quipped. 'I'll be back in a few minutes. I need to check if my x-ray results are through.'

I waited until Ellie had closed the door behind her before turning back to Floria.

'So, what happened?' Floria said.

'Slater tried to ambush me,' I said. 'The shot you heard struck a tree. After I'd pulled you clear of the car, I circled around behind him. Once I'd taken his weapon, he became quite talkative. He admitted giving Tom Morgan the ecstasy that killed him and covering up for Jodie after Davenport was killed.'

'How did he know we were coming back for the phone?'

'When you called, he guessed Jodie must have talked. He had two choices, run or face prison.'

'So, how did he end up getting run over?'

I paused for a moment, uncertain as to how much I should tell Floria about the conversation in the alleyway behind Slater's house.

'You're going to keep me in the dark again, aren't you?' she said, cynically.

'Not this time,' I said, with a smile. 'He tried to get me to shoot him, to end it there rather than face a trial.'

'He wanted you to execute him?'

'I thought he was serious, because he knew what he'd face in prison. He was being clever, though, just like he was when we tried the waterboarding trick. As soon as he was sure I wouldn't shoot him, he did a runner. The car hit him as he crossed the road.'

'Why didn't you shoot him in the leg or something?'

I laughed. 'Training, I guess. My instinct was to do just that but, as you should know, once there's no immediate threat, no court in the land is going to countenance shooting a suspect who's running away. If I'd killed him, it would be me now facing a jury.'

'And now he's dead,' she replied, with a shrug. 'And you've saved the taxpayer a fortune in trial costs. I won't lose any sleep over it, that's for sure. More than I can say for my boss, though. He's a bit strung out, reckons they can't find either of his phones.'

'At a guess, Slater was in the process of hiding them when we arrived,' I said. 'I'm sure they'll turn up.'

'No worries. I want to get out of here as quickly as I can. All I can think about at the moment is food. I'm bloody starving and they tell me I can't even have a brew until after surgery.'

The door opened. It was one of the nurses. 'They're ready for you now,' she said to Floria before closing the door again.

'Will I see you later?' Floria said to me.

'I'll be here when you come out of theatre, I promise,' I said. 'But before you go … one last question. It's about Tom Morgan's AWOL file. That wasn't a coincidence you asking me to look at it was it?'

Floria said nothing. She winked and simply smiled knowingly as the nurse reappeared, this time to collect her patient. I had my answer. Over her shoulder, I saw a familiar figure standing talking to Ellie. It was Wendy Russell, no doubt keen to find out what had been going on. It was going to be a long night.

Then, and only then, would it be time to head home. I yearned to see my family once more. At the very least, I owed them a brunch. And, after that, there was the small matter of a promotion board to prepare for.

Chapter 74

In June 2006, Sergeant Michael P Fitzgerald and Sergeant Andrew Masters, both of the Royal Service Corps, appeared at Cardiff Crown Court before His Honour Judge Jeffrey Rice-Jones. Both were charged with Abduction, Conspiracy to Rape, Assault occasioning Actual Bodily Harm and Unlawful Possession of a firearm. Masters was also charged with theft of two SA80 rifles from Prince Albert Barracks. Private Jodie Baker also appeared on unrelated charges of perverting the course of justice and assisting an offender.

Sergeant Masters pleaded guilty to all charges and was sentenced to 12 years imprisonment. He was dismissed from Her Majesty's Service with immediate effect.

Private Baker was sentenced to a term of imprisonment of eighteen months, suspended for one year. She was also dismissed from Her Majesty's Service.

Sergeant Fitzgerald pleaded not guilty. In November 2006, following trial, he was found guilty of Abduction, Unlawful possession of a firearm and Conspiracy to cause Grievous Bodily Harm. He was sentenced to 14 years imprisonment and dismissed from Her Majesty's Service with immediate effect. In sentencing, HH Judge Judith Etherington commended the bravery shown by 2nd Lieutenant Ellie Rodgers and Private Naomi Briscoe both during the incident that led to Fitzgerald and Masters being charged and at the subsequent trial. Of Sergeant Fitzgerald, Judge Etherington said he had shown no remorse, a predisposition to blame all others rather than accept personal responsibility for his actions, and that it was right and proper his sentence should reflect the very serious nature of his criminal behaviour.

In September 2006, following a lengthy series of discussions between the Crown Prosecution Service and the Service Prosecuting Authority with regards to trial venue and jurisdiction, Corporal Douglas R West appeared at Newport Crown Court where he entered a plea of guilty to charges of conspiracy to rape and an indecent assault at the 'Royal Arms' Public House in Cwmbran. He was sentenced to a term of seven years imprisonment and dismissed from Her Majesty's Service with immediate effect.

Following a thorough investigation, the Crown Prosecution Service and Service Prosecuting Authority agreed no charges would be brought against Captain Giles Pemberton.

In October 2006, at Cardiff Coroners Court, in response to an application made by solicitors appointed by the family of Private Angela Davenport, His Honour Judge James Heley QC heard evidence from the Royal Military Police and others at a second inquest into Private Davenport's death. As a result of new evidence submitted to the inquest by the Royal Military Police, the jury decided the initial verdict of suicide was unsafe. The new inquest found Private Davenport to have been accidentally killed during a struggle with Private Jodie Baker.

Also in October 2006, HH Judge Heley QC, sitting at Cardiff Coroners Court, heard evidence relating to the sudden deaths of Private Thomas Morgan and Sergeant Paul Andrew Slater, both of the Royal Service Corps. In reaching a verdict of accidental death in the case of Private Morgan, Judge Heley concluded that Morgan, when absent without leave from his Regiment and whilst hiding on a mountain top to avoid the Military Police, took an accidental overdose of ecstasy with fatal consequences. In his summing up in the case of Sergeant Slater, Judge Heley concluded that, on learning evidence had been uncovered implicating him in the abduction and rape of Private Angela Davenport, Sergeant Slater escaped from police custody using an unlawfully held firearm, discharged that weapon at pursuing officers and, when confronted by Officer 1A, a serving Metropolitan Police Officer, Sergeant Slater suffered catastrophic injuries when he ran into the path of a vehicle driven by other officers responding to the incident. Judge Heley recorded an Open verdict, there being no evidence to confirm whether Sergeant Slater intended to end his life or failed to see the oncoming police car.

Private Jodie Baker is now married and lives near Blackwood in South Wales with her husband – a former soldier – and two children. Private Naomi Briscoe served for two years before resigning in favour of attending university to study law. She now lives in Liverpool where she works as a solicitor in a criminal law practice.

2nd Lieutenant Ellie Rodgers resigned her commission in November 2006 after experiencing a mental breakdown. She returned to her home city of Liverpool where she now lives with her mother and step-father.

Chapter 75

November 2006.

Michael Davenport was taken by surprise when he received Robert Finlay's telephone call. Finlay – now a Chief Inspector, by all account – wanted to call on them. When Michael pressed for a reason, he wouldn't be drawn. Necessary to tie up some loose ends was all he was prepared to say. His curiosity aroused, Michael readily agreed and, as he replaced the telephone on the receiver, he wondered if might be something to do with newspaper articles he'd read reporting that an inquest into another other soldier who'd died in similar circumstances to his daughter was going to be re-opened.

As the kettle now boiled, Michael heard the rumble of tyres on the drive. Perfect timing, he thought, smiling to himself, and so typical of a copper. They can smell a brew going on from a mile away. He poured hot water into the teapot and then placed it on the tray of cups and saucers before carrying it through to the living room. As he reached the coffee table, the doorbell rang.

Cold air swept in behind the policeman as Michael closed the door behind him. 'I wondered how things are with you and Mrs Davenport?' Finlay said, as he sat down on the settee.

Michael thought for a moment, considering how best to respond to the question. The truth was, things were not good, for him or for Phyllis. His wife was on anti-depressants and their local GP had spent so much time with them in recent months, they now had her personal number. As for his own health, Michael was now on an increased dosage of blood-pressure pill and had been warned unless he began to take it easy, he was at significant risk of a stroke.

In the end, he just shrugged, and with the tea brewing, leaned forward to offer one of the biscuits Phyllis had suggested their visitor might enjoy. 'Like I said at the inquests,' he said, 'Angela was the light of our lives, our only child. Life goes on but it doesn't get any easier, and it doesn't bring her back.'

'Not for me, thanks,' Finlay said, declining Michael's offer with a polite wave of his hand. 'Do you mind if I ask whether you had a chance to read the transcripts from the inquest and trials?'

'I did, and thank you for arranging to have them sent to me. It helped with our closure ... well, to some extent.'

'I hoped it would be useful to read the witness testimonies away from the atmosphere of the court.'

'It did. In many ways it was like reading a court room drama from the TV ... gripping, in a perverse sort of way. There was enough there to make a decent book if anyone was minded to write it.'

'Perhaps you? It's something the public should be told.'

'I think not. I have a way with words, I know. But telling the story of how our daughter died ... that would be too painful.'

'For what it's worth, I recall what you said to the Press at the conclusion of the original inquest. It was very moving.'

Michael nodded. He remembered the day well; particularly the sense of bewilderment he'd felt on hearing the coroner's verdict. That confusion had developed into outrage as he and Phyllis realised just how powerless they were, and how downright impossible it was to discover the truth. He was all too aware how much they owed the man sat in front of him. Finlay had proved to be the key to finding out what had really happened to their daughter. 'You're a dad, Mr Finlay,' he said, solemnly. 'I'd wager there wasn't a father present who didn't ask himself how he might handle the kind of situation my family faced. We owe you a great deal. We knew it wasn't suicide. Angela wouldn't ... couldn't have done such a thing. It took you to prove it.'

'It was my job.'

Michael sighed and then smiled. 'If only it were that simple. If I'd known what that man had been doing to those girls, I'd have happily killed him, you know?'

'Sergeant Slater, you mean?'

Michael scowled in reaction to hearing the Sergeant's name before glancing toward the kitchen. Phyllis might well be behind the door, listening. Although his wife was curious, wanting to know why the policeman preferred to call on them in person, she had been unable to face him. She feared it would be bad news of some kind. Michael lowered his voice. 'We don't ever mention that name here,' he said. 'Not ever. So, what brings to all the way from London to see us again? Is it something to do with the new Deepcut inquests? I read an article last week that said you've been appointed to head the team re-investigating one of the cases.'

'I have.' Finlay returned his cup to the tray, reached inside his jacket pocket and pulled out a padded envelope that he placed, gently, on the coffee table. 'It's not that I came about, though. The last time I was here, I made you a promise …'

'To find out who was behind that video,' Michael said, interrupting. 'Phyllis and I are very grateful you kept it from the inquests. What's in the package?'

'I think you know, sir,' Finlay said.

Michael stared at the envelope. If it contained what he thought, the man sat opposite him was taking a significant risk. 'You're a brave man …' he said, falteringly. Hands shaking, he reached across the coffee table and ran his fingers over it, feeling the shape of the contents before peeling back the seal. Inside, there were two mobile telephones. His daughter's and one other.

'The second device is the phone used to record and send the video,' said Finlay.

'The inquest was told these were never found,' Michael replied.

Finlay hesitated before responding. 'Yes, that's correct, that is the official version.'

Tears forming in his eyes, Michael stood, nodded and then stood up. 'I'll just be a moment,' he said, quietly. 'I think Phyllis will want to see these are safe.'

'You asked about the Deepcut case?'

'Yes, only because we'd wondered if that was why you wanted to speak to us again.'

'There's something I should explain. When those deaths happened, I was a uniform Sergeant. I wasn't involved in any of the cases. Like many others, I always assumed the inquest verdicts were correct. What happened here, in Wales, what I learned about your daughter, how she'd stood up to her abusers and was planning to turn them in … it taught me to be more open minded. When I got back to London, I started digging.'

'Are you hopeful?'

'Early days.'

'Well, I wish you luck.'

Michael left Finlay sitting on the settee as he returned to the kitchen. Phyllis was standing at the open back door, staring out into the garden. Together, they examined the phones, confirmed one was indeed their daughter's and then, for over a minute, they held each other tight. By the time they remembered their guest and returned together to the living room, the room was empty. Hearing the sound of a car, Michael stepped over to the window and was just in time to see a small, yellow Citroen disappearing into the distance. As he turned away from the glass, Phyllis joined him and reached for his hand.

'I should have liked to have thanked him,' she said, forlornly. 'So this is it, then? No more shocks, no more surprises? Our girl can finally rest?'

'He's re-investigating one of the other deaths,' Michael said.

'Why, has something happened?'

'I didn't ask, and he didn't say. But I'm damn sure of one thing. If anyone can uncover the truth, it will be Robert Finlay.'

Post script and acknowledgements

Although this story is set in 2005, the issue of abuse, bullying and sexual exploitation of recruit soldiers remains a problem to the British Army of 2022.

In 2016, the UK Government introduced The Service Complaints Ombudsman for the Armed Forces to replace the office of the Service Complaints Commissioner who produced annual reports but had far fewer powers.

In each annual report since then, the Ombudsman has expressed concern at the over-representation of BAME people and women in the Armed Forces in the complaints system and the possible causes. In her first annual report of 2016, the Ombudsman said this[1]:

The Ombudsman is concerned about the continued overrepresentation of both female and Black, Asian and Minority Ethnic (BAME) Service personnel in the Service complaints system Tri-Service. The disproportionate representation of female and BAME personnel as complainants (21% and 10%) compared to representation in the Armed Forces (11% and 7%) not only continued for the third consecutive year, but actually increased for female personnel. Bullying, discrimination and harassment were more commonly the cause of complaints for these groups.

The Ombudsman recommended that the Ministry of Defence (MoD) commission a study by the end of April 2018 to determine the root causes of the overrepresentation of female and BAME personnel in the Service complaints system and that appropriate action was taken to try and redress the situation by the end of December 2018, including putting the appropriate support mechanisms in place. The MoD failed to act on that recommendation. In her 2020 report the Ombudsman wrote this in her report:

---

[1] Source – The Centre for Military Justice
https://centreformilitaryjustice.org.uk/

"Female personnel had nearly twice the rate of Service Complaints than males. Although this over-representation was found in all complaint categories, it was primarily driven by bullying, harassment or discrimination. The rate at which female Service personnel raised bullying, harassment or discrimination Service Complaints was four times larger than the equivalent figure for male Service personnel. The rate of reported bullying, harassment or discrimination Service Complaints by female personnel has not changed by a significant amount in the last three years.

In 2021, Producer Jane MacSorley and former Met DCI, Colin Sutton, published *Death at Deepcut*, a series of podcasts published through Audible that revealed a fifth soldier, Pte Anthony Bartlett had died in suspicious circumstances at Deepcut in 2001 and an additional seven soldiers died during their Phase I training at nearby Pirbright Barracks during the same period.

In 2022, the Army conducted a survey of soldiers that revealed the following: - There had been an observable increase in the reporting of targeted sexualised behaviours, behaviours that include coercive sexual favours and assault. Especially shocking was the proportion of service personnel saying they had suffered a 'particularly upsetting experience', which has significantly increased since previous surveys in 2015 and 2018. In 2018, 15% of service women reported a particularly upsetting experience (already an increase from the previous survey in 2015). In 2022, 35% of servicewomen reported a particularly upsetting experience in the previous 12 months. The figure for men is 13% (up from 2% from the last survey), also a huge increase.

The reason for this is unlikely to be increased confidence in reporting because, as the survey shows, those people are not in fact reporting these experiences, they are disclosing them to an anonymous survey. The explanation, of course, is that things are getting worse, not better. Lots of the behaviours categorised as a 'particularly upsetting experience' are criminal offences. They include sending unwanted sexually explicit material, revenge porn and sexual assaults. They range from unwanted sexual touching through to rape. The proportion disclosing rape doubled from 2% in 2018, to 4% in the 2022 survey.

The vast majority (65%) reported not having told anyone of their experience. The survey noted, 'there still seem to be significant barriers to reporting sexual harassment' including 'the perceived negative repercussions of making a complaint'.

In 77% of reported examples the perpetrator was male. Sexualised misbehaviour remains a common experience in the Army with women more likely to find this behaviour offensive than men. This novel was initially inspired by similar events reported to have occurred at Blackdown Barracks, Deepcut in Surrey during the late 1990s. It was motivated by the realisation that little appears to have changed since that time.

At Deepcut, four young soldiers died while performing guard duty. Initial police response to each incident is reported to have been poor, with little awareness of the need to treat the deaths as suspicious until shown otherwise. Subsequent communication issues between Surrey Police and the Royal Military Police is said to have resulted in key evidence being lost or never gathered. This was not the police service's finest hour. No prosecutions took place – despite evidence of sexual assaults, bullying and harassment. Inquests into the deaths resulted in unsatisfactory conclusions, criticism of investigations by Coroners, successful appeals and new inquests that continue to the current day.

Devon & Cornwall Police were appointed to undertake a new investigation, a House of Commons Defence Select Committee carried out an inquiry, the Adult Learning Inspectorate did an inspection and, finally, a full review was ordered by HM Government in 2004 to be led by Nicholas Blake QC. A BBC Panorama documentary – Bullied to Death – investigated the alleged suicides and a great deal of media attention is still given to the mysteries surrounding them. Despite all the interest and attention, many questions about Deepcut remained unanswered.

Even though I served for many years as a soldier and police officer, the experience of researching this novel proved extremely challenging. I met and spoke to young men and women who described shocking, life-changing experiences that occurred during their formative months as soldiers. On several occasions, I nearly stopped, so ugly and upsetting were the stories of bullying, sexual abuse and similar behaviours. The responsibility to represent these stories, authentically and with honesty, weighed heavily on my shoulders. I haven't named the people who spoke to me – that was a pre-condition of their willingness to do so – but they know who they are and I am indebted to them for the bravery they displayed in being prepared to speak. Many others will recognise at least part of their stories; some will have been through similar.

The title of this novel comes from the expression *CROW*, an acronym used in the services to describe young soldiers, fresh from their initial training. The term is believed to have originated during WWI where it was used to describe conscripts and recruits who 'Can't Read or Write'. In more recent times, it has been accepted as referring to 'Combat Recruits of War'. It is the Crows who, in the main, are the victims of the sexual harassment, abuse and assault described by those who were brave enough to tell me their stories from twenty years ago. *CROW 27* is an amalgam of those stories.

Writing a book is always a lonely experience. Sometimes, as was the case with *Crow 27*, it is a harrowing one. I hope reading that, after reading this story, you now have a better understanding of the some of the challenges young soldiers face, even before they reach the battlefield.

I owe a special thank you to freelance BBC Panorama Producer, Jane MacSorley, for the doors she opened to me and for her generosity and trust; to the *'Deepcut the Truth'* campaign for having faith in me; to a special group of former soldiers who trained at, and were posted to Deepcut Barracks for their openness, honesty and bravery when describing their experiences to me; to retired Captain Tina Jones, RLC (who tragically died before this novel was complete) for her encouragement, candour and courage while helping me with my research; and also to Lt Colonel John Nelson, former Royal Military Police Provost Marshall, Southern District, for his help while I researched and wrote, and for checking the draft manuscript.

I was warned by many contributors how difficult it would be to find a publisher brave enough to publish this story. They were right. Although commissioning editors felt moved to commend my writing and the importance of the story, some felt intimidated by the possibility of a reaction from the military 'establishment', others weren't prepared to take a punt on its commercial viability. 'Old news', one said. In the past, this story may not have seen the light of day. Today, thanks to the Amazon KDP system, it can.

My wife, Heather, my agent Broo Doherty (DHH Literary Agency) and former agent James Wills (Watson Little Literary Agents) all showed great patience and support while *Crow 27* was in embryonic form and throughout, as the story developed. They, like me, realised the stories of these young recruits needed to reach the eyes and ears of the public. I will always be grateful to them.

Finally, a thank you to Des James, Emma Norton and the team at the Centre for Military Justice. While people like you remain determined to achieve change and see justice for the victims, there will always be hope.

Prince Albert Barracks, as I'm sure you realise, doesn't exist. Neither does the Royal Service Corps. *Crow 27* doesn't seek to re-tell, re-invent, analyse or put forward any theory or interpretation on the events surrounding the real and very tragic deaths of four young soldiers at Blackdown Barracks, Deepcut in the late 1990s to early 2000s. It doesn't seek to undermine or call into question any official inquiry or verdict or to represent what really happened at Deepcut or any other barracks. Any soldier, police officer or civilian who believes they recognise a particular character, setting, Regiment, Corps or police service is mistaken.

Crow 27 is fiction.

Printed in Great Britain
by Amazon

10125279R00233